THE SECRET LIFE OF COWBOYS

Tyler

C.H. ADMIRAND

sourcebooks casablanca

Cover design by Randee Ladden
Cover images © cokacoka/iStockphoto.com; Evgeny_D/iStockphoto.com

The characters and events portrayed in this book are fictitious or are used fictitiously. Any similarity to real persons, living or dead, is purely coincidental and not intended by the author.

Published by Sourcebooks Casablanca, an imprint of Sourcebooks, Inc.
P.O. Box 4410, Naperville, Illinois 60567-4410
(630) 961-3900
FAX: (630) 961-2168
www.sourcebooks.com

Printed and bound in Canada
WC 10 9 8 7 6 5 4 3 2 1

To my great-great-grandmother,
Anna Garahan Flaherty

Chapter 1

HARDWORKING MAN WANTED.
MUST HAVE A STRONG BACK
AND EVEN TEMPERAMENT.
APPLY IN PERSON.
334 LOBLOLLY WAY
PLEASURE, TX

TYLER GARAHAN CRUSHED THE NEWSPAPER ADVERTISEMENT in his hand. Staring at the building across the street from where he'd parked his pickup, he dug deep for a confidence he sure as hell didn't feel.

"I don't have time to waste."

He needed this job. Hell, he needed any job, but this was the last one he'd circled in Sunday's paper. His last chance or he and his brothers would lose the Circle G.

He tried to swallow past the lump forming in his throat but couldn't muster an ounce of spit. Facing down the longhorn bull that tore ass toward him, wanting to skewer him in the part that made him praise the Lord he was a man, was the closest he'd come to being this scared.

He gritted his teeth, braced his arm against the door, and pushed it open. "I'm not scared."

You shouldn't lie, Tyler.

His gut clenched.

Trust in yourself, son.

Was it wishful thinking or had he just heard from

his grandfather on the other side? Shaking his head, he brushed his damp palms against the front of his jean-clad legs and closed the door.

Stalking across the street, he glanced up at the sign above the building. *The Lucky Star*. As if called up by a long ago memory, the lyrics to an old Kenny Rogers tune his mom loved played through his mind as he crushed the unease he refused to give in to and reached for the door.

The scent was the first thing that hit him, right between the eyes. Rain? How could it smell like a warm summer rain?

Focus on the goal. Get the job first.

But his concentration wandered when he noticed the mirrors on both sides of the entryway. What the hell was that about? He sneered. *A guy doesn't want to see himself walking into a bar. He wants to see the bar, check out what's on tap, and maybe if his luck is running high, flirt with his choice of curvaceous sweet things perched on a barstool.*

He grinned, savoring the image, because he hadn't had the time lately to get out on a Saturday night in search of a little female companionship. A knot of need started to form in his gut, but he ignored it and strode forward down the hallway lined with mirrors.

Tyler stopped dead in his tracks and stared. "Damn. What's the owner thinking?"

His gaze ran the length of the hallway and back—he wasn't seeing things—there were benches in front of the mirrors.

"Red velvet."

He didn't have to touch the seats to know what they

were covered with. His mother had a favorite lady's chair in her bedroom. A red velvet lady's chair.

"Hell," he muttered. They needed to hire him, if only to suggest a few major changes to increase business. No self-respecting bar owner would have mirrors or velvet in their place.

At the end of the hallway, a long, sleek ebony bar gleamed, and damned if every one of the barstools didn't have a red velvet cushion to sit on.

"Shit," Tyler muttered aloud. "I can't see myself working in a place like this."

"Well now, handsome," a husky voice purred to the left of him, "I can see you working here just fine."

He turned and felt his mouth drop open. *Beautiful. Stunning. Drop-dead gorgeous.* All of the above fit the little lady walking toward him with her hand outstretched.

"Name's Jolene Langley," she said. "Welcome to The Lucky Star, cowboy."

Lord, she was a looker. Belatedly, Tyler removed his Stetson, ran his hand through his still-damp hair, and grasped her hand. "Tyler Garahan."

Satin. Damned if her hand didn't feel like one of his mom's nightgowns. He'd done his fair share of laundry over the years and ought to know.

Her grip surprised him. It was firm. His gaze drifted from the top of her wavy red head to the tips of her fancy blue boots—a color only a female would wear.

"Emily!" she called out though her gaze never left his. "See something you like, cowboy?" She returned the favor by letting her gaze slide from the top of his tousled dark brown head to the tips of his worn leather boots. Her gaze lingered on his boots. He glanced down and swore beneath his breath; he'd forgotten to polish them.

"Em?" she called a second time.

"I'm coming," a soft voice answered. "Give me a minute."

He glanced in the direction the voice seemed to come from—somewhere just beyond the bar—and noticed small tables scattered in front of a stage.

"You have live entertainment in here?" He imagined some whiny soft rock band standing on stage, playing music that would get under his skin and have him reaching for a shot of whiskey instead of his usual longneck bottle.

Her laugh was as smooth as her skin. "You could say that, cowboy."

Irritation began to burn in his gut at the way she'd sneered when she called him cowboy. Hell, he was one and proud of it, but that wasn't as important right now as landing the job and saving the ranch. "Name's Tyler, ma'am."

"What's up, Jolene?"

The pretty redhead walking toward him had to be a blood relative to the one currently staring at the third button down on his worn denim work shirt. He hoped Jolene didn't look lower and notice the tear he tried to hide by rolling up the sleeves. The woman was getting under his skin—and not in a good way.

"Trouble, Em?"

Tyler finally tore his gaze from Emily's face and noticed what Jolene had: the huge splat of chocolate dead center between Emily's breasts. Firm and proud, cupped lovingly by a form-fitting, cropped T-shirt.

The saliva pooled in his mouth. He swallowed. The urge to devour the chocolate-covered confection caught him off guard. Digging deep for control, he realized he'd been too long without a woman: two months, three weeks, and four days... if he were counting.

He may be damned for it, but he let his gaze feast on the bounty before him. The two inches of exposed skin was tanned and taut. His gaze dipped to the hem of her denim mini skirt, and he had to swallow again. The woman had legs—curvaceous and toned, not toothpick thin—and Lord Almighty, bright green nail polish on her toes.

Emily smiled at Tyler and answered Jolene, "The spoon got caught in the mixer."

Jolene had a good three inches on Emily and an in-your-face beauty and sexuality that challenged him on every level, but there was something about the barefooted redhead with chocolate smeared across her cheekbone like a slash of war paint that tugged at his gut.

He had to fight against the urge to smile and replied, "Looks like the mixer won."

Emily lifted her right hand and the mangled spoon she clutched. "That's the second spoon today." Her sigh was long and low.

Jolene patted Emily's shoulder. "Why don't you just quit while you're ahead?"

"You know I can't until I beat the stress out of myself and this batter." Emily looked over at Tyler and asked, "Are you here to fix the sink?"

He shook his head. "Although I have been known to wrastle an ornery pipe into submission, I'm actually here about your sister's ad in the paper." For a split second disappointment clouded her pretty face and had him offering, "Maybe I could take a look at it before I leave."

Her smile blossomed slowly and was surely like a flower opening its petals to catch the rain. Before he could untangle his tongue, she said, "That's right neighborly, but I'll wait for the plumber. Oh... and she's my cousin."

"Really? You look enough alike to be sisters." Now that she was close enough to touch, he could see the subtle differences: the shape of their eyes—Emily's were long-lashed and almond shaped—and the curve of their lips—Emily's were fuller, and there was something indefinable about the barefooted redhead that went a whole lot deeper, straight to her core, a sweetness he hadn't found in long, long while.

If he were gifted with words like his New York City cousins, he'd have said there was something special about Emily and the way she seemed to smile from the inside out. But Tyler'd probably mess it up and compare her to one of the Circle G's milk cows.

Neither woman looked like they'd ever set foot on a ranch, and Emily sure as hell wouldn't believe him if he told her that certain breeds of milk cows had beautiful eyes and sweet faces. The steer he and his brothers raised for beef weren't pretty—well, they probably would be if he were another steer.

Shaking his head to clear it, he asked, "So did you save any of the batter?"

Emily's smile was slow and achingly sweet. "Enough to fill half the pan."

"Are you really going to bake half a pan's worth, Em?"

Emily grinned at her cousin. "No. That's why I decided to get another spoon and just eat the batter after

I nuke it for a few seconds. Then I'll start over with another batch."

Tyler could handle cooking meat and potatoes. Baking was a whole other ball game, but he was pretty sure it would take longer than a few seconds to cook brownies in the microwave. "That wouldn't be long enough to cook them, would it?"

Her slow, sweet smile eased under his worry about getting the job. "Brownies taste better half-cooked," Emily said. "Imagine how great the batter would taste warm and freshly whipped."

Tyler couldn't keep from grinning at the thought. Standing this close to her, he couldn't help but notice that without boots, the top of Emily's head would hit him mid-chest. He'd have to work at it to line up their lips, but if they were lying down—Whoa! Hold on there. Time enough to go there later, after he'd landed the job. *If he landed the job.*

"So, you're here about the position."

The hard edge in Jolene's voice had Tyler looking at her. Hell, a few positions came to mind and stubbornly got stuck there, making it hard to focus. Man, if he didn't need the money, he'd be looking for a nice quiet place to sample the chocolate-covered redhead. Head to toe and every luscious inch in between. Had she noticed him drooling over her cousin?

"I think you should hire him, Jo," Emily said, heading back the way she'd come. "See y'all later," she called out over her shoulder. "If you need me, I'll be upstairs whipping these brownies into submission. Bye, Tyler."

Lord, he'd get arrested if either woman could read his thoughts right now. One of Grandpa's favorite expressions came to mind watching the gentle sway of Emily's hips. The hitch in Emily's *git-a-long* was as delectable as the front of her had been, and damned if a line from a Trace Adkins song didn't start running through his brain, *We hate to see her go, but love to watch her leave.*

Damn, get your mind on the job, son.

Jolene asked him a question, but he was too preoccupied to pay attention. "I'm sorry, ma'am... what did you ask me?" *Lord, don't let Jolene wonder if I'll be able to keep my mind on the job and off her cousin. I need this job!*

Jolene was watching him closely. Finally the corner of her mouth lifted into a smile. "Are you here to apply for the position?"

"Yeah. I mean, yes, ma'am. I'm here about the job."

"You a hard working man, Mr. Garahan?" She reached out and brushed at the front of his shirt.

He shifted from one foot to the other, uncomfortable now that she'd touched him. Had she meant to? "Excuse me?"

"The person I need to fill the position has to be willing to work hard."

He rubbed his fingers along the brim of his hat and wondered how to convince the woman that he'd work until he dropped. *Doing's smarter than jawing.* "I give one hundred percent to everything I do."

Damned if she didn't reach out and touch him again, this time he twitched as her nail flicked unerringly over his left nipple. *Holy Hell!*

He stepped back. Had she meant to touch him like that, or did she simply have dead-on aim? Unease roiled in his gut. He couldn't flat out ask her. If he was wrong he'd look like a fool, blow the interview, and lose his chance at the job. "Ma'am?"

"What about your temperament?" she asked, taking a step closer to him, easily closing the distance.

"I'm easygoing most of the time." His eyes narrowed. Was she coming on to him, or was it some kind of test?

"So far, you have all of the qualifications I need. How's your back… strong?"

"Yes, ma'am."

She stepped around behind him, and he wondered why she couldn't take his word for it that his back was strong and had to see for herself. The small palm cupping the seat of his Levis was all it took to answer his unasked question and end the interview.

He spun around to face her. "I don't know what kind of game you're playing or what kind of *position* you're hiring for, but I don't think I'm the man for the job."

Hell, usually he enjoyed an aggressive female, given the fact that free time was next to nonexistent and getting down to the good part right off meant more time in the saddle, but he'd been attracted to Emily, not Jolene, and totally missed the fact that Jolene apparently had other things in mind. At least Emily had been honest in mistaking him for a plumber. He couldn't imagine what Jolene had mistaken him for.

"I believe you're just what we're looking for." She smiled, and he wondered if anyone ever told this woman flat out no.

"Take off your shirt."

Sheer desperation grabbed a hold of his roiling gut

and twisted it. Self-preservation warred with duty. "Look, I don't know what you're selling here, lady, but I'm not buying." He planted his heel, did an about-face, and strode toward the hallway. He could find another job. Had to.

"Position pays thirty dollars an hour, plus tips."

That stopped him dead in his tracks. *Damn*. How could he walk away from that kind of money? Without turning around he shot back, "What're the hours?"

She chuckled, and the sound grated on his nerves. "Seven o'clock to two o'clock, six days a week."

Tyler's hands shook as he did the math. Two hundred ten dollars a night? That was over a thousand dollars a week! He clenched them into fists.

"You could start tonight," she added. "And you can cash your check right here at the bar."

He could have part of the mortgage payment by the end of next week.

They could keep the Circle G.

Garahan men might be ornery when their backs were against the wall, but no one had ever accused a Garahan of being stupid. He turned back toward Jolene. "What do I have to do?"

She put her hands on her hips and called out, "Jennifer? Natalie?"

Hell, now what?

The sound of high heels hitting hardwood had him looking in the direction of the sound. The blue-eyed brunette and brown-eyed blonde walking toward him had to be blood kin. Without a word, they looked him over from head to toe and then began to circle around behind him.

"Lord love ya, Jolene," the blonde sighed. "We got us a live one."

"Are you a real cowboy?" the brunette asked, staring up at him like he was the embodiment of her childhood heroes all rolled up into one man.

He closed his eyes repeating his new mantra: I need this job… I need this job… Once he was calm, he opened them and answered, "Yes, ma'am."

"Hire him!" the blonde said.

The brunette narrowed her eyes and drew her mouth into a thin line. "Hold on sister, dear." She turned toward Jolene and asked, "Has he passed the test yet?"

His gaze shifted from the brunette back to Jolene. "Just how many kegs of beer will you expect me to move for that kind of money?" He hoped his back would hold out after putting in a full day at the ranch.

"Oh, we're not hiring you for that," Jolene said. "If you want the job, Tyler, take off your shirt."

Want? *No*. Need? *Hell, yeah*.

Need overrode want. Hell, he needed the money—fast. With his hands clenched into tight fists, he silently dug deep for the grit to do as she asked.

His gaze settled on the stage and suddenly everything clicked into place like the latch on the gate to the Circle G. The odd questions, the searching looks, waiting for his reaction to being touched suddenly made sense. For the kind of money she was offering, he'd bet every penny of it he would have to get up on that stage.

Drawing in a deep breath he cursed silently, the air inside the bar smelled like fresh rain too. They weren't hiring him to haul kegs; he was about to become their latest attraction! He lifted his hands and unbuttoned the top button. His fingers fumbled and beads of sweat formed at his temples. *Better get used to it. Hell, there'd be no getting used to it.*

The raptor-like gaze of the three women unnerved him, but hell, for the salary Jolene was promising him, he'd sell his soul to the devil if it'd save Grandpa's legacy… their ranch. Her amber gaze collided with his, and he wondered if his soul was already lost.

As the last button slid free, he couldn't bring himself to shrug out of the shirt. He felt so exposed standing there while the women in front of him watched him as if he was a prime cut of beef on today's blue plate special. It sure as hell wasn't the same as stripping down for one woman at a time.

Jolene's gaze met his. "Thirty dollars an hour, plus tips, Tyler."

Damn. His Celtic pride kicked in and their ancient family motto filled him: *Aut Vincam, Aut Periam: I will either conquer or perish!* He lifted one shoulder and let the shirt slide off. The collective gasp had him wondering if it was the thick ridge of scar tissue running along the line of his lower ribs or something else.

Then damn if the blonde didn't lick her lips like she was a cat and he was a bowl of fresh cream. "You'd better see if he passes the last test," she said with a glance at the bar. "Heck, even if he doesn't, I'd snap him up, Jolene."

The blonde walked around the bar to a door in the back, opened it, and yelled, "Gwen!"

A muffled reply sounded from below them. Just how many females worked at this bar?

"Are you ready for the last test?" Jolene asked.

Tyler's gut told him to pick up his shirt and hightail it over to one of the fast food joints. They only paid one-third of Jolene's offer, but at least he knew he could handle flipping burgers and the deep fryer. Well… maybe not the fryer, but he'd flipped burgers plenty of times for his brothers.

Indecision caught him off guard; it wasn't part of his makeup. He'd never been in this kind of tight spot before, but Dylan and Jesse were counting on him and he wasn't a coward. It wasn't in the Garahan blood. Three generations of Texas Garahans had faced Indian attacks, droughts, more than one deluge, and a handful of range wars. He would stick it out… no matter what she wanted.

A six-foot tall blonde appeared in the doorway and sauntered toward him.

Jolene smiled. "Gwen," she said slowly. "I'd like you to meet Tyler." Turning toward Tyler, Jolene smiled and nodded to the blonde giant. With a sly smile, she purred, "Pick her up."

A thousand questions raced through Tyler's head, but not one of them had included picking up the Amazon standing in front of him. "Now?"

Everyone but Gwen nodded.

He sighed and moved to scoop her up off her feet, but the woman backed away from him, hands raised up to stop him. "Not like that."

He stepped back and rubbed his now damp palms on his jean-clad legs. *Were they making fun of him?*

"I'm afraid I don't understand."

Jolene's laugh was as light as the afternoon breeze off the pond at the Circle G. "If you just stand still, Tyler, Gwen knows what I mean."

With a gleam in her eye, Gwen took a giant step forward and jumped. She reached for his neck with open arms and wrapped her legs around his waist, clinging like a burr to a horse's hide.

He had just enough time to blink, brace himself, and pray his back would hold out. He'd unloaded a truckload of hay before cleaning up to drive out here.

She settled against him. Hoping he wouldn't lose his grip, he slid his hands beneath her muscled backside.

Gwen leaned close and whispered in his ear, "Nice catch, cowboy."

He was too stunned to speak.

"One more thing." Jolene walked toward where he stood, legs braced apart, holding on for dear life, muscles screaming, tendons straining.

He hoped to hell he didn't have to go haul in any full kegs of beer for his next test. Poke him with a fork; he was done!

"You can set Gwen down now."

When he did as she asked, Gwen touched his cheek, smiled, and walked back toward the still open door.

Distracted and disturbed by what he'd just had to do, not quite sure what it proved, he didn't see Jolene move until she was crowding him so close he could feel her breath on his chin and feel the tip of her fingernail as it tapped in the hollow of his throat.

He sucked in a breath and held it, waiting to see what else she'd ask him to do. He hated being at this woman's mercy. *Suck it up, boy. Garahans go down fighting!*

Gee thanks, Grandpa!

Her gaze met his, and he sensed she knew he was fighting the urge to either step back or step forward.

Holding himself as still as the scarecrow in the Circle G's cornfield, Tyler waited.

She let her fingernail slide down his breastbone all the way toward his—Aw hell, she wouldn't.

She laughed—a sexy, sultry sound—as if daring him to move. "Thirty dollars, plus tips."

Thinking of the ranch and the sweat, blood, and tears three generations of Garahans had infused into the land, and not what he'd have to do to earn those tips, he froze. The sweat gathered at his temples began to trickle down the sides of his face, but he held his ground. He pictured his brothers as they rode hell-bent for leather toward the barn at the end of the day, arguing over whose turn it was to rustle up supper. He savored the memory of his mother pulling a huge turkey out of the oven during the holidays and his grandpa giving them all hell while smiling at the brothers with a gleam of pride in his eyes.

She dipped the tip of her nail in his navel and he jolted.

But he kept his hands at his sides and his face devoid of expression, even when she shocked the shit out of him, tucked her finger inside the waistband of his jeans, and yanked him flush against her saying the words he'd been both dreading and hoping to hear.

"You're hired."

Chapter 2

"Hey, Jesse, it's me." Tyler jammed his arm into one sleeve, switched the phone to his other ear, and repeated the movement, yanking his shirt back on.

"Did you get the job?"

Tyler rubbed at the ache in his temple. "Yeah—" Before he could say anymore, he heard Jesse yelling to Dylan, sharing the good news.

"When do you start?" his brother asked.

"Tonight at seven."

"Good news, bro," Jesse said. "Are you coming back to the ranch, or will you kill a few hours and wait in town?"

Tyler pushed his Stetson further back on his head so he could rub at the ache between his eyes. "I've got some forms to fill out."

"Uh, Tyler?"

He heard the sudden change in his brother's voice and should have realized his brothers would be worried about the money. Tyler had kept the grim reality to himself for too long and had had to lay their finances out on the table last night. The discussion that followed had been anything but brotherly.

"Yeah?"

"Will it be enough?"

Thinking of the way Jolene traced the tip of her fingernail from his throat to his navel, he gritted his teeth. "Yeah… just."

"OK. Good."

"See you around three o'clock."

"Dylan and I'll get up earlier and feed the stock; you can sleep in."

Tyler swore. "I don't need you to do my chores."

"Hell," Jesse bit out. "You're the one taking on the night job. It's the least we can do until you're used to hauling kegs and bending over all night stocking shelves."

"Jess—" Tyler hesitated. How could he tell his brother he wasn't going to be hauling any beer?

"Yeah?"

The image of Jolene's flame-bright hair and amber eyes mocked him, something that didn't sit well with him. Maybe he wouldn't have to say anything. He might find another job and only have to put up with this one for a few days. At least the money would help tide them over in the meantime.

But a barefooted, curvaceous redhead with a smear of chocolate on her cheek had him stopping to think things through. He wanted Emily—but he wanted to get to know her too. Despite the fact that he'd been without a woman for almost three months, he hadn't been hit this hard with need or want since his first taste of love at fourteen. There was no way he was going to miss out on the chance to get to know Emily better before sweet-talking her into bed. In order to do that he'd have to give the women of The Lucky Star a chance.

"Nothing," he finally said. "See you in the morning."

He snapped his phone closed and stared at it. What the hell had he gotten himself into? He should have taken O'Malley's offer six months ago and sold the ranch.

Who would tend the family graves? Where would your brothers live?

Damn he was getting tired of hearing voices in his head. "We could add a clause to the contract of sale about me tending the graves," he mumbled pushing away from where he'd been leaning against his pickup. "And my brothers could damn well live in the back of their trucks for all I care."

There's only one truck left that runs, the bodiless voice insisted.

Stalking back to The Lucky Star, Tyler wondered how the hell he'd make it through the next few hours let alone his entire shift.

Tyler walked in and noticed the group of females staring at him. Uneasy with the attention, he removed his hat and held it at his side.

"I'm glad you're back." Jolene said.

"You sound as if you're surprised I came back."

Jolene shrugged. "Let's just say it took you longer than expected to make a phone call."

She stared at him and wondered if he'd be as much trouble as the last cowboy wannabe they'd hired. Clay had spent way too much time on the phone sweet-talking one of the handful of women he juggled. They'd all been regulars at the club and the reason why Jolene now had her ironclad set of rules.

Added to her other worries, the prospect of training yet another dancer had her frustration growing. She hoped he knew how to move. "Any questions about tonight?"

Tyler looked away and his Adam's apple bobbed up and down.

Was he nervous? Who'd have figured a big old hunk of man like the one standing in front of her would be nervous about dancing? Watching the hint of color slashing his cheekbones, she wondered if stripping for an audience was the real problem.

"The routines are easy," she said, hoping to get to the heart of his worry in order to move past it.

"I'm not worried about that." He looked down at the tips of his worn and dusty boots.

"All right. Let's go over the house rules."

His head snapped up, and his dark eyes riveted to hers. "Rules?" He clenched his jaw and waited.

Now what? She didn't have time to deal with the cowboy's attitude now. She had to sit down with Emily and go over their receipts from last month, and they still had to decide whether or not they were going to cave in and pay the damned Rotary Club.

Centering herself, she rubbed her temples and drew in a deep cleansing breath. Looking right at Tyler, she held up her index finger.

"The customers pay to see a show, and we give them one. So unless you're bleeding or unconscious, I expect you to show up on time."

He nodded and she held up a second finger. "The customer is always right."

He looked like he wanted to say something but wisely kept his thoughts to himself.

Jolene held up a third finger. "They can look and touch but not grab or grope your package."

"My what?"

Outrage had Tyler's eyes bugging out and his face flushing crimson. Jolene tilted her head to one side and marveled at the fact that the man was actually blushing.

Shaking her head, she held up a fourth finger. "If you've got an itch," she told him, "scratch it on your own time and not in the ladies' room or men's room."

His eyes glassed over.

"Don't forget the hallway!" Jennifer added. "Those butt-cheek prints were really tough to clean off the mirrors."

Jolene had to agree. "We had to use two types of glass cleaner the last time one of the customers flashed her double Ds and waved a fistful of fifties in Clay's face."

Tyler opened his mouth to speak but no sound emerged. He nodded silently.

Satisfied that their newest employee knew and understood the rules, Jolene said, "Well if you don't have any questions, we've got a lot to teach you in just under two hours. Do you know how to two-step, Tyler?"

He nodded.

"Ever dirty dance?"

Tyler shook his head. "No, ma'am." All business, her newly hired dancer ran his hand through his hair and confessed, "At least not in public."

"All right then, Natalie," Jolene said. "Let's see if Tyler fits into Clay's costume."

"What kind of costume?"

"Don't you worry none, cowboy," Jolene purred, staring at his zipper. "All of your assets will be covered."

Chapter 3

EMILY SAT DOWN HARD ON THE STEPS. SHE'D NEVER HAD the wind knocked out of her looking at a tall, dark-eyed cowboy before. Then again, she'd been involved with a string of losers; the latest one had pulled the rug out from under her… go figure.

Shaking her head, she watched her cousin do what she did best… grab a hold of the reins and take charge.

Watching Tyler's expression and the way his color changed from grim to green, she felt sorry for him. She couldn't help it… she liked him. There was an innate kindness that she'd connected with right off. When he looked as if he'd swallowed sour milk, she realized that her cousin must be telling him the rules.

Thinking she might have to go to his rescue, Emily strained to hear their conversation.

"My what?"

From the tone of his voice and the way Tyler's face flushed crimson, Jolene must have mentioned the "look but don't touch" rule to him. That comment usually had that reaction from the dancers they'd interviewed for the job. Some walked away, not willing to follow Jolene's rules. Too bad for them the last dancer had agreed but hadn't kept his word. She had a feeling the gorgeous hunk of man she'd been blindsided by would. Emily hadn't been tempted by a good-looking man in six months. She didn't want to be now. Looking at the way Tyler kept backing up, she knew she wouldn't have a choice. She yearned to be alone with him, talk to him, sit on a front porch swing with him... hell, they didn't have a swing, let alone a front porch.

Sighing, she shifted and the bowl slipped in her grasp. She caught it before it hit the stairs, giving away the fact that she hadn't left. Heck, she couldn't; there was something about the dark-eyed cowboy that pulled at her, tugging at her heartstrings. Maybe it was the hint of desperation—he needed the job—or maybe his willingness to look at their sink. He was polite and easy on the eyes.

The image of Tyler catching Gwen was stuck in her mind and had her fingers fumbling, nearly dropping the bowl a second time. Damn but that was one fine-looking cowboy. Her blood began to hum, and her skin positively tingled remembering how tightly he'd hung on to Gwen for dear life. Her mouth went dry wondering how it would feel if his hands were cupping her bottom. The tingles spread and the humming built to a deafening roar as she remembered how he'd spread his legs to help handle the weight he held with his beautifully bulging biceps. Oh my God, he was hot.

Fanning her face, to cool her overheated flesh, she ran the tip of her tongue along her lips, catching a speck of chocolate. Savoring her favorite flavor, she let her imagination run wild, the focus being the tall, dark-haired hunk of cowboy tied to her bedposts, a bowl of chocolate, and her eager tongue. No! Step back from the fantasy and the dark-eyed, dreamy man, and no one would get hurt. She couldn't let her heart get involved again; it had been too painful the last time it had been stomped on and ground into the dirt.

"I don't have time for romance," she grumbled, scooping up a spoonful of batter. Licking her lips, she indulged in her favorite weakness, the chocolaty goodness, and dipped the spoon back into the bowl. Three spoonfuls later, she slowly smiled. "But I might be able to squeeze in some time for a walk on the wild side." The tall, dark, and studly cowboy looked interested enough to make it worth her while and one hell of a ride.

Emily slowly got to her feet. She needed to get back upstairs to one of her back-up boxes of brownie mix. Baking always cleared her mind. There was something soothing about mixing ingredients together, while her mind wandered and her hands were busy. She could usually work through most of her worries by the time the batter was smooth and ready to be poured into the pan.

A little while later, she'd successfully outwitted the mixer by using good old-fashioned elbow grease and her favorite wooden spoon, and she had two batches of warm and gooey goodness cooling on the countertop to show for it. "Time to get cleaned up and see how tall, dark, and handsome is doing downstairs." Mind clear, she was ready to see if she could distract the man she hadn't been able to stop thinking about. She showered quickly so she could spend more time on her makeup and deciding what to wear. Twisting her hair up off her neck, she secured it in place with a hair clip and studied her reflection. "If only I could do something about these freckles."

Knowing it was her only option, she dragged out the mineral powder makeup she used liberally to hide the offending spots sprinkling her cheeks and nose. A swipe of blush across her cheekbones, touch of mascara, and thin line of purple on her lids, and she was ready for lip gloss.

Leaning close to the mirror, she applied her favorite shade of lip color and pressed her lips together. Stepping back, she studied her handiwork and smiled. "Not bad." She laughed. "Better than the first outfit he saw me in."

Twirling to the left and then the right, Emily was satisfied with the body-hugging fit of her black denim skirt and deep green tank top. With a dab of lavender oil on her pulse points, she was ready to see if she could tempt the handsome cowboy who'd managed to work his way under her skin with his gentle teasing. Ready to do a little distracting of her own, she grinned. "It wouldn't be right if I'm the only one suffering."

He may think she was bubble-headed and scatter-brained—most people did at first—but she was ready to let him see the focused side of her personality. When she put her mind to it, she could do whatever she wanted. She had a gut feeling Tyler was different than the men she usually dated. There was just something about him. She couldn't say exactly why, but Emily looked forward to discovering what made Tyler tick as much as the need to talk him into her bed.

Stepping into her favorite pair of boots, she headed for the stairs. She was ready to attract and distract.

The steady beat of a familiar country tune throbbed in her veins. She looked to the left and then the right. Her gaze snagged and got stuck on the long, tall Texan standing on stage slipping out of his worn denim shirt. Every ounce of spit dried up in her mouth. She tried to lick her lips, but her tongue was paralyzed and her brain had completely shut down.

Thickly muscled pectorals smoothed, then bunched as he bent down and braced his hands on the back of a chair someone had placed on the stage. He leaned forward and his biceps bulged as he pressed more of his weight on the back of the chair. *Oh Lordy!*

Emily stared, transfixed by the sight. Even though she'd met him earlier, there was something different about him when he was center stage. His go-to-hell-and-enjoy-the-trip attitude commanded attention. When he straightened up and hooked his thumbs in the waistband of his leather chaps, her heart beat double time.

Even though she'd seen Clay do the same routine a hundred times, the impact of Tyler strutting across the stage in chaps and a tiny pair of black spandex briefs had her gasping for air and reaching out to steady herself. With one hand to her heart and the other braced against the wall, she wasn't prepared when his gaze to swung toward hers.

Before she could react, he unbuckled his chaps and let them fall to the stage.

Air… she needed air! Good Lord, he was gorgeous. He had the body of a Greek god and the arrogance to match.

The crowd erupted in cheers, whistles, and more than one moan of ecstasy, but the man didn't seem to notice. He waited to the count of ten, spun on his boot heel, and strode to the back of the stage like a gunfighter preparing to take his stance at the end of Main Street before a shoot out.

Drawn to him, she made her way through the crowd toward the stage. Emily stared. She couldn't look away; the back of him was as gorgeous as the front. Finally the cheers died down and as if on cue, the man slowly walked to the front of the stage where women waited, waving fists filled with bills. From where she stood Emily could tell they weren't the one-dollar kind. Two women waved fistfuls of twenties, and one long-legged brunette held out a handful of fifties!

Wishing she weren't a part owner in the club so she could push her way to the front of the crowd and monopolize the handsome hunk, she jolted when Jolene said, "Isn't he magnificent?"

Emily agreed. "There's something really special about him. You feel it too. Don't you?"

Jolene nodded and put her arm around Emily. "It might take a little while for him to settle in."

"You don't think he'll walk, do you?" If he left she might never see him again, and she had a deep-seated need to touch off that powder keg of passion she sensed lurked just below his *I-just-don't-give-a-damn façade*.

"I don't know," Jolene answered, "but the ladies love him."

Emily narrowed her eyes, watching the way the women lined up in front of the stage caressed the span of Tyler's shoulders and the sculpted muscles of his amazing pecs. She ground out, "Yeah, but it's against our rules to shove bills down the front of his briefs."

She knew Jolene must have seen it too when her cousin said, "Hell," and stalked over toward the stage.

Emily had seen the blonde with dark roots stuffing her hands, along with a few bills, into the front of the cowboy's clingy black briefs. When Tyler stiffened and jerked back, Emily got a good look at his face.

He looked mad enough to spit nails, that or brand something with his red-hot gaze. She blinked. Gwen jumped into the fray and had the blonde by the arm and was leading her toward the door.

The silent message rippled through the crowd as the women frantically waving bills paused to watch the woman who dared to go one step too far in her adoration of the handsome hunk on stage.

Why couldn't the women be content with just having the opportunity to look at someone as beautiful as Tyler? He was the stuff dreams were made of... well, Emily's dreams anyway.

Although the man on stage continued to move down the line, allowing the semi-circle of women surrounding the stage to trail the tips of their fingers on his arm, his shoulders, his chest, and for a brave few, a quick squeeze of his amazingly taut buttocks, he never once showed any emotion. Tyler had absolutely no expression on his face, but that didn't seem to bother any one of his adoring public.

Then he turned to face her. Their gazes met and the bottom simply dropped out of her stomach. His eyes, hot and dark, just barely visible beneath the brim of his black Stetson, seared her right through to her soul.

He lifted his chin a notch as if daring her to comment on the fact that he stood before a group of wild women in a pair of spandex underwear. Body-hugging spandex that lovingly caressed each and every muscle of his sculpted backside. Lord above, he had abs to die for too, with roped muscles leading beneath the elastic band riding low on his hips. He sparked a series of fantasies Emily had had in mind for some time, just waiting for the right man to share them with. Her fingers itched to caress, her hands to grab a hold of him and not let go until she'd gone through her imaginative repertoire.

"He cannot be real," Emily whispered as the image of the handsome hunk spread eagle on her bed, eyes hot with passion, wrists securely tied to her bedposts roared through her.

"He's all too real." Jolene sighed. "And mad as hell."

The image faded with the music. Tyler tipped his hat to the crowd and swept his chaps from the floor. Flipping them over his shoulder, he strode off stage as if he hadn't a care in the world.

Emily had seen that expression on her cousin's face before. "We'll face him together, Jolene. I don't think we'll have to worry about him taking out his anger on us."

"How do you know?" Jolene asked walking toward the door at the side of the stage.

Emily shrugged. "I've got a feeling about him. He might yell some though."

The stage door burst open a few moments later. Emily had forgotten just how tall he was; he towered over Jolene, and her cousin had a good three inches in height over Emily.

Tyler looked like a storm cloud about to explode with thunder and lightning. "You never said anything about women shoving their hands down my shorts and taking a layer of skin off my dick with their claws!"

Emily hadn't expected anyone to be that bold or that Tyler would be hurt. She felt his pain.

"I had no idea anyone would try anything like that." Jolene kept her voice even, her tone soothing.

"One of your customers broke your rules," Tyler ground out.

"I'm sorry, but it's not my fault—" Jolene began.

The anger and tension coiling within the big man had Jolene backing up into Emily, yet he only pushed his hat to the back of his head, and his expression changed from visibly angry to one of cold arrogance. "It's your club... your rules."

Emily looked at her cousin and was catapulted back in time to the day the Stalter brothers cornered little eight-year-old Jolene on the playground. She hugged her cousin and marched forward, drilling the tip of her pointer finger into Tyler's rock-hard chest. "It's our club and the rules usually work for our dancers and the club."

Tyler's gaze swung from Jolene to Emily and her heart kicked into overdrive. The anger swirling in the depths of his velvet brown eyes changed to an untamed emotion, something dark, dangerous, and compelling.

Emily couldn't look away. He blinked, and for a split second, she saw his face contort in anguish. He blinked a second time and it was gone, leaving the heady mix of anger and passion that called to her on an elemental level as deeply as the anguish she'd seen there.

Tyler Garahan was a man of many levels, and Emily planned to discover each and every one.

"Your shift's not over." Jolene's voice was soft but firm. "Are you going back on your word?"

Tyler's anger seemed to dissipate. He shook his head. "Once a Garahan gives his word, you can count on him to keep it."

"You looked like you were getting ready to walk."

He closed his eyes and sighed. "I'm sorry, Jolene. I'm not used to being on stage standing in front of God and every one of those screaming women like that." His

Adam's apple bobbed up and down as he struggled with what he was feeling. "I didn't count on getting mauled like that. My temper got the better of me."

"So I can count on you to stick?"

Tyler looked from Jolene to Emily and then back. "Yes, ma'am. I've never gone back on my word before. I'm sorry for giving you reason to doubt me."

Jolene nodded. "I need to be sure I can count on you, Tyler."

Emily knew why they needed to keep The Lucky Star afloat and making money; what she didn't know yet was why Tyler needed the money when he so clearly didn't want to be up on the stage at The Lucky Star stripping for tips.

Damn. Even before he started, fate had stacked the deck against him. Grandpa's ranch would be lost to them if he didn't get the promised pay. "You can count on me."

He swayed on his feet and realized that he hadn't stopped to eat before his shift. Although he wasn't a great dancer, the moves Jennifer and Natalie had taught him, combined with the fact that he'd been up working since four o'clock this morning, hit him like a ton of bricks. He needed to sit down, eat, and sleep, and not necessarily in that order. Pride kept him going, but he was smart enough to know he'd have to work hard to make up for nearly quitting on Jolene. "I need some air, but I'll be back in a few minutes to help clean up."

Jolene nodded. "Take a break. You earned it."

He moved through the crowd.

"Hey, handsome, where are you going?"

Tyler sidestepped the leggy blonde reaching for him and bumped into a pretty little thing with long dark hair and a mouth just made for sin. "Excuse me, ma'am." Tyler touched the brim of his cowboy hat.

"Do you always talk like that?" the brunette purred.

Tired enough to be confused, he asked, "Like what, ma'am?"

The woman giggled and slipped her arm through his. "Why don't we go someplace real quiet?"

He was the first to admit he enjoyed women, but one at a time. His attention had been snagged by a chocolate-covered redhead earlier. Now that the anxiety of performing his first strip/dance number was abating, all he really wanted was a cold beer, a hot meal, and a soft bed—preferably empty—because as soon as his head hit the pillow, he'd be down for the count.

Looking down at the dark-haired woman and her slick, red, I-just-want-to-suck-you-dry lips, he shook his head. "Maybe some other time." Tipping his hat, he kept walking.

"Don't get lost, Tyler!" He looked over his shoulder and there stood Emily, Jolene, Jennifer, and Natalie. His sigh was long and deep. "I swear I'm just going outside for a breath of air that doesn't smell like perfume."

Damn if Jolene and Emily didn't look at him like he was crazy. "Doesn't the mix of half a dozen different scents make your eyes water?" Hell, it did his. When they just stared at him as if he were from another planet he shook his head. "Ten minutes, and I'll be back."

Emily moved toward him. "You look like you could use a hot meal."

Relieved, he nodded. "Yes, ma'am. I'll be right back."

She reached out to grasp his hand. "I'll rustle up some bacon and eggs for you." She squeezed his hand before letting it go. "Come on upstairs—"

"You can cook just as easily in the downstairs kitchen, Em."

Tyler looked from his boss to the lovely Emily and shrugged. "I'd appreciate it no matter where you cook it, ma'am."

Emily frowned at Jolene. "Fine. Come on back to the downstairs kitchen; it's behind the bar."

Tyler touched his fingers to the brim of his Stetson and made his way through the crowd.

He felt someone slipping their hand into his back pocket, leaving what felt like a credit card or a room key. He was too proud to accept the first, and he'd be damned if he'd accept the second. The promise of sexual release just wasn't what he was after. Now that his anger left and he was able to think straight, all he wanted was to breathe air that wasn't laden with too many sweet-smelling perfumes so he could clear his head and chow down on the promised meal. He reached into his back pocket and handed the room key back to the sultry looking brunette. When she pouted, he shrugged and kept walking.

Once he made it outside, he breathed in deeply. Cool night air filled his lungs. He marveled that Texas air could smell so good. He'd been all the way to Tennessee once, and the air just didn't smell the same there. No offense to folks from Tennessee, but he'd take a lungful of good old Texas air anytime.

Staring up at the stars, he ignored the steady stream of women moving past him, trying to get him to talk to them. His mind wandered until it settled on the chocolate-covered redhead who'd gotten under his skin. He'd been poleaxed by Emily Langley, and he intended to explore his fascination with the woman, her excellent curves, and her sweet-looking mouth. Ten minutes later, he made his way to the downstairs kitchen and found Jolene sipping from a steaming mug while Emily had her back to him frying bacon. "Ain't nothing that smells better to a man with an empty stomach than well-cured pig frying."

Jolene chuckled and smiled. "Have a seat, cowboy."

He sighed. "Name's Tyler."

Jolene grinned. "I know it, but you all dressed up like a cowboy is going to help bring business into The Lucky Star. It'll be good for the both of us."

Emily had yet to turn around, and he had a deep-seated urge to see if her face was as pretty as he remembered. "Everything OK over there?"

She turned around and his heart just flipped upside down and sideways. She had a smear of bacon grease on her tank top right between her amazing breasts. He tried hard, real hard, not to notice. But when her gaze dipped down to where he'd been staring, he knew he'd failed. "You… um…"

"Darnit." She sighed. "I get so involved cooking, I don't always notice when I get some of it on me."

Jolene laughed, drawing his attention back to his boss. "I've got some stain lifter that'll take that right out, Em."

Emily turned back to the frying pan and lifted the rest of the bacon out to drain on the paper towel–lined plate next to the burner. "How many eggs and how do you want them cooked?"

If Tyler wasn't so tired, he'd offer to help; even so, he felt he owed it to her to explain. "Thanks, Emily. I'm so tired, I don't think I could stand up long enough to fry up some eggs."

She grinned and his heart flipped back into place. "Fried it is. How many?"

He wasn't starving, so he only asked for three.

While he ate, the women kept him company. He listened to their quiet conversation and was surprised at how comfortable he felt. He hadn't expected to be. When Jolene pushed her chair back, he got up and held her chair for her. "See you tomorrow… er, later tonight, boss."

Jolene smiled at him—a genuine smile and not the phony one she'd given him during his interview. "I'm counting on it." She patted Emily on the shoulder. "See you in the morning."

Now that they were alone, Tyler didn't know what he wanted to say first. He'd been struck by her beauty first thing… the chocolate had just added to his fascination with her. He lifted his mug to his lips and sipped. "Thanks for the hot meal."

She smiled at him. "My pleasure. You looked like you were going to keel over any minute if I didn't feed you."

Lord, her smile tied his tongue up in a knot. He loosened it enough to say, "Might have."

When he got up and started to rinse his plate in the sink, she joined him. "Here," she said, placing her hand on his. "Let me."

They both stopped and looked into one another's eyes. Tyler couldn't say he minded that she was quiet around him. Maybe he got to her the way she got to him and her tongue tangled up a bit. The thought of tangling tongues with Emily Langley had his libido warming up. He'd been fed and now had energy to spare.

"Emily, I—"

"Need to put something on that scratch."

The pained look in her eyes had him wondering what caused it. Her next words answered his unasked question. "I'm so sorry I didn't think about it before I fed you." She glanced down reminding him of the reason he'd nearly thrown away his chance to save the Circle G.

"It, uh, doesn't bother me all that much."

Her face flushed a lovely shade of pink. Mesmerized, he reached out and touched the tip of his finger to the delicate line of her cheek, stroking it down to the edge of her jaw. "You're distracting, Miss Emily Langley."

She cleared her throat and managed, "Likewise, Mr. Garahan." She blinked and seemed to get her thoughts back in order. "Still, you don't want an infection, and you seriously don't know where that woman's nails have been."

Emily's words had his stomach clenching. "Yes, ma'am. I'll be sure to take care of it."

She visibly relaxed and brushed her hand along the top of his shoulder. "Promise?"

The feather-light stroking motion was doing crazy things to his insides. He covered her hand with his and pulled her up against him so her hands were trapped between them. "You're gonna make it hard for me to sleep tonight."

Her eyes widened. "Really?"

He bent his head until their lips were a breath apart.

"Let me show you why." She licked her lips, and he shuddered with need but held back. He didn't want to scare her off. She was like a filly that needed gentling, coaxing.

Tyler brushed his lips across hers once, then twice, before settling them against her full lips. Her honey-sweet taste shot to his head like three fingers of his grandpa's favorite Irish whiskey. He struggled against the need to devour and settled for a taste of her creamy skin, pressing his lips against her temple and the tip of her nose, before he finally pressed them to the top of her head.

Holding her against him was pure torture. He didn't know how long he'd have to wait before convincing her he would be worth the time to get to know. One thing he did know was that he'd be locking lips with Miss Emily again… soon… real soon.

He eased back from their embrace, running his hands from her shoulders, along the surprisingly toned length of her arms, until he had her hands in his. *It felt right.*

"'Night, Emily."

She tilted her head up to meet his gaze and softly smiled. "Goodnight, Tyler."

Chapter 4

UNABLE TO THINK OF ANYTHING BUT THE GENTLE KISSES they'd shared, Emily watched Tyler leave the kitchen. She couldn't remember ever being kissed as if she were fragile, yet something precious to be savored.

Setting the kitchen to rights, she couldn't get him out of her mind. She couldn't explain the reason why, but something about him just seemed right. Her past boyfriends had just been good to look at, but after getting to know them, she hadn't been attracted to the person beneath their flashy surface, bright-white smiles, and fake suntans.

Despite his rough and tumble exterior, Tyler as a person attracted her. He was a gentleman... the real deal... she could tell by the way he treated Jolene, Gwen, Natalie, and Jennifer. The bonus, as far as she was concerned, was the fact that he was a man of his word and seemed deeply bothered that he'd nearly gone back on it.

She'd seen him struggle with his conscience and knew it had more to do with the circumstances surrounding the incident that had him ready to give up, but when he'd had a moment to get a hold of his emotions, he was ready to stick by his word. She'd love him for that alone.

"Whoa there," she told herself, making her way upstairs to the bathroom. "No reason to toss good sense to the wayside. It's way too early to start tossing around the L word."

She enjoyed being in his company, and cooking for a man never bothered her. It didn't matter if the person was male or female, cooking soothed her the same way baking did. What she hadn't counted on was the way she'd been drawn to him. He seemed so lost when she'd wandered downstairs and found him talking to Jolene. And tonight after the show, he'd been exhausted. She'd fought the need to wrap her arms around him and tuck him into bed… her bed… finally deciding to coax him into the kitchen and feed him. They'd chatted as if they'd been friends forever.

She sighed, remembering how it felt to be held in his arms and kissed so tenderly. No way would she let him walk away from what they'd started. She needed to experience the pleasure of being held in his arms again, against the steady, strong beat of his heart. She sighed and brushed the hair out of her eyes so she could stare at her reflection in the mirror above the sink.

"You're a liar if you think just being held by that tall, dark, handsome hunk of cowboy is going to satisfy the itch that's twitching in your belly." Her reflection shrugged back at her. She was only human.

Emily reached for her toothbrush and tube of toothpaste. Squeezing out a thin line along the bristles, she brushed her teeth while wondering if she was jumping the gun where Tyler was concerned. "He might just want to see if he can talk me into bed."

Her reflection stared back at her as if silently asking: "So?" She grinned. "I'm already interested enough to jump at the chance. But what if it ends after one night?"

She ran her hands under the warm water and splashed her face before reaching for the apricot scrub, squeezing some onto her fingertips. Working the cleanser into her pores, she weighed the pros and cons of beginning a relationship that might only be short-term.

"There's the benefit of having a tall, dark-haired, dark-eyed hunk in my bed." She rinsed her face and reached for the hand towel hanging by the sink. "He looks like he'd be the devil in bed… but he kisses like an angel."

Hanging the towel back on the hook; she sighed. "Lord, that is one complex man: in-your-face sexy on the outside, but shy, sweet, and honorable on the inside." She shut off the light and headed down the hall to her bedroom. "I think I'll have to take my time getting to know him."

Getting undressed for bed, she decided. "Whatever is going to happen will happen no matter how much I stress over it. Fate and destiny can be truly evil bitches sometimes."

Under the covers, she rolled over onto her side. "I'm willing to get to know him better and take the chance that he might want the same thing."

Closing her eyes, she prayed, "Lord, please let him have as much trouble sleeping tonight as me."

"Ty?" a deep voice called, rousing him partway from an exhausted sleep.

"Five more minutes, Grandpa," he struggled to open one eye, knowing the irascible old man would be standing at the foot of his bed with either a glass of cold water or a cup of fragrant fresh brewed coffee, depending on his grandfather's mood.

"Did he just call you Grandpa?"

"Yeah, he did. Must have been a rough night at The Lucky Star if he's seeing Grandpa."

Too tired to open both eyes, Tyler forced his one eye to focus and then moaned. "Musta been dreaming."

The two men standing on either side of his bed grinned simultaneously. Alike enough in looks to be taken for twins, even though they hadn't shared a womb at the same time, his brothers were different enough in personalities to drive a saint crazy. And Lord knows neither the man he'd been dreaming about, who helped to raise them, nor either of his brothers would ever qualify for sainthood.

"Bro," Dylan ground out, "if you're dreaming about Grandpa and this ranch you need to get out more."

"Yeah," Jesse added, "and find yourself a fine-looking female."

"Hell, Jess," Dylan snorted. "Any female, at this point, would do. I think our big brother's in dire need of a woman with quick hands and a soft heart."

A redhead with a huge splat of chocolate in the middle of her T-shirt came to mind. Her beautiful face settled in his mind and stuck. *Emily*. She was a woman worth the time to get to know. Her beauty had hit him between the eyes and stunned him, her curves had his libido and imagination working double time, but the woman beneath the surface was what counted. And he had a bone-deep feeling she was a woman worth knowing. But would she want to get to know him too?

He scrubbed his hands over his face and moaned, "Is that coffee fresh?"

Dylan lifted the mug to his mouth and grinned. "Was about two hours ago." He sipped and Tyler groaned.

"I'm up, damn it." Tyler pushed himself up against the headboard and held out his hand toward the mug.

Dylan shook his head. "You're still in bed." He smiled and lifted the cup to drink. Swallowing a mouthful, he licked his lips. "Hot and sweet, just like I like my women."

"Coffee," Tyler ground out.

His brothers shared a look and backed up.

"Nothing doing. Not until you're on your feet, or else you'll drink it and fall right back to sleep." Jesse stared at the middle of Tyler and frowned. "You lose a fight with a cat last night?"

The image of a blonde with dark roots and nasty claws came to mind. "No. Why?" The lie came just a bit too easily to his lips.

Jesse lifted one of the steaming cups he held and pointed at Tyler's stomach. "You've got a couple of serious scratch marks there."

Emily had been worried about the possibility of infection. The little redhead had kept him tossing and turning most of the night, remembering her soft laughter, cheerful smile, and captivating demeanor. She'd cooked him breakfast and kept him company while he ate. Talking to her had been a pleasure—like they were old friends. The gentle kisses they'd shared had been achingly sweet and whet his whistle for more. Holding her against him had been pure torture. He'd had a taste, and he craved more.

"You want to tell us about it?" Dylan leaned toward the bed and waited.

Shaking his head to clear it, Tyler focused his thoughts

where they needed to be—the present—and that cup of coffee he wanted. Unwilling to own up to the truth of what happened, he shrugged. "Must have been a staple from one of the boxes." Tyler needed caffeine if he was going to stay one step ahead of his brothers—make that one lie ahead. He threw the covers off, got out of bed, and stalked toward his brother. "Now, gimme that cup!"

Jesse shoved the chipped stoneware cup at him, sloshing coffee over the rim. Tyler grabbed the cup, switched hands, and using his brother's shirt like a towel, wiped his wet hand on the front of Jesse's clean white T-shirt. Slipping his fingers through the handle, Tyler tilted his head back and took a long slug of coffee.

Swallowing a moan of pure caffeine-induced pleasure, he looked over at his brother and admitted, "God, I'd have had to hurt you if you didn't hand that cup over."

Jesse glanced down at the wet spot on his shirt and held up his hands. "Yeah, I'm shaking in my boots, Ty."

"Come on," Dylan urged. "We're burning daylight."

Tyler gulped down more of the coffee. "I'm coming." He started to follow his brothers out of his bedroom, but Dylan put a hand to the middle of Tyler's chest and grinned at him. "You might want to put pants on first."

At his suggestion, Tyler looked down. "Hell." He was too tired to put pants on. "Why should you care if I eat breakfast in my boxers or not?" he demanded, following close on his brothers' heels.

"Because Lori's in the kitchen making you breakfast," Dylan bit out.

"Yeah," Jesse added. "You know Grandpa's rule, when it's just us men… anything goes… but if there's a woman in the house, we wear our damned pants to breakfast."

Taking another swig of coffee, Tyler wondered if there was more to Jesse wanting him to put on his pants. They'd all grown up together—Jesse still didn't have a thing for Lori, did he?

Time to test the waters and find out. "She's seen me in less—" he began only to find himself pinned to the wall just outside his bedroom door with his little brother's arm wedged up against his throat.

"Shut. The. Fuck. Up." Jesse pressed harder, cutting off Tyler's air.

Just when the room started to fade to gray, the weight lifted and he dragged in a much-needed breath of air. Rounding on his brother, hands curled into fists at his sides, Tyler rasped, "What the hell is your problem?"

Dylan reached past him and dragged their younger brother down the hall. "You two can fight later. We've got chores. Come on, Jess."

"He's got no call to be talkin'—"

The rest of what Jesse was going to say was cut off by a sweet, soft voice calling out that breakfast was ready.

Tyler stubbed his toe on something cool and hard. Shaking his head to clear the last of the fuzziness away, he reached down and picked up the coffee mug where it had fallen in the scuffle.

"Wasn't even worth calling a fight," he mumbled rubbing at his throat. "Damn... that hurts." Looking down, he swore. He'd be inciting a riot and asking for round two if he showed up in the kitchen in his form-fitting boxers. Hell, it wasn't the style of them that might offend the woman his brothers must have coerced into cooking for them while Tyler worked nights. When a woman was in your damned house, you had to dress for breakfast... no more showing up naked or in your boxers. Grandpa's rule had been handed down generation to generation, and as people said, "If it ain't broke..."

Growing up, his mom had been strict about it. After she died, Grandpa had stepped in, doing double-duty as their only parent and the ranch's owner and, therefore, their boss. The old man hadn't been too particular about briefs or boxers at the breakfast table, as long as the three of them hustled their butts and got the animals fed and watered on schedule.

Retracing his steps, he wondered how serious it was between Lori and Jesse. They sure as shit couldn't afford to pay Lori, so why would she... And then it hit him right between the eyes and he grinned. Jesse must have sweet-talked her into doing it.

The youngest of the trio had inherited their grandfather's Irish charm. Far as he could tell, Jesse had all of the charm, since Tyler and Dylan pretty much communicated with as few words as possible to as few people as possible... well, unless the situation warranted it.

He was grinning to himself as he turned around to grab the pair of jeans he'd left on the floor where he'd shucked them off last night. Stepping into them, he pulled them up his legs, fastened the button, and brushed against the raw abrasion low on his belly.

He drew in a breath and remembered Emily's concern-filled warning. Stopping in the bathroom, he checked for signs of infection. Worried enough about his working parts to take extra care, he rummaged in the medicine cabinet and found cotton balls and some antiseptic.

"Shit!" Sucking in air between his teeth, ignoring the cold stinging sensation along his now semi-erect shaft, he dabbed on some first aid ointment and pulled his boxers and jeans back on.

His mood grim, Tyler stormed into the kitchen, ready to tear ass.

"Morning, Ty."

The petite blonde holding a steaming cup of coffee out so he could grab it smiled at him and half of his mad just melted away. Not sure he could trust himself not to say something that would get his brother riled again, he nodded and accepted the offering. He blew across the surface of the liquid then sipped. Perfect temperature. He swallowed a mouthful and eyed his brother, gauging his mood before saying, "Thanks."

"Don't mind him, Lori." Jesse eyed him like he was an opponent, rather than one-third of the reason Tyler'd sold his integrity last night—for more than he'd hoped to earn but still a hell of a lot less than they really needed.

Her smile was sugar-sweet. "A good-looking, grumpy man like your big brother just needs something to line the ache in his empty belly."

She turned around and reached for the plate she'd left on the countertop. Filling it with steak, scrambled eggs, fried potatoes, and toast, she laid a hand on Jesse's shoulder and reached past him to give Tyler the plate.

Tyler looked right at his brother and grinned. "You can cook for me anytime, Lori."

Lori's smile broadened. "That's the plan. At least until you're ready to quit working nights." She placed a plate of crisply fried bacon in the middle of the table, totally at ease in the Garahan kitchen. Bustling about topping off coffee cups, her gaze flicked from where his brother still sat and then back.

Tyler looked at his brothers and wondered just how much Lori knew about their financial situation. Probably a lot more than he'd be comfortable with and not a topic he wanted to discuss over breakfast.

"Since neither one of my brothers can boil water without melting the pot handle—"

"Hey!" Jesse grumbled. "It wasn't my fault that I got distracted."

Dylan nodded at their brother and said, "That's his story and he's sticking to it."

Jesse reached across the table to grab at Dylan, but Dylan gave him a brotherly shove, pushing him back in his chair. Tyler shook his head at their usual morning routine. One out of the three of them usually woke up in a bad mood and took it out on the other two. Good thing they didn't do it all at the same time, or they'd never get anything done.

"You're always welcome, Lori." He slid his chair away from the table and got to his feet. "The cooking is definitely a bonus."

"If y'all are finished, I'll just clean up." Picking up empty plates and stacking them with the silverware piled on top, she set them in the sink to rinse before loading the dishwasher.

Not used to having someone serve them with a smile—heck, his brothers would have just as soon punched him good morning as hand him a mug of hot coffee—Tyler handed her his empty mug and said, "Thanks for breakfast. Tastes better when you don't have to cook it too."

She didn't turn around when she answered him. "My pleasure, Tyler."

Dylan grabbed him by the arm and tugged him toward the back door. "We're burning daylight, bro."

He noticed that their younger brother took his time leaving their blue-eyed cook. The door slammed behind them, but Tyler was too focused on getting through the morning without falling down to bother picking a fight with the youngest Garahan—a sure sign he was not himself this morning. He'd make up for it and razz Jesse later.

Outside, Tyler asked, "Do you think he's serious about Lori?"

Dylan shrugged. "Don't know. Might be."

"I heard there was a lot of kicking and screaming before the ink was dry on her divorce decree."

Dylan shook his head. "Man, and all of it wasted on that pisspoor excuse for an ex-husband of hers."

They walked into the barn, gathered what they needed, and saddled their horses. Tyler's first chore of the day was to ride fences with his brother and repair any breaches so none of their cattle would wander off their ranch. The routine chore would let him work up a sweat and forget about money and a certain redhead with whiskey-colored eyes for a while.

The sun soaked into his aching bones. Maybe he should have washed down a couple of aspirin with that second cup of coffee and taken the time to stretch out the kinked muscles low in his spine.

"Ty?"

Jerking back to attention when Dylan called his name, he put his back into it, lifted the fallen post, and steadied it while his brother fastened the wire. Tucking the wire cutters into his back pocket, Dylan pushed his hat to the back of his head, probably hoping to grill him some more about his new job.

"So what's the owner like?"

"Short."

Dylan's snort of laughter had Tyler grinning as he swung up into the saddle.

"Must be tough on him, having bouncers taller than he is."

Tyler squeezed his thighs against his mount. Recognizing the signal, his horse started walking. "I didn't exactly say my boss was a he."

About to swing up into the saddle, Dylan paused, and his head whipped around. "Your new boss is a woman?"

"With a capital W." The words slipped out before Tyler had a chance to think about what he was saying. He hoped Dylan wouldn't try to pick his brain the rest of the ride back to the ranch house. He didn't have much left and would need it to be on his toes come time to drive into town and show up for work.

"Damn," his brother muttered after a few miles of riding alongside him in silence. "She's gotta be a redhead."

It wasn't a secret the Garahan men were partial to redheads. He frowned, wondering just how much to tell his brother. He'd never done anything he was too ashamed to tell his brothers about before. It wasn't that he'd never been naked in front of a female before. Hell, he'd been fourteen and horny as a bull with a three-day hard-on when Jenny'd met him out by the pond one sultry summer night.

God, she'd been so hot and wet…

"Tyler!"

"What?" The image of the blue-eyed blonde with bounteous breasts faded as the irritated face of his younger brother came fully into focus.

"I asked you how many cases and kegs you had to haul last night?"

Should he fess up? "Not that many." And hell if that wasn't the truth. *None wasn't all that many.*

"So it's just the hours then," Dylan said, bringing his horse up alongside Tyler's.

He nodded. He supposed the hours had something to do with his mood. Lying was getting a whole lot easier. *Should he be worried about that?*

"Jesse and I don't want you to think we aren't going to pull more weight around the ranch while you're working nights, earning the rest of the feed bill and mortgage payment."

Tyler noticed the lines of strain around his brother's eyes and the grim set of his jaw. Dylan looked as if he wanted to go three rounds and then some. Tyler had a pretty good idea who his brother would start with. "It isn't Mike's fault the bank called in our loan."

Dylan's jaw clenched and his eyes narrowed.

Bulls-eye.

"Yeah, well he's the one—" Dylan began only to be interrupted by Tyler.

"The one who fought to have the mortgage extended three times," Tyler ground out. If anyone had tried to help the Garahan brothers save the Circle G, it was their childhood friend Mike Baker. Too bad he was a blood relative of Tyler's former girlfriend, Linda Lee.

"Lot of good it did us."

"He bought us three months," Tyler grumbled.

"And look where it got us," Dylan bit out.

Tyler nudged his mount forward. They had two more sections of fence to ride before heading in for a break. "We didn't lose the ranch," Tyler said. "And if I'm going to be taking—"

Shit! He'd almost spilled his guts. Damn this tired; if he wasn't careful, he was liable to tell Dylan everything that happened since he left the house yesterday afternoon.

"Taking what?" Dylan demanded, eyes narrowed, mouth grim.

Thinking fast, Tyler improvised. "Taking a beating during the day at the ranch and orders from a little bit of a woman and her redheaded cousin at night. So stop riding my case about it."

Dylan's expression went from grim to gray. One thing about the men in the Garahan family: they'd work until they bled, but taking orders from a woman, well that was a whole other story and probably the reason there'd been so many crusty old bachelors in their family.

"You're right," his brother agreed. "Sorry."

Tyler swallowed against the lump of lies lodged in his throat. If he could remember to keep quiet about what he was doing at The Lucky Star to earn his pay, no one would be the wiser.

Chapter 5

"It'll be close," Emily said, adding the next set of numbers into the calculator, "but I think we'll have enough to pay the taxes, liquor supplier, and chip away at the mortgage."

Jolene paced in front of the upstairs kitchen table, their makeshift office while they renovated one of the storerooms downstairs. "Maybe we should have waited another month before buying this place."

"You know that we'd have lost out; there were three other bids for this place." Emily shut her eyes, grateful for the moment's rest. She'd had precious few hours of sleep last night thanks to one tall, dark, and deadly handsome cowboy's tender kisses.

"A penny for your thoughts, cuz." Jolene leaned her hip against the counter and crossed her legs in front of her. The smug smile told Em she didn't need to explain why she was tired. Jolene always could read her like a book.

"Wondering where we would have ended up working if you didn't convince us this place would be a gold mine."

"Well, I may have been a bit hasty," Jolene said softly.

"I'm always first to give credit where credit is due, honey," Emily said, pushing her chair back to stand up. She stretched the kinks out of her spine and walked over to where her cousin stood. "Your idea was inspired, the location fabulous, and our new headliner… to die for."

"And?" Jolene was waiting for Emily to spill her guts. Damn, the woman really did have the ability to read minds.

"He's got this really rough but handsome exterior, but inside he's got this sugar-sweet, gooey center that a woman would have to be dead not to fall for."

"Are you falling for him already?" Jolene didn't try to hide her exasperation.

"Maybe, but this time, I'll be ready when he walks."

"What makes you think he'll walk?"

Emily didn't know that he would; it was just a part of the pattern of her past relationships. "He might surprise me and stay."

"Way to go thinking in the positive, Em."

"The past has always been—"

"Among my favorite interests," Frank Emerson, President of the Pleasure Preservation Society, boomed from where he stood in the doorway.

Annoyed that he'd come upstairs uninvited, Emily walked toward him. "I don't believe we heard you knock."

His smile was just a shade off and definitely not sincere. "I'm sure you two were talking too loudly to hear me when I knocked just now."

Liar. Emily knew he hadn't; the man had a habit of walking in unannounced to catch his prey off guard while he went in for the kill, usually walking away with whatever he wanted. "I don't suppose you can read?"

His eyes narrowed before he acknowledged what she'd meant. "Surely the sign that says *private* on the door at the bottom of these stairs doesn't refer to your fellow businessmen and women in town?"

Jolene cleared her throat, and Emily knew she was about to say something that would make her and Emily feel better but would just alienate the head of the damned society. Emily sent a warning look that Jolene grudgingly heeded. "What do you want, Frank?"

He took his time answering, while glancing about their kitchen, no doubt taking it all in so he could file it in his damned report on the one historic building in Pleasure he hadn't been able to get his hands on. "I'd hope to get you two ladies to change your mind and join in our campaign to bring tourism back to Pleasure."

Jolene mumbled something beneath her breath, which Emily was grateful couldn't be heard across the room where she and Frank were standing. She smiled and said, "We'd like to think we're doing our small part here on Loblolly Way, Frank."

His eyes narrowed again. Not a good sign. "Nevertheless, we need business owners like yourselves to donate to the cause and help us keep history alive in Pleasure."

Jolene actually laughed and Emily wished she hadn't. "Why, my dear Mr. Emerson," Jolene began, "I do believe we're doing just that. Wasn't it the Donovan sisters who founded our fair town?"

He nodded.

"And weren't those dear women the same Donovan sisters who opened the town's first bawdy house?"

His jaw clenched and Emily could swear she heard the sound of teeth grinding.

"Be that as it may," he said, "we at the Preservation Society have a vision for the town and it—"

"Doesn't match ours," Jolene purred. "So while we

appreciate you coming all the way over here, we're not ready to make that donation just yet."

When he stood there staring at Jolene, Emily took his arm and turned him around so he was facing the hallway that led to the stairs. "We'll be in touch when we're ready to write that check. Y'all have a great day."

"But—"

"Emily will walk you downstairs, Frank, in case you've forgotten the way out."

Emily wished Jolene would escort Frank out of their place but knew that would only end in disaster. Jolene couldn't keep her mouth shut around a royal pain in the ass like Frank. "It's right this way." He grudgingly followed behind her.

By the time they'd reached the bottom step, she could hear voices. "Now who do you suppose that could that be?"

Frank actually smiled... a real smile. "Ah, I've asked my colleagues, Anne Marie Gonzales, President of Pleasure's Women's Club, and Janet Gorman, President of the Rotary Club, to meet me here."

Emily groaned aloud. "And you did that because?"

"My dear Ms. Langley, nonprofit organizations such as ours depend upon the generosity of those who have lucrative businesses to make donations that will keep our coffers filled, so that we can continue to do our good works."

He turned and smiled, hand extended toward the blonde. "Janet, good of you to join us." Turning toward the black-haired woman, his smile broadened. "Anne Marie, I knew I could count on you."

The women stared openly at Emily. Lord, she wasn't

ready to face the three of them, especially alone. It was one thing to have to deal with Frank, but these two uptight, bitchy women would just put a crimp in her day. She walked over to the door she'd left open and hollered up the stairs. "Jolene!"

When her cousin answered, she called out, "We got us some visitors, come on down."

She had the satisfaction of seeing the twin looks of disbelief on the ladies' faces that neither one had been quick enough to hide when she'd shouted for her cousin. She knew they didn't like her and Jolene, and it was no secret the women didn't think she or her cousin were ladylike, but she didn't really care. She'd met their type before. All showy and good intentions on the outside, but that did not match the vinegary center that made them miserable to have to deal with.

Jolene rushed through the door and, before Emily could warn her, made a face. "Well, well," she drawled. "Look what the cat dragged in."

"Be nice, Jolene," Emily urged.

"Maybe," Jolene whispered. "Depends on what these two want," she said out loud.

Affronted, the women looked at one another, and Anne Marie drew in a deep breath, threatening to burst the pearl buttons on her cashmere sweater set before launching into a boring monologue about the history of their town and how donations to their clubs would be the only way their organizations would be able to preserve the finest aspects of their town.

"That's all well and good, Anne Marie," Jolene said quietly, "but what exactly do you intend to do with the funds we turn over to you?"

Stumped, the woman looked helplessly at Janet.

Jolene turned toward her as well. "Janet? How do you intend to spend the donation I may give to the Rotary Club?"

"Well I'd definitely start with… that is to say, possibly I'd…"

Jolene sighed. "Just as I thought: neither one of you has a fiscal plan as to what you intend to do with any funds received from tax-paying businesswomen like myself and my cousin."

After grinning at Emily, Jolene added, "Perhaps another time. Y'all know the way out?"

With that she turned her back on the group and started to walk away.

"I'd think very carefully about your decision, Ms. Langley," Frank Emerson said slowly. "I'd hate to see your establishment lose money due to lack of business."

Jolene smiled. "We're doing just fine bringing in the crowds. Goodbye, Frank."

She turned to leave again and this time Anne Marie stopped her. "I, for one, have been meaning to bring up the topic of your establishment at our next meeting. The good people of Pleasure shouldn't have to drive past such a den of iniquity as this on their way to the feed store and center of town."

Jolene's jaw clenched, and Emily recognized the sign as the point of no return with her cousin's temper.

"I know exactly what you mean, Anne Marie," Janet simpered. "The good folks of this town should know about what goes on in a place like this."

Jolene actually smiled at that. "Why, Janet honey, wasn't that you I saw sidling up to Dave and Joe after they'd finished the finale last week Thursday? Surely you reported back to your club all about it. Especially the lap dance."

Janet paled, not a good look with the black pantsuit she always wore when conducting official Rotarian business.

"You've not seen the last of us," Anne Marie warned.

"Promises, promises." Jolene grinned at Emily and tugged on her hand. "Don't all y'all let the door hit ya where the good Lord split ya."

"Jolene," Emily rasped. But her cousin's comment was enough to have the trio drawing in a collective breath and leaving.

"Finally," Emily said as the phone rang. "I'll get it."

Jolene shook her head and reached it first. "Jolene here."

The expression on her cousin's face changed radically. The humor was replaced with a hint of fear and a whole lot of temper. Jolene opened her mouth to speak, then changed her mind, and disconnected without saying a word.

"Who was it?" Emily demanded.

"Damned if I know."

"What did they want?"

"Money."

"Jeez, Jolene," Emily said, walking to where her cousin stood by the bar. "Was it one of Frank's vice presidents?"

Jolene shook her head. "I'm not sure who it was, but he's called here once before... you remember that first day we were open for business and Jake Turner walked in?"

Emily smiled at that. "Ah yes, the gorgeous, clipboard-carrying fire marshal."

Jolene frowned at her. "Well, whoever it is called then too, asking for the same thing."

"Money," Emily said.

"Right."

"How much?"

Jolene shrugged. "Five thousand."

"Dollars?" Emily had trouble conceiving of such an amount in cash. "When did they want it by?"

"Actually, I never really found out. I hung up before he could tell me when he wants the money."

"Aren't you worried that someone is trying to extort money from us?"

Jolene grinned. "Not especially, since we've already got the buzzards circling overhead, waiting for us to slip up so we end up donating to their damned clubs."

"But, Jo," Emily said, "this is different. Shouldn't we call the sheriff's office?"

"And tell them what, that the Preservation Society ganged up with the Rotary Club and the Woman's Club, and are harassing us for money?"

"No," Emily wrapped her arms around herself trying to keep the warmth from escaping. "That someone is threatening you for money."

"Oh that."

"Yeah," Emily agreed. "That."

"But I told you I never find out when he wants the money or what he'll do if I don't pay… I hang up first."

"Jo, honey?"

Surprised at the subtle change in Emily's tone, her cousin paused. "Yeah?"

"Did Aunt Susan drop you on your head when you were a baby?"

Jolene laughed out loud. "Shut up, Em."

"Must have been more than once to have such a lasting effect on your poor injured brain like this."

"Bite me, Em."

"No thanks, Jolene."

"Good thing I love you."

"Back at you, cuz."

A few hours later, Emily grinned at Natalie, grateful for the distraction from their earlier visitors and the worrisome phone call. "It's definitely a new look for us. Whose idea was it to dress up like bad news cowgirls?"

Jennifer's face lit up. "It was my idea," she said. "Don't you just love the wine-red boots?"

Emily shook her head. "You know I really love the black pair I always wear."

Natalie smiled and patted Emily's arm. "We know, honey, but I think Jennifer's right about the overall look. All of us dressed alike is bound to make a statement, and people will know who we are."

"Hell's bells, Nat, they already know who we are."

"But not the droves of new customers who'll be bound to find their way to our door after Tyler's debut last night."

Emily smiled in spite of herself. Heaven help her, the man had certainly made an impression on her... and every other woman in their club last night. "Word of mouth has worked for us so far." She looked over at her friends and nodded. "The black leather bustier is a definite plus. I'm so glad Ronnie was able to get them on short notice." She skimmed her hands from the bottom edge to up beneath her breasts. "It feels real good. How cool is it that Ronnie's shop, Guilty Pleasures, could get the special order for us in time for tonight? A little chilly on the chest though." She shivered and her breasts threatened to spill out over the top. Emily made a mental note to be careful or else she'd get arrested for showing more than just her cleavage.

"Once the evening crowd pours in, it'll warm up considerably," Natalie reassured her. With a glance to her left and then her right, Natalie laughed and said, "Damn, we look fine. We so owe Ronnie!"

The three women twirled in front of the mirrored wall in the hallway, checking themselves and each other out.

Emily hesitated. "I'm still not sure about dressing alike."

"Come on, Em." Jennifer reached out to grab Emily's hand. "Try it this once," she urged. "If you were working in another club, odds are you'd be wearing black slacks and a white button-down shirt." She paused for effect. "Isn't this black leather so much cooler?"

Emily laughed. "All right, Jen. But tomorrow, I'm wearing my favorite boots."

"Only if you polish them," Jennifer retorted.

The three friends started walking back toward the bar. Natalie nudged Emily with her elbow. "Jolene said you had your belly button pierced."

Emily shrugged. "Yeah, so?"

"Why don't you wear a hoop or something?"

"I gained a few pounds, and now I don't."

Natalie narrowed her eyes and stared at the thin line of skin showing between the top of the low-rise skirt and the bottom edge of Emily's bustier. "I think you'd look great with one."

Gwen looked up from where she stood behind the bar and groaned. "Please tell me this is Halloween and all y'all are going trick or treating."

Jolene patted her on the arm. "We know how you feel about displaying what the good Lord gave you, Gwen."

Em could tell Jolene was trying not to smile, so she kept her mouth shut. Gwen would be a hard sell; their friend hated to draw attention to what Gwen considered her worst feature. In Emily's opinion, it was Gwen's best asset, but their friend had always been embarrassed by the size of her breasts.

Gwen's face darkened. "I'm always on time for my shift, but I'll be damned if you'll get me in one of those Debbie the Dominatrix outfits."

Emily laughed. "Please… do you see us carrying any whips or chains, Gwen?"

The other woman frowned. "I used to room with a girl in college who had this catalogue where you could get all kinds of kinky stuff. Debbie the D costumes were always sold out. Besides," Gwen added, "if I have to rough anybody up because they start groping our dancers, you know what'll happen."

Although Gwen didn't say it, Emily sensed what their friend wanted to say. "Jolene, I think she's right. These bustiers are strictly for looking good in; they seriously inhibit movement. If I almost popped out and flashed because I took a deep breath, then Gwen with her totally bodacious tatas would blind the first person she had to escort to the door."

Emily looked over at Natalie and Jennifer. When they made eye contact, Jennifer nodded.

Gwen swore. "Not funny."

Emily frowned. "I'm not trying to be. You need to focus on bartending and bouncing… or it is bouncering?"

Gwen relaxed her stance. Her relief at not having to change out of her signature black T-shirt was evident.

Natalie grinned. "We're going to look fabulous tonight! I've got a couple of extra belly button rings upstairs, Em."

Jolene's gaze swung from Natalie toward Emily, and her expression changed from thoughtful to smug.

Emily recognized the look in Jolene's eyes.

"I double-dog dare you to wear one tonight."

"Jeez, Jolene. We're not kids anymore."

"A dare's a dare."

"Oh all right."

"Good." Jolene rubbed her hands together smiling gleefully. "I've got a couple upstairs that you can pick from if Natalie doesn't have what you want."

Her gaze met Jolene's and held. Rather than argue, which is what her cousin expected, Emily ignored her and changed the subject. "Got any body glitter left, Jen?"

"I've got just plain sparkle or 'hey cowboy, I'm ready to ride' extra sparkle."

A half hour later, sporting glitter-dusted shoulders and cleavage, and flashing belly rings, the women took turns checking each other out one last time.

"If you change your mind about the plain gold hoop," Natalie said, "I've got the cutest cubic zirconium horseshoe belly ring."

Emily rolled her eyes. "You would."

Jolene grinned then motioned for everyone to come closer. When they did, she gestured for them to link arms. Huddled like a football team receiving instructions from their quarterback, they waited. "All right ladies," Jolene kept her voice low and even, "tonight, we're not only going to be headlining our new star entertainer, but I was able to secure a last minute radio ad so I expect a full house."

Jennifer looked at her sister and said, "Nat and I are ready."

Emily grinned. "Good news travels fast, and I'm sure word has gotten out about our new dancer. Mavis Beeton was here two nights ago, but missed Tyler's debut last night so she'll probably be here with Ronnie in tow."

When Jolene grinned at her, Emily laughed. "Did you see the way Mavis was leaning with her head to the side so she could get a better look at Joe's backside?"

Jolene snickered. "We'll have to watch her intake of Mega-Margaritas."

Natalie chimed in, "Oh just let Mavis enjoy the eye candy. She never touches… she just looks."

Jennifer nodded and grinned. "We're going to totally rock tonight ladies!"

The group high-fived one another and then Jolene glanced down at her watch. "Joe and Dave will be here in about twenty minutes. Where's Tyler?"

"Sorry I'm late, boss."

Good Lord, Emily thought. He was even better looking with his clothes on, and if that didn't mess with her concentration, Emily's mind did a little side trip remembering how great he looked half-naked. The man was totally ripped. There was just something about the long line of his dusty jeans and torn and bloody cotton shirt…

Oh my God! Emily moved toward him. "Where are you hurt?" Tyler looked at her and, wonder of wonders, his deeply tanned face pinkened. "It's nothing much." He cleared his throat and added, "Ma'am."

Jolene moved toward him, but Emily waved her away. "You've got a club to run, cuz." She tugged Tyler's arm. "And I remember where the first aid kit is."

Tyler dug in his heels, shaking his head. "I'm fine. I just need to wash up."

Emily agreed with the second statement but didn't think the man currently frowning down at her felt anywhere close to fine. He looked like he'd just gone nine rounds and lost. "I'll just show you to the upstairs bathroom; there's a shower up there."

He didn't budge. Wondering what had happened to the closeness they'd shared late last night, and if he was always this stubborn, she tugged his arm again. She thought they'd been laying the groundwork, getting to know one another. It was a given that they were attracted to one another. A blind, deaf man would have recognized the signs. Distracted by the niggle of worry planting itself in her brain, she tugged on his arm again.

Jolene ended the man's indecision. "Go on up with Emily. Natalie and Jennifer have to go over tonight's routine with Joe and Dave too. By the time you're finished, the guys'll be here, and she'll only have to go over the routine once."

He nodded. "Jolene, I'm sorry I'm late, but I got caught up and then the bull—"

Emily's heart stumbled in her breast. Did this poor guy just get off work? "The rancher you work for must really be a jerk if he demands such long hours from you."

Tyler's head tilted to one side. He looked as if he

were about to say something then thought better of it and instead nodded in agreement. "He can be."

"Do you get paid overtime?" she asked leading the way to the back of the bar and the staircase to the second floor.

"No."

"So he's a skinflint too?" She shook her head and tugged him up the stairs. "Unbelievable."

"He's got bills to pay, same as you and your cousin," Tyler ground out.

She appreciated the way Tyler defended his boss. Loyalty was a trait she admired, but still. "Hmmphf." She tossed her hair over her shoulder and slanted a look out of the corner of her eye and had to look up. The cowboy was tall, but he sure as spit wasn't skinny. Lord, his muscles had muscles. The tips of her fingers tingled with the need to reach out and test their firmness and strength, just as she had touched the breadth of his shoulders last night. She flexed her hands, before balling them into fists to keep from reaching out and grabbing hold of him.

"Here we are." Back in control, she opened the door to the upstairs apartment hallway. "Just give me a minute to pick up a few things; I didn't realize we'd be having company."

"I just need to take a quick shower," he said, following along behind her into the tiny bathroom.

The low whistle of appreciation had embarrassment staining her cheeks. She'd left her bra and panties drying on the shower rod… her black lace bra and skimpy panties.

Jeez! "I, uh…" she snatched the underwear off the rod.

Tyler cleared his throat, and she noticed he seemed to be trying to look anywhere but at the delicate underwear clutched to her breast then groaned out loud when she noticed the open box of tampons someone had left on the back of the toilet. *Perfect.*

His gaze locked with hers and she wondered just what the big man was thinking. Was it the skimpy underwear or the feminine protection? It had been years since she'd been embarrassed by the good-looking male cashier at the grocery store, the one who always managed to be the only one open when she'd had to buy the darned things.

Tyler took a step closer to her, crowding her. But the vibes pouring off of him weren't the same as last night. Last night he'd been gentle, careful with her… right now she wasn't sure what he was thinking. There seemed to be a dangerous edge to him tonight. Unfortunately, she didn't have the time to test her theory right now; she had to get back downstairs and had to make sure Tyler did too. They were expecting a full house. She backed away from him, right into the broken corner of the vanity cabinet with her hipbone.

She muffled her moan of agony; her hip hadn't been right since she'd landed on it tussling with the Stalter brothers defending Jolene all those years ago.

"Hey, are you all right?"

His concern wrapped around her like a warm hug.

She drew in a breath and ignored the ache. It'd go away sooner or later. It always did. "I'm good."

All at once, his demeanor changed until he was the man she remembered from last night. She smiled, knowing she was going to enjoy getting to know this complex cowboy.

"Look, I don't want you to go to any trouble. I can go back downstairs and use the sink in the men's room to wash up." He started to back up, but she scooted past him.

Their bodies brushed against each other and her nipples saluted his amazing pectorals.

Gazes locked, need clamoring for attention, neither one spoke. Words weren't necessary. The tingles morphed into sparks that threatened to ignite the air around them. Emily wondered, was he the tinder or the flint?

"Well," she said when he continued to stare at her like she was a frosted cake and he was just dying to start licking from the top down until he could bite the sweet confection at the center.

Lord, where did that fantasy come from? She shivered, looked up, and got distracted by the heat in his dark brown eyes. She was going to have to remember that one and see if she could convince him to act it out later. "I'll, um… let me just get you a towel."

Shifting her burden to the crook of her left arm, she stepped out of the bathroom and walked to the linen closet. Fumbling with the cabinet door, she was finally able to open it, reach in, and grab a fluffy white towel. She dropped her underwear and tampon box on the shelf before bringing Tyler the towel. But when she tried to hand it to him, he frowned down at her.

"Don't you have a dark blue or brown one?"

Now why on earth would he care what color the towel was? "You're kidding right?"

He shook his head. "I've pretty much stopped the bleeding, but I don't want to ruin your towel."

Emily sighed. It would be a bit longer before she'd get back downstairs at this rate, but he seemed to need reassurance right now. "You won't. Why don't you show me where you've cut yourself?"

"I didn't."

"But you've got blood on your shirt."

He shrugged. "Widowmaker pushed me into the fence and scraped me up some, but that doesn't qualify as a real cut."

"Please don't tell me that's the name of the bull you mentioned downstairs."

He grinned, and his crooked smile went right to the soft spot in her heart reserved for rascals and rogues. At least that's what her grandmother had told her all those years ago. Granny should know—she'd married a rogue of her own. Emily watched the way Tyler relaxed once they were alone together and that niggle of worry eased—for the moment. Funny, when other people were around, he was more reserved and treated her as if they hadn't shared the tender moment that kept her awake most of the night. But alone together, he let his guard down.

"Emily!"

Jolene's voice had her looking over her shoulder. "Be right there." Turning back to Tyler she said, "If there's anything else—" Her voice trailed off as she got caught up in the desire plain as day in his velvet dark eyes. The desire called to her now, as it had last night, but was more insistent. She drew in a breath, felt her breasts pushing the bustier to the limit, and had the feminine satisfaction of watching his eyes glaze over. A definite mood lifter.

She shivered. She couldn't help it. She'd never been so attracted so fast or been desired so desperately.

He grabbed her hand and yanked her close. "I just have to taste you again." He dipped his head and sipped from her lips.

Emily moaned. She'd been expecting to be devoured after the way he tumbled her against him. The soft, hesitant kisses he trailed along the line of her jaw had the spit drying up in her mouth and every last thought evaporating from her brain. Passion she could have handled; Tyler's devastatingly gentle exploration had desire curling in low in her belly.

She melted against him and it was his turn to groan. Drawing back, he rasped, "I wasn't sure last night, but darlin', you surely taste like sin."

She snuggled closer. She'd wanted to take a walk on the wild side with him, now was her chance to light the fuse. Her earlier fantasy returned with a vengeance: Tyler naked in her bed, tied to her bedposts. It ramped up the sensual tension holding her by the throat. Sliding her fingers through his hair, she grabbed hold and tugged his head down until their lips were a breath apart. Ready for a taste of the passion she sensed lurked beneath the surface, she rasped, "I feel a sin coming on."

Lips fused, hearts pounding, she let her tongue tangle with his and groaned in pure pleasure when he slid his hand down her spine to pin her to him. Heat to heat, her brain fizzled and every thought evaporated save one: kissing Tyler. She moaned and he took charge, changing the angle of the kiss, destroying her when his tongue left hers to tease the inside edge of her bottom lip.

Her legs buckled, but he held her up and plundered. "You're addictive, Miss Langley, and this small sampling won't be enough." He paused then asked, "Will you meet me later?"

Emily smiled. "Your place or mine?"

His gaze smoldered with the passion he held in check. "Yours is closer."

She licked her lips and pulled his mouth back to hers.

"Em, what's keeping you?" Jolene's voice cut through the haze of passion surrounding them, and they jumped apart like guilty teenagers who'd been caught necking on the front porch swing.

Emily looked over her shoulder and was relieved Jolene hadn't caught them in an embrace. There was a time and place for that, and it wasn't here and now. Tyler was definitely a temptation Emily planned to indulge in later—not too much later.

"Sorry," Tyler said. "It's my fault."

Jolene shook her head. "We have a show to rehearse, and the phone's ringing off the hook with people wanting to know all about our new act. The radio ad's working."

"Can you give me five minutes?" Tyler asked Jolene, but was looking down at Emily.

Jolene sighed. "Focus people! Come on, Em."

Emily felt herself being dragged away from Tyler and all she could think to do was dig in her heels. "I'll be right down, Jo."

Her cousin shook her head but finally gave in. "You've got one minute," Jolene said before turning to leave. "Clock's ticking."

When they were alone, Emily reached up to touch the side of Tyler's face. Trailing the tip of her finger along the strong line of his jaw, she whispered, "You're a hard man to walk away from."

He grinned, and his eyes twinkled. "Not if you're thinking of coming back."

Their gazes met and held. Emily's belly fluttered again at the promise of passion burning brightly in his warm, dark eyes. "I've… uh… got to get to work."

He seemed to draw within himself, and Emily wondered what was going on in that brain of his. He was definitely a man with many moods, but she'd keep up.

Before she could ask, he stepped back. "You'd better go downstairs. I'll be down shortly." He sounded resigned.

With the door between them, Emily tried to sort out her feelings. Lord, they were a jumble. Lust ran hot and deep for the dark-eyed, broad-shouldered cowboy, giving her ideas that they would definitely explore thoroughly later. But she'd also sensed he was hiding something, or maybe that something on his mind was too much of a burden to carry alone. She didn't wonder why she wanted to fix it, simply accepted that if she could, she would. "Emily!"

Jeez.

Sprinting toward the stairs, she hollered. "Keep your shirt on, Jolene. I'm coming."

Chapter 6

Tyler breathed a sigh of relief when Emily answered the summons from downstairs. The combination of her amazing breasts threatening to spill out of her black leather bustier and her honey-sweet lips made his skin itch to haul her back into his arms, kiss her senseless, flip her around so she was bent over the vanity, and sink into her lush, warm body.

Oh man. He'd definitely gone too long without a woman. He didn't think Emily was the one-night stand type, and even if she had been in the past with someone else, that's not what he wanted from her. He wanted more… was afraid he wanted close to all. Shrugging out of his shirt, he toed off his boots and shucked his jeans over his raging erection. Naked, he stared at his reflection and grimaced. "Son, you are in desperate need of soap and hot water before you can even think about getting busy with that amber-eyed filly."

He reached out and flicked on the spigot, turning it to just shy of scalding. Instead of dreading what he had to go downstairs to do, his mind was filled with the taste of a sweet little redhead who had a body made for sin and mouth made for pleasure.

Groaning, he ignored the worst of the aches and pains he'd acquired during the day. Pushing past them, he concentrated on getting through the next few hours. Then, he planned to sweet-talk Emily Langley into bed.

Showered but shirtless, Tyler made his way back downstairs. The song playing in the background had him cringing, but the sight of the two guys on stage bumping and grinding to Big and Rich's tune about saving a horse had his stomach roiling. *Please don't ask me. Lord above, please don't let them ask me—*

"So, big guy." Jolene walked toward him. "Feeling better?"

His gaze shot from the stage to his boss's whiskey-colored eyes. Remembering the way she'd made him feel, like he was a piece of meat, had the words sticking in his throat, but better there than said. Once said, he'd probably be fired, because what he wanted to say wasn't fit for anyone to hear.

When she merely arched her brow at him in question, he nodded. The line of tension in her shoulders eased just a bit, and she turned back to the dancers on the stage.

"That's fine, boys. Now," she said, turning back toward him, "since Tyler's here, Jennifer is going to run through the new routine she's come up with."

"But I thought—"

Jolene looked over her shoulder at him and smiled a sugary sweet smile that made the roiling in his gut churn harder. She and Emily might look alike, but their personalities were entirely different. He'd work for Jolene, but he didn't have to like it.

"What?" she asked. When he didn't answer, she shrugged and turned back to the group of people waiting for them.

I thought all I had to do was strip. The words burned in his mind, but he'd be damned before saying them aloud. Hell. He could do a decent two-step, especially if he'd been drinking and one of his brothers dared him to, but what these guys were doing? No way!

Jennifer got up on stage and started to go over a few of the moves and his heart plummeted. Double hell. He stared down at his feet: they'd never be able to follow along the intricate pattern she'd worked out and his tired brain would never be able to remember half of what she was saying.

"Problem, Tyler?" Jolene asked, laying a hand on his forearm.

Unease swamped him, and before he could call the words back he'd uttered the painful truth. "I can't dance like that."

Her hand clenched his arm, and he could have sworn she drew in a sharp breath, but it could have been the music blaring all around them. His gaze met hers and for a heartbeat, he saw something close to fear flash in her eyes. He hadn't meant to say anything.

"I'm sorry," he began, shaking his head, "but I need this job and can handle a simple two-step, but—" It had been hard enough to reconcile himself to the fact that he'd be taking his clothes off in exchange for the cold hard cash to dig the Garahan brothers out of debt. His mind still reeled at the prospect of his brothers finding out.

Natalie walked over and looked up at him. "I could work with you," she offered.

"Nat—" Jennifer began.

Natalie shook her head, cutting Jennifer off with a look. "We worked on the routine together, and I have a few ideas where it could be simplified."

"But Nat—" Jennifer looked fit to be tied, but the little brunette standing in front of him didn't budge. Was she defending him?

"No one is going to be looking at his feet, Jen."

Tyler's breath whooshed out as her words hit him right between the eyes. "And just where the hell do you think they'll be looking?" he demanded.

Natalie didn't seem to mind that he'd nearly shouted the question. She tilted her head to one side and said, "Your shoulders."

"Your abs," Jolene rasped at the same time Jennifer blurted out, "Your ass."

Damned if the three of them weren't grinning at him like it was Christmas and he had an armful of presents... or was he the present? Shit. Words were beyond him. He'd had his fair share of women, but he hadn't been surrounded by them or the focus of such attention before. It would definitely take some getting used to.

"Girls," Emily said, walking toward the group, "give the poor man room to breathe." She handed him a white cotton shirt.

Grateful, he slipped his arms in the sleeves and pulled it on. Working the buttons through the buttonholes, he didn't feel as exposed; he felt better.

"Now what's the problem?" she asked, folding her arms beneath her breasts. "I thought you needed Tyler to go over the new routine."

The movement plumped up her leather-encased breasts, and his brain shouted, *Grab the woman and run!* Every fiber of his being strained to move toward her, but he fought against the razor-sharp need and what he wanted to do with this woman.

Get a grip! Needing to get control of the situation, he repeated, "I can handle a simple two-step, but I can't do that fancy footwork."

Natalie moved to stand beside Emily. "I'm going to work with Tyler on his routine." She nodded to her sister. "Jen's got a great one worked out, but I think I know a way to simplify it so Tyler's comfortable with it."

Emily nodded. "Good idea, Nat." Her gaze met his. "Are you willing to let Natalie teach you?"

Watching him way too closely for comfort, Emily's gaze swept from his feet to the top of his head. His body reacted to her perusal. But instead of bringing up the kiss they'd shared and their plans for later, she asked, "How's the cut?"

Not what he expected her to ask, given the way she'd given him the once over. He'd seen the lust reflected in her eyes and, from the way she'd rubbed against him and kissed him back, knew they'd likely burn up a set of sheets before too long.

But last night they'd shared something special. Her caring about him was a bonus he hadn't expected. Something warm unfurled inside of him.

He looked at her, not just the creamy exposed skin he longed to sample in a few unexposed places, but at her as a person, and was secretly pleased she was worried. "I'm fine."

"Did you put something on it? Clean it out good?"

He couldn't help but smile; the lady was all business right now, focused like before, but not on the passion raging inside of them waiting to be set free. She'd flip-flopped to the caring side of her that drew him in like a man dying of thirst. "Yes, ma'am."

She smiled up at him, and his gut clenched.

Jolene interrupted. "If y'all are done jawing over there, Nat and Jen have work to do."

"So, Tyler," Natalie began, "how about I show you a few steps? I've got this great idea for your finale… by the way, how's your back?"

With a heavy sigh, he walked over to the stage. He was going have to work hard to earn his keep tonight.

Jolene and Emily walked down the mirrored hallway toward the front of the club. "What do you think of our cowboy?"

Emily sighed. "He has a name."

Her cousin shrugged. "I can't seem to get past his gorgeous exterior… sue me."

Emily snorted with laughter. "Come on outside for a minute. I want to see if Ronnie and Mavis are here yet. They promised they would be here early."

An engine picking up speed had Emily looking up as they stepped through the door. A car was heading in their direction, a little too fast for comfort. "Kids," she mumbled. "Did we push the speed limit all the time when we were that age?"

Jolene shook her head. "I can't remember that far back."

They laughed. It felt good to stand in the evening air, sharing a little quiet time with her best friend. Emily thought she heard the engine cut back like it was slowing down. "It was a long time ago."

The sound of a shotgun blast had them both freezing a heartbeat before Emily yanked Jolene down to the sidewalk. The five-pointed star hanging above their door tilted precariously but didn't shake loose, even though it was now peppered with holes.

Time stood still for a heartbeat, then snapped back into motion.

Heart racing, pulse pounding, Emily looked at Jolene. Her cousin's eyes were wide with shock. "What the hell just happened?"

Emily shook her head. "Someone's just having themselves a time at the expense of our sign." They both looked up, and Jolene sighed. "That wasn't cheap, damn it."

It was Emily's turn to sigh. "Isn't that the point?"

"I know," Jolene said, "but we don't have enough money to buy another one right now."

Emily stared up at the swaying sign. "I think it gives it an old-time look, maybe just what Frank Emerson had in mind when he told us we needed to keep things historically accurate."

When Jolene chuckled, Emily knew they'd be all right, now that the moment of sheer terror had passed. It wasn't every day she and Jolene got shot at… well, were in the way while their sign got shot at. Thinking back to one of Emerson's visits, she wondered out loud, "Wasn't there a rumor that someone was always shooting up the sign outside of this place when it was Donovan's?"

Jolene shook her head. "Leave it to you, Em." She waited a few minutes and then asked, "Are they gone?"

Emily nodded, struggling to her feet. "Long gone by now." Before she could process the fact that her knee wasn't working properly because it had gone numb, the feeling came back with a vengeance, giving way to sharp pain. "Damn it!"

"What?" Jolene reached out to help her up, but then stopped.

Emily saw surprise flicker in Jolene's gaze a moment before Jolene's brow wrinkled and her cousin groaned. "I can't bend my arm."

Emily looked at the arm Jolene held out and asked, "Is it your elbow?"

Jolene winced. "Yeah."

"It must have happened when you hit the sidewalk."

"I wouldn't have hit the sidewalk at all if you didn't yank me down."

Emily stood and was sorry she had. Her knee ached.

Jolene nodded and Emily asked, "Did you recognize that car?"

Emily shook her head, then remembered one of their customers talking about someone in town turning sixteen and getting a brand new shotgun for his birthday. She wished she could remember who it was. She'd have to ask Mavis.

Jolene shrugged. "I heard the Baxter twins have been causing trouble lately, maybe they decided to bring it into town for a change of pace."

"That's who the birthday boys were," Em said. "The Baxter boys."

She tried to take a step and sucked in a sharp breath as pain tore through the joint when she put her weight on it.

"Can you walk?" Jolene asked at the same time Emily asked, "Can you move your arm?"

"Lord, aren't we a sorry pair. Our biggest night so far and we're outside acting like a couple of old women." Jolene shook her head. "I like my idea of those twin shotgun toting hoodlums riding around town with one of them in the back of their daddy's pickup truck picking off signs, streetlights, and the occasional scarecrow."

Emily couldn't help it: she giggled. "I like your idea too, but last I saw there weren't any scarecrows in the center of town."

"Omigod!" Natalie and Jennifer rushed toward them.

Suddenly they were surrounded and everyone began to talk at once, asking questions and demanding answers.

"Did you see who shot at you?" Dave asked at the same time the other male dancer demanded, "What kind of car was the shooter driving?"

Jolene and Emily looked at each other and then back at the men. "No," Jolene answered the first question.

"I didn't notice," Emily said, answering the second. "Besides," she said, looking up, "they were aiming for our sign, damn it." Anger sprinted through her. They'd had it special ordered and paid over two hundred dollars for it. She needed to walk off some of her mad. Not thinking, rolling with her temper, she put her full weight on her injured knee and ended up on her hands and knees.

"Em!" Jolene cried out, but Emily couldn't answer her. She was too busy trying to catch her breath, controlling the need to hyperventilate to counteract the shards of pain slicing through her aching knee.

Biting back the need to let go, struggling to keep everything inside, she closed her eyes. She didn't sense the movement or the man who scooped her up and cradled her against his warm, broad, muscled chest.

The heat and solid feel of him surrounded her. Relaxing in his arms, she leaned on his physical strength, wondering if he'd loan her a bit of what she sensed went bone deep in him: Strength. Courage.

"Hang on, Emily."

The clean, spicy scent of Tyler combined with the muscled mass of his powerful body went to her head like a double shot of tequila.

"Let's get you two inside before whoever took pot-shots at you decides to try a second time."

Tyler couldn't decide which bothered him more: the echoing sound of shots being fired knowing Emily and her cousin were somewhere outside and in the middle of it, or the sight of a bruised and battered Emily.

Her silence unnerved him.

Hell, so did the last few days. Grandpa had always told him to take the good with the bad. *How else how will you know to recognize the good?*

Fitting her more snugly against him, trying not to inhale her soft scent or notice the way she melted against him, he stepped inside The Lucky Star.

Funny how the long, mirrored hallway didn't seem odd anymore. His life was definitely going down a path he'd never imagined. He busted his ass all day long at the Circle G, same as always. Only now he scrubbed off the evidence of the day's hard work, got dressed, and then drove nearly an hour only to get undressed again.

Go figure.

Perverse, that's what Grandpa always said life was. Like the beauty of a wild horse, begging you to climb on and take it for a ride, only to get on its back to be bucked off. But any man worth his salt, or his grandfather's good opinion, ignored the lumps and bruises and got right back on that wild horse hanging on for what could be the ride of a lifetime.

Something told him the little woman he held against his heart would be worth the ride. Walking over toward the front of the stage, he bent and carefully set Emily on the nearest table. It was a struggle to ignore the way her snug black leather skirt inched higher. A good long look at her first-class legs reminded him that they'd agreed to meet later. Now that'd have to wait. "Let's have a look."

She squirmed as if trying to find a comfortable spot on the hard surface before trying to straighten her leg. Having taken his share of spills and life's hard knocks, her sharp intake of breath and way she swayed told him just as much as looking would.

He squatted in front of her and rested his hands on his thighs. "Take a deep breath." He knew it hurt like a sonofabitch but didn't offer her any sympathy, afraid she'd break down; and anyway, as his brothers liked to remind him, he was useless as tits on a bull once a woman started crying.

Emily swore and he was impressed; he'd never thought to string *cocksuckingsonofabitch* together in one breath. He couldn't help himself; the snort of laughter escaped before he could hold it in.

Jolene narrowed her eyes, glaring at him. "You think this is funny, cowboy?"

He cleared his throat and inclined his head toward where Emily sat, her eyes suspiciously glassy. *Damn.* He decided to go with the truth. "No, ma'am." He paused then added, "Ain't never heard anyone think to use those particular, ah..." He flicked his gaze back to Jolene. "Adjectives together before."

The sound of her hissing out a breath didn't bode well for him, but her anger didn't worry him right now; Emily's knee did.

"Verbs."

Not recognizing the deep voice, he looked over his shoulder and was surprised to see a man standing there. Dave and Joe were still outside waiting for the law to arrive—he'd called them as soon as he'd heard the shotgun blast—so it was up to Tyler to protect the women. He drew in a deep breath, straightened to his full height, and turned to face the stranger. "Not unless you use the word bitch first. Bar's closed."

"Not because of any violations I've written them up for this time." The light-haired stranger turned his attention to Jolene.

"Jake," she rasped. "What are you doing here?"

Tyler stopped and unclenched his fists. "You know this guy?"

Jolene nodded, and the man looked from one woman to the other demanding, "What the hell happened?"

The look Jake and Jolene shared told Tyler they were acquainted, so he answered, "We didn't get that far yet." Sliding his gaze toward Jolene and back to the man standing beside him, who was obviously as frustrated as Tyler, he nodded. "First we're going to clean up Emily's knee and then we're going to see if I can convince her to go on over to the emergency room to have it looked at."

"No."

The whispered word had him walking back over to where he'd deposited her. "Someone can go with you, so you're not sitting there all alone for hours." He always hated that particular part of going to the emergency room—the sting of antiseptic and needles would be the rest of why he only went if he was unconscious and had no say in the matter.

He felt sorry for Emily. She looked shell-shocked. Wondering how his boss was handling the situation had him glancing in Jolene's direction. Damned if she didn't have a similar expression on her face.

Jennifer's voice slashed through his thoughts and drew his attention away from the sorry looking pair of redheads. "Well, well, if it isn't the big bad fire marshal."

"Now, Jen," Natalie said, "he doesn't have his clipboard with him today."

"I was just doing my job," Jake said, looking at the group of women. "Can't we let it go?" he asked.

Jolene shrugged and Tyler figured that was as close as the newcomer would get to an answer. Needing to get Emily to agree, he pressed her. "Your knee's swelling; you should get an X ray."

"No."

He could feel his temper simmering. "You always this difficult?"

"You always this bossy?"

He snorted to cover the laugh he didn't think she'd approve of. "When it matters."

Steering clear of the real reason—his gut-twisting need to protect the little redhead he'd tangled tongues with and fallen hard for—he tried to get her to agree to go to the emergency room. If he timed it right, he planned on tangling a whole lot more of them together as soon as humanly possible.

"Do you have any ice?"

A few minutes later Jennifer returned with a bag of frozen peas, antiseptic spray, and cotton balls.

"I thought you were bringing ice?"

"Frozen peas'll work better."

Shrugging, he reached for the spray and cotton balls first, and handed the bag of peas to Emily, fighting the need to scoop her up and never let her go. *Females were trouble*. According to his grandpa, redheads were double the trouble. *But twice the fun*. Tuning out everyone else in the room, he locked his gaze with Emily's. "This might hurt some, but you need to clean it out and keep the swelling down."

She angled her chin higher and nodded at him.

After her initial intake of breath, Emily was quiet.

He stood slowly and moved back a step only to bump into something solid. "What the hell?"

"She might have water on the knee or a cracked patella," Jake said, inspecting Emily's scraped and swelling knee from where he stood just behind Tyler.

"Don't you have somewhere else to be?"

Jake's gaze slid over to where Jolene stood talking to the deputy who had arrived while Tyler'd been busy tending to Emily.

"I'm checking to see that those violations weren't just temporarily fixed."

"What violations?" he demanded, reaching for the antibiotic ointment and bandage Jennifer was handing to him.

Instead of answering, Jake stared at Jolene.

Tyler shrugged. He didn't have time to talk. He had a woman to convince she really needed to go to the hospital. "Emily—" he began, keeping his voice even.

"No hospitals," she interrupted, her voice was firm and her mind obviously made up.

Instead of telling her that he thought she was hard-headed as well as stupid, he noticed Jolene looked really pale. Emily noticed at the same time. "Jolene, your elbow still bothering you?"

Her cousin had one arm wrapped around herself and didn't look as steady as she had a little while ago. She was probably still reacting to the shooting and Emily's injury. Time to start deflecting some of the lawman's questions.

Before Tyler could get the words out, Jake stepped in and bit out, "I think Miss Langley needs to sit down."

The deputy questioning Jolene nodded, waiting while Jake took her by the arm and urged her to sit.

Satisfied Jake would take care of Jolene, Tyler turned his attention back to Emily and couldn't help but notice her damned black leather bustier again. It cupped and lifted her ample breasts up as if for a thorough tasting. He had planned on sampling the creamy flesh just begging to be tasted after his shift was over. But now… well, he'd have to wait.

She drew in another breath and need hit him hard and deep. They'd have to put off getting to know each other intimately a day or so, until the swelling in her knee went down… but then again… she could just lie back while he took his time sampling the skin at the top of her thigh, the base of her throat, the valley between her breasts. Oh yeah, he could just imagine taking his time tasting all that fire and cream confection. He could be careful, and they could go slow.

Swallowing hard, he dug deep for control and zoomed in on the conversations going on around him.

"Do you two have any enemies?"

Emily looked at Jolene, and they both shrugged at the same time.

The deputy wasn't satisfied with either woman's response. He asked, "Has anyone threatened you?"

Jolene shook her head. Emily mimicked the movement.

Tyler could swear he heard the lawman grinding his teeth together. "I want you both to list your enemies, or those that you think might want to do you harm—"

"Oh for heaven's sake," Emily said, struggling to her feet and rounding on the lawman. "Did you not know that those wild-eyed Baxter twins got a pair of shotguns for their sixteenth birthday?"

The deputy snapped his black notebook shut and stared at Emily. "Just doing my job, Miss Langley."

Tyler eased her against him, and she was grateful she could lean against his strength and take the weight off her leg. Answering the deputy, hopefully setting him straight, she said, "And we appreciate it, but don't make this into something it isn't. I've been in town six months, and we don't get much action here, except for the occasional high jinks of the local teenagers, but that's no reason to make it into a murder investigation."

Jolene added her two cents. "You should be concentrating on someone who's riding around town with a twelve gauge shotgun and load of bird shot."

"How do you know what caliber it was?" the deputy asked.

Emily looked at her cousin and wondered why they had to spell it out for the lawman. She shrugged, and Tyler loosened his hold on her but didn't let go. "Can't you tell the difference by the sound?"

When the lawman didn't reply, she continued, "We grew up down South. Just because we don't own a shotgun, doesn't mean we don't know what one sounds like."

"Emily," Tyler soothed, "I think the deputy has enough information now."

Jake looked in their direction and nodded. "If either Miss Langley remembers anything of importance," he said, "we'll be sure and give you a holler."

When the deputy was gone, Tyler turned and asked Jolene, "What are you and Emily going to do about tonight?"

"Sleep."

Emily snickered.

Tyler could feel his temper simmering again; he tamped it down. "You two could have been killed."

Emily looked at Jolene and sighed. "True. The bird shot could have broken the chain holding up that big old star and it could have landed on your head... or mine."

Jake's lips twitched, though he fought against smiling.

Tyler had to admit they had a point, and he was overreacting. "Well, what if it hadn't been bird shot?"

Emily and Jolene shared a look before Emily turned to Tyler and rasped, "Then I'd be rounding up a posse to hunt down the dirty varmints who shot the heart out of our sign in cold blood."

The picture Emily painted loosened the tension in the room. Jake chuckled and Tyler joined in; soon everyone was laughing together. When they grew quiet again, Tyler said, "Just so you ladies know, while no one was seriously injured, I'm still not leaving you alone tonight."

Jake nodded. "The two of us will stay."

“And sleep where?” Jolene demanded.

The men shared a look before Tyler glanced her way and had Emily’s toes curling.

“Wherever we have to in order to be here to protect you two stubborn redheads.”

“Who says we need protecting?” Emily sounded annoyed, but Tyler didn’t give two damns.

“Who says they weren’t aiming lower and missed?”

Chapter 7

"YOU LADIES OUGHT TO GET SOME REST IF YOU'RE NOT going to go to get those X rays."

Emily wanted to shout at the dark-eyed cowboy that she was fine and didn't need any damned X rays, but she knew that was unfair to Tyler. His concern went bone-deep and sent the man into full-on protective mode. It was nice. It'd been some time since anyone other than their close-knit group of girlfriends had cared.

She sighed and reluctantly agreed. "Come on, Jolene, we could probably use to take a break. Gwen and the girls can open for us."

Jolene stood with Emily. "Well if y'all are sure, we'll just take a break and have some sweet tea."

Emily dug deep for a smile that was a little rough around the edges. No use complaining about her sore knee or looking for sympathy; she wanted her knee mobile. Glancing up at Tyler she sighed, long and deep. She needed to be mobile for later. "Be back in fifteen minutes."

"We'll check on you in an hour," Tyler promised.

"Who died and put you in charge?" Jolene grumbled.

Tyler flicked his gaze at Jolene, then turned to look at Jake, as if for back-up. *Men digging in together for the battle*. Emily's heart felt just a bit lighter for having noticed. "Come on, cuz. We're taking a break, and they can all be in charge. That way, chaos will reign while we're upstairs, and you can come back down, wave your magic wand, and fix it."

Jolene's lips twitched, just as Em had hoped. "You can be such a bitch, Emily Langley."

Emily's felt the smile blooming up from her toes. "I know, honey, but you love me anyway."

Her cousin sighed as they hooked arms and walked toward the door that led to their upstairs apartment. Halfway up the stairs, she wished she'd asked for help. "Damn that hurts."

"I know. Me too, but we're almost there," Jolene coaxed. "Does it hurt when you walk or just when you bend it?"

"Yes."

Jolene stopped and started to laugh. "Only you, Em."

"I have to go to the bathroom."

"Need a hand?" Emily stared at Jolene who shrugged and said, "I've still got one arm that works just fine."

Emily shook her head. "Nope. I'm good." Inside the bathroom, Emily realized it wasn't quite as easy as she'd thought, maneuvering with a bum leg, but with a hand on the edge of the sink, she managed to sit and pee.

"Hey, Jolene?"

"Right here," her cousin called from the other side of the door.

Emily snorted. "I knew you wouldn't leave me in my hour of need."

Jolene's laughter warmed her heart. "Not even if you wanted me to."

"Do you think we should be worried about whoever it was riddling our perfectly beautiful lucky star with holes?"

"Uh uh. I agree with you. Remember the other day

when Mavis stopped by and was telling us about the Baxter twins?"

Emily struggled to her feet and washed her hands. Pleased that she'd managed the task alone, she started to repair her eye makeup. "I loved her description of them: 'just two wild-eyed Texas boys, shooting off their mouths and showing off with their brand new birthday shotguns.'"

"Yeah. Old man Peterson was fit to be tied when he caught them shooting up the weather vane on top of his barn."

"Mavis nearly bust a gut laughing, describing the old goat's attack rooster chasing after those boys."

Jolene was silent, and Emily wondered if she was still there. "Jolene?"

"Hmmm? Right here," she called out. "I was just thinking: do we really want two men staying overnight, telling us what to do and when to do it?"

When Emily didn't answer fast enough, Jolene called out, "Everything all right in there?"

Emily grabbed hold of the edge of the sink to steady herself and reached behind her to open the door. "Yep. Just wanted to get rid of the mascara under my eyes before we go back downstairs… after we take a little rest."

Jolene opened the vanity drawer and pulled out a bulging makeup bag. "If we don't have it in here," she said with a grin, "honey, you don't need it." She paused and said, "You didn't answer my question."

Emily looked at her cousin's reflection and shrugged. "I kind of like that Tyler and Jake are worried about us."

Jolene frowned. "Skip that part and get to the part where they're going to be telling us what to do and how to be sure to lock the doors and windows."

Before Jolene could build up any steam, Emily stopped her. "Don't you just love it when a man you're interested in goes into full-on protective mode? His jaw clenches, his eyes narrow, and he starts surveying the territory around him like he was a sheriff waiting for the Dalton Gang to ride up and start shooting."

Jolene's lips twitched. "You surely do have a fanciful mind. Maybe you ought to try submitting some of those ideas to Harlan over at the *Pleasure Gazette*."

Ignoring the suggestion that she write for the town's local paper, Emily said, "Seriously, Jo, you can't tell me the handsome fire marshal doesn't just set off a few bells and whistles, and have your guts churning and your pulse pounding when he turns and looks at you."

Jolene bit her lip, fighting not to smile, but ended up giving in. "He is good-looking, isn't he?"

Emily agreed. "Nearly as yummy as the big bad cowboy you have working for you."

Jolene smiled. "You two seemed pretty friendly upstairs earlier."

Remembering the taste of him and the long, hard length of him, Emily sighed. "The man's lips should be licensed as lethal weapons."

"I'm here for you, honey," Jolene said. "Tell me more."

They were laughing when a deep voice called out, "Is everything all right up here?"

Jolene whirled around, smacking her elbow against the door jam. Her low moan had Tyler moving forward and barking out orders. "Emily, sit down for God's sake and take some weight off that knee."

Emily remembered that it was concern that sharpened his voice and had him telling her what to do. Man, she hated when anyone did that, but she sat on the edge of the tub, mostly because Jolene had turned green before every ounce of color drained from her face.

"Where are you hurt, boss?"

Jolene was too busy trying to breathe and not pass out, so Emily answered for her. "She hit her elbow"—she paused—"she landed pretty hard on it outside earlier."

Tyler maneuvered Jolene over toward the toilet and made her sit down on the lid. "Can you move it?"

Jolene shook her head, and Emily knew it was much worse than Jolene had let on.

"Why didn't you say anything earlier?" Tyler's voice sounded harsh.

Emily frowned up at him. "Because that's the way she's made."

He slid his gaze over to where she sat and shook his head. "Women."

"We're a lot stronger than you give us credit for," Emily blurted out. He glared at her and shook his head again, which really ticked her off. "Jerk."

He opened his mouth but ended up clamping his jaw shut without saying a word and turned back toward Jolene. "What hurts the worst?"

Jolene took her time answering him. "It hurts to move my arm, but the elbow hurts the worst."

"Do you want me to drive you ladies to the emergency room?"

Jolene got her gumption back with a vengeance. "You're the new headliner here, Tyler. After the advertising I paid for, we need you downstairs. We're expecting a crowd."

Conflicting emotions rushed through him: relief that

the show would go on and he'd be able to collect more money toward the mortgage bill, and resignation that he'd have to go on stage again tonight.

He nodded. "What about Natalie or Jennifer?" he asked. "Can't one of them drive you?"

Jolene shook her head. "I need them here if I'm going with Emily."

"What about Gwen?" Tyler asked.

"She's our bartender and bouncer. I need her here."

"Then who's going to make sure the both of you get checked out?" he demanded, unable to keep his frustration under control.

"That would be me," a now-familiar deep voice answered from behind them.

"Jake," Jolene sounded relieved.

"OK," Emily answered, tilting her head to one side, while she studied first her cousin and then the man standing just outside the bathroom.

Tyler wondered just what was going on here. The fire marshal had definitely helped earlier, but now he wondered if there was more to the man's motives than just being helpful. The set of his jaw and his stance—as if Jake were poised ready for a fight—indicated the man's involvement was more than just the need to be useful.

Testing his theory, while at the same time doing his damnedest to protect the women, Tyler said, "I'm sure we can find someone else to drive them. Besides, I'm sure you're busy, doing random inspections."

The fire marshal moved to a fighter's stance, flexed his hands into fists, then raked his hands through his hair. Definitely the sign of someone who was emotionally involved with the situation. "I said I'd drive them." Jake braced his feet apart and crossed his arms over his chest.

Tyler pushed one more button to be sure he could trust the guy. "I already offered to drive them."

Jolene sighed. "And I've already told you that I need you to do your show tonight, Tyler."

Her voice had an edge of desperation to it, and he wondered why. Not moving until he was satisfied with the arrangements for his new boss and her cousin, he imitated Jake's stance.

Tyler sensed it was a struggle for Jake to keep a lid on his frustration, and his next words confirmed it.

"Look," Jake said, "Jolene needs you to do what she hired you to do."

The expression on Jake's face was hard to read. Tyler was ready to pound on the guy if he added anything derogatory about Tyler's job at The Lucky Star. But Jake didn't do more than appear very concerned about Tyler's boss.

Finally, Tyler nodded. "I'd be obliged if you'd drive them over to the emergency room and stay with them."

Jake's gaze met his and the silent communication between them was all that was needed. Jake would protect the women while Tyler did what Jolene needed him to do.

"I'll be here when you get back," he told them.

Jake nodded, but Emily blurted out, "That could be hours from now!"

Tyler helped the women out of the bathroom and toward the stairs. "I'll wait."

"But what about—" Jolene began, but he didn't let her finish.

"I said I'd be here."

"Won't you be expected home tonight?" Emily asked.

Tyler wondered if what she really wanted to know was who would be waiting home for him, and almost asked her if that's what she meant. At the last minute, he was able to stop himself from looking foolish. They were a long way from asking each other those kinds of questions... for now. Besides, his gut told him that even though they hadn't flat out asked, neither one was in a relationship right now. Ever since he'd broken it off with the brunette from over in Amarillo, he'd developed a sixth sense about lying women. Emily didn't strike him as the type who would smile and lie to his face.

The other man nodded as he placed a protective arm around Jolene and led her toward the stairs. "I meant it about hanging around tonight," Jake said. "I'll keep you company."

"Appreciate it," Tyler said, slipping his arm around Emily's waist. The woman had amazing curves. His arm fit snugly in the gentle inward sweep between her waist and hips. He clamped down on the need flaring to life inside of him and eased her toward the stairs. *Later*.

When Emily's step faltered, Tyler didn't ask, he swept her into his arms and braced to catch an earful. But to his shock, Emily didn't say a word. After a few moments the rigidness left her body as she relaxed against him.

Contentment swept up from his gut right to his heart. *This woman mattered*. He couldn't even begin to guess why now, why her, but was Irish enough to accept that fate often had more to say about the path of a person's life than a sack-full of good intentions.

As he followed Jake down the stairs and past the bar, Gwen called out, "Natalie needs you back in five to go over the dance steps."

He cringed at the thought of getting back on that stage. "Be right back."

Fate was a fickle son of a bitch sometimes. After he and Jake were satisfied that the ladies were settled in the car for the short ride over to the hospital, he headed back inside. He had a job to do and the sooner he did it, the sooner he could get back to where he wanted to be… right there beside Emily.

"I told you to keep them from opening for business tonight, not permanently!" The head of the Pleasure Preservation Society stood with his back to the room.

"It's not my fault," the other man was quick to explain. "My sister's boys are good kids with dead-on aim. They hit their target."

Emerson glared at him.

Jim Dooley continued. "Hell, they're only sixteen; how were they to supposed to know the women'd get too close to their target?"

Emerson's mouth opened and closed. Was Dooley serious? "They had to notice two redheaded women on the sidewalk in front of the bar."

Dooley nodded. "Hell, Frank. They're just a little trigger happy's all… they haven't got a mean bone between 'em. Besides, the women didn't get hurt."

"Just tell them to lay low for a couple of days," Emerson said. "We can get a rumor going about The Lucky Star and its owners so that people will line up behind us while we continue our campaign to change the town's name." At Dooley's blank look, Emerson grumbled. "We need everyone in town behind us, or we can't get enough votes."

"Are you worried about that?"

"Pleasure's an old town with shady beginnings; the odd thing is most of the townspeople were born and raised right here and proud of their beginnings. We'll need to be very persuasive to convince them to change our Take Pride in Pleasure Day celebration and rodeo to Take Pride in Emerson Day."

"What about my nephews? Sheriff McClure's deputies are sniffing around asking questions."

"I'll handle everything," Emerson promised.

Chapter 8

DURING THE FIRST BREAK, TYLER WALKED OVER TO THE bar where Gwen did double duty as bouncer and manager. "Any word?"

Her gaze slid over toward his and rested there for a moment. "Worried about your job, cowboy?"

Tyler clenched his jaw to keep the words from tumbling out, words that no lady ought to hear. These women were a tough bunch, but he admired what they accomplished together. "It was a simple enough question."

Gwen shrugged and then turned toward the raised voices at the other end of the bar. "So was mine."

His hands fisted at his sides, and he consciously relaxed them. *Women.* He remembered his mother reminding him to pick his battles. Tyler nodded, realizing that now was probably not the time to get into it with Gwen.

The raised voices reached a screeching crescendo, and a curvaceous blonde went flying backward. Without a word, Gwen stalked from her post to wade into the fray, grabbing the woman standing with her hands on her hips by the back of her skimpy shirt. The brunette's shocked surprise turned to anger in a heartbeat as she pointed to the blonde at their feet and said, "She started it."

The woman pushing to her feet looked as though she wanted to do serious damage to the one who'd knocked her down, but when Gwen reached out a hand to help the blonde up, Tyler watched the look change from anger to innocence.

"I didn't do anything," the blonde wailed as Gwen tried to yank her up, but the woman changed her mind, deciding to stay on the floor.

"Need any help?"

Gwen looked over at Tyler as if surprised that he'd followed her. She shook her head and turned back to the catfight. "Easy or hard, ladies?" Her words were short and sweet, just the way he and his brother Dylan preferred them. He smiled thinking of his brother and Gwen together… too bad she wasn't a redhead.

"What are you talking about?" the one in the skimpy shirt demanded.

"Yeah!" the blonde echoed.

"Real slow to catch on," he said with a nod in their direction.

The right corner of Gwen's mouth lifted, but before the smile could soften the hard look on her face, she cleared her throat and answered for the troublemakers. "Fine then. Hard it is."

In a move that shocked the shit out of him, Gwen lifted both women off the floor so their feet were flailing as she hauled their pretty little asses toward the front door.

Never doubting that Gwen could handle herself, Tyler followed along behind, just to make sure the women didn't decide to turn on The Lucky Star's impressive bouncer. Stepping around Gwen, admiring the way her biceps flexed under the added weight of the squirming women, he opened the front door.

"Why, Gwen, honey," Jolene drawled, "how nice of you to arrange a coming home party."

Gwen's sharp bark of laughter told Tyler here was a woman he wouldn't mind having for a friend.

"Just cleaning up a bit while we waited for you." Gwen shook her head as she set the women on their feet and shoved them out the door.

Tyler wasn't surprised to see Emily's knee wrapped up with an ace bandage, but Jolene's arm in a sling took him aback.

"Well, boss?" he asked, ushering the women inside.

"Jo?" Gwen looked as if she wanted to press Jolene, but then she retreated behind the mask of indifference he was used to seeing on Gwen's face.

Jake walked in behind the women. "Tell them."

Tyler nodded to the other man. With a look, they communicated their like intentions. They would put together a brief plan for how they'd handle things tonight once the bar closed down. The women would have to go along with the plan.

No exceptions. No excuses.

"Just a sprained elbow," Jolene said, nodding at Emily, "and a bump on the knee."

"That's not what the emergency room doctor had to say."

Emily agreed. "Well of course not, they couldn't charge as much if they called it that. They had some fancy medical terms, but in plain English, it's a sprain and a bump."

"Which we wouldn't have if Emily didn't go in to protective mode and yank me down to the sidewalk."

Tyler watched the play of emotions on Emily's face. Lord, what a show. He loved redheads and the way they shot straight to boil. Impressed, he gave Jolene a break and said, "You might have been hit by some of the shot. Just looking at the sign, you could tell they weren't that far away when they fired."

"Gee thanks, cowboy," his boss grumbled.

He hated that nickname and the way it got under his skin. He closed his eyes and counted until he was calm again. "It's—"

"Tyler," Jolene said for him. "I know, but I like the way you get all grumpy and insulted when I call you cowboy… cowboy."

Emily giggled. "Don't mind my cousin," she said. "She's always been perverse that way. Besides, she's just being difficult because I had to help her pee before."

"Way too much information, Em," Jolene bit out.

"Well, who knew how hard it'd be with only one arm?"

Tyler struggled not to laugh. Hell, if *they* thought it was tough, trying peeing with one hand… He almost said it, but caught the knowing look Jake shot his way. The guy was growing on him. Men understood other men… but women. He sighed. They sure were work sometimes.

"Well?" Natalie asked.

"What's the verdict?" Jennifer demanded.

Emily repeated what she'd told him. "Sprained elbow—"

"And a bump on the knee," Jolene added.

"Does it hurt bad, Jolene?" Natalie asked while Jennifer turned toward Emily and asked, "Shouldn't you be sitting down?"

While Jake eased Jolene into a chair, Tyler clenched his hands in frustration because he'd been too focused on what his boss was doing to notice Gwen had stepped around him to help Emily sit down.

"Just a bad sprain," Jolene said, reaching for the bottle of pain reliever Natalie handed her, while Jennifer tossed Emily another bag of frozen peas. "Did you break it?" Joe asked walking up to the group.

Jolene sighed. "Sprained."

Dave sidled up alongside of Joe. "Did you tear the meniscus?"

Emily grimaced but answered, "Just a bump."

Tyler's gut clenched. "I've been there, and if you don't keep it up and ice it, the swelling'll take longer to go down, and you'll be limping for the rest of the week." Emily didn't react the way he thought she would; she nodded and shifted the peas on her knee. "Maybe I could keep it up for the rest of the night." The women closed ranks and started talking, effectively shutting him and Jake out. *Female trick*, he mused, but it wasn't going to work until he'd finished asking his damned questions.

Besides, Tyler wasn't used to being ignored, especially when he was determined not to be. "Where's the list of instructions?" he bit out, his tone sharper than he intended.

But neither woman seemed upset by how he sounded. Jolene shrugged and immediately cringed, closing her eyes and drawing in a slow, steady breath.

"That's it. You should be lying down." Jake moved toward Jolene, but before he could slip his hands beneath her legs and lift her up, Gwen's next statement stopped him.

"Jo just needs to sit awhile," she said, looking from Jake to Tyler and then back again. "The crowd will distract her. Don't fuss."

A new song began to play, a familiar George Strait

tune this time, and the lull in the conversations around them picked back up again. Tyler looked at Jake and noticed the other man scanning the crowd, probably for the same reasons Tyler was about to.

"We spoke to one of the deputies at the hospital," Emily said, with a look over her shoulder toward the front of the bar.

"And?" Gwen prompted.

Emily shook her head. "Can you believe it? They really are serious about looking for suspects."

Jolene sighed. "I don't know why they won't listen to us. You'd think they'd believe us when we told them what we heard."

"One look at our sign and anyone with half a brain could see it was bird shot… otherwise there wouldn't be much left of our star."

Emily sighed. "I guess we'll have to let the law do what the law will do." Tyler followed Emily's logic and agreed wholeheartedly, but there was a hitch in his gut that had him going over the "what ifs." Damned disturbing. How the hell could he and Jake protect the women during the day when he had to be home in the morning? There was a section of fence that he'd intended to repair in a remote part of the ranch, stock to be tended to… the usual chores. Then there was that damned elbow pipe under the kitchen sink he'd promised his brothers he'd replace. He had a knack for plumbing. Neither Jess nor Dylan could sweat a pipe without it leaking.

As if the other man could read his mind, Jake spoke up. "I've got a few days of vacation coming and I—"

"No." Jolene's refusal was short and sharp.

"Well now," Jake rumbled, "I'm just going to assume that you're in pain and not thinking clearly, Miss Langley."

Jolene's mouth rounded in shock but no words came out.

Emily pushed to her feet again and moved to stand beside her cousin. "Although we appreciate your offer, Jake," Emily said, "there's no reason to take any time off. The Baxter boys'll be laying low for a few days. At least that's what me and Jolene did when we—"

Tyler watched as the two women shared a look that reminded him of himself and his brothers. "You want to finish that particular story, Emily?"

She flushed a pretty shade of pink. "Maybe later."

With a glance around the bar she nodded toward the other men, who hadn't said anything more after inquiring about the women but hadn't left either. "No need to worry about us though. Joe and Dave help out with the heavier jobs around the bar, so we're not without extra muscle if that's what you're worried about."

If a man could spit flames, Tyler thought the fire marshal just might. The man was angry and wasn't hiding it. He was obviously more than interested in Tyler's boss. Tyler had taken the man's measure and liked what he found. He knew he was overreacting, but knowing Jake could check in on the women during the day while Tyler was at the ranch eased some of the uneasiness that had caught Tyler off guard.

"Let's get one thing straight, ladies," Jake said, looking from one redhead to the other. "We're not certain your lives haven't been threatened. You're both injured and moving slower than you normally would."

"But it wasn't a killer," Jolene insisted. "It was the Baxter brothers."

Emily sighed. "While we appreciate that you're worried about us—" she began, only to be interrupted by Jake.

"If Joe and Dave are downstairs hauling kegs and the shooter shows up, you won't be able to hide fast enough."

Jolene looked at Emily and they both slowly stood, shifting until they were standing shoulder to shoulder. "We don't intend to hide."

"Of all the stupid—"

"You'll want to watch what you say to my cousin," Emily warned, eyes blazing, chin lifted in defiance.

Tyler couldn't hide his admiration for the women. They weren't going to hide, and they didn't like to be told what to do. Hell, if that didn't add to his growing fascination with Emily.

"At least I'm not too stubborn to recognize the truth when it kicks me in the ass and knocks me off my feet," Jake grumbled.

"Men," Jolene grumbled. "Can't live with them"—she paused and smiled up at Jake—"and you can't live with them."

Jake looked at Tyler for help. He smiled and shook his head. "I need to make a call if I'm going to be staying in town tonight."

"You're on in five, Tyler." Jennifer reminded him.

"That's all I need to check in."

He walked over toward the other side of the bar where his cell phone reception was stronger. "Hey, Jesse. Where's Dylan?"

His brother grumbled something into the phone, but damned if Tyler could figure out what he'd said. Tired and just plain irritated, he bit out, "What?"

His little brother actually growled before saying, "In the kitchen under the sink."

Tyler swore under his breath. "Well, tell him to cool his heels. I said I'd fix the damned pipe."

It was Jesse's turn to swear, and Tyler could tell by the colorful string of adjectives that his little brother had had a day similar to his.

"Look, I'm going to be tied up here in town tonight," he paused and nearly bit off his tongue when Jennifer called his name. He covered the mouthpiece of his phone, but not before a deep chuckle sounded on the other end.

"Man," Jesse said, "I told Dylan you'd find yourself a woman now that you'd be able to spend more than twenty minutes at a time in town."

"It's not what you think." But how the hell could he explain just exactly what he would be doing in town without telling Jesse the whole of it? Embarrassment coupled with shame, mingled with worry.

He braced himself to accept the fact that if he wanted to keep his lies straight, he'd have to keep them simple. A lie of omission was still a lie. Wasn't it?

Just tell them the truth, Tyler.

Ignoring the sage advice his grandfather had raised them with, he raked a hand through his hair and dug deep for a calm he didn't feel. Hearing his grandfather's voice in his head all the time was wearing on him. *Just like your new job.*

When Jennifer called his name again, Tyler ground out. "Be right there."

"So, bro," his little brother drawled, "she gonna use a short rope on you?"

Disgusted with himself first and his brother second, he bit back what he wanted to say, the words sliding down to settle in his gut, churning in it until it ached. "They've got some extra inventory that came in late today that I didn't have time to unload."

"They got you doing more than stocking shelves?" his brother wanted to know.

More than you can imagine. "Yeah." Tyler thought of the new angle in his routine, reminding him of the "test" he'd had to pass before being hired, and the big old girl he would have to haul up from a dead lift later tonight. His tired muscles at the base of his spine were still screaming from a hard day's work at the ranch. He didn't even want to think of pulling the move Natalie had planned every night with a different woman… no telling how big or heavy they'd be.

"Where're you gonna bunk tonight?"

The hint of concern warmed his heart. Jesse wasn't steamed at him any longer. Good thing he was steamed enough at himself for putting himself in this position in the first place.

He hated lying and detested being lied to. So he told Jesse the one truth he could. "They've got an apartment above the bar with a couch."

"Hell, Ty," his brother grumbled. "The least they could do after the night you put in working for them is find you a room with a bed."

"Yeah." But both rooms, and beds, were already occupied with two amazing looking redheads who right now were bruised and battered.

"I'll be home in the morning."

"OK."

"Don't forget to tell Dylan to leave the plumbing alone; he'll only make it worse."

The string of muffled expletives had Tyler sighing.

"Too late," Jesse added a bit too cheerfully.

He'd have his hands full when he got back to the ranch tomorrow.

Emily knew Tyler'd be busy with his phone call and then his upcoming number on stage. She scanned the crowd sitting at the tiny tables they'd set up by the stage and smiled when she noticed Ronnie Del Vecchio sitting beside Mavis Beeton. "Jolene, I'm going to go over by Ronnie and Mavis."

Jolene nodded. "I'll check with Gwen and see how business is doing tonight."

Limping but mobile, Emily wandered over. "Hello, ladies."

The women both smiled, and the older woman waved to the empty seat beside her. "I hear tell you had a spot of trouble before Ronnie and I got here."

Emily sat down and nodded. "Just a bit. Some fun-loving teenager shooting up our new sign."

"Are you both all right, dear?"

She nodded at Mavis. "Just a couple of bumps and bruises. It took us by surprise, and I yanked Jolene down onto the sidewalk."

Mavis nodded. "I'd have done the same." She reached over to pat Emily's hand.

Ronnie smiled at Emily. "I hate to change the subject, but you and your friends look absolutely fabulous."

Mavis nodded in agreement. "You do sell the nicest

things in your shop, Ronnie." Placing a hand on Emily's arm, leaning close, she confided, "Did you know that Ronnie has the most amazing lubricant oil?"

Em looked from the dark-haired younger woman to the gray-haired one and smiled. "Do tell, Mavis." The two were thick as thieves, despite their age difference, and staunch supporters of The Lucky Star.

Mavis sipped from her oversized margarita and Emily grinned; they'd special ordered the big glasses with Mavis in mind and named their new signature drink the Mega-Margarita. The woman just loved them. "Ronnie's such a dear; she special orders it for me."

Emily already knew that the owner of Guilty Pleasures offered special order services. "Ronnie's a smart business woman."

"…by the gallon."

Struggling to keep her mouth from dropping open and flat out asking what Mavis would need that much oil for, she swallowed and nodded. "I'm sure that comes in handy."

Mavis murmured her agreement and sipped. "I just can't seem to keep enough on hand, so when Ronnie came up with the idea to order the king-size for me, I jumped at the chance."

Ronnie took a pull on the longneck and grinned. "Mavis, you are my best customer."

Mavis patted her curls and leaned toward Emily again. "Between Ronnie's shop… especially the back room… and you and your cousin's place here, a woman could forget about life's troubles and just kick back for a while and admire the eye candy."

Emily smiled at Ronnie and then followed the

direction Mavis was looking. Her heart tumbled in her breast and began to beat wildly. He was tall, darkly handsome, and going to be all hers.

"If I were thirty years younger and hadn't known that man since he was in diapers, I'd grab him with both hands and never let go." Draining her drink, she licked her lips and sighed.

Swallowing a chuckle, Emily signaled and Gwen nodded. "Why don't you and Ronnie enjoy the next round on us while you tell me about Tyler?"

Mavis patted Emily's cheek. "You're such a lovely young woman. You'd be perfect for him. He and his brothers have always been hard workers, but tough times can harden a man."

Before Emily could ask anything, Mavis continued, "I think that gorgeous cowboy is looking this way."

Emily turned and her gaze collided with Tyler's. The heat between them flared high and wild and every last thought in her head evaporated. She could swear she saw the steam. "Yes, ma'am," she answered.

Mavis sighed loud and long. "Well, well. I repeat, I think you two are perfect for one another." Her smile was just this side of wicked, "If you need any ideas… I've got a little extra oil you can borrow."

Emily knew that Mavis could run circles around her. "Oh I want him." She smiled at Tyler and had the satisfaction of seeing his step falter. "And I plan to keep him busy for a long, long while, starting tonight."

Ronnie snickered, while Mavis simply nodded, turning to reach for the Mega-Margarita Gwen had brought over to the table, she added, "If you need any advice, you just ask, honey."

Emily didn't doubt for a minute that the older woman would have some interesting advice to share. "I will, thanks, Mavis." Em settled in to watch Tyler do what he did best.

Her man stood center stage, and her heart nearly pounded its way out of her chest. He was so beautiful. The way he walked, stood, talked… add to that his innate kindness and need to protect, and she was a goner.

While he wowed the crowd with his moves, a new worry got under her skin like a sliver of wood. Women were clamoring to get closer to the stage, bills clutched in their fists. Anger swelled up from the pit of her stomach as jealousy settled in for the long haul.

She fought against the overwhelming feeling and realized it would be tricky being a part owner of the club and being involved with their popular headliner without showing the sticky tangled emotions curdling in her belly.

Shaking free from the feeling, she leaned toward Mavis and asked, "Ever ride a bucking bronco?"

Mavis laughed. "Honey, my first husband was as wild in bed as he was riding the rodeo circuit."

Ronnie leaned close. "I didn't know you were married to a rodeo cowboy."

The older woman's smile was slow and sweet. "Lord, I loved that man." Her eyes narrowed. "I got arrested for shooting the bull that threw him then stomped the life out of him. But they dropped the charges three days later."

Emily didn't need to ask Mavis what happened; she could figure it out, but her heart still hurt for the woman, knowing she'd lost the man she loved to a rodeo bull.

Emily's gaze followed Tyler's movements and her head felt disconnected from her body. Good Lord, what would she do if something like that happened to Tyler?

"Life can be hell on earth," Mavis said after taking a healthy swallow. "But if you're lucky, you'll find yourself a man to make your time here worth every moment."

Tyler strutted toward the front of the stage and hefted the birthday girl as he'd been told to do. The man's muscles bunched and strained, but he lifted the curvy blonde with an ease that had Emily wondering if he enjoyed this particular part of the routine.

As if she'd read her mind, Mavis warned, "You keep on ignoring that green goddess swirling inside of you, dear. Your handsome cowboy isn't going home with Cindy Hamilton."

"You know her?"

Ronnie nodded. "Mavis knows everyone in Baylor County."

Emily sighed. "Was I that obvious?"

Ronnie and Mavis looked at one another and then the women around them. "Only to us, everyone else is too busy trying to catch that big man's attention, while you already have it."

The smile started on the inside of her. Emily knew that her friends were right. She did have Tyler's attention for the next little while. If she had her way, she'd stick, then maybe if she were really lucky, Tyler'd be around for more than just a few night's worth of tangled, sweaty sheets.

She was suddenly exhausted and needed to rest up before Tyler's shift would be over. She'd miss the finale, but heck, if Tyler was a man of his word, and she'd bet on it that he was, they'd be sharing their own special finale later. Wouldn't they? He wouldn't change his mind just because of what happened outside earlier, would he? It was just a bum knee, they could work around it. "Ladies, I'm beat."

"You rest up now, dear." Mavis patted Emily's hand.

"See you tomorrow," Ronnie called out over the raucous crowd.

A quick look over her shoulder satisfied her that there were no problems in the club at the moment and that Jolene was chatting with Gwen. "See y'all tomorrow." Emily walked over and said, "I'm going upstairs for a little while."

"You want company?"

"Maybe," Em told her. "Come on up when you're ready, and I'll make us a cup of tea. We never did have a chance to have one before."

It took longer than normal, but she made it up the stairs without a hitch. Busying herself with the mundane task of heating tea water, she opened the cabinets and gathered mugs, the tin of Earl Grey, and honey for her, sugar for Jolene. Settling down to wait for the kettle to whistle, she noticed the tiny under-the-cabinet microwave and snorted. As if she'd use ever use that to heat tea water.

"Doesn't taste the same," she muttered aloud.

The steady beat of the country music she loved eased the tension between her shoulder blades. That first sip of hot tea soothed the tightness in her throat.

"Don't borrow trouble," she told herself, hoping the stern tone of her voice would keep the worry Jake and Tyler had planted in her brain from growing out of control.

Her cousin walked in and all Emily could think was that Jolene looked like something the cat dragged in.

"You should sit, Jolene. You don't look so good."

"News flash, Em," Jolene snipped, "you don't either."

Emily chuckled. "Jolene Langley, I swear—"

Her cousin snorted with laughter. "I know you do, honey, but we can work on that sad trait."

Emily couldn't help it; she laughed. And from the look on Jolene's face, it was just what her cousin intended.

"We're in sad shape."

"Been worse off," Emily admitted. Busying herself, making her cousin a cup of tea, she said, "We've been through a lot since grade school."

Jolene eyed her over the rim of her mug. "Yes, ma'am."

"Did you ever wonder what would have happened if we hadn't stuck up for each other?"

"A pair of smart-asses like us?" Jolene asked, making Emily smile again.

"We were, weren't we?"

"If we could have kept our mouths shut," Jolene drawled, "we might not have ended up starting so many fights." Jolene sipped from her mug and Emily did the same.

"Not in our nature though," Emily admitted. "Is it?"

"Nope."

Sharing a cup of their favorite tea helped them both to relax for the first time since Emily'd heard the roar of that engine.

"So," Jolene began, "do you think that hardheaded fire marshal and my newest headliner are really going to spend the night?"

Emily sipped and nodded. "Absolutely. Didn't you see the hard look in Tyler's eyes?"

Jolene shook her head. "I wasn't looking at him, exactly."

"Why, Jolene Langley," Emily drawled. "Are you stuck on the big bad fire marshal?"

"His name's Jake."

"You know, I don't believe I was ever properly introduced. Does handsome Jake have a last name?" Emily asked.

"Turner."

"Is he married?"

"How would I know?" Jolene protested just a bit too strongly.

"Hmmm..." Emily watched Jolene closely and murmured. "He's single then."

"Oh for God's sake, Em—"

Emily leaned across the table and snagged her cousin's hand. "Not his sake, Jo... yours. You've got to forget about your ex—"

Jolene shot to her feet, upsetting the chair. It cracked against the hardwood floor. "I do not want to talk about it."

Emily's temper spiked, shooting straight to boil—an even match for Jolene's. She shoved her chair back so hard it hit the cabinet behind her, rattling the plates and cups inside.

Before she could blast her cousin, the door to the apartment flew open and Jake burst inside. "What the hell's going on up here?"

The door banged against the wall and swung partway closed. His gaze swept the room before coming to rest on the two of them.

Before Emily or Jolene could answer, Tyler shouldered his way through the half-closed door. "What's—"

He looked from one woman to the other and sighed.

With a glance in Jake's direction, Tyler summed up the situation enough to have him fisting his hands at his sides and rounding on Emily. "You scared the shit out of Jennifer and Natalie," he said to both women through tightly clenched teeth, but he was glaring at her.

Of all the things he could have said, he picked the one thing that left Emily feeling guilty.

"I—"

"Don't you think you've given them enough to worry about for one day," he said, definitely on a roll, "without having to worry that someone was waiting upstairs for the two of you to finish the job?"

"Oh, leave her alone, Tyler. Everyone's blowing things out of proportion. You men need to settle down and stop spoiling for a fight to satisfy your need to pound on something since you weren't there to catch the kids who did this."

Tyler turned slowly. "Hell." He turned toward Jake. "Anyone else up here besides these two?"

The other man shook his head. "I don't think so, but now that you're here, I'll check the bedrooms."

"Like I said, Em," Jolene drawled, "the men are blowing this way out of proportion."

"Would the two of you sit down before you fall down?"

Tyler's exasperation and frustration came through loud and clear in the set of his broad shoulders, deep grooves etched between his dark eyebrows, and jerky movements.

The man was fit to be tied. And didn't that just bring that earlier image back to mind? Tyler tied to the bedposts with silk scarves… his velvety brown eyes blazing with desire while he twisted against his silken bonds, his abs, pecs, and biceps bunching and bulging beneath his sun-browned skin, drawing her attention to his…

Emily couldn't look away; the image in her mind was too real. The man she wanted in her bed was too sexy to be ignored, even if he wasn't on the same page at the moment and looked ready to kick ass and take names. Hell's bells, when did the prospect of an ass kicking become such a turn-on? Tyler had her tied up in knots of sexual tension until she couldn't think straight. *Jeez!* What a time to lose her mind.

"Jolene," a deep voice rumbled, "would you please sit down?"

Emily turned toward her cousin and saw that Jake was trying to get her back into the chair.

Taking pity on the men who were only trying to help them, Emily rasped, "I'm sorry, y'all were worried. Jolene and I were just having a discussion."

Jolene snorted. "You could say that."

"Sounded like an argument to me," Jake ground out.

"Heated discussion," Emily said, her lips twitching to keep from smiling. "I'm sorry, Jolene, and I won't bring up the subject again."

Jolene glared at her, but after a quick glance at Jake and then Tyler, she nodded and sat down in the chair Jake had righted.

"Now," Jake said, eyes hot and dangerous but hands gentle as he eased Jolene down onto the chair, "you want to talk about it?"

Jolene shook her head, and Tyler threw his hands up and uttered a comment that had Emily seeing red.

"You're either a very brave man, Tyler Garahan," Jolene began, a satisfied smirk on her face, "or a very stupid one."

Jake's face broke into a smile, and Emily noticed that her cousin was noticing too.

"Are you two going to stay up here away from the crowd and rest up?"

"It's not resting if they're going to be throwing chairs at each other—" Jake began.

"My chair tipped over," Jolene grumbled, "when I got up too fast.

"And I stood up too fast and hit the cabinet behind me by accident." Needing to do something with her hands that wouldn't get her into more trouble—like grab a hold of the delicious, dark-eyed cowboy staring at her with growing desire and testing each and every muscle in the man's amazing body—Emily smoothed her hair back over her shoulders, hopefully hiding the fact that they were shaking with need.

From the way the men were staring at them, she had a feeling they had a very good idea of just what had happened before they'd come running to the rescue. She and her cousin had trouble tolerating stupid people… especially if those people were men. "Um… thanks for coming to the rescue—" Emily began only to be interrupted by her cousin.

"But we didn't need any help."

"Jolene Langley!" Emily said, immediately contrite. "She's just feeling poorly and doesn't know what she's saying."

"Are you two ready to simmer down?" Jake asked.

Brave man, Emily thought smiling.

"I'm about ready to call the sheriff, if you two don't sit down and shut up."

Tyler's words had Emily mentally hog-tying the man and slapping a piece of duct tape over his big mouth. Then she'd haul him off to bed and get back to acting out her latest fantasy. She had a few really long scarves in her top drawer... she smiled, thinking that she was just the woman to handle the job.

He frowned, and she thought, *Men. Totally clueless.*

The longer he stared, the more Emily wondered if what she was thinking wasn't such a secret any longer.

And then he smiled, and Emily realized that he might be clueless where women were concerned, but he sure as heck was beautiful.

Lord love her, she'd always been a fool for a dark-eyed, broad-shouldered cowboy.

Chapter 9

EMILY FELL ASLEEP WAITING FOR TYLER. SHE COULDN'T say what it was that woke her from a deep sleep, but she knew something must have. Blinking, wiping the sleep from her eyes, she shifted in bed and groaned.

How could she forget about her knee? Damn had she really fallen asleep and missed her first chance to get all tangled up with the man?

The rhythmic snoring from the bedroom down the hall from her eased her mind that Jolene was still asleep, but didn't give her a clue about where Tyler was. Annoyed at herself first and Tyler second, she wondered why he hadn't just snuggled up in bed with her if he couldn't wake her. *Double damn.* Too honorable, he probably wouldn't. She sighed and heard another sound. Not able to decide if the noise she heard was someone downstairs in the bar or a little creature with black, beady eyes looking for a midnight snack that had disturbed her sleep, Emily strained to listen.

Thud. Thump.

Heart racing, hand to her breast, she sat up in bed. "That's no mouse!"

Tossing the covers aside, she swung her legs over the edge of the bed and stood at the exact moment glass broke and someone cursed. She didn't waste any time, and she wasn't going to lie in bed waiting for whoever it was to come upstairs.

She limped to her cousin's room. "Jolene," she rasped, shaking her cousin's shoulder.

"Mmmpf..."

"Jo, wake up!" Her stomach began to churn. "Someone's downstairs in the bar."

Her cousin mumbled something into her pillow, but Emily couldn't make it out.

"Jolene. Wake up!"

Her cousin lifted her head and groaned. "The guys are downstairs. Remember?"

"Fighting?"

Jolene swore beneath her breath and mumbled, "How would I know?"

They both heard the splinter of either a chair or table being smashed. Jolene shot up in bed and was out from under the covers before Emily could straighten up; they'd nearly knocked heads. "Somebody's wrecking our place!"

"Before you woke up, I heard some loud noises, then something broke and somebody cursed. Maybe whoever broke in took out Tyler and Jake and is trashing the place."

The look on her cousin's face changed from fear to anger. "Then let's go get the sonsofbitches!"

Emily grabbed a hold of Jolene's hand. "We don't know how many there are." She wasn't afraid exactly, just being cautious; it was a new feeling for her.

"Probably three or four, if they got the jump on the guys."

Emily hesitated. "Maybe we should call 911."

But Jolene was already moving toward the closet. She reached in and pulled out a hockey stick, which she immediately handed to Emily. She reached inside again, this time pulling out a Louisville Slugger.

So much for calling 911 or being defenseless.

Jolene motioned for her to follow, and Emily nodded. As they crept down the stairs, sweat beaded on Emily's forehead and between her breasts. She shivered and looked down. Damn! She forgot she'd been too tired earlier to look for her favorite T-shirt to sleep in. When Jolene had pulled two miniscule nightgowns out of her top drawer and had tossed the silky black one at her, she grabbed it and put it on while her cousin had donned the copper-colored chemise.

"Sonofabitch!" a deep voice yelled.

The women froze on the steps, their eyes wide and backs pressed hard against the handrail.

"Jo," Emily whispered. "Was that Jake?"

Jolene turned toward her, and from the look on her cousin's face, Emily realized they wouldn't be waiting. "Not sure… could be, but this is our place," Jolene rasped. "And no one is going to break into it or hurt one of our men if I have anything to say about it."

She grabbed the bat in Jolene's hands, holding her cousin in place. "But Jo, what if—" Another thud echoed in the night, this time followed by a series of loud curses and what sounded like someone getting punched.

Their eyes met and their gazes held. Emily nodded. "Hell, if you're going, then I'm going. What are a few more bumps?"

Jolene grinned and Emily was ready. They tiptoed the rest of the way down.

"Jake," Tyler ground out, "can't you hang on to those two while I take care of the others?"

The grunted response said it all. "Hang on." Tyler finished off the knot he could tie in his sleep. It'd hold. "What's the problem?" he demanded coming up from behind the man.

"These two are so drunk, they're slippery," Jake explained. "I can't hang on to either of them long enough to tie them up."

Tyler watched for a few minutes and sighed. "You grab here," he pointed to the one young man's belt. "And I'll grab his buddy."

Just then the four teenagers they'd caught breaking into the bar got their nerve back. "Hey what gives?" one yelled, while the other three mumbled and cursed, but Tyler could hear the underlying edge of fear in their voices.

"You broke in to our friend's bar and tried to steal a keg of Shiner Bock... my favorite beer," Tyler told them.

"And we stopped you." Jake shook his head, asking, "What were you kids thinking?"

"Hey," the same one answered, "we would have gotten away with it if you guys weren't here."

"Yeah," another one spoke up. "We heard this place is run by a bunch of women."

"They'd be a cinch to steal from," said another.

"Shit." Jake swore. "Behind you!"

Tyler spun, ready to fend off another intruder. All he could see was someone in the shadows swinging something at his head.

He dipped to the side, and the blow glanced off his shoulder. Used to being quick on his feet, he straightened up and grabbed the weapon and the intruder.

Silken curves crashed against him as a mass of curls swept across his naked chest. His body shivered in response as recognition slammed into him. “Emily!”

“Tyler?”

Rage, hot and potent, boiled through his gut, spewing from between his lips. “What the hell do you think you’re doing?” He’d nearly tossed her to the ground after grabbing… “And what the hell did you try to hit me with?” he demanded, reaching for the weapon clutched in her hands. “A hockey stick?”

Someone turned on the dim lights behind the bar as he looked from the weapon to the woman holding it. She was dressed in a silky black slip that rode high on her thighs, exposing the curvy length of her well-toned legs. Lust hit him hard, low, and inside. The sight of all that cream-colored flesh got his heart pumping and parts of him standing at attention. Jake appeared at his side with a baseball bat in his hands. Tyler shook his head and looked over at the other shadowy figure, knowing it was Emily’s hardheaded cousin.

“What are you two doing?” Tyler demanded.

“What does it look like?” Jolene ground out.

“Protecting our bar,” Emily answered.

“Together they just might have half a brain,” Jake grumbled.

“I’ll have you know—” Jolene began only to be interrupted by the sight of the teenagers tied together, sitting up, leaning against the bar, like an old time photo of an outlaw gang that had been brought in for the bounty on their heads, slung together in front of the sheriff’s office for the photo that would record the deed for posterity.

"My, my," she drawled. "What have we here?"

Emily chuckled. "I do believe our men have done our work for us and gift-wrapped the culprits with a bow. If y'all had waited, I've got this roll of red ribbon upstairs."

"Whoa," one of the boys rasped. "Did you know they'd be such babes?"

Tyler kicked the bottom of the boy's boot for noticing. "Shut up."

The one next to his friend groaned. "Man, have we died and gone to heaven?"

Jake nudged the boy's buddy, repeating Tyler's words, before asking, "Don't you know you're in serious trouble?"

"Tyler—" Emily began.

"Holy shit!" one of the boys groaned. "Ty, is that you?"

Tyler flicked on the overhead lights and shook his head. "Timmy, can't you keep out of trouble for just one week?"

"Shoot, Ty," the tallest of the group answered. "We were just gonna get us some free beer."

"You're not old enough to buy beer," he reminded them.

"Heck," Timmy answered, "we weren't going to buy it; we were gonna take it."

"Do you realize that stealing is a crime?" Emily rounded on the group of boys with her hands on hips and her hair spilling wildly over her shoulders. One look and Tyler's concentration flew right out the window. Earlier he'd raced upstairs, ready to take Emily up on her earlier promise only to find she'd been fast asleep, her silky red hair spread across the white of her pillow. Lust had him by the throat, but he couldn't do anything about it, and he hadn't been able to wake her up. Without an invitation from the pretty lady, he wasn't going to be crawling into bed beside her.

The whispered comments caught his attention. He didn't have to look at the boys to know they were still staring at the women... his woman in particular. "Close your eyes, boys," he ground out. "You're not old enough to look at either Ms. Langley in their nightclothes."

"Hey, we didn't get the beer; the least you can let us do is take in the eye candy, man. How old do you think they are, Timmy?"

Tyler reached out and rapped Timmy on the head. "Don't answer that or I'm calling the law instead of your uncle."

"Jeez, Ty. Ain't no harm in looking."

He ground his teeth together. "Look boys, you've already committed one crime—"

"That's right, Tyler," Emily said, walking over to where he stood.

When he looked down into her upturned face, he felt the floor shift beneath him. Her beauty reached out and grabbed him in a choke hold while need for her roared through him like a three alarm fire. He fought hard for control and won. "Yeah?"

"The only crime that's been committed here so far is breaking and entering," Emily said, nodding to the group struggling to loosen the knots in the length of rope that linked them together. "You and Jake stopped them before they got away with the keg."

"Which we may be willing to overlook." Jolene stood on the other side of Tyler and poked him in the arm. "Are you paying attention?"

She was waiting for him to say something, but he

was distracted looking down at Em. Jolene shrugged and finally flat out asked, "What do you suggest we do then, call these boys' families or Sheriff McClure?"

The protests from the boys didn't mean as much to him as what the women wanted. He'd like to keep Timmy out of trouble, but only because he'd known the boy since he was a toddler. He didn't know the other boys well, but he'd seen them around town. They were pretty much harmless, just being drunk, stupid, and sixteen.

"I think you all owe Ms. Jolene and Ms. Emily an apology," Tyler suggested.

"It'll be up to them what we do with you," Jake added.

Jolene slipped around Tyler to where her cousin stood, and they linked arms, staring down at the boys.

"Can't you untie them?" Emily asked. "It seems cruel to have their hands and feet tied like that."

Tyler shook his head. "They haven't apologized yet. Besides, why don't you decide what you two want to do with them first," he said, looking down at the boys. "Then we'll see."

Jolene and Emily leaned in close to consult with one another, and Tyler was struck by the beauty of the women. Jolene sure was a looker, but Emily was the one who had his heart stuttering. Her black nightgown skimmed the tops of her thighs. Her riot of red curls spiraled over her cream-colored shoulders, just begging him to reel her in for a long slow tasting. A curl slipped forward and got caught on the edge of her nightgown, dragging his attention to her amazing breasts. He couldn't blame the would-be beer-nappers for staring, but he didn't have to like it, especially since he'd been denied the promised taste of her earlier and been sleeping in a chair down by the bar.

Side by side, the sight had his gut clenching again. Two fiery haired angels… battered and bruised but beautiful. *Damn, he had it bad.*

"Hey, Ty," Timmy called out.

When Tyler didn't answer, the boy called him again.

Emily turned around and the laughter in her eyes told him the juvenile attention didn't bother her.

"Er… Ms. Jolene," Timmy said, clearing his throat, "we're sorry."

"Yeah," one of the others chimed in. "We didn't mean to steal your beer… well, we did, but we didn't mean…"

"To get caught?" Jake suggested and the group fell silent.

"We're sorry, Ms. Emily," Timmy added. "Can we make it up to you?"

Emily and Jolene looked at one another and then the men. "Maybe. Are you boys afraid of hard work?"

They all answered at once. "No, ma'am."

Jolene and Emily smiled. "Well then, I think we can let these boys loose before their families get here and charge us for cruel treatment, if they promise to come back later this afternoon. I've got some stock that needs shelving and a sign that needs re-hanging."

The group of boys looked at one another, and Em would bet they knew who'd shot their lucky star out front. They looked up at Tyler, and Timmy answered for the group, "Yes ma'am."

"I know Timmy's Uncle Ned," Tyler said. "When he hears that his nephew tried to steal a keg of Shiner, he's toast."

"Is that true, Timmy?" Emily asked.

Timmy hung his head then shrugged.

"Tell her, Timmy."

"Do I have to, Ty?"

"Yep." If it hadn't been his boss and her cousin that they had tried to steal from, he might not be as hard on the boys. When he was their age, he and his brothers had pulled a similar stunt, but that wasn't the point. One of Timmy's friends was bound to know who'd been taking target practice on the sign hanging outside of The Lucky Star. With any luck, he'd get the names out of Timmy and have the teenager and his friends watching out for the Langley women.

"My Uncle'd skin me alive if he thought I tried to steal from you."

"Why did you?" Jolene asked.

Timmy looked at the boy sitting next to him. "Steve double-dog dared me." Hanging his head in shame, the boy sighed.

"Well that makes sense to me," Jolene said. "Let them go please, Tyler."

"Are you going to call their families?" Jake asked coming to stand beside his friend.

Emily and Jolene shared a look and shook their heads. "Not this time," Jolene said slowly. "And not if all y'all show up by three this afternoon ready to work."

"But if one of you is late, we'll call Sheriff McClure and press charges," Emily added.

"You sure?" Tyler asked the women.

Emily nodded and Jolene urged, "Untie them, please."

Tyler shrugged and did as she asked. "Hand over your keys, guys."

"No way—"

"You've all been drinking, and not one of you is

going to drive home," Tyler told them. "You can either walk home or call for a ride."

"But if we tell them to pick us up here, they'll ground us for life!"

"What's wrong with here, boys?" Jolene drawled.

Not one of them could look her or Emily in the eye. "Um… nothing, Ms. Jolene."

"Shoot, you know why," Timmy grumbled. "On account of what Ms. Gorman told my Uncle Ned."

"I'd start walking if I were you boys," Jake suggested.

"I'll call Dylan and ask him to call your uncle and tell him you got caught drinking with four of your friends, and that I wouldn't let you drive home. He might pick you up by the time you reach our ranch."

Timmy's shoulders slumped further. He looked from one man to the other and then at the Langley women. "All right. Thank you, ma'am," he said to Jolene and then told Emily the same.

"Don't waste the lesson all y'all have learned here tonight," Emily warned.

"No, ma'am," one of the boys called out. "It was a lesson well learned."

"We're glad," Jolene answered.

"Amen to that," another boy said. "We learned that redheads are way hotter than blondes."

Emily groaned and Tyler chuckled. "Start walking, guys."

Once the grumbling group left, Jake walked over to where Jolene was leaning against the bar and asked, "Where's your sling?"

Tyler noticed the way Jolene had started to lean toward the fire marshal, but then stopped when he asked that last question. Saying the Langley women were prickly was like saying a skunk had a slightly unpleasant smell. Besides the fact that these women spelled trouble with a capital T, reminding him of an old Travis Tritt song, they were like two peas… one pod. He shook his head. May as well tell it like it was. "Difficult as hell," Tyler mumbled.

Just then Emily shivered. *Was she cold?* He leaned close and checked her eyes, just to be sure it wasn't a delayed reaction to the night's events. Up close they were a killer shade of amber, like his grandpa's favorite whiskey, but clear as a bell.

She shivered again.

"Cold?" Before she could answer, he shrugged out of his unbuttoned shirt and wrapped it around her. Cradled in his arms, she felt like she was the missing piece in his life—the piece that made everything else click into place. Wary, he realized he'd have some thinking to do.

"Em," he rasped. "I really need to talk to you… alone."

She looked up into his eyes and smiled. "I'd like that."

"If you're going to ride her case about helping me defend our bar, do it here and now," Jolene warned. "So I don't have to chase you down to take a piece out of you."

"Man," Tyler said, "I can't catch a break. Somebody shooting up the outside of your place, chicks fighting in your bar, these knuckleheads breaking in to try to steal a keg, and now my boss riding my case for trying to lend a hand."

"Never a dull moment," Jake said with a smile.

"You don't think you could maybe thank me, do you?" he asked Jolene.

She shrugged.

"Come on, Jo," Emily coaxed. "Tyler and I need some time alone, can't you give him the third degree later?"

Jolene threw up her hands in the air and started grumbling. "You think you have had a hard day, cowboy?" she asked. "*We* were outside when those shots were fired at *our* sign, and in the emergency room when those chicks were fighting in *our* bar, and tonight we had the bejeezus scared out of us when those kids broke in trying to steal one of *our* kegs."

Tyler nodded in agreement. "I'm real sorry, Jolene." He looked at Jake. "Are you sticking around or going on home?"

Jake looked at Jolene. "Sticking around." He nodded in their direction, "Why don't you two go have that... talk."

Tyler's jeans pocket vibrated before he could grab a hold of Emily and run.

"Is that a cell phone in your pocket, Tyler," Emily drawled, "or are you just happy to see me?"

He stared at her, shook his head, and then answered his phone.

When she laughed, he felt the heat creeping up his neck to his face. *Damn if his mouth hadn't been hanging open like a schoolboy*. He needed to get some alone time with the woman before she drove him right over the edge. He clenched his jaw tight and answered through his teeth.

"Yeah?"

"Hey big brother," Dylan greeted him. "You see tonight's news?"

"No, why?"

"The Lucky Star was one of the highlights."

All thoughts of getting busy with Emily flew out of his head. Tyler's gut iced over and sweat broke out on the back of his neck. God help him, if his secret was out, he'd never be able to live this down. Dylan and Jesse would never let him forget he'd shucked his clothes to—

"You still there?" his brother asked.

"Yeah. I'm here."

"Why they hell didn't you tell me?" Dylan demanded.

"I didn't think it was important." What a cop out and so unlike him that Tyler's icy gut started to churn.

"It sure as hell is important," Dylan bit out. "You have to know it's not worth it," his brother continued.

He felt like the scrapings off the soles of his boots, a mix of horseshit, ground-up pissed-on hay and dirt… the dirt being the cleanest part of the mix. Not knowing what to say, he grunted and rubbed a hand across his middle to ease the noxious roiling.

Best to let his brother vent his spleen and get it over with. Dylan would only hound him until Tyler'd fessed up the whole truth anyway.

"Tyler!"

Great, now Jesse had the phone. "Yeah."

"When did you start thinking with your dick instead of your head?"

Tyler let out the breath he'd been holding and wondered just that. "Probably about the time I peeled off my shirt."

"Damn, did the shooter get a piece of you too?" his brother asked.

"Shooter?" *What the hell?*

"Hey, Dylan," he heard Jesse yell, "I think big bro hit his head during the shootout!"

By the time he'd convinced his brothers that the story was highly exaggerated and that he was fine and everyone who worked at the bar was fine, he was vibrating with need from standing so close to paradise and not having the opportunity to taste it.

Emily was waiting for him to finish the call. When he disconnected, she reached out a hand to him.

Linking his fingers with hers, he looked down at their joined hands. His was tanned and broad, hers was pale as cream and slender in comparison... but they fit... really well. His gut tightened anticipating fitting together other parts.

"You 'bout ready to come upstairs with me, Tyler?"

He swallowed against the dryness in his throat. "Yes, ma'am."

"You seem willing enough," she teased, drawing him closer. "Are you ready and able?"

He ran his free hand through his hair and tugged her along behind him as he made a beeline for the stairs.

"See you later, Tyler," Jake called out as the couple sprinted past where he stood with Jolene.

"Sleep tight, Em," Jolene yelled. "Don't let the cowboy bite."

Chapter 10

Emily couldn't keep up or catch her breath. "Tyler, wait!"

"Can't, ma'am," he rasped, swinging her up and holding her against his heart. "Gotta have you."

He took the stairs two at a time and reached the top in half the time it would normally take her to climb the stairs. Impressed she giggled. "Why, Mr. Garahan, I do believe you're in a hurry."

He squeezed her against him and kissed the top of her head as he opened the door to the upstairs hallway. Disappointed that he didn't seem to want her as much now that he'd run up the stairs, she sighed. "Thanks for the lift; you can set me down now."

The deep chuckle rumbled against her side and had her looking up. The heat in his gaze made her weak with anticipation. Desire, hot and strong, was there plain as the nose on his face.

"What part of 'I can't wait' didn't you get?" He rasped, power and pure male muscle working in tandem as he stalked down the hallway. "Which one?"

She didn't dare ask him what he was talking about; she didn't want to break the sensual spell his impatient desire was spinning around them. "Second on the left."

He shouldered the door open and kicked it shut with his boot.

Emily's heart stumbled in her breast as he spun

around and let her legs slide free, but kept his arms vised around her, crushing her between the hard, hot, muscled length of him and the cool wood door.

She moaned his name, and he pinned his hips to hers, holding her like a butterfly against a swath of black velvet. The image shifted to one of pure pleasure as he lowered his lips to her ear and rasped, "I want to take my time with you, Emily Langley, but I don't have the strength to wait that long."

His lips teased the edge of her ear as he nibbled a path down the tendon in her throat. Warmth swept up from her toes, as desire began to build. "Let me have you now, Emily," he begged. "We can go slow later."

Bereft of words, overwhelmed by need for this man, she tilted her head back and tightened her arms around his neck. Sliding the tip of her tongue along his bottom lip, she bit it and had the satisfaction of watching his eyes glaze over. She needed to torture him as much as watching him and wanting him had tortured her.

His lips took hers in a ravenous kiss; using teeth, tongue, and lips, he drove every thought from her head but one. *Now*.

He came up for air before diving down to sample the deep V of skin above her silky black chemise, licking and nipping the skin until the heat from his mouth seared a path from the depths of her cleavage to the base of her ear.

"Tyler!"

He reared back, nostrils flaring, mouth in a firm straight line. Unsure what he waited for, trying to ignore the way her heart opened to him, ready to let him in, but afraid if she did he'd leave, she murmured, "Please?"

His grin was quick, but lethal. "Yes, ma'am."

His mouth fused to hers as his hands got busy slipping the straps off her shoulders and easing the silky bit of nothing off of her. His groan of pleasure sprinted through her as he filled his hands with her breasts, teasing them into hard, pointed peaks as his head lowered to sup from their bounty.

"I can't—" *Breathe. See. Stand.* Pick one; all she could do was feel. Tyler was igniting flames of desire in so many places at once her brain couldn't keep up.

Her breasts ached and her lips tingled... and then he found the lacy thong she'd put on earlier with him in mind.

Naked. She didn't know how he'd managed it so quickly, but she'd lost her chemise, her lacy thong, and her mind. "Now," she demanded, pulling him closer. "I want you naked, now."

His head reared back, but his hands never stopped moving. His callused fingers traced her curves, setting off sparks as his hands swept around to grip her backside with his strong capable hands.

"Later," he promised as he eased back. "Gotta protect you." Her brain didn't register what he was saying at first. Tingles zinged through her system, setting the sparks he'd ignited to flames. She reached for him, but he shifted until she could see what he was reaching for. His hands were strong and sure as he ripped open the small square packet.

His erection was huge, straining against the denim of his worn jeans. "Let me help." Emily grabbed the tab of his zipper and fought against the urge to yank, knowing she might hurt him. Slowly sliding the metal zipper down, his groan of pleasure fueled hers as she reached around to help him out of his jeans. His mouth found hers, tantalizing her with a soul-searing kiss.

"Now?" he rasped.

"Now," she agreed.

In one smooth, swift move, he filled her to bursting. Before she could adjust to the hard, hot length of him stretching her, his hips began to move. Plunging fast and deep, his hips set the pace, while his mouth stoked the fire.

A scream of pleasure raced up her throat, but his mouth found hers again, muffling the sound. When her legs gave out, he slid his hands beneath her backside and lifted her, holding the injured one still, wrapping the other one around his waist.

Mine, she thought. "Tyler, I—"

"Come with me, darlin'."

The tight knot of pleasure he tied around her burst as his lips latched onto her breast and he drove deeper inside her.

Shocked pleasure set off tiny fires that still raged out of control. She couldn't move or make her brain function long enough to speak. A moan slipped from between her lips.

Tyler couldn't bring himself to move. Didn't want to leave the hot, wet, wild woman he'd just taken against a door.

His brain started working again, and his first thought was, *a door for God's sake!* What was he thinking? She'd been injured; he should have at least made an attempt to make it to her bed.

"Emily?"

"Mmmm?"

"Darlin', I'm sorry—"

"For the pleasure, the lovin', or rendering my brain totally useless?"

His lips twitched, and his heart tumbled closer to the edge. "I should have at least made love to you the first time in a bed."

She kissed his throat. "And that would be because?"

"You're hurt."

"But you didn't wrap my bad knee around your waist," she told him. "You only wrapped the good one around you. See?" Damned if she didn't flex her good leg and tighten it around him.

"Give me a minute."

"Take all the time you need, Tyler; you are not leaving me tonight."

"That a fact?"

"Oh yeah," she murmured. "I've got this powerful need to test your back."

He dropped his forehead against hers and moaned. "You're going to be the death of me, Ms. Langley."

"But what a way to go."

Her lips found his and something deep inside of him clicked, like a tumbler in a lock falling into place. He eased her legs down, watching her eyes darken with desire. "I'm gonna fill that need soon, Em. Let me take you to bed."

Her smile devastated him and said yes.

He bent to pick her up. His legs were a little shaky, but it had been a full day and he had to admit, this little woman packed a hell of a punch. Setting her in the middle of her bed, he looked his fill, marveling that her womanly curves could be packed into such a tiny package.

"You're overdressed." Emily reached up to unbutton his shirt.

Tyler shrugged out of it, need strumming through him like a live wire. He couldn't wait that long to be naked in bed with his Emily.

His. He liked the way that sounded.

Her eyes widened, and his ego ramped up a notch. He didn't think much about how he looked, other than whether he was clean or dirty. The look on her face told him more than words that she liked what she was seeing. Desire for her began to build again.

He crawled over top of her, stealing a kiss as he settled the angles and planes of his body on top of her glorious curves. "Now where were we?"

Her smile was slow and sweet. "I've got this fantasy," she rasped.

His throat went dry. "Do tell, Ms. Langley." She traced the tips of her fingers along the edge of his jaw, distracting him. Had she been bluffing about fantasizing about him? "You don't have to tell me now—"

"I'm working up to it." She slid her hands down to his shoulders and around to his back. "You were looking at me earlier like I was a frosted cake," she rasped, licking her lips before pressing them to his collarbone, "and you just couldn't wait to lick your way down to the gooey center."

Tyler closed his eyes and laid his forehead against hers. He'd need patience to listen without rushing her. "Do you have a gooey center, Em?"

Her cheeks flushed. "Only for you, Tyler."

"I'm obliged to test that theory," he breathed against her cheek. "How 'bout if I start right here?" He slid the tip of his tongue along the line of her jaw, nipping at her chin before kissing it. "You do taste delicious… but I think I need to sample more."

Emily groaned and squirmed beneath him.

"Mmmm, here." His lips found hers and he moaned aloud. "Cherries: tart but sweet. My favorite."

"Tyler—"

"I've got a ways to go before I get to the sweetest part. Are you gonna deny me that taste?"

The strangled sound and lift of her hips were all the answer he needed. Nibbling and licking a path beneath her chin and between her breasts was pure unadulterated pleasure. Her skin was like satin, her scent a cool combination of lavender and rain.

Sliding his tongue to the left, he circled the tip of her breasts with a deliberate slowness that had her grabbing a hold of his butt, pressing him against her warm, wet heat. "Not yet, darlin'."

"Tyler, I can't wait."

"Yes you can. I've only tasted your cherry-sweet lips and just started on your buttercream breasts."

Her body was on fire! Everywhere he touched tingled before fizzling and erupting into flames. Lord, what had she started? "I want you now." She couldn't take any more of this torture.

"We'll get there, darlin'," he promised. "There's this stretch of skin that curves in by your belly," he said, licking and nipping until her eyes crossed.

"But—"

"I'll surely come long before I get to your amazing backside."

Her giggle surprised her. She'd never laughed when making love before.

He paused as if he'd sensed something was wrong. He lifted his head and saw the worried look on her face. He swallowed the chuckle, knowing she needed reassurance that he wasn't angry or insulted. "Laughing while you're loving makes it sweeter."

Her heart just tumbled right on up and over that first peak and began the tricky slide down into love. "Tyler, I've never laughed before when—"

His dark eyes gleamed. "I don't care what happened before," he ground out. "It's what's here and now between us that counts."

She nodded.

"Do you trust me not to hurt you?"

She didn't hesitate. "Yes."

"Excellent. Now where was I?" His eyes darkened with desire, and her breath hitched in anticipation. His hands kneaded her hips before sliding around to lift her amazing backside. "I've been wanting a taste of this sliver of skin you're always flaunting."

Before she could ask which skin, his lips and tongue were sampling the skin near her belly button. She wanted to tell him that she'd gained weight and didn't want him to notice her there, but the words slid right back down her throat as his tongue dipped into her navel, sending shock waves zinging from her breasts to her toes.

"Tyler, I can't wait. I've got to have you now." She was desperate and demented. He was making her crazy.

"Not before we ride out your fantasy, darlin'. Just one more flavor I have to sample."

She tensed; she wasn't ready for him to taste her there… yet. They'd only made love once, and her heart wouldn't be able to get over this wild-eyed cowboy if he up and left her in the morning. "Tyler, please stop."

His head jerked up, and the dark and dangerous look he sent her had her shivering on the sheets. "You playing games with me," he ground out, "or do you really want me to get up and walk away from you?"

She reached out a hand to touch his heart. "I do not want to you walk away from me." He was visibly trembling beneath her hand. Was it anger or passion? "I'm sorry," she confessed, slipping both hands around his neck and drawing him down close enough to press her lips to his. "I may have fantasies about you—"

"Hell, Emily, how can I think when you're promising more delights than I've—"

She wouldn't let him finish. "And I'd love to act out each and every one with you, but I'm not quite ready to let you make love to me with your mouth... yet." She deepened the kiss and drew back slowly.

He sighed. "I guess I could wait to taste that gooey center I just know will taste like honey."

Said center throbbed with need, and she wondered if she were crazy. "I'm not trying to tease you." She sighed. "I can't believe how hot and bothered you get me. I swear I wasn't even going to tell you about that particular fantasy."

"Ever?" he asked pulling her in close and holding her.

The fire settled down to a warm and cozy glow. "Well, not yet at least," she said, "until I know you better."

Tyler didn't press her. "I can wait, Emily," he said, licking his lips, "knowing that you'll let me know when I can sample your honey-sweet center."

Crazy. Insane. Idiot. All of the above fit, but she was

so lost in the gift he'd given her, she could only nod. He wouldn't rush her; he'd let her tell him when she was ready to share that most intimate way of loving.

Rolling onto his side and taking her with him, he pressed his lips to her temple. "I'd like to sleep with you for a little while before I get back to where I left off."

"But I—"

He drew her backside up against the hard, hot length of him and chuckled. "I can work around where I'm dying to taste. By the time you're ready for me to dip my tongue in for a thorough tasting, you'll be so hot for me, you'll be begging me to lick, sip, and nibble my way to that gooey sweetness you've been dreaming about, darlin'."

Shocked to the core and rendered speechless, Emily lay in Tyler's arms, wondering how to tell him that he'd gotten her juices flowing and her heart pounding and may have changed her mind. *Tease*. Hell, she'd be teasing if, when he actually settled between her thighs and grabbed a hold of her backside, pulling her in, she hesitated, not willing to trust that part of her to him yet.

"You have a mean streak in you, Tyler Garahan."

"You might want to remember that, darlin', for the next time you drive me crazy with your amazing brain."

"My brain?"

"It's so wickedly wonderful. Gotta love a redhead with an imagination."

She reached around and pinched his backside. "Is that all you like?"

"I must not be doing it right if you have to ask," he grumbled. "Let me hold you for a little while, Emily. I need to build up my strength so I can love you at sunup."

Sliding farther down that slippery slope toward love, she snuggled closer. "That's only two hours from now."

He chuckled. "I'm glad you're keeping up, darlin'." He kissed the top of her head and slid his arms around her waist and snuggled closer, so not a breath of air was between them. Back to front, like spoons in a drawer. "You might want to rest up for me."

"Is that an order?"

"Hell no," he said, slipping his hand beneath her hair and moving it off her neck to nibble the tiny bit of skin beneath her ear. "Just a suggestion. I usually wake with a raging hard-on, and I've been wanting you something fierce since I first saw you standing there in all your chocolate-covered glory."

She eased his hold on her and turned over so they were face-to-face. "You could give a tease lessons, Tyler."

His grin said it all. He was hard, hot, and waiting for her. "You've got a smart mouth, darlin'," he rasped. "I've just got to taste it again."

"But I thought you wanted to sleep with me?"

His mouth curved as his lips lowered. "We can sleep later."

"You're not mad at me because I won't let you—"

Tyler groaned. "I'm so hot for you, Em, that it'll kill me to take the time to explain how I feel."

Her eyes filled with tears, and he knew he'd have to pull back from the edge long enough to reassure her. "I don't just want to grab a quick lay in your bed and leave."

Her lips twitched as her tears fell. "Don't forget the door."

His gut clenched, and his heart stuttered. "Lord above woman, and if that doesn't tell how much I want you, how every damned breath you take in that double-damned black leather contraption you wore earlier tormented the hell out of me, then you're not as smart as I thought you were."

"Tyler," she crooned, pulling him back to where she wanted him. "Shut up and kiss me."

His groan of frustration said more than words. "Don't mind if I do."

Their tongues tangled and the hitch in her heart smoothed out. "I've got a need for you, Tyler, that scares the breath right out of me."

He pulled her close and held on for dear life; she would later swear he trembled in her arms. "I'm right there with you, darlin'."

"Emily?"

"Mmmm..."

"Can you reach my pants?"

"Whatever for?"

"I've got to be inside you, but can't if I don't protect you."

Hell's bells. It wasn't that far a slide into *headoverheelsgrabyoubytheheartlove* after all. Pressing a kiss to where his heart beat like thunder, she angled her body over the side of her bed and snagged his pants. "Here you go, sugar."

He grabbed the jeans and the promised protection while she struggled to get her brain wrapped around the fact that he wasn't just here for tonight. He was sticking long enough to care whether or not he wore a condom when they made love for the second time that night.

"Damn."

"Need help?" she moved closer, waiting for him to tell her what he needed.

"Nope, but I've only got one condom left."

Her shocked expression must have hit his funny bone. He started laughing, and she tried to smack him. "Whoa there, filly—"

Stunned, she connected with her fist, surprising him. "Did you just call me a filly?"

"That right, darlin', you're my redheaded filly, and I just love your fractiousness."

She tried to move out of his grip, but he only tightened it, drawing her in, lining her up until he was poised above her. "I'm a fractious filly?"

"God, Emily," he groaned, "can we talk later?"

She sighed, " I guess—" She never finished what she was about to say. Tyler eased back and drove all the way home. When he touched her womb, she admitted what her heart had known all alone. Hell or high water, she was in for the long haul and down for the count.

Lifting her hips, she matched his strokes, grabbing onto his muscled backside for dear life. They came together in a wild explosion of sheer glory. When the dust, and her heart, settled, she pressed her lips to his throat and sighed. "Are you ready to talk now?"

Chapter 11

"WHAT'S THE EMERGENCY?"

"Why did you call the meeting?"

"Are we going to—"

"If you would all calm down, we can get down to the reason I called this emergency meeting." Frank Emerson scanned the faces of his executive board and wondered if he shouldn't have kept the meeting between himself and his two vice presidents. *Too late now.*

The treasurer of their group, Mavis Beeton—the one he was most concerned about—spoke up, "According to the by-laws of the Society—"

"Not now, Mavis," he interrupted. "We have an urgent situation on our hands. Everyone knows how hard we've worked, saving historic landmarks and rebuilding downtown Pleasure."

His board nodded their agreement; although the expression on Mavis Beeton's face left no doubt that she was not happy he interrupted her... again.

"And you are all aware that there are only three businesses left that will keep us from achieving our goal and fulfilling our mission statement of rebuilding the downtown area and recreating Pleasure's illustrious past."

"I don't see why you won't leave them alone," Mavis mumbled. "They pay their taxes, and on time too!"

Emerson raised his eyes to the ceiling, not daring to say what he was thinking. It would truly shock the old harridan. He still needed her, so he wisely kept those thoughts to himself. He turned to his vice presidents. "Any progress on the strip club?"

"Those young ladies happen to be friends of mine," Mavis interrupted.

Stanley stared at her, then shook his head. "So far, no response to our repeated requests to either close their doors permanently or close and then reopen as a bar, in keeping with the tenets that coincide with our mission statement."

Dooley spoke up, "I've been pushing for a response from the owner of the lingerie shop and adult toy store. I think she's going to cave under the pressure—"

"You should be ashamed of yourself, John," Mavis stood up and crossed her arms. "Ronnie Del Vecchio is a very nice young woman and happens to be a friend of mine too."

Trish Stewart snorted. "Would a nice woman run a shop like that?" Not waiting for an answer, she continued, "I think I'm wearing the owner of the new age shop down." Her smile told Emerson that she'd been following his advice and sending in "customers" to cause trouble for the owner. He'd have to ask her the details later.

"We have a deadline, people," Emerson reminded everyone.

He looked from one face to the next and slowly rose to his feet. Placing both hands on the table in front of him, he leaned forward and ground out, "We have to resolve the situation with these last three holdouts, now. Our new website is scheduled to be launched in two weeks."

Mavis Beeton scribbled something down in her steno notebook, irritating the heck out of him. She was his worst detractor, always countermanding whatever he wanted with some reason or another as to why his course of action and way of thinking was wrong. When she lifted her head and met his gaze, he knew she was about to do it again.

Braced for her argument, he waited.

"Mr. Emerson." She paused, and looked from one member to the next. "I was born right here in Pleasure, Texas. A Beeton has lived and worked in this town since it was founded by the Donovan sisters. Although I think what you're doing to resurrect tourism in our town is admirable, I think you're forgetting one very important point."

He opened his mouth to speak, but Mavis held up her hand and forged ahead. "This town's first business was a bawdy house, owned and operated by the town's founding mothers. You are doing them an injustice by trying to eradicate the closest thing we have to a bawdy house and petitioning to have the town's name changed."

Emerson waited until she leaned back in her seat before he acknowledged her words. "Thank you for the reminder. If there is no further input, I suggest we adjourn." He paused, then asked, "All those in favor?"

Everyone's hand was raised.

"Meeting adjourned."

"Em, what are you doing?"

Emily brushed a lock of hair out of her eyes with the back of her forearm and snorted. "A smart woman like you should be able to figure it out in one." Cracking the egg on the edge of the small measuring cup, she reached for a fork and began to beat the egg until it was frothy. Surprised that her cousin had yet to say anything derogatory, Emily looked up and her gaze collided with Jolene's.

"What?"

Jolene pulled out one of the kitchen chairs and sat down. "Sleep well last night?"

Emily smiled, still feeling the glow from their early morning bout of lovemaking. "Mmmm... didn't get much sleep, but I do feel loose."

Jolene narrowed her eyes at her cousin. "Now, you're just bragging."

Emily smiled.

"I just had a call from Shannon McKenna."

Emily nodded. "Ronnie's friend."

"Yeah."

"How's business over at the Mysts of Time?"

"She was calling to find out if we'd been having any problems lately."

Emily paused to look at Jolene; their gazes met and held before she added the water and oil to the brownie mix and started to beat it with strong, swift strokes. "What kind of problems?"

Jolene leaned over to swipe her finger along the chocolate on the inside edge of the bowl. Tasting it, she sighed. "Mmm... good."

"Jo," Emily protested, smacking her cousin's hand with her spoon to keep her from sampling any more. "What did Shannon say?"

Her cousin got up and started to prowl around the kitchen, her movements slow and deliberate. "You know how pretty her front window display is?"

Em thought about it as she scooped the batter into the

square, glass baking pan. "I love the ivy she painted on the window. When you look through it, it's like you're standing in the woods, peering through a break in the vines into an enchanted world illuminated by candles of every shape and size. Why?"

She brushed her hands on her backside and walked over to the stove, pulled the oven door open and slid the brownies onto the wire rack. "These'll be ready in about thirty minutes."

"Someone shot out her window and the stained glass sign hanging in it."

Emily shivered. "When did this happen?" Even as the question was leaving her lips, Emily sensed she knew when. "Yesterday? Same day they shot at our star?"

Jolene nodded.

"Then why didn't we hear about it?"

"We're a small town, except for the outlying ranches that surround us, but I'm guessing the law is busy, what with the trouble out by Zeke Eldridge's place."

Emily sighed. "Did they ever find out who left his corral open?" She had a sneaking suspicion it was old man Eldridge himself, looking for some company. It had been awhile since his cows had run off and had to be caught and returned.

They looked at each other and Jolene said, "I think Mr. Eldridge is sweet on the county dispatcher."

Emily shook her head. "I'm just as sure his heart belongs to Mavis Beeton."

Jolene snorted. "She's been trying to turn that man's head since way before we moved here."

"Longer," Emily said, "if the county rumor mill can be believed."

Their laughter died and Emily asked, "Do you think it's a coincidence?"

Jolene stared at her for a long time but didn't answer. Finally she asked, "What do you think?"

Emily shrugged.

Jolene opened the oven door and peered inside. "Hey, these look ready."

Emily rolled her eyes. "Only if you want to eat them with a spoon… which you know I do prefer. They need more time."

"Why don't you call Ronnie and ask her to meet us at Shannon's? We can powwow over there."

A short while later armed with a plate filled with gooey chocolate brownies, the cousins walked over to the Mysts of Time. Emily's heart hurt looking at the stark opening that used to be the storefront.

The door opened and wind chimes tinkled, announcing their arrival, although no one seemed to be in the shop.

"Be right there!" a voice called out from somewhere toward the back.

While they waited, Emily and Jolene browsed through the shop. "Take a look at these crystals." Jolene wandered over to the display.

Emily walked over to the other side of the shop, her interest caught by the assortment of pendulums and tarot cards. "These are really beautiful." She reached out to touch the cool sleek teardrop-shaped hunk of amethyst.

"You should really let the pendulum choose you."

Emily looked up at the proprietress of the shop and then again at the display. Oddly enough, one of the pendulums was moving slightly… the one that had caught her eye.

Shannon smiled and pointed to the swaying teardrop. "That one would be a good choice." When Emily simply nodded at her, she continued, "You should ask it a few questions to see which direction it moves for yes, no, and maybe."

"Actually, we're here to ask you a couple of questions about what happened here."

Shannon's eyes narrowed. "What do you think happened?"

If the tone of the woman's voice didn't tip Emily off that she was frustrated and upset, the way she was glaring at Em and Jolene would have.

"Same thing that happened over at our place."

Shannon's eyes flicked over to Jolene and then back before she sighed. "I'd heard that someone else lost a front window, but I was too busy over here trying to sort through the damage to bother to find out who it was."

Jolene looked around the shop. "Actually it wasn't our window, but somebody shot our sign full of holes."

Shannon finally noticed the plate of brownies in Jolene's hands and said, "Want some coffee to go with that?"

"Sure," Jolene answered.

"Thanks," Emily said at the same time.

"Come on in the back, and I'll start a pot."

Shannon walked to the back room and held a batik curtain aside, gesturing with her hand for them to precede her.

While Shannon moved around the tiny kitchen filling the pot with water and measuring out the scoops of ground coffee, they talked about their favorite chocolate dessert recipes. A few minutes later, coffee was dripping cheerfully into the pot. Shannon filled a pitcher with milk and placed it next to the sugar bowl on the table before sitting down.

When it was ready, Shannon got up and filled their mugs with coffee. When she placed them on the table, her brow was furrowed. “You haven’t heard what happened to Ronnie Del Vecchio, have you?”

Emily and Jolene exchanged a wary glance before Emily answered. “No, but Jolene asked her to meet us here.”

Shannon McKenna looked out of the window facing the back alleyway. “Someone broke into her place last night and mangled half of the stock in her back room.”

Emily’s temper started to boil. “She had the coolest selection of vibrators and toys.”

Shannon nodded.

“There’s definitely a link here, Shannon.” Jolene grabbed a hold of Emily’s hand and squeezed it once before letting go.

Emily recognized the signal and instinctively readied herself for battle. “You’re not in this alone anymore, Shannon.”

“We’ve got your back,” Jolene said. “Where’s Ronnie?”

“Sorry I’m late,” their friend called out joining them.

“Have a seat,” Shannon said, “and some coffee.”

“Thanks.” Ronnie took a long drink, set her cup on the table, and splayed her hands on either side of it. “Do you think we’re being targeted because we’re *women* business owners?”

Shannon tilted her head to one side. “Maybe.”

“Have either of you received an anonymous phone call asking for money?” Jolene asked.

The women looked at one another before answering. “One,” Shannon answered.

Ronnie shrugged. "I had two calls demanding I close my shop because of the stock in my back room, and two calls demanding money."

"Was it the same voice each time?"

Ronnie thought about it and shook her head. "The ones demanding money were. The ones telling me to close up my shop weren't."

"It was the same person demanding I close down The Lucky Star both times. I'm not sure about the calls demanding money," Jolene said. "I was pretty steamed at the time, so I wasn't exactly paying attention to who was behind the phone calls."

"What's wrong with women owning and running their own businesses?" Ronnie asked.

Shannon got up to pace. "There are other women running stores in town."

Jolene agreed. "There's Lettie and Pam Dawson and Minnie Harrison."

Emily smiled. "Those ladies practically run things around here. They've been carrying on their family businesses for years."

Ronnie shrugged. "I've only been in town a couple of months and haven't had a chance to meet everyone."

Shannon stopped pacing and turned to face the group of women and explained, "Lettie runs the food side of the general store, and Pam the hardware side. Minnie runs the feed store."

"This town, and the ranchers who live on the outskirts, couldn't survive without those stores."

Emily paused with her cup halfway to her lips. "I think I know why we're being targeted."

Jolene leaned close. "Well?"

"Have any of you heard about the First Annual Take Pride in Pleasure Day?"

"Sure," Ronnie answered as Shannon sat back down. "Mavis Beeton stopped by a couple of weeks ago to ask if I'd be competing in the rodeo. I'm not sure how she found out I used to be a barrel rider, but what does that have to do with anything?"

"Maybe nothing," Jolene said.

Emily shook her head. "Maybe everything." Locking gazes first with Jolene, then Shannon, and finally Ronnie, she said, "Our businesses are the only ones in Pleasure that have anything to do with *pleasure*."

"And your point would be?" Shannon asked.

"Did you also happen to hear from Mavis that the Preservation Society and Women's Club are petitioning the town council to have the name changed, or that they're creating a new website to advertise the new name and town celebration?" Emily asked.

"What else would they call a group of women who get together if not the Women's Club?" Ronnie wanted to know.

Emily rolled her eyes. "No silly, the town's name."

"What's wrong with it?"

Jolene smiled. "Not a thing. Those Donovan women knew what they were doing when they opened the town's first business. They just called it *Donovan's*. Cowboys and drifters started stopping in for a good meal and smooth whiskey."

"And then they added the upstairs rooms and brought in a couple of working women," Emily added.

"The town boomed after that," Jolene continued. "People started settling down, drawn to the charming women who started it all with one excellent saloon and bawdy house."

"So you think there's a connection between the move to get the town council to change Pleasure to something else?" Shannon wanted to know.

Ronnie shrugged.

"But why extort money from us?" Shannon wanted to know.

"I'm guessing they have to pay for the new website somehow," Jolene said, "and I heard attendance at the Preservation Society meetings has been down lately, so their coffers are low."

"But if they change the town's name, they have to change the name of their celebration too." Ronnie was starting to tap her fingers on the table.

Shannon nodded. "Take Pride in Emerson Day sounds a lot more plain vanilla than Take Pride in Pleasure."

Jolene looked up, her eyes blazing with anger. "Why those two-bit, penny-ante thieves!"

Shannon and Ronnie shared a look but didn't comment.

Emily did. "And now you're thinking what I'm thinking, cuz."

Jolene all but growled. "Those crooks want to clean up town and get rid of The Lucky Star because we have strippers." She looked at Shannon. "They want to get rid of the Mysts of Time because they don't understand the concept of your shop or anything that has to do with New Age." Sighing, she let her gaze meet Ronnie's last. "They want to get rid of Guilty Pleasures because of your back room and your collection of adult toys."

When she was finished, Emily spoke up. "But we aren't going to give in! We won't let some pain in the butt from Colorado take over our town and change its damn name."

Jolene nodded and added, "Or let them run us out of town. Jeez, it's just like a page out of the past when the Dooley sisters tried to close down Donovan's."

"I think it's time we started spreading the word around about what's been happening to our businesses, starting with Lettie, Pam, and Minnie."

"Don't forget Mavis," Jolene interrupted. "She can spread rumors like a wildfire."

Everyone smiled at the image of the older woman charging forward, stopping at each business and spreading the word. Emily grinned at Jolene, "Why don't I just give Mavis a call?"

Jolene asked Shannon for a pen and paper. When she handed it to her, Jolene said, "OK. Let me just write this down. Em, you're calling Mavis. Shannon you call Lettie and Pam, and Ronnie's calling Minnie."

Shannon smiled. "It's time to kick butt and take names, ladies."

The group stood up. Jolene put out her hand first. Emily laid hers on top of it, then looked at Shannon and Ronnie who quickly did the same. "We're staying and we're not letting anybody change our town's name!"

Vows said, strength in numbers, the women left to put their plan into action.

Chapter 12

Tyler's battered ribs ached as he shifted beneath the sink to get a better grip on the damned pipe. Plumbing was a bitch. Repairing the damage Dylan had done to a perfectly good, albeit leaky, pipe was going to be next to impossible.

Just like the Langley women. He smiled as he worked, thinking he'd be back at The Lucky Star tonight and could sample another taste of his redheaded filly. His smile widened. *She really hated me calling her that.* But she had clung to him when he'd finally dragged himself from her bed. She had a firm and agile body with a wickedly sensual mind, but it was the whole package that sucked him in. He liked her as a person too.

Hell, just admit it, son. He shook his head, glad that he was hearing his grandpa in his mind again. It comforted him.

He was so far gone over her, he hoped she wouldn't step back from him when she found out he was broke, his family ranch was failing, and that he'd rather stay home at night than party in town.

He shifted again, this time getting just the angle he needed in the tiny space to apply the right amount of pressure and loosen the connection. He caught the elbow pipe before it smacked him in the head. *Time to pay attention, son.*

The near miss with the pipe reminded him of last

night and how close he'd come to knocking Emily off her feet. Of course he hadn't known it was Emily at the time, but the fact still remained, he'd almost punched her out. The knowledge vibrated through him, irritating him more than the damned mangled pipe.

"Fucked up," he mumbled. "Why don't I just bend over and you can fu—"

"Watch what you say in front of Lori."

Jesse's demand was punctuated with a swift kick to the bottom of Tyler's boot. He absorbed the impact and the knowledge that something more than friendship was on his baby brother's mind where Lori was concerned. He'd have to give some serious thought to just what that might mean to the Circle G. They'd had women stay out at the ranch before, not many and not that often, but they'd each had a girlfriend they'd thought was the one and wanted to share their love of their ranch with. So far the Garahan men were batting zero for two and Jesse was up at bat.

"If I didn't have my head stuck underneath this ancient excuse for modern plumbing," Tyler bit out, "I might have noticed I wasn't alone."

He grabbed hold of the top edge of the cabinet and shimmied his way back out, working hard to contain his groan of pain as his ribs bumped against the cabinet trim. Lifting his forearm, he wiped the sweat off his forehead and reached for the glass of water he'd left on the kitchen table.

"Ty," his brother growled, and that's when Tyler noticed the quiet woman stacking the breakfast dishes on the other side of the kitchen.

Man, he'd thought she'd left when he'd started

swearing. Not long on conversation or useless words, he mumbled an apology.

Lori's eyes widened; it must be the gritty sound of his voice, a combination of a hell of a night and lack of sleep. He hadn't minded corralling the group of teenagers who had snuck into the club as much as the fact that they'd tried to steal from Jolene and Emily. He'd called Timmy's uncle and knew the kids had all made it home… sore feet and all. If his grandfather were still alive, he'd have told the boys that the walk was good for their souls.

He had, however, definitely minded leaving Emily alone in her bed, the soft satin-smooth feel of her arms and legs wrapped around him, and the way she'd pressed her lips to his heart. But he had a ranch that needed running and a repair to the damned pipe his brother had mangled.

"Tyler?" The soft sound of his name being called dragged him back to the moment and the job he needed to finish.

"Hey, sorry, Lori." This time she must have heard him.

She nodded and flushed the prettiest shade of pink. "That's all right."

Lifting the glass to his lips, he gulped down the rest of the cool well water and rested the glass against his hot forehead. Texas weather wasn't for everyone, but he liked the heat, was raised on it, and accepted it as part of ranching on the outskirts of Pleasure, the only place he'd ever lived, and the ranch he'd bleed for.

Bleeding made him think of the Langley women, and the trouble they'd had since he started working there. They'd been lucky so far. He had a feeling it was just kids but had heard from Mrs. Beeton the other day that some of the local do-gooders had been by the club to harass Jolene and Emily for donations, but that the Langley women hadn't been willing to buckle under the pressure to change up their club.

Hell, they're pretty much stuck on having their way about how the club was run, down to what he and the other guys had to wear on stage. He thought it was tough working the ranch with his brothers, but it didn't compare to how it felt to strip down to the damned spandex briefs the redheads insisted he wear.

"Damn."

"What now?" His brother paused in the doorway about to follow behind the woman Tyler noticed Jesse couldn't seem to stay away from.

"Just thinking out loud." Why couldn't he just wear black underwear? Cotton was more comfortable.

His brother grunted and headed outside following right behind Lori. Tyler couldn't keep from muttering, "Like a love-sick calf."

Tyler'd been in love just long enough to recognize the signs of a man who had it bad. If Jesse didn't watch out, he'd be married before he realized he'd been hog-tied to that blue-eyed little filly.

Stretching to relieve the ache in his lower back; he reached for the new elbow pipe he'd been carrying around in his pickup for a week. "Dylan should have waited," he mumbled settling beneath the sink once more.

Working to fit the pipe into place without using too much force, so that the threads would seat properly, he wondered why the hell Emily and Jolene had come downstairs armed for bear. They could have waited upstairs until he and Jake had taken care of things. "Good thing for them Jake and I were paying attention, or they could've ended up with more bumps and bruises."

Shifting so he could slip out from beneath the sink again, he wondered when he'd stop replaying the near miss over and over in his head, when he could be replaying making love with Emily.

He chuckled thinking of the gorgeous redhead ready to clock him with the hockey stick, dressed in that skimpy excuse for a nightgown. His heart kicked into overdrive remembering the feel of getting tangled up with Emily after she'd tried to brain him. The beats evened out and another part of his anatomy started to get hard thinking of her compact, curvy body flush against him when he'd pinned her between himself and her bedroom door.

"Hot as hell today," he mumbled to no one in particular. Good thing because he didn't feel like talking to anyone anyway.

Sorting through his tools, he was careful to put them back the way he'd found them. *That way you'll have 'em when you need 'em.* It felt good to work with his hands at something different for a change, not that he didn't like ranching; he loved it. *Lived for it. Breathed it.* But fixing something broken added a layer of satisfaction on top of the life he loved.

Swiping his arm across his forehead again, he wondered if the temperature would break one hundred degrees before noon.

"Hotter than a randy bull with a pen full—"

The sound of feminine laughter, sharp and irritating, had his hackles rising.

"Shit." There was only one female who laughed like that... his ex. Self-preservation in the form of the need to disappear filled him. He snatched up the toolbox, snapped the lid shut, and sprinted for the basement, all the while praying, "Lord, please don't let her come inside." He paused halfway down the stairs and held his breath, listening.

"I thought Lori said Tyler was in the kitchen. Where did he go, Jesse?"

Tyler jolted at the sound of Linda Lee's voice. He didn't have the time and couldn't dig deep enough for the patience to face his one-time girlfriend. *Come on, bro*, he silently prayed, don't tell her anything.

"Well, now," he finally heard his brother say, "he might have been here earlier, but he's not here now."

I owe you one, Jesse.

A few moments later, Tyler heard footsteps, a high-heeled staccato, clipping away from where he stood crouched on the cellar stairs, sweating bullets. The back door slammed and he grinned heading the rest of the way downstairs. "I will pay you back, little brother."

Toolbox stowed, he sprinted up the staircase wondering if he'd run into his little brother again before he had to head on into town tonight.

A few hours later, exhausted but still standing, Tyler slammed his truck door closed, ran a hand through his hair, and jammed his Stetson back on his head.

Sore in places that reminded him of last night's fight, he made his way over to The Lucky Star, hoping his boss and her curvaceous cousin were feeling better than he was.

The comforting beat of Texas Swing greeted him as he stepped inside and made his way down the hallway.

George Strait's music always seemed to unlock the tension deep inside of him like a cold beer on a hot day. Feeling better than he had in awhile, he smiled walking toward the black lacquered bar and the pretty redhead behind it.

Emily's heart turned over in her breast and began to beat faster. Tyler's smile was as welcome as the bright sunshine after weeks of rain. It eased the knot of tension between her shoulder blades and had her heart fluttering in her breast. Lord, he was so gorgeous. That tall, muscled length of him was all hers. *Hell's bells,* he even admitted he loved her mind! If that didn't beat all.

Her tired brain sent signals to all of those places he'd spent time getting to know last night, and every damned one of them was paying attention. She tingled from head to toe and everywhere in between.

"Hey there, sweet thing."

His deep voice sent a riot of shivers up and down her spine. He looked good, tasted good, and sounded good. How's a body supposed to concentrate? "Hey yourself, handsome."

"Jolene giving you busywork?"

She smiled at him. "Keeping the books is just one part of the job. We all pitch in with chores wherever we need to. The bar needed polishing before we open up tonight."

Lord, don't let this man be like her other loser boyfriends. Her desire for him wasn't the only thing tangled up this time. She'd only just realized how deeply the man moved her when she'd lifted her gaze from her chore and saw him walking down the hallway. Her heart was on the line this time.

Her relationships always started out great: that giddy rush when your gazes first connect and you know, you just know, that the touch of his fingertips slipping across the curve of your cheek to slide beneath your ear would leave you in a puddle—her favorite move in the prelude to a kiss that would solidify her commitment... and had done so with her last three loser boyfriends. But Tyler Garahan was different. As solid as they come, he'd stood up for her and her cousin, and she had a feeling the protective streak in the man went all the way through to the bone. She had to admit he challenged her on all levels and that had never happened before. But more importantly, when push came to shove, the man understood and respected the word no.

He hadn't gotten angry with her, and he hadn't tried to change her mind. He was content to wait until she was ready to move to the next step in their relationship. She'd spent the night in his arms and had been reluctant to let him go this morning. The long, tall, dark-haired Texan smiling at her had her toes curling, her juices flowing, and her mind screaming: *Take me now... we can finish polishing the bar with your amazing backside!*

Tyler in her bed. Lord, didn't that just send another shiver up and down her spine. It worked its way up from her toes, and the sound of her concentration fizzling as it evaporated shook her to the core. *Damn. Too late. Color her gone!*

"You know, my brother Dylan would just love you."

She shook her head, wondering what he was talking about. It was work struggling to pay attention since he'd sidled up to the bar. Jolene would ride her case no end if she thought Emily was slacking off while everyone was working.

"Dylan?" Lord, while he'd been talking, she'd been stripping him naked in her mind. Her hands started shaking. She set her cloth down, reached for a bar towel from the neat stack, and wiped the sweat from her palms.

The slow curving of his lips, lifting into a crooked grin did things to her insides that were probably illegal in forty-nine out of fifty states. But this was Texas. She felt her lips curve upward, mirroring his smile.

"Yeah," Tyler nodded. "He's a man of few words and appreciates the same in a woman."

Their shared laughter eased another knot of tension, this one low in her belly. What she was beginning to feel for the man went much deeper than attraction. She reached for the soft cloth and picked up where she'd left off polishing the top of the bar.

"I didn't know you had brothers."

He hesitated, as if he'd only just realized he'd told her something personal—something she knew she'd only share with someone she'd come to consider a friend, or perhaps more, and figured he would feel the same way.

He nodded, then said, "Two."

The silence between them was no longer comfortable. Wondering if it was him or her, she tried to re-establish the easy rhythm between them. "I don't."

He grinned at her. "You want one?"

Her bubble of laughter surprised them both. "If Dylan doesn't like to talk, I don't think he'd want to hang around with me."

Tyler's gaze swept from the top of her head down to

her hands then back. "You'd be wrong about that," he said. "All of us Garahans are real partial to redheads."

He didn't seem uncomfortable with the confession, and Emily noticed he'd been staring at her hands. She dug deep not to give in to the impulse to reach across the bar and grab him.

Tyler cleared his throat and nodded toward her still-moving hand. "You'll wear a hole clean through the wood if you don't move to another spot."

She froze. Tension crackled in the air between them.

Emily felt her toes curl over the edge of the precipice and the wind blowing in her face. Digging deep to pull back from the lure of unbridled passion simmering in his velvet brown gaze, she drew in a deep cleansing breath. She wanted him right here, right now, on the bar. Needing to keep her mind on the job and her hands busy, she kept polishing and asked, "So what's your other brother's name?"

"Jesse."

She huffed in frustration, guessing he was back to one-word answers. "You're not all that talkative yourself."

Tyler's laughter sounded rusty and told her more than words could. He'd relaxed and opened up about his family and had been comfortable with her. From the wary look on his face, he hadn't intended to. Were all men this stingy with sharing bits and pieces of themselves at the start of a relationship? It must be a man thing and one she intended to work through until they were on even footing. She wasn't going to be the only one investing time and attention in what they'd begun last night. He was voracious in bed and that had her mind conjuring up the last time they'd made love early this morning.

Emily licked her lips and looked up. Her gaze collided with his, and she drew in a long, deep breath. *Oh yeah*. Deep, dark, delicious passion beckoned to her. Her black leather bustier pinched, but she didn't pay it any mind; she was too busy watching the way Tyler's eyes glazed over. She'd have to see if Ronnie had something sexy in her shop that would get her cowboy's juices flowing like hers were. *Hell, life was too short not to be happy... or make a handsome hunk wait for another night of mind-numbing sex.*

His eyes grew impossibly darker. He was still interested even after the night they'd spent burning up the sheets. She really liked that about him. He was honest with her and told her he wasn't just a one-night stand. She'd hoped, and now she knew.

Meeting his direct, questioning gaze, she didn't hide what she was feeling. She wanted to nip at the skin at the top of his hip and lick a path from his breastbone to his navel. Her hands itched to glide down the length of his spine before gripping his amazing backside while she devoured him one lusty bite at a time. She hadn't had the time last night; he'd overwhelmed her with his need. Not that that had been a bad thing, but it was surely her turn to make his knees weak and his heart stumble.

Holy crap!

Tyler's Adam's apple bobbed up and down, his nostrils flared, and he clenched his hands into fists. Her man was ready, willing, and able. But was there time? Ready to risk her heart and her cousin's wrath, she smiled at him wanting to hook her thumbs in his pockets to yank him in for a thorough tasting.

"So you like redheads?"

Chapter 13

Tyler's tongue got stuck to the roof of his mouth. If he was reading the unspoken messages Emily was sending him, she was his for the taking, right here, right now. She hadn't been turned off by their door-banger. He'd wondered about that driving home this morning. He usually had more finesse, but Emily Langley had short-circuited his brain.

Hot, sweaty, sheet-tangling, brain-burning sex. How the hell was he going to make it through his shift later, knowing she wanted him as badly as he wanted her? Nodding his head to hide the fact that he was momentarily unable to speak, he dug deep for control.

Emily made her way down the bar, polishing in smooth circular movements. "You really are a man of few words, like your brother... Dylan."

He finally managed to loosen the knot in his tongue. "Yeah. Natural redheads are a personal favorite of mine."

He let his gaze dip down to her amazing cleavage before he caught the direction of his lust-addled brain and stopped. Hell, he'd almost let it slide down past the Mason-Dixon line of propriety in public. It didn't matter that Natalie and Jennifer were on the other side of the room talking to Jolene, he didn't want her to think he would disrespect her. Alone and in bed was a different story. It would be just the two of them.

He looked up at her, hoping he hadn't blown the good

thing they'd started. She was grinning at him. She knew what he'd been thinking, and she wasn't mad. Relaxing, he let out the breath he'd been holding.

Hell yeah! He liked redheads just fine. The one on the other side of the bar, taking another damned deep breath displaying her best assets while smiling at him just about had him panting, as she hog-tied him with the seductive power of her smile and the promise of passion in her warm, amber eyes. He wondered what other fantasies her agile mind could come up with. Just the thought of it had him chomping at the bit, but he could wait to finish the first one and wouldn't push her. She'd be worth the wait. He cleared his throat. All he could think about was letting the gorgeous redhead, with the promise of heaven in her eyes, take him upstairs and have her way with him. Hell, he'd even let her borrow his rope, so she could tie him to the bedposts while she let her sexy mouth fulfill the promise in her eyes, but that was one of his fantasies. Maybe they'd get to it before too long.

He held out his hand and locked gazes with her. "I just had this really great idea."

She set down her cloth, her eyes never leaving his, and as if in a trance, walked around the end of the bar to take his hand.

He lifted it to his lips and pulled her into his arms, then tilted her face up with the knuckle of his pointer finger. She licked her lips, moistening them. Fire shot straight to the part of him currently standing at attention, painfully straining behind the zipper of his jeans.

"Kiss me back, Emily." Molten amber seared him. He dipped his head and took her lips in a kiss that had his heart pounding as he pulled her toward the stairs. "I need you… now."

She yanked him toward the pantry. "In here."

He went with the moment and the lust that had him by the throat. As she closed the door and locked it, sealing out the world around them, he dipped his head and feasted on her breasts.

He slipped the tip of his tongue beneath the edge of her bustier. *Sweet. Hot.* "God, you taste good."

"Mmmm." She leaned back against the low cabinet and pulled him close. "My turn," she said, unbuttoning his shirt, brushing her hands across his chest, and smoothing the soft cloth off his shoulders. "I just love your broad shoulders."

While he tugged at her leather top, she pressed her lips to his breastbone. The warmth of her mouth drugged him until his eyes crossed and his hands cupped her shoulders with a strength she knew he was keeping in check. "More," he rasped, sliding his hands down her spine, kneading her denim-covered backside, and pulling her hard up against his erection. Emily was so hot, she worried that the club's supply of matches would spontaneously combust.

Mouths fused, tongues tangled, they drove each other closer to the edge, and all she could think was: *Yes! Now!* The door rattled as someone tried to open it. "Emily, I know you're in there… we're gonna open soon, and I need you out here."

They looked at each other and he whispered, "I think your boss is looking for you."

"I'm busy," Emily answered, pulling him closer so she could press her lips to his. "Why can't I get enough of you?" Her moan of desire must have been just a little too loud.

Jolene rattled the doorknob and called again, "Emily!"

"Are you gonna get in trouble if we don't open the door?"

Emily placed her hands on either side of his head, amazed that he'd worry about her. "My cousin likes getting her way, but it's my turn. She had her way yesterday. Go away, Jolene."

Tyler eased back so he could cup her face in his hands. The kiss he pressed to her lips was soft, tentative. "I thought I could be satisfied with a quickie, Em, but I want more."

She melted against him and sighed.

"I rushed you last night. I'm not sorry and wouldn't change one moment of what we shared, but tonight you deserve my undivided attention when I make love to you."

When she smiled up at him, he held her hands to his heart. "I promise you will enjoy the ride. I think I missed a couple of places last night, and I've got a hankering to sample some more of your buttercream skin."

Emily couldn't think; her imagination was working overtime, processing the erotic images Tyler planted in her brain. She leaned against him, hoping her legs wouldn't just fold up like a lawn chair.

"I plan to drive you crazy later," he promised kissing the breath out of her. "If we don't relieve the powder keg of sexual tension soon, one of us is gonna explode." Tyler straightened Emily's clothing and she buttoned his shirt. Smoothing her hands along the breadth of his shoulders, Emily inhaled slowly, savoring the solid feel of him beneath her fingertips before tracing the outline of his mouth. "What if I can't I get enough of you, Tyler?"

"Don't let's borrow trouble, Em." He ran the tips of his fingers along the length of her jaw and pressed his lips where his fingers had been.

His tender touch lined her belly with a slow sweet ache that she'd never felt before. Afraid to put a name to it, she rested her head against the broad expanse of his chest and closed her eyes. "I'm afraid I'm in over my head."

He tightened his arms around her and rested his chin on the top of her head. "That makes two of us."

"*Tyler?*"

"Good grief, now they're looking for you."

"Is it going to be a problem that we're together?" He hoped it wouldn't be but had to ask. Women could be territorial about things that made absolutely no sense at all.

"No," she leaned up on her toes and brushed her lips across his. Clothes straightened, Emily opened the door just enough to peek around it. Satisfied that no one was waiting to give her a hard time, she slipped out. A few minutes later, Tyler did the same, closing the door behind him.

"Hey, Tyler," Natalie called out. "You 'bout ready to go over tonight's routine?"

The sigh slipped out before he could catch himself. "Can't we just stick with the one I'm doing?"

When Natalie rolled her eyes at him, he knew she wasn't upset that he really didn't want to learn another routine.

Emily was back at the bar setting up glassware. Her

eyes met his and he wished they were alone back in the pantry or upstairs in her bed.

"You've got a couple of routines under your belt now, Tyler," Natalie reassured him. Thinking clearer now that Emily wasn't standing so close, messing with his brain, he knew he had to take her out to the Circle G. He wanted to make love to her out by the pond. He couldn't wait to ask her.

"...and the crowd just loves you," Natalie continued.

He didn't know how he felt about that. On the one hand it was good for business, so it reflected in his paycheck and his tips, but the flip side was that the females sure couldn't wait to run their hands all over him when they lined up in front of the stage. Hell, half the time it annoyed him, making him feel like an object, and the rest of the time he worried that he'd end up meeting one of the women outside of the club when he was in town. He wasn't sure, but he thought he'd seen Mrs. Beeton at the back of the crowd last night... awkward didn't even begin to describe how he felt about that.

In his gut, he knew the gorgeous redhead watching him like he was a hunk of brownie warm from the oven and she'd just die if she didn't get to take a bite was the reason he really hadn't noticed too many of the customers or thought about what he was doing up on stage too much.

"Aren't you listening?" Jolene asked walking toward him.

Years of training had him answering, "I... um... yes, ma'am."

"Don't call me ma'am," Jolene grumbled.

"Oh, give him a break, Jo," Emily said, folding clean

bar towels and storing them in the cubby beneath the bar back.

"Why should I?" Jolene asked. "He's giving Natalie a hard time."

Natalie tilted her head and looked up at their boss. "I don't mind."

"Sorry," he said. "I don't mean to harass you when you've been nothing but patient with me, Natalie."

She rolled her eyes at him, reached out, and grabbed him by the arm. "Come on, we don't have a whole lot of time to rehearse."

Not sure when he'd have another opportunity to get this close to Emily, he resisted for a moment, but Emily was nodding at him to go with Natalie. "Later, Tyler."

Emily wasn't tired anymore... a brief taste of Tyler had rejuvenated her, knowing she'd have an opportunity to sample more of the dark-haired Texan currently driving her crazy.

She wanted to blame it on her hormones but knew it might be what her heart whispered to her, scaring the breath out of her... he might be *the one*. What worried her most was that she didn't know a whole lot about him; maybe it was time to find out more. "Who does Tyler work for during the day?"

Jolene reached for a bottle of water and opened it. "I don't know."

"Maybe Natalie or Jennifer knows."

"You can ask later... our cowboy's got some work to do before I let you distract him again."

Emily shook her head and with an absolutely straight face said, "I'm sure I don't know what you're talking about."

Jolene snorted. "You mean tall, dark, and studly wasn't locking lips with you in the pantry?"

Emily's smile was just this side of smug. "A lady doesn't kiss and tell."

Jolene laughed. "Good thing you're no lady… by the way, was it as good as I'm imagining?"

Emily grinned. "Better."

Jolene nodded and smiled watching the stage where Natalie was working with The Lucky Star's headliner. "It was our lucky day when he walked into the bar because of that ad."

They both watched as Natalie put Tyler through the paces.

"There's just something about him that's so physical."

"Could be because he works a ranch for a living," Emily bit out. When Jolene just stared at her, she let out a huff. "Honestly, Jolene, didn't you remember him talking about Widowmaker the other day?"

Jolene shrugged. "If you know he works at a ranch, why did you just ask me about what he does?"

Emily just shook her head. "I know he works on a ranch; there's a half a dozen just outside of town. I was wondering which one."

~

"You're a natural, Tyler," Jennifer called out encouraging him.

He gritted his teeth and started counting again. "Natalie, please?" He hated to beg, but he was sore all over from the last couple of days. "Isn't this one new step enough?"

She stopped moving and turned toward him, her

eyes searching his face for something. What, he sure as hell didn't know, but he wasn't about to prod her. He'd take the much-needed break while she thought it over. Maybe he could sweet-talk Emily into taking a break with him… alone.

"I think our man's 'bout done in, Nat." Jennifer waved a water bottle at him.

He grabbed it. "Thanks."

"You need a couple of aspirin?" Jennifer was watching him closely—too close for comfort.

He paused, swiping the sweat from his face with his forearm and nodded.

"I've got some stashed behind the bar." Natalie went to get it.

"Who do you work for?" Jennifer asked. "That is, when you're not working for Jolene."

"A rancher."

Jennifer rolled her eyes at him, "Well there's news. Which rancher?"

"Does it matter?" He didn't want anyone at the bar to know his business. If they were like most women, and this nosy bunch seemed to be, once they found out that he was on the verge of losing his ranch, the story was bound to make the headlines of tomorrow's newspaper right alongside the mystery of who peppered bird shot through the wooden star hanging outside the club. Either that or word would get back to his brothers about his night job. Once that happened, he was seriously screwed.

So he wasn't talking to anyone except Emily… later when he drove them out to the ranch.

Tyler tipped the water bottle back and drained it.

When he came up for air, his gaze collided with Emily's. She was staring at him and hell if that didn't make things stir behind his zipper again. Relieved to still be in his jeans, and not those damned spandex briefs, he smiled remembering how amazingly responsive she was and how sweet she tasted.

She fanned her face, and his smile turned into a wolfish grin.

"Here you go." Natalie took his hand, turned it over, and shook out two pills into his palm. "I just had this great idea for your entrance."

Tyler took the pain relievers, knowing he'd need them to face the crowd tonight.

A little while later, Toby Keith was singing about Gene and Roy, *his new cue*. Settling his Stetson just a bit forward, he touched the buckle holding his chaps. Wishing he were wrangling ornery cattle instead of standing on this stage, he drew in a breath and walked out to the center.

"Sister dear," Jennifer said, hugging Natalie, "I bow to your greatness."

"That's some imagination you've got, Nat," Gwen said with a smile.

Emily heard their conversation but wasn't really listening. Tyler had reached center stage as the song ended. He lifted his head and unerringly picked her out of the crowd.

The heat in his gaze scorched her. Emily's body tingled in places she hadn't remembered she had until Tyler's lips had set off a conflagration that she'd yet to control. She couldn't wait to get him alone again and drive him crazy. Maybe she'd start by kissing a path across his amazing abs, but his muscled chest just drove her to distraction… she might start there instead. Too many choices and way too much time before she could get started.

The music changed and his hips moved to the beat, and still he didn't look away. Emily's body went haywire as the tingling gave way to shivers. Lord, she wanted his mouth on her again. She was craving another taste of that gorgeous hunk of dark-haired cowboy. She had to admit, she had it bad.

As the crowd sang along with the chorus, agreeing to save a horse by riding a cowboy, his hips began to undulate, captivating her.

She licked her suddenly dry lips, and he stiffened for a second before reaching for the coiled rope Natalie had left on the stage.

"I struck gold the day I hired that man," Jolene drawled joining them.

Tyler rotated his wrist in small circular motions, gaining in speed. With the flick of his wrist, he let the rope fly. The lasso landed around the bride-to-be, as planned, where she stood at the front of the stage.

Emily's stomach clenched. She knew it was part of the act but that didn't mean she had to like it. "You'd think someone about to get married would be playing cowboy with her fiancé," she grumbled.

The woman squealed in excitement as Tyler tugged on the rope and drew her closer. "Please don't tell me he's going to lift her up onto the stage," Emily rasped. "His ribs have got to still be sore from that bull and the tussle with those boys last night."

Tyler bent down on one knee, removed the lasso, and hauled the woman up into his arms in one smooth movement.

With every fiber of her being, Emily wished she could trade places with the tiny blonde. That's when she knew she was in deep trouble.

The way the blonde was clinging to Tyler got under Emily's skin like a sliver of wood. Ready to tear ass over to the stage to remove the parasite, Emily realized she'd have to deal with it. This was part of his job… she didn't have to like it, but it was part of who he was and what he did.

An old Chris LeDoux song started playing and she relaxed as the words filled her. And just like the song said, now that she had Tyler in her bed, what would she do with her cowboy if she decided she didn't want to keep him, but he didn't up and ride away? Worse yet, what if he got his fill of her after tonight?

Breathing deeply, she inhaled the calming scent of lavender that she'd dabbed on her pulse points. Back in control, she looked up as a drop-dead gorgeous blonde strode into the club.

"Welcome to The Lucky Star." The greeting was automatic, but the response from the blonde wasn't what she expected.

"It can't be the same Tyler."

"You know Tyler?"

The blonde looked over her shoulder and grinned. "Tyler Garahan is one gorgeous hunk of Texan with dark brown eyes that hold the promise of heaven when he looks at you."

Oh God! Emily's legs turned to water at the knees.

Who was this woman? While Emily struggled with the realization that the man she'd burned up the sheets with last night, and had been contemplating starting a relationship with, was about to be greeted by his girlfriend/fiancée/wife—whichever noun fit—the crowd roared.

Before she could get her brain back into gear and ask the blonde just what her relationship to Tyler was, the blonde had moved through the crowd toward the stage and was currently hog-tying the bride-to-be.

That wasn't part of the act, was it? Looking over to where Natalie and Jennifer stood with their mouths open, she knew it wasn't. One look at Jolene and she knew her cousin was going to roll with it, pretending it was part of the act, at least until it had gone too far. No point in overreacting unless it was called for.

With a smug smile of triumph, the blonde brushed her hands together, tilted her head back, and gave a really good imitation of a rebel yell. *Hell, I thought they only did that back home*.

The glazed look in Tyler's eyes changed to one of wary recognition as the woman stalked over to where he stood.

Damn. He did know her.

As Emily got closer, she heard the other woman ask, "Got any more of that short rope, Tyler?" and Emily's heart just dropped like a stone, shattering on the floor at her feet.

That'll teach her to start thinking about a pair of boots under her bed and long nights filled with good old-fashioned lovin'.

The blonde looked up and made eye contact with Emily, but before Emily could make her brain and mouth work in tandem, the bitch of a blonde gave her a smug little look that said, "*I was here first*."

She actually thought about backing down for about three whole seconds. Then her brain kicked in. No way in hell was she going to let go of Tyler now, and she sure as hell wouldn't give him up without a fight.

Worry creased lines between his brows, but the she-devil kept tossing hungry looks at Tyler, like he was a big old piece of meat skewered on a stick, drenched in barbeque sauce.

"Excuse me," Emily said, wading through the crowd. When she was just a few feet away, she decided to go with plan A: be nice to the bimbo. "I'm sorry, ma'am," Emily said, adding an extra helping of sugar to her voice, "but customers are not allowed to tie up other customers, nor are they allowed to manhandle the entertainment."

Proud of herself, she waited for the woman to answer her. The slow-eyed look the blonde flicked in her direction before ignoring her completely had Emily's blood shooting straight to boil. No f-ing way was she going to put up with being ignored.

Time for plan B: "I did say it nicely the first time," Emily announced as she curled her fingers into a tight fist.

Chapter 14

"TYLER, HONEY," THE WOMAN ACTUALLY PURRED, "I'VE missed you."

"Linda Lee, go home," he ground out. "I'm working."

"Oh honey, if you call this work, you're doing it wrong." Her irritating laughter chased a set of chills up his spine. Lord, he'd forgotten how much he hated that sound.

"I'm going to have to ask you to leave."

His former girlfriend turned and glared at Gwen. From the way the crowd backed away, Tyler knew the other women in the crowd had the sense to recognize the command in Gwen's voice and most obeyed it.

"I'm not ready to go yet," Linda Lee drawled. "Thanks for the offer, but I'm gonna wrastle me a cowboy and bring him on home."

"I don't think so, blondie!" Emily's fist connected with Linda Lee's nose.

Tyler felt his mouth go slack. *No*. He did not just see his little redheaded filly clock Linda Lee in the nose… did he? He closed his mouth and barely controlled his snort of laughter. Hell, it wasn't funny… well, actually it was, but he couldn't let the outraged women surrounding the stage catch him laughing at one of their own.

As he watched, the woman he'd gotten tangled with nearly a year ago cupped her nose with both hands. Bright red seeped through her fingers.

Aw, hell.

"Well," Gwen said, loud enough to be heard over the crowd, "I guess you're ready now." She plucked Linda Lee from the stage, whipped the bar towel hanging from her back pocket, and handed it to the woman as she hauled her through the crowd.

Shaking his head in wonder, he looked over at the diminutive redhead. She stood cupping one hand loosely in the other. He had to respect a woman who knew what she wanted... him... a definite turn on. *Damn!* "Nice jab."

Emily rolled her eyes at him and walked back over to the bar.

Linda Lee squealed like a stuck pig, and he fought the need to cover his ears to block out the sound. *Hell*, he thought, *at least his ex had stopped laughing*.

Jake stopped in front of the stage. "You want me to call the law so you can file a restraining order?"

Tyler chuckled. "Kiss my ass."

The other man grinned up at him. "Uh... no thanks. By the way," Jake drawled, "there're two brunettes over by the left side of the stage in a heated debate." He nodded in their direction and cocked his head to one side and repeated what he'd overheard, "Can you really give a woman the big O with just a look?"

Tyler laughed out loud. "I guess good news travels fast."

Jake joined him and then said, "You're a real crowd-pleaser, son."

"Give me a break," Tyler ground out.

Jake laughed. "The boss and I might, but I'm not sure Emily will."

Tyler scanned the crowd for Emily, found her by the

back door, and felt one of the knots of tension in his gut ease up. He was worried the scene with his ex would change things between them.

Ten minutes later, he'd changed and come back out front, and found everyone but Emily.

Had he read her wrong? Shaking his head, he knew he hadn't. What they'd shared last night had been too hot to handle and they'd both been ready, willing, and able to get burned again tonight. Between their interlude in the pantry and the lusty looks they'd shared while he was on stage tonight, he knew he hadn't misunderstood, but after Linda Lee walked in things had changed. Hell, Em fought for him. He wasn't about to give up on something this good just because she'd gotten cold feet.

"Women," he bit out.

"Something on your mind, cowboy?"

"Nothing worth repeating, boss."

They stared at each other until Jolene finally broke eye contact and looked away. "When you're ready to talk about it," she offered, "let me know."

Snatching the hat from his head, he raked his fingers through his hair, jammed his Stetson back on his head, and stuck his hands in pockets. "Look," he said, drawing her attention back to him. "I haven't seen Linda Lee in a few months."

"Hmmm." Jolene adjusted her sling. "Is that really her name?"

His chuckle surprised the both of them. "Hell."

"Been there, don't intend to go back."

He wondered if Emily had been right there alongside of her cousin in whatever hell Jolene had been referring to. He'd have to ask her later. "Real name," he answered. "Do you know where Emily is?"

"No." The nervous way she was scanning the near-empty club had his gut roiling.

"When was the last time you saw her?"

"Right after that blonde bimbo, um Linda Lee, gave the performance of her life and Emily slugged her."

Rubbing the back of his neck, Tyler was torn between pride and worry. Pride won out.

Jolene sighed and said, "She's probably outside getting some air. She doesn't like to use her fists, but she will if she has to."

"Thanks, boss." Tyler sprinted down the hall and out to the street.

Outside, he nearly passed by the figure standing half-hidden in the shadowed alley. A flicker of movement in his peripheral vision had him pulling up short. He walked over and nearly swallowed his tongue. "Linda Lee?" *Not Emily.*

"Tyler, honey," she breathed. "I knew you'd come back for me."

He held up his hands to keep her from wrapping herself around him again. "How could I, when I thought you'd been asked to leave and not come back?"

"You know, I've been thinking about what you said," she tossed her hair back over her shoulders and gave him her best sultry look.

At one time it would have worked. He was a flesh and blood man… not one made of stone, but he had a gorgeous redhead on his mind right now… one he was still looking for… "I'm done talking, Linda Lee. Just go home." When she licked her lips and stepped closer to him, he stood his ground and reminded her. "You were the one who hated the ranch and ended things."

"Maybe I was hasty."

"I've thought about the rest of what you'd said, and now I agree. Ranch life isn't for everyone, especially a woman who's used to city-living like you."

Her smiled shifted into a full-fledged pout. "I've changed my mind." She traced the tip of her fire-red fingernail along his jaw.

He felt nothing. It was long over between them and time for her to see reason. "I'm finished playing your games."

The woman had a body made for loving, but he wasn't interested in her. His mind took a short trip back to the pantry and the redhead who'd set him on fire. His cell phone vibrated in his pocket. He pulled it out and flipped it open. Jolene had texted him.

He scanned the message, not really paying attention to what Linda Lee was saying until he heard the words, "*...brothers would love to hear how you're spending your nights*."

Her threat brought his full attention back to her. "What?"

The triumphant smile got under his skin like a splinter. "Or do Jesse and Dylan know you're a stripper in a club?"

It wasn't the words so much as the way she'd said them. It made him feel dirtier than the time he'd skidded through a pile of horseshit, trying to break one of their stallions. He'd had manure in places he'd forgotten he'd had.

Knowing it was the only way to handle her, he bit out, "What do you want?"

Her tone changed from vinegar to sugar. "After I

walked in and saw you up on the stage tonight, honey," she rasped, "I only want you."

Her hands reached for him, but he sidestepped her grasping claws.

Undeterred, she purred, "I remember how you like it, baby."

Before she could remind him of a time he'd already moved past, a time he didn't want to remember, he shook his head. "Don't push it, Linda Lee. It's over."

His phone vibrated again. He flipped it open and read the text message. "I've got to go." He started walking toward the door.

"I think I'll pay a visit to the ranch tomorrow."

Her words stopped him cold. "Why?"

"I've got a hankerin' to visit with your brothers."

Her smile was pure bitch. She hated his brothers almost as much as she hated the Circle G. When their eyes met, he knew what she had in mind, and it had nothing to do with preserving his dignity. But the need to talk to Emily overrode all else, distracting him, and the only thing he could think of to keep Linda Lee from bothering him at work and messing up things with Emily was to bribe her. *Damn*. He didn't have anything Linda Lee wanted… actually, he did, but he was a one-woman man… and his woman was Emily. Wracking his brain didn't help. Finally, he played the only hand he had left. "Meet me tomorrow at the Tasty Freeze."

Like flipping a switch she went from bitch-mode to syrupy sweet. "Where?"

Opening the door, he answered, "The ice cream place by the Feed Store."

"Is this your idea of a cornball date?" Tyler didn't

stick around to answer or hear the rest of what she was saying. Jolene's text let him know Emily was over by the park. His body was tired, but his heart was filled with hope. He ran down Loblolly and skidded around the corner onto North Main. The park was just ahead.

Emily turned and smiled when she saw Tyler running toward her. He didn't ask, he simply reached for her, and she wrapped her arms around him. Grateful for his warmth and strength, she put the scene with the lasso, and the jealousy, from her mind and settled against him. Just being in his arms again felt like coming home after being alone against the world for too long.

She inhaled his scent—a unique combination of the soap he used and a hint of horse, but beneath it was all Tyler. She pressed her lips to the hollow of his throat and sighed.

Tyler's arms tightened around her, and he laid his cheek on the top of her head. "I was worried that you'd get the wrong idea about Linda Lee."

Emily eased back in his arms but didn't let go, and glanced up at Tyler. He needed a shave. Her fingers itched to touch his cheek. She liked the feel of his whiskers as much as she loved the feel of his cleanly shaven face. Her hands tingled, anticipating being able to take her time exploring the rugged contours of his amazing chest and abs.

He was sticking around for more, and she was looking forward to each step in their relationship. They'd hit a snag at the beginning, but things would only get easier from here. The sound of her name on his lips grounded her. She looked up at him.

"Would you come back to the ranch with me?"

Her breath snagged in her breast; this was a huge step in the direction she wanted to go. "I'd love to."

Taking her hand in his, he held her against his side as they walked back to his truck.

Chapter 15

Tyler held the passenger door open and Emily got up on her toes to brush her lips across his cheek. "Thanks."

Tyler rounded the hood and opened the door. "What?" he asked when she grinned at him.

"You've got a slide-over-here-honey seat!"

His eyes crinkled with laughter. "Well, what are you doing all the way over there?"

She scooted over, snuggling against the solid warmth of his side and sighed. "I've always wanted a pickup truck with one of these seats."

When he raised an eyebrow in silent question, she laughed. "So I could do this." She slid her arm around his waist and laid her head on his shoulder. He turned the key in the ignition and in one smooth move wrapped his arm around her so they were hip-to-hip.

As they drove toward the edge of town, she sighed. "Isn't this nice?"

He squeezed her hip but kept his eyes on the road, as if they'd done this a thousand times. She liked the way he answered her with a touch or a stroke; it was as if they'd been lovers for a long time instead of just one night. The feeling of forever was tantalizing, but she didn't want to push too hard, too fast.

"Which direction are we headed?"

"East of town. Why?"

"Mmmm," she murmured. "Just checking. I haven't spent much time out of town and am sorry it's dark and I'm missing the scenery."

After driving for a while, Tyler slowed the truck to a crawl and made a right-hand turn. The headlights hit a sign on the gate, a G inside of a circle. "What does it stand for?"

"It's our brand. My great-grandfather wanted to keep the name of the ranch simple and in the family. That's why it's the Circle G."

Emily wondered if she should point out that he hadn't been honest with her about the rancher he worked for. She knew the only way their budding relationship would have a chance was to be honest with one another. Beginning the way she planned to continue, she asked, "So when you were talking about your boss at the ranch working side-by-side with you, did you mean one of your brothers?"

He paused with his hand on the door handle and cleared his throat. "Not exactly."

"So you were just being evasive?"

"Kind of?"

Irritation started to work its way beneath the happiness she'd been riding high on since he'd come to find her in the park. "Like now?"

He let go of the handle and pulled her to him. "I didn't plan on getting involved with anyone at the club."

"Why did you?"

His smile was slow and sweet. He shrugged. "I couldn't seem to help myself."

She relaxed and the irritation waned. "So you figured—"

He kissed her forehead, the tip of her nose, and her

cheek. "If I wasn't going to be getting close enough to be friends with anyone at the club, they didn't need to know I owned a ranch with my brothers."

"So you are the owners?"

He sighed. "For now."

The tension radiating from the man beside her was palpable. Not sure if she should press him for details, she was smart enough to put what Mavis had told her and add two and two together and come up with a likely scenario. The ranch had fallen on hard times, and Tyler had had to find work to help make ends meet.

She reached for his hand and squeezed. "It must be hard for you."

He nodded and reached for the door, opening it. "Sit tight."

While she admired the fit of his jeans, he pushed open the big gate. He got back in the truck, drove through and put it in park again, got out, and shut the gate. The road leading toward the ranch was dark, and Tyler fell silent.

"Have you changed your mind?"

He snorted, swallowing his laughter. "Not hardly, Em. I've wanted you here… to see you at our ranch."

She settled next to him again and noticed the tension leaving him by degrees.

"I wanted to bring you here, to the Circle G, the place that matters most in my life… my reason for living… for breathing… and the reason I had to take on a night job to help pay the mortgage and feed bill. We might be just scraping by, but someday this ranch'll turn a profit."

He shook his head as if to clear it. "Enough about me, Em. Tell me something about you."

The gift of trust that he'd just given her, sharing what

was important in his life, touched her. How could she not do the same?

"I grew up down South but didn't have your typical happy family. My dad died when I was young and it changed my mom. She never was the same; she'd lash out at me for things that really weren't my fault, until I started wondering if maybe it was." She looked up at him and sighed. "Jolene's mom ran off to be a buckle bunny. Her dad took it real hard. So she and I started spending more time with each other. We both had bad attitudes and smart mouths, so we usually ended up in trouble, having to defend ourselves."

Tyler chuckled.

"You think that's funny?"

"Just the part about the two redheads currently in my life having bad attitudes and smart mouths. You were saying?"

"When Jolene called to say she was moving to Texas and had bought a bar sight unseen, I moved with her."

"So you two have always had each other's backs?"

She smiled. "Yep."

"My brothers and I have too."

"So you three raised a little Cain in your youth?"

His laughter made her smile widen. "Apparently not as much as you and your cousin. Here's our turn."

The road forked and he turned left, away from the two-story house she could see ahead of them. "Where are we going?"

"There's a spot out by the pond where the night air is sweet as sugar and the grass is soft as air."

Emily blinked back tears. Tyler's love for his land was heartwarming.

As if he sensed her mood change, he brushed the tips of his fingers along the curve of her cheek. "It's where I want to make love with you, to share a part of me that goes soul deep." He pulled off the road and parked. Reaching behind the seat, he pulled out a worn quilt. "My great-grandmother stitched it together when she was a bride."

"It's a family heirloom. Won't the damp grass ruin it?"

"It's made of sturdy fiber, just like all the Garahan men."

Emily wrapped his words around her like a hug. They'd learned more about one another in the last hour than she'd expected to find out in a month of Sundays. Each new discovery was as devastatingly intimate as each new spot Tyler had touched with his lips and tongue the night before.

"Come on, Em," he said, opening her door and reaching for her hand. He spread the quilt on the grass as the cool night breeze rippled across the pond. Emily breathed deeply. "Is it the water or the grass that smells so sweet?"

Tyler shook his head. "I'm not sure, but it could be the damp Texas earth. I don't rightly know. Smells good though, doesn't it?"

His hesitation waiting for her response was one more gift to hold to her heart. "Mmmm."

When he reached for her hand, she went willingly. He eased her down on the soft cotton bed he'd made for her. The beauty of each gentle touch combined with the magic of the night filled her heart to bursting. As if she were a present, he slowly undressed her, savoring each and every curve he uncovered. She was tingling with awareness, mindless with need, and ready to explode by the time he'd bared all of her to the cool night breeze.

When he started to unbutton his shirt, she shook her head to clear it. While she loved the way he worshipped her body, she wanted to show him the same tenderness, sharing the gift they were making together. She brushed his hands aside. "My turn." Her hands stroked the long sinewy muscles, testing the tensile strength of muscle and bone that were part and parcel of the long, tall Texan she'd fallen in love with. She pressed her lips to his throat, his chest, his hip.

When nothing remained between them but the night and the thin layer of protection, Tyler whispered kisses across her heart and eased into her with a long, strong but loving stroke that made her feel as fragile as her grandma's bone china.

She lifted her hips to welcome him and would swear she heard his control snap. "God, Em," he rasped grabbing her hips, rearing back for a second before his nostrils flared and his eyes went dark with desire. "Now!" His fingers dug into her hips as he kicked it into overdrive, pounding into her with a speed that made her head light and her heart thunder.

"Come with me, Emily."

His raspy plea sent her spiraling over the edge. As the night gave way to dawn, he emptied himself into her and groaned like a man dying of thirst scenting water.

Wrapped in each other's arms, cocooned in his great-grandmother's quilt, they drifted off to sleep.

Tyler woke slowly, savoring the feel of Emily in his arms, as the air warmed by degrees and the scent of sun-warmed grass wafted over them. He had a never-ending list of chores to tend to and a woman he didn't want to leave long enough to do them.

Emily pressed her lips to his chin and stretched. "Have I told you how good you look in the morning, Tyler Garahan?"

He chuckled. "I'm sorry I missed my chance to say it first." Pressing his lips to the sensitive bit of skin beneath her left ear, he nuzzled closer. "I've got chores that need tending to, but if we hurry, there's a Texas-sized breakfast in your future before I have to get to work."

"I guess I could call Jolene for a ride."

He didn't want her to leave… not when he'd been imagining her here at the Circle G and finally had her out by the pond. They'd loved each other like crazy, and his body strained to attention, hoping to do it all over again.

"Can't you stay for a little while?"

"What will I do? Won't I be in the way?"

He grinned. "You could ride out with me or hang out at the house. That is if Jolene could spare you for the day."

Tyler could tell from the way she was frowning that she was giving it serious thought. She probably had a hundred things to do herself. Then it hit him: maybe she didn't know how to ride a horse. "Do you know how to ride?"

She smiled. "I've ridden a couple of times back home. I can keep up. Besides, Jolene probably won't worry about where I am 'til noon."

"I've got so much to do; I'm not sure where we'll start today."

Emily bit her bottom lip, trying to hide the fact that she was disappointed. "Do you have to leave right now?"

He nodded. "Normally, I'm already up and in the saddle by now."

Her wicked smile did things to him that could not be

legal. He clenched his jaw. "I guess I have a few minutes to spare." He reached for the edge of the quilt and unwrapped Emily flushed with morning. Their passion rose like a tidal wave and they willingly went under.

Energized from tangling with her cowboy, Emily smiled. "Good morning, Tyler."

He squeezed her beautiful backside and grinned. "Back at you, Em. Time to get dressed."

By the time they arrived at the ranch house, there was no one in sight.

"You've got a porch swing!" Emily ran up the steps and sat down, pushing off with her feet and looked up at Tyler like he'd just given her a gift.

"You can sit here while I rustle up breakfast."

She pushed off a couple more times, closed her eyes, and sighed. "Lord, I love it here. Pretty land, sexy, gorgeous man, and a porch swing."

"I like it here," he said, holding out his hand. "Come on, you need to eat if you're going riding with me."

While she set the table, Tyler whipped up steak, eggs, bacon, and home fries, unwrapping and nuking a plate of biscuits. "Lori made them yesterday; she said all I had to do was warm them up."

"Lori?"

He turned and smiled, pleased at the hint of jealousy in her amber eyes. "Our cook."

"Why do you need a cook if you can cook?"

"Time's precious, and we're so far behind, we might never catch up without her help. She's a special friend of Jesse's."

"Oh. That's all right then." She reached for one of the warmed flaky confections. "Got any honey?"

Tyler set it out along with the butter dish. "Help yourself, darlin'."

By the time they'd finished eating and he'd gone over his list of chores for the day, Emily was exhausted just listening to the number of jobs to be finished by sundown. As agreed, she rode out with him to the south end of the ranch. The air was clear and the sun was hot, with no cooling breezes off the pond to refresh them. Up ahead she could hear the sounds of bawling steer and men yelling.

"What are they doing?"

Tyler squinted and answered, "Rounding up the half a dozen or so steer that got through the breach in the fence. Come on, they won't bite."

"The steers or your brothers?"

He laughed, "It's steer... singular or plural, and don't worry, I won't let either one bite you, darlin'." Tyler took off his glove and put two fingers in his mouth and whistled.

His brothers turned and stared as if they were seeing a ghost. Emily wasn't sure what that was all about, but she'd ask Tyler later.

"Dylan, Jesse," he said when they rode close enough to hear, "I'd like you to meet Emily Langley."

Jesse pushed his Stetson back off his forehead and asked, "The boss?"

Dylan surprised her by answering, "The cousin." He tipped his hat. "Pleasure, ma'am."

Jesse did the same, and she knew that they'd paid attention when their mother had taught them to be gentlemen. They might lead a rough life and work endless hours, but they were gentlemen to the core.

"Tyler's letting me tag along today to lend a hand."

Dylan's grin was every bit as devastating as his older brother's. "Is that a fact?"

"Yeah," Tyler said. "Let's get started."

"We ain't never had one of Tyler's women ride out with us to work the ranch," Jesse said, riding alongside Emily.

"His women?" Wondering how many there had been would kill her, but one look at the man and she had to admit, in all fairness, he probably spent most of his spare time beating them off with a stick.

"Shut up, Jess."

His little brother just laughed. "Come on, Emily," Jesse urged. "If we get there before Tyler, you get to hold the post."

It wasn't quite as easy as she thought it'd be, but she was game and wouldn't admit that the damned thing was heavy. Bracing her feet apart, she held the post and her ground. Tyler's slow sweet smile was all the encouragement she needed to keep going. Lord, the things his eyes said; when he looked at her made her head spin.

When the posts and barbed wire had been repaired, Tyler called out, "I'm taking Em back to the house for lunch."

Dylan angled his shoulder and his horse in between Tyler and Emily. "Well now, I think I'll tag along just to make sure you don't expect her to rustle up some grub for you."

Jesse caught Dylan's drift and squeezed in between Dylan and Emily. "I wouldn't want you to feel obligated to do any of the dishes we left in the sink, Emily. I'll ride along to make sure you rest up some."

Emily looked up at the sound of a feral growl. "Good Lord! Do you have wild cats out here?"

Dylan threw back his head and laughed, a deep masculine sound. “Naw,” he snickered. “Just big brother over there making sure me and Jesse watch our step around someone as pretty as you.”

She felt her face flush beneath the brim of her borrowed hat. Emily pressed her knees against her horse’s side and gently tugged on the reins. Her horse obeyed and headed around the Garahan brothers over to where Tyler rode, jaw clenched, eyes narrowed, staring at the distant horizon. “I like your brothers.”

He made a rude sound that she supposed was his nonverbal reply, but she did notice his hands eased their grip on the reins. “I like them sometimes too.”

“Race you back to the barn!” Jesse challenged and was off like a shot, with Dylan hot on his heels.

“Don’t mind those idiots,” Tyler warned.

“I don’t,” she admitted. “I think they’re sweet.”

His guffaw caught her off guard.

“What?” she demanded.

“Uh… nothing… just don’t tell my brothers what you think about them.”

After he spent a little extra time showing her how to rub down her horse, water, and feed him, Tyler walked with her from the barn to the house. “Lori should be here.”

The sound of low feminine laughter and deep rumbling voices gave life to the ranch house, soothing some of the worry Tyler had unknowingly put there with his warning about his brothers.

“And that’ll be Jesse in there trying to coax a smile from her.” He reached for her hand. “Come on, Em.”

While the men took turns washing up so they could eat, Emily noticed she was covered in dust from head to toe. "Sorry, Lori," she said, backing slowly out of the room. "I didn't realize I was so dirty."

The blonde was tall but slender. "Don't mind a bit of dust; can't be helped if you spend your day outside working the land."

"But my boots are probably covered with all kinds of icky things."

Dylan's burst of laughter caught her by surprise. "Ranching's man's work."

"Oh really?" she asked. "I suppose you don't remember who helped you hold up fence posts today."

"He's just teasing you," Lori warned. "All the Garahan brothers like to tease."

"Sorry—" Dylan began.

"I didn't want you to think I'd visit and not lend a hand."

"Ignore my brothers," Tyler said, squeezing her shoulder, then kissing the top of her head. "I do."

"I need to wash my hands."

Tyler gestured toward the kitchen sink, and she asked, "But don't you prepare meals in here?"

Exasperated he walked over to where she stood staring at the spigot. "It's dirt, maybe a little horse manure mixed in, but Texas dirt is welcome in this ranch house."

With each word his love for the land and his ranch came through, the same as it had with each fence post they'd pounded back into submission and each strand of barbed wire they'd restrung.

"You love it," she whispered, reaching out to stroke his cheek.

Heart in his eyes, he nodded. "Best wash up, darlin', or Dylan's liable to eat your lunch."

"You snooze," the middle Garahan brother called out, "you lose."

Emily washed up and was back at the table in minutes, amazed at how welcome the Garahans made her feel. Looking from one handsome face to the next, she shook her head. "Jolene would just shrivel up with envy if she knew the company I've been keeping today."

Dylan shook his head, passing the bowl of potato salad. "So what do you do at the bar, Emily?"

She helped herself to a scoop. "I keep books, order stock, that sort of thing."

Jesse snickered. "How many kegs of beer has our brother hefted this week?"

Emily wondered what kind of a question that was. "Kegs? Tyler doesn't haul kegs, he—"

Tyler nudged her under the table. Her gaze swung to his, and the pleading look in his eyes stopped her cold. *What was going on here?*

Dylan and Jesse shared a look before changing the subject. She'd have to grill Tyler later to find out why he didn't want her to talk about what he did at the club.

After the meal was over and Emily's offer to wash up was declined, she asked to use the landline to call Jolene.

"Well hello there, stranger," her cousin drawled. "Sleep well last night?"

Emily felt too good not to laugh. "I surely did, cuz. Did you?"

Jolene grumbled something not repeatable and mumbled, "Hang on."

While she shouted at someone to keep their shirt on, Emily could tell from the sound of Jolene's voice that something had happened and Jolene needed her.

"Can you talk about whatever is going on?" Emily hoped she would be able to solve it over the phone because she really didn't want to leave the Circle G yet.

"Can't. When are you coming back?"

"I was going to ask Tyler to drive me in tonight." The silence on the other end of the line said more than words. "Why don't you have Natalie or Jennifer come and pick me up?"

Jolene's sigh was heartfelt. "I owe you one, Em."

"Yeah," she said. "You do and you will."

She turned around and walked into a solid wall of muscle. "Trouble at The Lucky Star?"

"I'm not sure. Jolene couldn't talk right now, but I need to get back and see what's going on."

"I can't drive you—"

Emily put her hand to the middle of his chest and smiled up at him. "I know. I asked if Natalie or Jennifer would drive out and pick me up."

"Oh," he said. "OK." Pulling her into his arms he hugged her to his heart. "I'm glad you came."

Emily pressed her lips to his. "I'm gladder you asked me to."

"Jeez, Ty," Dylan groaned. "Not enough women to go around, so if you're not gonna share, take it outside."

Emily's laughter mingled with Tyler's as they walked outside, and then she remembered the quilt. "Oh no! Your grandmother's—"

"Quilt?" he finished, nodding. "I hung it up while you were in the bathroom."

Relieved, she sighed. "Oh good—Tyler," she rasped reaching for his hands, "there's something about this place that just pulls at your heartstrings."

His eyes darkened, and his jaw clenched. "You feel it too, Em?"

She tilted her head to one side and looked up at him. "The air's sweeter out here than in town, especially out by the pond... it's almost magical there."

He reeled her in and hugged her tight. "Grandpa always told us to find a redheaded filly who loved our ranch as much as she did us."

"I'd have liked to meet him."

Tyler grinned. "He'd have taken to you right off."

"It's scary, isn't it?"

"What?" he asked.

"How quickly you get used to having someone in your life."

"Me?" he rasped.

"You," she whispered.

"Kiss me back, darlin'."

"My pleasure, Tyler. You know, if you ask me nicely, I can come back."

"Consider yourself asked." Tyler dipped his head to capture her lips.

When he drew back, he couldn't help but think about the way he never had any time to do anything or go anywhere. The Circle G was a demanding responsibility that he loved but that left little to no time off for fun. If he planned this right, they could steal a little time together on a date.

"Can you meet me later for dinner? I'll leave here early so we can spend a little more time and be together."

She grinned up at him. "Sounds an awful lot like a real date."

He shook his head. "I wish there were more hours in

the day, Emily. I'd take you out and introduce you to everyone I know—take you to the movies, dinner, wherever you'd like to go. But for now, we'll have to settle for whatever time I can squeeze in between jobs and sleeping."

Tyler pressed his lips to her forehead, the tip of her nose, and then her chin. "Hmmm... someplace quick and easy. How about five o'clock at the BBQ Pitt?"

"I'd love to."

An hour later, Emily was listening to Mavis Beeton grumbling about the royal pain in the butt that she worked with on the Pleasure Preservation Society. "Can you believe that that man had the audacity to suggest that I come over here and encourage you young ladies to close the doors to your club?"

Emily's stomach churned. She glanced over at Jolene. Her cousin was staring down the mirrored hallway. "Not gonna happen, Mavis."

The relief on the older woman's face was endearing. "You know I've worked hard for that group over the years," she said, "but that doesn't seem to mean anything to that horse's ass."

Emily chuckled. "I really don't know Frank all that well."

"If you met him once, you know all there is to know."

Ronnie Del Vecchio walked in and the women turned to greet her.

"What's up?" Emily asked.

"Have you heard the latest rumor going 'round town?" Ronnie asked.

Mavis snorted. "Which one? The one about The Lucky Star closing down and reopening as an old-time saloon?"

“No.” Ronnie shook her head. “The one about the town council voting to change the town’s name from Pleasure to Emerson.”

Chapter 16

IMAGES OF THE FIERY REDHEAD HAD STAYED WITH HIM AND continued to fog his brain long after she'd ridden off with Natalie. Em riding alongside of him, sweating with him while they muscled fence posts into place, and laughing while he and his brothers teased one another and her. Kissing her on the back steps... loving her out by the pond.

Tyler drove half a block past the BBQ Pitt before he realized it. He turned around and pulled into the lot and saw Emily. She waved and smiled when he pulled into the space next to hers. "Sorry I'm late."

"It's a beautiful day, and I didn't mind waiting for you."

Emily noticed the lines of strain around his eyes and wanted to hug him to erase them, but wasn't sure if they'd gotten to that point in their relationship yet... PDAs weren't for everyone.

Tyler took the decision out of her hands when he walked over to her and pulled her into his arms. Resting his chin on the top of her head, she heard him breathe deeply. "I'm mighty glad to see you, Em."

When he pulled back, Emily slipped her arm through his. "It's been a really long time since I've been asked out. I understand more than most people that sometimes life sucks you in and before you realize it, you lose large chunks of time that you can't ever get back."

Tyler held open the door for her and followed her inside. "Hey, Bonnie!" he called out.

"Well, hey there, darlin'," the buxom brunette waitress called out. "I didn't think we'd ever see you again. How's things out at the Circle G?"

"Hanging in," he said with a grin. Squeezing Emily closer to him, he said, "I'd like you to meet my girl, Emily Langley."

Bonnie smiled. "It's a pleasure. Tyler doesn't get to town much, and when he does, he usually brings his good-looking brothers with him. It's nice to see him with a female for a change."

Tyler shook his head. "Man, I'd forgotten that you don't have an off switch."

The waitress snickered. "You love when I talk, 'cause I fill you in on what's going on in town so you can catch up when you come in every six or seven months."

Tyler sighed. "Busted. How about a booth near the back?"

"Follow me."

Once they were settled, she asked, "What can I get y'all?"

"What would you like, Em?"

She didn't hesitate. "I'd love a margarita."

"What do you have on tap?"

Bonnie shook her head at him, but looked at Emily. "He asks me every time, and every time I repeat the list and still he'll ask for his favorite down-home Texas-brewed beer... Shiner Bock."

Tyler shrugged and Bonnie smiled. "I'll be right back with your drinks. Why don't you take your time and decide what you want to order."

When she headed for the bar to place their order, Tyler moved over closer to Emily. "I'm really glad they still have booths in this place."

"Sounds like you come here a lot."

He laughed. "My brothers and I used to make it into town a couple of times a month and we'd always eat here. They have the best food in the world. It's been hard to get away lately with the way finances are."

When she just stared at him, he asked, "What?"

"I like the way that sounded before," she said. "When you called me your girl."

He grinned. "I'm a one-woman man, Em… and I don't plan on sharing you with anyone."

Emily linked her fingers with his and smiled, and he wondered what he'd ever seen in his ex or any of the other women he'd dated. There was something different about Emily that went bone deep, making what they'd shared in the last few days truly special.

They'd lived, worked, laughed, and loved more than he'd thought possible in such a short span of time… it was scary and amazing. And that was when it hit him: he didn't worry about sharing his life with Emily; it seemed natural to just do it. The fact that she wanted to be with him and learn about his life at the Circle G was icing on the cake, which had him remembering that one particular fantasy that they'd yet to play out. His mouth watered just thinking of working his way to Emily's honey-sweet center.

He focused on Emily's beautiful face, and her sweet smile drove every thought from his head. Her cream-colored skin and fiery auburn hair spilling wildly over slender shoulders, with a strand nestled in her impressive cleavage, had his libido humming.

"Taking a little side trip there, Tyler?"

He didn't think Emily was upset with him, but he didn't like to be put on the spot. He shifted on his seat and nodded his head when he saw Bonnie walking toward them. "We're ready to order."

They both ordered ribs, and when their meals arrived, they ate companionably.

Emily wiped her mouth on her napkin and said, "I've seen that you really do work 24/7. Don't you ever have time off for good behavior?"

Tyler shook his head. "We did when we used to have a couple of hands working for us, but times are hard right now, and we can't afford to pay anyone."

She sipped from her glass lost in thought. "You know the deal Jolene and I made the other night with Timmy and his friends?"

"Yeah." Focusing on her mouth made it hard to think straight. He blocked the image from his mind.

"Did you ever think of asking him to volunteer out at the ranch?"

"He works out at his Uncle Ned's."

"Does his uncle have ranch hands working for him or is he in a situation similar to the Circle G?"

It was funny: Tyler didn't mind talking about the ranch and its financial burden with Emily. *That was new*. He'd always kept his troubles concerning the ranch from everyone except his brothers, and hell if he hadn't tried to keep the extent of their dire situation from them, thinking he could fix it.

"He's got a couple of hands working for him, so he could probably spare Timmy for a couple of hours a week."

Emily leaned close and pressed her lips to his forehead. "Well then, what do you think of my idea?"

Warmth radiated from the spot, easing the growing ache behind his eyes. "It's a good one, but I can't pay Timmy."

She rolled her eyes. "Hello! Did you not hear the volunteer part?"

He scratched the back of his head. "Yeah, but—"

"Don't let your pride get in the way here, Tyler," she brushed the tips of her fingers along the line of his jaw. "If you talk to Timmy, you could offer to teach him something about ranching or raising horses or something... you think of what... in exchange for a couple of hours of manual labor from him."

"But he already works for his uncle. What could I teach him that he doesn't already know?"

"I'm sure you can think of something."

The sound of her exasperation had him chuckling.

"Are you laughing at my idea?"

Her quick temper warmed his heart. His woman was a delight, no matter which mood she was in. "No, ma'am."

"I hate when you call me that."

"I know, darlin', but I didn't want you to think I wasn't respectful of your idea."

"Oh, well... all right."

"Or mindful of your temper."

She narrowed her eyes at him. "Will you at least give it some thought? From what I saw, you and your brothers could surely use a hand, and you'll drop from exhaustion if you try to keep up this pace working at the ranch and for Jolene and me."

He knew she was right, but he hated asking for help.

Her next words surprised him and had him wondering

if she could read his mind. "It's not as if you're asking for a handout. You're offering something more valuable than the almighty dollar, your time and your experience, and you're sharing it with a young man who will remember what you've taught him the whole of his life."

She crossed her arms beneath her breasts, and his brain switched gears until all he could think of was getting Emily into bed until she teased, "I'm so glad you could manage to squeeze me into your busy schedule."

He felt his face flush. "Time isn't something I seem to have a lot of lately," he explained, "but it's all the more special because I get to spend it with you."

Emily reached for his hand. She squeezed it and held tightly to him. "Thanks for last night and today, Tyler. You made everything special for me."

"My pleasure, Em." He got up and pulled out her chair. "We'd best be getting back or Jolene'll send out a search party."

As he'd hoped, Emily laughed, and the sound of it soothed his soul. He held out his hand to her. Their eyes met and something solid and strong moved between them. Something worth keeping. "Come on."

Emily turned and waved to Bonnie before saying, "I'm coming."

Tyler pulled her close and pressed a kiss to her cheek. "You will be later, darlin'," he rasped. "I promise."

Emily reached for his hand. She squeezed it and held tightly to him.

Jolene and Jennifer were waiting when they walked into the club. "We were worried about you."

"No need," he said. "We're here."

"You're on in five," Jolene told him.

"Not a problem." He hauled Emily in for a quick kiss before sprinting down the mirrored hallway. "I'll just get changed and be on stage in five minutes."

"See you later." Emily brushed her hair out of her face and smiled to herself. It had been an eye-opener spending daylight time with Tyler. He put everything he had into working at his ranch and still had energy to spare to come and work for them. He was kind, sweet, and hell on her heart.

"Care to share what you're thinking, cuz?" Jolene asked.

"A smart woman like you ought to be able to figure it out." Emily wanted to savor her time with Tyler a little while longer before sharing it with Jolene.

Halfway through the evening, she heard a rumor about Tyler and that blonde bimbo. The worry that the blonde from the night before wasn't quite out of Tyler's life got stuck in her brain like a maggot, until she knew she'd drive herself crazy unless she asked Tyler about her.

She walked over to where Jennifer was standing, mumbling, "Time to take the bull by the horns."

During his first break, Tyler walked toward her with a smile on his face. "Miss Langley." He tipped his hat and said, "Jennifer said you wanted to see me?"

Her heart just tumbled over in her breast. Lord, he got to her on all levels. She had to steel herself not to let that distract her from the need to clear the air and keep the honesty at the heart of their relationship. She cleared her throat and asked, "So who exactly is the blonde to you?"

Tyler's sigh was loud and long. "No one special."

Emily snorted. "Just someone who thinks she's still your girlfriend?"

The flush of bright crimson tipped her off that her words had hit their intended mark. "Old girlfriend then," she said more to herself than anyone else.

"Jesus, Em," Tyler ground out. "It's over between us, has been for months." He tipped the brim of his hat back, and she got a good look at the frustration on his face.

She nodded. "All right, I'll give you that much, but it didn't look like she knew it was over between the two of you."

Tyler ground his teeth together. "Look, I'm not asking you about any former lovers of yours—" As soon as the words were out, a pained expression settled on his handsome features.

Emily glared at him, willing him to either confirm or deny that he had been out with the woman.

"Sorry," he apologized, "but that's all she is to me." He paused then added, "Trust me, Emily."

She may spend the rest of her days with a big L tattooed in the middle of her forehead, but she needed to trust that he was being honest with her. Without honesty, the basis for their relationship would crumble. She nodded and asked, "Are you staying tonight?"

"I can't, but I'll be back tomorrow after I finish up at the ranch."

She ignored the twinge of uncertainty and rose up on the tips of her toes to brush her lips lightly against his. When he growled low in his throat, she took the kiss deeper. "I really love the way you taste."

"You're killing me, Em." With a yank, she was plastered against the warm, hard length of his amazing body.

"The feeling's mutual, Tyler."

He dipped his head to sip from her lips, and she offered all that she was feeling, and then she gave more.

"Save some of your sweetness for me."

Emily traced a cross over her heart with her pointer finger.

Tyler smiled.

Emily hated that she had to go to bed alone after the night of loving she and Tyler had shared out at the ranch. It was becoming a habit, spending the night with him. But he was dog-tired after the finale and had already told her he couldn't stay. She'd be a shrew to suggest that he stay and let her sap the rest of his strength after she'd seen how hard he worked from early morning until they'd stopped for lunch. She knew he'd spent the rest of the day that way too.

"Being noble sucks," she grumbled. "Being alone instead of cozied up in bed next to my man sucks more."

With a sigh of regret, she sat up and flicked on the light by the bed, reaching for the romance novel she'd started to read the other night… before Tyler distracted her.

The stairs creaked, and she paused to listen. Had it been her imagination? When they creaked a second time, she was out of bed and in Jolene's room in a flash, nudging her cousin awake. "Jolene," she rasped. "Wake up!"

"Hmmmm?"

Jolene sat straight up in bed, rubbing her eyes. "Who? What? Where?" The stairs creaked closer to the top this time. "Em," Jolene turned toward the door, "someone's coming upstairs."

Emily groaned. "No kidding."

"Do you think it's Jake?"

"Why would he be sneaking up the stairs?"

Jolene rolled her eyes and whispered, "So he doesn't wake us up."

"But we're already awake," Emily pointed out. A knot was forming in Emily's belly. "OK. So what's the plan?"

"We need to be ready in case it's not him."

"Who else would it be?" Emily rasped. "Damn. Tyler took the hockey stick." She wished he hadn't; she felt better armed.

"Jake's got my bat. Oh. Wait. I know!" Jolene rummaged through the stack of shoeboxes piled in the corner of her room and came up with a black stiletto pump. She handed it to Emily. "Here. I'll use the other one."

Their eyes met. "Ready?" Jolene asked.

Emily grabbed a hold of the shoe, spiked heel pointed out, intending to do major damage. "Ready."

"You go first," Jolene nodded toward the still dark hallway.

Emily stopped and glared at her cousin. "Throwing me under the bus already?"

Jolene shook her head. "My elbow's still stiff. You've got the use of both arms and can swing your weapon to inflict maximum pain."

Their gazes met and held. "OK," she agreed.

Jolene nodded but didn't move out of the way. Side by side, as they'd faced more than one enemy in the past, the cousins walked toward the kitchen.

As they drew closer, Emily moved to stand in front

of Jolene. "You're supposed to be behind me, Jo," she whispered. "I've got a better chance of clocking them on the back of the head."

Worry creased her cousin's forehead. "And if that doesn't slow them down?"

Unease skittered up Emily's spine, chilling her to the bone. Ignoring the goose bumps, shaking off the feeling, she rasped, "Then you run like hell for help."

Jolene grabbed a hold of the strap of Emily's chemise. Em paused, waiting. Jolene whispered, "I've got your back."

And just like that, Emily's fear melted. Clutching her weapon, she pushed the door open and rushed at the figure. Determined to make her one shot count, she raised her arms up over her head and brought her weapon down.

The intruder spun around, grabbed her wrist, and squeezed it hard, forcing her to drop the stiletto before pinning her arms behind her. Adrenaline sprinted through her system. Panting from exertion and fear, she couldn't quite catch her breath. Squinting to see in the darkness didn't help until she was yanked forward against a rock-hard chest. Recognition slammed into her with the force of a blow.

"Tyler?"

"Emily?"

With the flick of a switch, the room was bathed in the soft glow of incandescent light. Jolene stood with her hands on her hips and a pair of black velvet stiletto pumps at her feet.

"What the hell are you doing?" Tyler demanded.

With her breathing semi-normal, Emily bit out,

"Protecting our club." Glaring up at him, she turned his words back on him. "And what the hell are you doing sneaking up here in the dark?"

Still plastered against him, the hard planes of his body set off a series of sparks beneath her skin that threatened to flare out of control. Needing to calm down, she looked up at him and asked, "Well?"

"I was halfway to the ranch when I realized I didn't want to spend the night without you, Emily."

"Damn," Jolene swore. "Good answer, cowboy." She turned and walked back to her room. "See y'all in the morning."

Emily reached for Tyler's hand and looked up at him. "Hey there."

He smiled. "Hey yourself."

Noticing the shadows beneath his eyes, she reached out to cup his cheek in her hand. "You look dead on your feet."

When he shrugged in answer, she tugged on his hand and smiled. "Come on, let's go to bed."

Tyler stumbled and caught himself before tripping. He'd been this tired before, but the need to touch her, press up against her until they were flesh-to-flesh and heart-to-heart overrode his need for sleep.

Following where she led, he looked at the door as she closed it and grinned. "If that door could talk."

Her laughter was low and sweet. "The tales it could tell."

He sat down on the bed and pulled off his boots. They hit the floor with a thud and just lay there. For a heartbeat, he wished he could do the same.

"Tyler?"

Emily's hand on his arm, shaking him, woke him. "Shoot, Em. I'm sorry. I—"

"Let me help you with that." She unbuttoned his shirt and helped slide his arms free. "I don't know how you can work all day at the ranch and then come into town and work for us. How long do you think you can keep this up?"

She'd urged him to his feet and had managed to get him out of his jeans while he'd been wondering where he'd get the strength to manage the task alone. "Thanks."

Her smile did things to his insides that he wished he had the energy for.

"Come on over here," she coaxed. "I've got this need to hold you tonight."

"Em," he rasped. "I can't believe I'm saying this, but I'm too tired—"

She touched the tip of her finger to his lips. "Shhh. I just want to hold you."

With Emily's help, he made it to the bed before he fell asleep on his feet. Good as her word, she wrapped her arms around him and pulled his back against her soft, sweet skin. "So good. Lord, you feel like heaven."

Pressing her lips to his shoulder, she soothed, "Close your eyes, Tyler. I'll be here when you wake up."

When Tyler opened his eyes, the sun was shining and Emily was smiling down at him. "Good morning, lover."

He grinned up at her.

"How'd you sleep?"

He laughed. "Like a rock." Running his hands over her shoulders, he rolled and pulled her beneath him, nuzzling her neck. "Thanks for not making me feel like I was a disappointment."

She snorted. "News flash, babe. I'm not such a nymphomaniac that I'd expect you to perform when you're so obviously dead tired."

"Good to know, Em. I'm glad we can share these intimate details of our lives without hurtling accusations at one another."

She tilted her head to one side and stared at him, wondering if he was being straightforward or sarcastic. "That wouldn't be productive."

He shook his head. "No, ma'am."

Straightforward. Good. "Soooo," she said, squirming so that the hard, hot length of him was lined up right where she wanted him. "You up for a quickie before breakfast?"

"I love a woman who can read minds." He kissed her, a long, deep, drugging kiss and reached for the foil packet she held in front of his face.

Sheathed and ready for action, Tyler gripped her hips, marveling at the womanly curves he'd had the pure pleasure of sleeping with last night. There was something more intimate about falling asleep in your lover's arms that rushed through him like a hit of whiskey. "Hang on, darlin'," he warned. "This is gonna be a wild ride."

Later, over breakfast, they laughed and teased one another like old friends. When Jolene joined them, he got up and cooked eggs for her too.

She thanked him and asked, "Have you heard the latest about Take Pride in Pleasure Day?"

He shook his head and scooped up another forkful of eggs.

"The town council's voting to change the name of our town."

Tyler laughed. "Not happening in this lifetime."

"That's not what Mavis and Ronnie told us yesterday."

Tyler sighed. "If you heard it from Ms. Beeton, it's the truth."

Emily frowned. "That's what we were afraid of. Is there anything we can do?"

Tyler thought about it. "I could spread the word to the ranchers. We've been known to change a few minds when we get together and ride into town."

"You'll help?"

"I've lived in Pleasure all my life. Garahans have worked at the Circle G for over one hundred and fifty years; you can take my word to the bank, we'll help."

"Thank you, Tyler." Jolene's smile was nearly as bright as Emily's. "I've got some paperwork to finish up. You coming, Em?"

Emily turned and smiled at Tyler before answering, "I'm going to be tied up most of the day."

"See you tonight." The sound of Jolene's laughter followed her down the hallway.

"Were you serious, Em?" Tyler didn't think he could stand working all day with the image of Emily tied to her bedposts stuck in his head.

She grinned. "What if I was?"

"Man." The burn in his gut matched the ache in his heart. "I've got to get back to the ranch."

Emily stood up and walked over to where he was sitting, leaned down, and kissed him. He pulled her onto his lap. She sat down, shifted to get comfortable, and got his full attention. "Think about me while you're working," she whispered, letting her tongue trail around the edge of his ear before nipping at it.

"You know I will." He groaned as she licked a spot of

skin beneath his ear. Fire shot from his neck to his lap. "You're killing me, Em."

She chuckled. "But what a way to go."

"Seriously," he mumbled, squeezing her to get her to stop, "I can't be distracted working with the stock. I have to pay attention."

"Hmmm... OK! How about an image of me wrapped in burlap mucking out stalls."

His groan came from his heart. "Burlap or cellophane, it doesn't matter what you wear, darlin', I'll already be thinking about you too much."

Contrite, she apologized. "I'm sorry, Tyler. I don't want you to get so distracted that you get hurt."

Mollified, he nodded. "But you still wouldn't mind if I thought of you while I was taking a break?"

Her smile warmed him from the inside out, and all he could think about was the long hours in between now and tonight when he'd see her again. It wasn't soon enough for a man about to go under for the third time.

Recognizing the look in Tyler's eyes, Emily shook her head. "I don't have time to get busy with you, Tyler. I wouldn't be able to think straight, and after I balance the books this morning, I've got to take inventory." She slid off his lap and stood up.

"I thought you were going to be tied up?" His confusion was sweet.

"I just hinted at the literal meaning to get a rise out of you." When his face flushed, she couldn't keep from laughing. "I just love the way your eyes get all dark and dangerous when you're feeling hot and bothered."

He narrowed his eyes and stared at her. She knew he wasn't happy with that last statement, but she wasn't finished. "And the way your nostrils flare out when you grab a hold of me right before you—"

"Damn, Em." Tyler pushed to his feet and reached for her.

Emily shook her head and pressed a hand to his chest. He pulled her to her feet and she sighed. "I didn't mean to make you crazy."

"Lord have mercy, darlin', you're killing me."

He laughed, and she was totally taken with this side of him. They were relaxed in each other's arms, and at ease sharing bits and pieces of their lives, working together toward a common goal. Amazing.

"You're a complex woman, Emily Langley."

Charmed, she smiled. "Likewise, Tyler Garahan."

"So will you let me kiss you goodbye?"

She sighed and smoothed her hands around to his back and pressed against the broad chest she spent the night snuggled up against. "What are you waiting for?" she teased.

He dipped his head and captured her lips. His tongue traced the line of her bottom lip, and she sighed. When his tongue tangled with hers, she fought to keep control or else they'd wind up back in bed and wouldn't have the time to spend together later. Focusing on just kissing him, she eased her hands up higher on his back. When he groaned, she eased her hold and stepped back.

"We really need to say goodbye."

"I wasn't finished saying goodbye," he grumbled.

She shook her head. "You weren't talking—"

"Why use words, when deeds are more effective?" Taking her hands in his, he brought them to his lips. "Save some of your sweetness for me, darlin'."

Emily sighed and leaned into him. "You're a hard man to walk away from."

"Not if you're planning on coming back."

"One last kiss," she whispered, pulling him close.

Tyler packed a punch. By the time they'd parted, her legs were weak and her mind was muddled.

"See you later, darlin'."

"I'll be there." Watching him walk away, she shook her head and looked up at the clock… she was already counting the hours until she'd see him again.

"Tyler."

He turned around and groaned. He didn't want to be here today with Linda Lee, but a Garahan always kept his word. Opening the door to the Tasty Freeze, he flinched when his ex brushed against him. He should have told Emily about this.

"Hey there, Tyler," a gray-haired man called out. "It's been a long time."

"Hi, Joe. I've been working."

The old man nodded. "Your grandfather would be right proud of what you and your brothers have accomplished out at the Circle G." He paused and nodded in Linda Lee's direction. "I don't believe I've met your girl."

Tyler shook his head. "We're just friends, Joe."

Joe shrugged and said, "If memory serves, you're partial to butter pecan."

Tyler grinned. "Still am, but I'm not sure what the lady'll have."

Linda Lee spoke up. "I'd like two scoops of the same, please."

"Coming right up."

While Joe scooped ice cream into tall sugar cones, Tyler rubbed a hand along the back of his neck to ease the tension building there. Not telling someone something was the same as lying… wasn't it? The stiffness in his neck was radiating down to between his shoulder blades. When Joe handed them their cones, Tyler thanked him and paid the man. "Where do you want to sit?" Linda Lee swirled her tongue around the top scoop and eyed him suggestively.

He sat down at the first empty table. "Linda Lee," he bit out, "stop it."

Tyler couldn't believe the overtly sexual way his ex was pulling the top of the cone into her mouth. It didn't have the effect she obviously hoped for. It was a complete turnoff.

"Stop what?"

"I want your word that you won't stop by the ranch anymore."

She pouted. Damn, she was going to be difficult. "And I want you to stay away from The Lucky Star."

She lowered her lashes and looked up at him coyly, then leaned forward trying to distract him.

He shook his head. "Give it up, Linda Lee. I'm still waiting for you to give your word."

Her eyes met his over the tops of their cones, challenging him.

Tyler shook his head and got to his feet. "I've got to go, Linda Lee, and I don't have time for your games. Just tell me you'll steer clear of the ranch and The Lucky Star."

"Whatever you say, Tyler."

The sugar-sweet tone was more of a warning than the challenge in her eyes. She wasn't going to go away or give up without a fight.

Damn. He turned on his boot heel and walked away before he said something that would get her going. Once she started harping on something, she wouldn't let it go. Best to retreat for now. She'd give up eventually… wouldn't she?

Chapter 17

The last few days had been quiet—too quiet. Tyler's neck itched, and he constantly looked over his shoulder. He kept expecting his ex to show up unannounced at the ranch with a car full of shoes and clothes.

"What the hell's ailing you?" Dylan bit out, shoving a precut fence post into the ground and holding it upright.

Tyler jolted. "Nothing." Man, he had to get a grip and focus on the job.

Dylan snarled at him, but Tyler didn't look up until he'd fastened the barbed wire and snipped it off. Wire cutters in hand, he pointed them at his brother. "You're the one with the problem."

His brother shook his head and stalked back to the pickup. "Funny thing," Dylan drawled. "But instead of Emily coming back out to the ranch, Linda Lee Baker stopped by the house yesterday."

Tyler froze. *Damn it to hell.* He never should have fucked or trusted that woman. "That a fact?" Dread slid into his stomach and lay there burning, like Jesse's gut-rotting chili. Emily had been too busy to spend more time out at the ranch—not that he hadn't asked her.

Grabbing another post hefting it up on his shoulder, Dylan walked back over to the next one they needed to replace. They'd already yanked it out, and Tyler used the posthole digger to smooth out the bottom and sides of the hole so the new post would set right. When he finished, he swiped his forearm across his forehead and straightened up. It was a warm one.

Dylan set the post, and Tyler thought that would have been the end of it. The middle Garahan brother wasn't long on words and used fewer on most days than Tyler did.

Hoping his last sentence had used up Dylan's morning quota, Tyler was surprised when his brother rasped, "So congratulations, I guess."

Tyler's head snapped up. "What?" Dread curled icy fingers in his gut and flayed it raw.

Dylan was grinning down at him. "I always thought your ex was just a good lay, but hey, if you're set on marrying the woman."

Hell, he was damned if he tried to keep Linda Lee from talking about his night job, and all but leg shackled if he didn't own up to the truth.

There was no easy way out of the hole he'd dug himself. Tyler's frustration built, fueling his temper until it burned hot and bright. The sudden need to pummel his fists into something washed over him. Dylan just happened to be available.

Tyler came up out of a crouched position swinging, surprising his brother. He had the advantage until Dylan got lucky with a punch that was low and inside, knocking Tyler clean off his feet. As he sucked in a breath, Dylan grabbed him by the front of his shirt and rapped his head against the ground. A small cloud of dust wafted up before settling back down beneath Tyler's head.

"You want to explain what the hell's wrong with you today?"

Tyler motioned for Dylan to get off him. When he did, Tyler was finally able to catch his breath, but it was still painful. After all these years, he should have remembered that move. Heck, their grandpa had taught it to all of them, but Dylan was the only one who ever had to resort to fighting dirty.

He sat up and shook his head. The ringing stopped. "Forgot you don't punch like a girl anymore."

Dylan grinned at him and swiped at the blood trickling from the corner of his mouth. "If you want to blow off some steam, we could still go a few rounds, but hell, we've got a good two hours left before we're finished up out here."

Tyler let his brother help him up. They'd continued working side-by-side as if the fight never happened. Finally, he couldn't take it anymore, he had to ask, "Is that all she said?"

Dylan nodded. "All that made sense anyway."

"My asking her to marry me made sense?" *Not to Tyler*.

Dylan shrugged. "Like I said, I was expecting to see Emily, not Linda Lee."

They got their rhythm back and worked in silence, replacing downed posts and trampled wire. Dylan hefted one of the last posts and held it in the hole. "You marrying Linda Lee didn't make sense at first, but once she'd explained how you'd been calling her every day since she left… and proposing when you two met in town the other day…" His brother let the sentence hang and shrugged again.

Tyler cut and twisted the wire into place. The ice in his gut morphed into a slow burn as the dread intensified. "She's lying," he rasped. "When the hell would I have had the time to call her when I spend all my time working our spread with the two of you?"

Dylan stared at him.

"I didn't ask her to marry me." His gaze met Dylan's. "You were dead on, bro. We burned each other up in bed, but that's all we had."

"Thought as much." Dylan hefted another post. "I'm partial to Emily myself, but why would Linda Lee lie?"

To get her way, *the bitch*. Same as she had when they'd been dating. Hell, they never went anywhere except to bed after the first few drinks they'd shared. Guilt smacked him in the back of the head. Maybe he did owe her something, but it sure as hell wasn't the rest of his life. "I did meet her in town, but the ice cream was supposed to be a bribe to shut her up and make her go away."

"Didn't work," Dylan grumbled. "Does Emily know?"

Tyler's shoulders slumped. "Not yet."

"What are you going to do about it?"

Tyler straightened up and sucked in a breath as pain shot through his side. "Damn, did you have to hit the same side as Widowmaker?"

Dylan pushed his Stetson back off his forehead and stared at Tyler as if he'd lost his mind. "I'm just doing what Grandpa told me to do," he said. "Going for the weak spot."

Tyler nodded. "Nobody ever beat Grandpa in a fist fight."

Dylan took off his gloves and slapped them against his thigh. Dust wafted around his jean-clad leg. "Want help with Linda Lee?"

Hope speared through Tyler. "You mean it?"

Dylan nodded and hooked his arm around Tyler's neck. "You just go get cleaned up and head out to work. Jesse and me'll come up with something."

Tell them the truth.

He shook his head. *Can't do it yet, Grandpa.*

"Maybe." If he let his brothers help him out of this latest jam, they'd hold it over his head and he'd owe them. "I'll think about it." Tyler shoved him and snatched the keys dangling from Dylan's left hand. "But I still get to drive."

His brother shoved Tyler, knocking him off balance while Dylan sprinted for the truck laughing. "Keys are for wimps."

Tyler watched his brother disappear inside the cab of the truck. A few minutes later the engine roared to life. Tyler got into the passenger's side and asked, "Where'd you learn how to hot wire a truck?"

His younger brother grinned and shook his head. "It'll cost you if I tell you."

Grateful he had brothers to help with the workload at the ranch, amazed that they hadn't killed each other over the years, Tyler wondered why he just didn't fess up and tell them the only job he'd been able to get was taking off his clothes. He had plenty of skills, but they all involved working on a ranch.

He thought about their reaction and the endless razzing he'd have to endure and decided to keep quiet awhile longer. Besides, he couldn't afford the jail time he'd have to do for killing his brothers, even if it was in self-defense. Well maybe not self-defense actually, more like permanently shutting them up once they got going riding him about working in a strip club. Hell, if he found out one of his brothers was stripping for money, he'd ride him mercilessly too. It's what brothers did.

Well. That was it then. He couldn't tell them yet. Just keep on working nights at the club, not sleeping much, and working days at the Circle G.

Dylan parked the truck by the barn. As they dropped off the spare wire and posts he asked, "You thinkin' about Linda Lee?"

"No."

His brother grunted. *Dylan's favorite response.*

Tyler smiled. "I've got to get to town. See you in the morning."

Wiggling toes painted a mesmerizing shade of gold-dusted crimson, Emily nodded. "You were right," she tilted her head back and drained her glass. Licking her lips, she sat back and grinned at Jolene. "I do prefer harlot red."

"I can read you like a book, cuz." Jolene reached for the blender pitcher and filled their glasses. "You keeping track?"

Emily laughed. "Honey, once I start drinking José, I don't bother to keep track." She felt positively loose all over, slightly anesthetized thanks to the mind-melding effect of a couple of margaritas. "No salt."

"Hell's bells, Em." Jolene grinned at her. "Drink up. I'll do the rim up pretty with the next one."

Toasting one another and their brightly painted toenails, she drank deeply.

Lifting her empty glass, Emily waited while Jolene poured. "Wait!" Emily jolted, pulling her glass back.

Margarita sloshed over the wide brim onto the back of her hand.

"You made me spill," Jolene grumbled.

"Salt." Emily licked her hand then drank the mouthful in the glass and handed it to her cousin. "You promised."

"Oops. Sorry." Jolene dipped her finger in the pitcher and rubbed it around the rim until it was wet enough then turned the glass upside down in the plate of salt.

Emily supervised while Jolene salted the rim of her glass. After making her cousin dip it twice, she confessed, "Jolene, I'm in love."

Jolene stopped pouring for a moment to stare at her. "I'd have to be blind and dumb not to see that." When Emily remained silent, Jolene prompted, "And?"

Emily sighed. "I heard from Ronnie, who heard from Mavis, who's best friend's brother owns the Tasty Freeze, that Tyler was having ice cream with that blonde bimbo."

"So is it true or a rumor?" Jolene asked.

Emily shrugged. "Mavis likes to gossip, but she wouldn't intentionally make up something to hurt someone."

Her cousin nodded. "Then I trust you gave him hell." Jolene sipped and leaned back against the back of the bar stool. "Why didn't you come get one of my black stilettos to finish the job?"

"Because I got distracted, and I keep waiting for him to tell me."

Jolene snorted into her glass. "You should never let your glands do your thinking for you, cuz."

Emily set her empty glass down on the bar and started to push to her feet. She wobbled. "I can't help it. But I wanted to kick him all the while I was kissing him."

"You gonna tell him you know?"

"I guess."

Jolene laughed watching Emily try to stand without swaying.

"Damn it, Jolene. You were supposed to keep track," Emily rasped clutching onto the edge of the bar for dear life, afraid she'd fall flat on her face if she moved one step to the right or left.

"I *am* keeping track," Jolene bit out.

"Our magic number is two." Why Emily felt the need to remind her obviously tipsy cousin was beyond her.

"And we're almost finished with the second *blender full*."

Shock cleared her head for a second before things got all fuzzy again. "You're an evil woman, Jolene Langley."

"But you love me anyway," Jolene grinned and divided the rest of the pitcher into their glasses.

"I wanted salt again." Emily pouted, reaching for the glass her cousin handed her. "Tastes better with salt."

"Drink up, cuz," Jolene said. "We're doing shots next."

Half an hour later, they'd stripped down to their underwear. "Much better." Emily mumbled. "Too hot before."

Jolene giggled pointing at Emily with the empty shot glass in her hand. "You don't match."

"Do too." Emily glanced down just to check.

Jolene shook her head at her. "Bra's black, bikini's not."

Emily shrugged. "It's a mix and match set. I've got another pair just like this upstairs."

Emily shot to her feet and paused, amazed that she wasn't at all wobbly. "Besides," she pirouetted so Jolene could see, "it's a thong."

"Only you, Em." Jolene got to her feet. "We need

something…" Looking around at the empty club, she sighed. "Music. That's what's been missing."

"I like George Strait."

"Gentleman George," Jolene nodded. "I do too, but then we need something faster that we can dance to."

An hour later Gwen walked into the bar and groaned, unable to believe what her eyes were seeing. Pulling her cell phone out of her back hip pocket, she hit the speed dial. "Jennifer, we've got a problem."

Ten minutes later Jennifer and Natalie ran into the club and stared up at the bar. Jennifer nodded at the cousins. "How long have they been like this?"

Gwen shrugged. "I don't know. I called you as soon as soon as I walked in and saw them."

"How much do you think they've had?" Natalie asked.

Gwen laughed. "They're strutting on the bar in their brand new boots and underwear. I'd say enough."

"I think we need to get Jo and Em down off the bar and get them dressed before the guys get here."

"Shit." Gwen looked at her watch. "They'll be here soon."

Jennifer watched the cousins bumping and grinding to Gretchen Wilson singing about a redneck woman. "I think they're winding down."

Gwen shook her head watching the way Natalie tried to help Jolene put her good arm into the sleeve of her shirt, but their friend was still dancing and it wasn't working.

Jennifer wasn't having any better luck with Emily.

"What the hell's going on in here?"

"Perfect." Gwen rubbed at her temple. "The big bad fire marshal's here."

Gwen walked over to get between Jake and the dancing Langley cousins. "It's Margarita Monday," she said, forcing a smile. "You're overdressed. Jo, honey," she crooned, seeing that Natalie hadn't made any headway getting their boneless friend dressed. "Time to get your clothes on."

Not daring to look over her shoulder to see if the fire marshal had moved or still stood rooted in front of the bar staring, she gently shook Jolene.

"You're no fun, Gwen."

Mindful of Jolene's elbow, she helped Natalie put Jolene's shirt on her then together they pried her boots off and poured her into her jeans.

Jennifer threw her hands up in disgust. "I can't get Emily to cooperate."

Gwen shook her head. "They're just a little too relaxed right now to fully comprehend what we're doing," Gwen told her. "Let me help."

It was trickier getting Emily's boots off and into her jeans, but fifteen sweaty minutes later, the cousins were presentable enough to get them upstairs without worrying about anyone walking in and seeing them strutting on the bar in their underwear.

"How will we sober them up enough to talk to them?" Jennifer's question was a good one.

Too bad Gwen didn't have a ready answer. "Our horse-saving, tequila swigging, redneck women here will have to sleep it off." She sighed, wishing she'd been in on the fun. It had been quite awhile since Jolene had let loose and partied, but there had been a time…

"I'll help Jolene upstairs," Natalie offered. "You two get on either side of Emily there."

Emily wobbled then giggled and Natalie sighed. "She doesn't look too steady."

After wrestling the two up the stairs and into bed, the women went downstairs to do damage control.

"Does this sort of thing happen often?"

Gwen tried not to take offense, but Jake's question seemed to set her off. "I don't see where it'd be any concern of yours if it did." She had the ultimate satisfaction of seeing the man's face turn red a moment before steam began pouring out of his ears.

"I'm sure they'll both be downstairs in time for the first act," Gwen said. "Why don't you come back later?"

Jake narrowed his eyes and glared at her. Gwen shrugged. She had a bar to run, without Jolene and Emily for the next few hours. She didn't have time to listen to the fire marshal's jealous ranting.

Chapter 18

"JOLENE?"

"Mmmmpf..."

"Wake up." Emily poked her cousin in the head until she lifted it up to look at Emily.

"What?"

"I think my tongue has hair on it." It felt positively icky, and she was afraid to touch it. "Does it?"

Jolene rolled over onto her side, narrowed her eyes at Emily and said, "Stick it out."

Emily did as she was asked.

"Uh huh."

"Uh huh, what?" Emily demanded. "Do I or don't I?

"Yep," Jolene said without missing a beat. "Same shade as your hair."

Emily's stomach clenched, and for a moment before her head cleared, she wondered how that was possible. Then reason returned and she snorted. "You're such a jerk." At least Jolene hadn't lost her sense of humor. "Um, Jo?"

"Mmmmpf..."

"Do you remember getting undressed?" A bad feeling that something happened that she couldn't quite recall started to fill her.

"I'm still dressed."

"Yeah, but I mean before."

Jolene shifted her weight and sat up. "What time is it?"

Emily looked at the clock beside Jolene's bed and then down at her cousin's bare feet. The harlot red paint on her toenails had her gut churning. "Nine o'clock. Um… I think we may have had a little too much tequila."

"Honey, you can never drink too much tequila," Jolene purred, a sure sign that she was feeling more like herself.

"I've got that song by Big and Rich running through my head—"

"Which one?"

"The one about riding the cowboy."

Jolene started humming the tune and a vague memory of stripping to the chorus filled Emily with dread. "I think we stripped in the bar."

"Now why would we do that?" Jolene didn't sound as sure of herself as she had a few moments before.

"Because you were trying to convince me to tell Tyler that I know he met his ex-bimbo in town, and I was trying to work out how to ask him while we kept drinking. And you know too much José can mess with your mind." Emily started wringing her hands. "I remember dancing on the bar…"

"So?" Jolene said. "We've done that before."

"In our underwear? With our boots on?"

Jolene grinned. "Well maybe not quite dressed like that." She tilted her head to one side and stared at Emily. "How do you know you weren't dreaming?"

Emily sighed. "Because it would be real strange that we had the same dream."

Jolene frowned. "I didn't say I did."

"You didn't say you didn't."

Jolene shook her head at Emily. "Let's not worry about it right now. We have aspirin to take, water to drink, and a club that started the night without us."

"In their underwear?" Tyler's gut clenched. His imagination was working overtime and his libido was a half a second behind, picturing the curvaceous Langley women dancing on top of the bar in all of their lace-covered glory. The thought of Emily in particular baring so much of what she'd been sharing with him settled into his gut and began a slow burn. Jealousy wasn't a new emotion to him, but it hadn't happened in a long, long time.

"And boots," Jake grumbled, taking a pull on his beer. "Damned if Jolene wasn't all but buck naked."

"And your problem would be?" Tyler asked, though he suspected he knew just what Jake's problem was and how the other man felt.

Jake's gaze met his and held. "I don't intend to share."

Tyler nodded. "I don't intend to share Emily either. So what did you see when you walked in before?"

"They were up on the bar in their skimpy underwear with their arms flung wide open, heads tilted back, singing their hearts out."

"And...?" Tyler prompted.

"I keep remembering how perfectly those damned scraps of lace cupped their breasts."

The slow burn in Tyler's gut warned him that his temper was about to erupt. Struggling for control, he ground out, "I'd forget what Emily looked like and wouldn't spread any tales about it."

"You've got it bad friend," Jake pressed him.

"Ever since she laid her lips on mine."

"As far back as that?"

Tyler drained his glass of sweet tea and set it on the bar. His break was nearly over and it was nearly time for the finale. "Just so you can't say I didn't warn you."

Jake nodded.

Tyler was about to remind Jake not to talk about Margarita Monday, but his tongue got stuck to the roof of his mouth watching the gentle sway of Emily's jean-clad hips; there was just something about the movement that mesmerized him. He couldn't get enough of her. There were so many facets to the lady that got to him—deep in his heart somewhere that hadn't been touched in a long while.

Linda Lee never had that effect on him. Well, she had an effect on him, but only his dick had paid attention where Linda Lee had been concerned. Funny... more of the women in his life had been blue-eyed blondes with a wild streak a mile wide and a sex drive that matched his, than redheads.

Nothing wrong with that.

He just couldn't figure out why this one redhead got to him. Tyler rubbed a hand over his heart, remembering the way Emily liked to press her lips there after they'd loved and were enjoying the afterglow, wondering at the deep ache there, not remembering a time when he'd ever felt like this.

"Hey there, cowboy." He stiffened, refusing to believe that Linda Lee'd show up at the club again, telling himself it was just his tired brain messing with him. Hell, it must be guilt for not telling Emily he'd met his ex in town for ice cream. He'd wanted to but the timing just never felt right.

"You all right, Tyler?"

The concern in her voice just didn't fit with the real Linda Lee Baker. It was part of her act, a damn fine one at that. Hell, she should have been on the silver screen.

He sighed; there was no avoiding her. The woman was obsessed with the idea of getting back together with him. Then he remembered his brother's promise of help, the one Tyler hadn't gotten around to accepting. Garahans stuck together; maybe Dylan had tried to nip Linda Lee's lies in the bud even though Tyler hadn't taken him up on his offer.

"Did you talk to Dylan?"

Her smile hardened into a grimace. "Your brother doesn't understand what's between us."

Tyler did a mental head slap. Damn the woman was thick. "Look I don't have time to talk to you right now. I've got to work."

The look on her face softened. "Don't worry about me, babe. I'll just sit over here and watch."

He nodded and walked toward the door by the stage. *What the hell was he going to do now?* Dylan's idea to stonewall Linda Lee hadn't worked. Or had it? Maybe she lied about that too. Tough call with that woman.

Man, he never should have dipped his wick in that poisoned well. He shivered. It was like his grandpa was standing beside him, handing out his favorite bit of advice. Of course, the old man would follow it up with a warning that he and his brothers should marry young and make sure the woman could handle life out at the Circle G.

Times like this he really missed the advice. He sure could use some now. Looking over his shoulder, his gut clenched. Linda Lee licked her lips and watched him like she was the cat and he was a bowl of fresh cream.

~

"Oh crap," Gwen groaned. "Trouble's back."

"Anyone in particular?" Jolene drawled, turning to look in the same direction as her friend. "Didn't you throw her out the other night?"

Gwen smiled. "Looks like I'll get to do a repeat performance."

"Joe said he saw her and Tyler at the Tasty Freeze too," Emily said, watching the way the blonde was eyeing up Tyler. "That makes four people. So it must be true."

Gwen and Jolene looked at each other and Gwen said, "Joe told us, but isn't that only two people? Remember? Mavis's best friend told her who told Ronnie."

Jolene waited before asking, "We started to talk about this before, but you never answered me... did you? If you did, I don't remember. So what are you gonna do about it?"

"Oh hell, y'all know that I'm stuck on Tyler. We had so much fun the other day... a real date. He took me out for dinner at the BBQ Pitt and introduced me to Bonnie, the waitress there, as his girl."

"Honey, I know. It's kind of corny but sweet," Jolene said.

Emily shrugged. "I know, but it's the sweetness of the fact that he wanted her to know I was his girl."

Jolene smiled at Emily. "That cowboy is just full of surprises... corny but adorable."

"So what are we going to do about the blonde?" Gwen asked.

"I don't know," Emily said, "but I can't let that bitch steal my man!"

Gwen agreed. "So what are you gonna do about him taking her out?"

"I haven't actually asked him yet, and I don't think he realizes that I know. Besides, I really want him to *want* to tell me about it."

Jolene frowned while staring at the blonde. "Don't wait too long. Hey, Em… I thought you broke her nose?"

Emily frowned. "It felt like it, but she may have had a nose job… harder to break someone's nose after that."

Gwen nodded. "Bled a lot, but it's not swollen. Too bad you didn't break it."

Jolene chuckled. "I think my darlin' cousin would like to try a couple of those moves on our tall, dark, and hunky headliner."

Emily sighed. "After I get him to fess up about his ex." She scrubbed her hands over her face and sighed. "I'm really stuck, and it's just a little scary. I've never felt like this before." It hadn't been all that hard to confess. Time to get down to the business of cleaning house. "So what are you going to do about her?"

"How about if we just roust her up some?" Gwen's grin was contagious.

"I think I'll go along with you and watch." Jolene tossed her hair over her shoulder and glared at the blonde bimbo.

Emily wasn't going to be left out. "Hey, wait! He's my guy."

Gwen froze and Jolene, not paying attention, walked into her back. "Damn it, Gwen!"

"Curse later, Jolene. Our Emily has just outlined her territory, and you know how we all protect our own."

Emily's mouth still felt like somebody jammed a wad of cotton in it, thanks to overindulging in José earlier, and she just couldn't drink enough water to moisten it. Looking at the dark-eyed cowboy and the blonde bimbo salivating in the crowd, she knew she wouldn't back down now that she'd staked her claim. "That man's mine and worth fighting for!"

As she got closer, she realized it wasn't going to be a quick and easy job after all. The bar was packed, and the blonde was now eyeing them as if she were sizing them up. Emily walked over to stand on the other side of Jolene, the three women presenting a united front.

Gwen wasn't smiling when she said, "Surprised you came back after last night."

"You'll have to leave," Jolene told her flat out.

Emily nodded. "You're poaching in my territory and messing with my man. You'll want to leave now before I hurt you."

"Like the other night?" the big-busted blonde sneered. "Not gonna happen. Just who do you think you are?"

Jolene's smile was lethal. "This is my place, and I reserve the right to kick out the people I don't want inside it."

The woman eyed Jolene up and down, then did the same with Gwen before saying, "Look, I'm not here to cause trouble."

"You already are." Gwen crossed her arms and gave her best impression of a staff sergeant ready to rip a green recruit a new one.

"Don't I even get to order a drink?"

Emily looked around her and noticed what Gwen and Jolene hadn't: everyone was watching and waiting. How they handled this incident would set a precedent for dealing with ornery clientele in the future. Although it burned her butt, she had to swallow her pride.

Emily wanted her gone more than anyone, but sensed it wouldn't be without a scene worth calling the law over. Common sense returned and she relented. "I don't see as how ordering one drink could hurt," she said quietly. "As long as you leave as soon as you finish."

The look the woman gave Emily was anything but friendly. She couldn't keep from wondering what Tyler had ever seen in her… well, if he had been able to see past his ex's two obvious assets.

"I'd like a cosmopolitan." The blonde had the nerve to imitate Gwen's stance, crossing her arms beneath her impressive breasts.

Bitch. Emily didn't like women who flaunted their big boobs to get what they wanted… mostly attention.

"I'll take care of it, Gwen." With a look, she knew Gwen and Jolene understood; Emily went to get the blonde's damn drink. A few minutes later she returned, drink in hand, and knew she had missed something important from the look on Jolene's face. "Jo?"

Her cousin turned toward her and a brief flicker of pain flashed through Jolene's eyes. *This would not be good*.

"I don't believe you," Gwen said before turning toward Emily to reach for the glass. "Here's your drink." Gwen handed it to the woman. "You've got five minutes," she said, looking at her wrist, "starting now."

The blonde looked ready to spit. The woman sipped her drink and glared at Gwen.

Perfect, Emily thought. She was ready for a good fight. It had been a hell of a day and from the looks of it… it wasn't over yet, with just half an hour until closing time before she could corner Tyler.

Without looking at her watch, Gwen reached for the woman's glass. "Time's up."

"Hey! I wasn't finished."

"Yeah," Gwen drawled. "You are."

Stepping in between the two, Emily put a hand out. "You've been asked nicely once," she said. "I got your drink, and now you should leave while it's still your choice."

"How do you think Tyler would feel," the busty blonde began, "knowing you kicked out his fiancée?"

Emily felt the blow all the way through to her spine. Bracing against the pain, she drew herself up for more, sensing the blonde wasn't finished and that she wouldn't go quietly.

"He didn't say anything about being engaged," Emily rasped, unsure of how to deal with the hurt lancing through her without letting it show.

"This should speak louder than words." The woman flashed a diamond ring right under Emily's nose.

It's not what you think, her heart warned, while her brain tormented her, *you've been had by a black-haired Irishman with a soft Texas drawl.*

"Doesn't look like it fits too well," Jolene said.

Emily looked first at Jolene, then at the woman's left hand. Jo was right; it was too big.

"Tyler surprised me with the ring the other day when we met in town." The woman's voice escalated with her irritation.

"I'll just bet," Gwen drawled.

The blonde glared at Gwen. "He's been working so many hours he didn't have time to have it sized." She was loud enough to be heard over the crowd.

"Why didn't he just wait to give it to you?" Jolene asked the question Emily didn't want to know the answer to but needed to hear. She wanted to believe in trust alone, but what with Linda Lee showing up again, and Tyler having been seen in town with her, she was working hard to go on faith.

"We just couldn't wait to tell everyone that we're getting married." The woman's screech echoed as the song ended and the house lights flicked on.

Chapter 19

TYLER STALKED OVER TO WHERE THE WOMEN WERE standing. "What kind of lies are you spreading now, Linda Lee?"

At the sound of his voice, the blonde's acid turned to sugar. "Why nothing, honey, just showing off the engagement ring you gave me the other day when we met at the Tasty Freeze."

The look Linda Lee gave Tyler was odd. Emily thought it looked like a challenge. Something was definitely going on here and from the look in Tyler's chocolate-brown eyes, he was fit to be tied. His words confirmed her suspicion. He looked right at Emily when he said, "We're not engaged."

"But Tyler, don't you want to know what Dylan and Jesse had to say about it?"

He stiffened, turned back toward the blonde, shoved the hat to the back of his head, and waited, not answering.

"They can't wait for me to move in."

Emily's heart faltered, even though she knew the bitch was lying. She'd been out to the ranch and spent a morning working alongside the Garahan brothers. They struck her as being the type to work until their fingers bled and would go to the wall for one another. "Funny," Emily drawled, "neither Dylan nor Jesse mentioned your name when I was out riding fences with them the other day."

Emily had the satisfaction of seeing Linda Lee's jaw go slack and her eyes glaze over. When the look of shock was replaced with a harder, meaner look, she knew the woman was deliberately trying to destroy what Emily and Tyler shared.

"Tyler made a special trip into town during the day just to pop the question. It was so sweet, we were sharing a butter pecan ice cream cone—"

"That's not what happened and you know it, Linda Lee," Tyler said, drawing Emily's attention away from the annoying blonde. "Go on home." He turned toward Emily again. "It's not what you think."

She looked from Tyler to the busty blonde. Emily might not have a whole lot of luck picking the perfect man until she'd met Tyler Garahan, but she'd always been adept at reading body language. The way the blonde was standing, arms crossed beneath her breasts and her gaze flicking back and forth between Tyler and Emily, told Emily the blonde was worried. From the way the bimbo with the double Ds kept looking at her, Emily just knew the woman was waiting for a reaction.

The bitch was definitely lying!

"I can explain."

Tyler's pleading look wasn't what swayed her; it was the cat-waiting-to-pounce-on-its-prey look on the bimbo's face as she said, "Just like you explained to your brothers about working here?" Linda Lee all but purred.

"Is there a problem here, miss?"

Emily spun around. One of the sheriff's deputies was walking toward her. Judging by the grim look on his face, he was either uncomfortable being inside the club or had had a run in with the busty bimbo before.

She had a hunch who called. A look toward Jennifer and Natalie confirmed it. When they waved at her, she waved back, grateful that they'd called in reinforcements. Emily pushed a lock of hair out of her eyes. "Absolutely. That woman over there," she pointed as she spoke.

"What's the problem?"

"She was asked to leave and refused." Emily didn't care how the woman left, as long as she didn't have to look at her smug smile anymore.

"Are you Jolene Langley?" he asked.

"No. Jolene's standing over there."

"Obliged, ma'am." He tipped his hat and walked into the fray.

Tyler was easy to spot, standing head and shoulders above the average female in the crowd. At first glance, he appeared to be relaxing while he conversed with the lawman. The longer she looked, the more she saw. Tyler was angry and looked ready to do serious damage to the blonde who'd tried to stake her claim in Emily's territory.

Lovers like Tyler Garahan came along once in a lifetime. Emily would be damned before she let some two-timing bitch on wheels take away her man. But it wasn't just his handsome face or killer body or the long nights of loving they'd shared. They'd connected on a deep level, sharing parts of themselves that would cement their relationship, building something solid that would keep their growing love strong and healthy. Tyler and the deputy were talking quietly. It was weird, but when Tyler stepped in to protect the blonde, it only added to his appeal. His innate need to protect was just one more facet to his personality that she loved.

It was time she told Tyler all that her heart held. She loved the man to distraction. There was no reason to keep it all to herself. Love was meant to be celebrated, shared.

Emily Langley loved the tall, dark Irishman… even the part that annoyed the crap out of her—his overprotective streak—but she'd work on not letting it bother her. The rest of the package fit, and she was smart enough to know that men like Tyler Garahan didn't walk into her life more than once in a lifetime. Deciding it was time to prove to the blonde, and anybody else in the room with ideas that involved tying a short rope around the tall, dark Texas cowboy, that he was spoken for, Emily walked toward Tyler.

He looked up and their eyes met. She smiled and ran the tip of her tongue along her top lip. Her man's eyes darkened as desire burned bright in his gaze. *Oh yeah*. He was worth the fight and then some. She pushed through the crowd to stand beside Tyler and stared at the angry blonde until she knew she had the woman's full attention.

Tyler looked down at her. "I can explain about the other day—"

"I'm listening."

"Hell, Em," he said, taking off his hat and raking his fingers through his hair. "I thought I could bribe her with ice cream to keep her out of my life."

"Why didn't you tell me?"

"Hell, darlin'," he said, "I can't hardly think straight when you're around."

She hooked her arms around Tyler's neck. With a

look and a tug, he was hers for the asking. When she had his lips right where she wanted them, she brushed hers across his, a tantalizing, teasing taste of the man she would continue to fight for… dirty if she had to… because she wasn't going to lose her man over a blonde bimbo and a misunderstanding.

"I'd have to be dumb as dirt to let you walk out of my life, Tyler."

Desire shimmered and an emotion she hoped to see shone back at her. "You're one smart woman, Emily Langley."

"Loco maybe," she admitted, "but my mamma raised me to use my wits."

"Lucky for me, you paid attention." Tyler bent his head and took her lips in a soul-searing kiss that branded her as his in front of everyone.

When he tucked her in at his side, Emily couldn't resist the verbal jab, "Langley women don't back down from a fight."

"You bitch!" Claws out, jaw clenched, Linda Lee launched herself at Emily.

She braced herself. *This is gonna hurt!*

But the expected impact never happened. Tyler anticipated his ex's move, curled his body protectively around Emily, and spun so his back took the brunt of the vindictive woman's body slam.

Before Emily could react, the lawman had the blonde cuffed. "You have the right to remain silent—"

She didn't need to hear the rest to know that disaster had been averted. She would have stood proud and tall, and taken her lumps, but Tyler had taken that decision out of her hands.

"Thanks," she rasped. "I owe you."

His grin was positively wicked. "I'm sure I can think of some way to even things out. We can talk about it later." His smile turned her inside out.

"I think that can be arranged." Lord, she didn't just love this man; she needed him. "Have I showed you what you can do with a mug of hot coffee and a cup of ice?" she whispered.

He looked thoughtful, bent down so only she could hear, "Who gets to drink the coffee?"

She smiled and burrowed deeper into his embrace. "I do."

His eyes darkened with desire. "What's the ice for?"

"For me to cool you off after I heat you up."

Tyler's Adam's apple bobbed up and down. "It sounds like I'd probably die from ecstasy, but I was wondering if you'd want to finish up your other fantasy before we tackle a new one."

Emily's smile could have been her silent answer, but it was too important to him. He had to ask, had to be sure. "I need you to tell me, Emily. I want to make sure we're both on the same page, and you're just as willing as I am to take our intimacy to the next level."

"Tyler, I'm so in love with you, it scares me."

He hugged her tight to his heart, and she could feel him trembling. "I was afraid to hope, scared you'd be mad that I took Linda Lee out, even if it was to try to talk sense into her to tell her it was over between us. I just got too distracted by your charms and forgot to tell you." He paused, "God, I'm so glad you love me, Em, because I love you too."

He leaned back and locked gazes with her. "Does

this mean you're ready to share that gooey sweetness with me?"

"A smart man like you got it in one." When his eyes narrowed at her, she tugged on his arm. "Yes. Yes and yes!"

She turned around to look for Jolene and noticed her standing by the front entryway talking to Jake. "Hey, Jolene!"

Her cousin looked up, saw the two of them, and smiled. "You punching out now?"

Emily looked up at Tyler and nodded.

"See you in the morning."

Tyler wrapped his arm around Emily and started hauling ass toward the staircase. "Can't you walk faster?"

Caught up in his urgency, knowing the reason for it, she shook her head.

"I can fix that." Tyler swept her into his arms and took the stairs two at a time.

"I guess you're not as tired as I thought you'd be."

He grinned but didn't take his eyes off the stairs. "It isn't easy hauling a woman upstairs after spending the day ripping out and planting new fence posts, and then working my butt off on stage in front of a raucous crowd, but I aim to please."

Emily turned her face against his broad chest and breathed in his scent... outdoors... clean with just a hint of whatever spicy soap he'd used before coming to work. "I'll see if I can take your mind off your rough work schedule, Tyler."

His arms tightened around her as he strode through the doorway at the top of the stairs and turned toward her bedroom. "I've got a lot on my mind," he rumbled.

"I don't mind working hard to get what I want," she purred.

From the way his eyes narrowed and his nostrils flared, she knew he was ready, willing, and able for action.

He hadn't put her down yet, but she couldn't say that she minded. His strength was another thing she really loved about her man. "Impatient?"

"Hell yeah." Setting her down in the middle of the bed, he stepped back and started to unbutton his shirt.

"What about the coffee and ice cubes?"

He tossed his shirt aside and reached for the hem of her tank top. "That fantasy will have to wait," he murmured, pressing his lips to her bared cleavage. "I've gotta hankering to taste you again."

More than willing to help him get what he wanted... what they both wanted... she reached around behind her and unhooked her bra. Her breasts spilled into his waiting hands. His grin sent a thrill all the way down to her toes. He pushed her back against the bed, unbuttoned then unzipped her jeans, and dipped his tongue in her belly button. Slowly sliding it up, he licked his way north, then abruptly turned left before he reached her breastbone.

His lips nipped and his tongue flicked across the flesh on the underside of her breast, circling ever closer to the peak that ached for his touch, tormenting her until she writhed and arched toward him, offering herself.

He pulled back and ran his hands from her waist up to her ribs letting his thumbs brush across her nipples. They hardened at his touch.

Words formed in her brain and exploded into tiny particles of fractured thought as his mouth replaced his hands.

"God, you're responsive."

Speech still beyond her, Emily managed a throaty rumble.

"The thought of how sweet you're going to taste when you trust me enough to love you this way has been driving me quietly crazy."

"But you never said anything."

"What was there to say? You needed to trust me and wanted to wait. I can be patient if I have to be."

Emily wanted to respond, but he'd moved his attention to the side of her neck, pressing moist kisses on a tantalizing path stretching from beneath her ear to her shoulder.

"The wait's been driving me crazy."

She shuddered in surrender and opened her heart and her body.

Tyler's gut clenched at the sight of Emily in the throes of passion. She was a goddess! Fiery waves spilled over her shoulders, cupping her breasts, brushing against his jaw as he dipped his head to taste, to sup from her lush well of generosity. Switching to her other shoulder, he worked his way up to that sensitive spot at the base of her neck.

She moaned, thrashing beneath him.

He pushed her shoulders back against the bed and swept his hands beneath her, lifting her hips, sweeping her jeans and the tiny scrap of lace off of her, freeing her. Awed by the beauty of her, he shook his head. *She was his for the asking*. He'd already tasted her cherry-sweet lips and the bounty of her buttercream skin, time to get to the honey-sweet center.

Cupping her taut backside, he lifted her to his mouth and let his tongue and lips show her what he held in his heart.

Her fingers bit into his shoulders, her thighs tightened against him as she raised herself up, allowing him to touch the very heart of her.

He devoured her, feasting until she cried out his name.

"Hold on, darlin'," he rasped. "Trust me, you'll enjoy the ride."

He straightened up, reached into his pocket, and pulled out the foil packet he'd need to protect her.

"Need any help?"

He shucked his jeans, smoothed on the condom, and leaned over her. "Nope. I'm good." He lifted her hips again and slid home.

Her hands cupped his butt, then clenched hard when he tried to pull out. "Easy," he rumbled. "I'm not leaving... just getting down to business." He thrust forward, and she lifted her hips to receive him again and again, building toward what they both wanted.

He drove into her, arching his back, holding her hips flush against him, calling her name as he came in a blinding flash. Gasping, he held her to his heart and traced the letters *TG* on her sweat-slickened back.

Branded... she was his!

He eased them onto the bed, pulling her on top of him, not willing to pull out of her just yet.

Her breathing gradually slowed, matching his. Tyler tightened his grip on her and reveled in the wonder of the woman in his arms. She'd believed in him when the odds had been stacked against him. She trusted him when anyone else would have turned and walked away.

She was a spitfire—a generous lover who'd captured his heart and seared his soul branding him with her initials deep inside of him. As he drifted off to sleep, he reveled in the knowledge that he wasn't ever going to let her go.

Chapter 20

"You get lucky last night?"

Tyler looked over his shoulder at his brother and grinned.

"Damn, bro," Dylan grumbled. "I think you should let me and Jesse have a turn working at that bar. You shouldn't be the only one getting laid; it's just not right."

Tyler wisely kept his mouth shut and shook his head.

But his brother was like a dog with a juicy knucklebone. "Grandpa taught us to share."

Tyler snickered. "He sure as hell didn't teach us to share women, Dylan."

Dylan shoved his brother out of his way and led his horse into the corral. "He would have if he'd thought about it."

Tyler laughed and stuck his foot out. Dylan went down hard on his knees but used the momentum to tuck and roll, springing up, catching Tyler off guard. "You want to negotiate who gets to take a turn going to The Lucky Star tonight, Ty?"

As quick as that, the brothers glared at one another, tempers simmering. Tyler slowly rose to his feet, hands loose at his sides, knees bent ready to take his brother out with a flying tackle. He tensed, preparing to spring.

"You two going to fight and waste these longnecks I popped open for you?"

"Jesus, Jess," Dylan ground out. "Just hold on… don't drink mine; it'll only take me another minute or so to convince Ty to let me fill in for him at work."

Jesse snorted, tipped his head back, and took a long pull from the beer in his left hand.

Tyler eyed the ones still gripped in Jesse's right hand. The dark brown glass was slick with moisture. Nothing better on a hot day than a cold beer. He and his brothers preferred the longneck variety. "Damn." He was tired and thirsty, but sleep was a long way off, and as much as he enjoyed pounding on his brother, he could fight with Dylan anytime.

He reached for the beer and took a long pull. "If you knew what I did at work, you'd change your mind."

"Yeah right," Dylan tipped back his head a chugged half the bottle.

"You do lay your life on the line every night, big brother," Jesse quipped.

Tyler's guts tied themselves into a knot that would hold a calf hog-tied. *They have no idea.* Maybe it was time to fess up and share the burden not being honest with his brothers had become. *Just get it said.* "I strip for money."

Dylan choked mid-swallow and beer shot out of his nose.

Jesse snickered. "Don't waste the beer." He turned to Tyler. "That a fact?"

Tyler could feel his face flame with embarrassment. It wasn't something he would joke about. They were his brothers, damn it; they should realize that. "You think I'm telling tales?"

Dylan had finally stopped coughing and was wiping tears from his eyes. Tyler couldn't remember if snorting beer hurt, so he figured the cuss was laughing at him.

What had you really expected, son? "Like I'd make something like this up."

"It's a regular honky tonk," Jesse said, watching him, "just like over in Wichita County, with kids shooting out the front of the place on a weekly basis." Jesse waited for him to agree.

But Tyler couldn't lie. He was tired of trying to shield his brothers from the truth to save the family name and reputation. Shaking his head to clear it, Tyler asked, "You been there lately?" He waited for an answer, knowing neither brother had had time to go into town since he'd started working at The Lucky Star. They were working their fingers to the bone, dead tired falling into bed at night, same as he was. The only difference was that he got undressed before he finished his shift at the bar.

His brothers just shook their heads and walked away. "Telling tales just like Grandpa," Dylan muttered. "It's your turn to rustle up supper, Jess," he called out over his shoulder as he strode toward the ranch house. "It's Lori's night off."

Jesse called out, "Yeah, yeah, coming!" Turning back toward Tyler, he looked as if he wanted to ask him something.

Tyler waited, but Jesse ended up shaking his head and walking away.

"I told 'em, Grandpa." Tyler sighed. "And they accused me of telling tall tales."

At least you tried to come clean, the voice in his head sounded firm. *That counts for a lot in my book*. Tyler kicked at a clump of dirt with the toe of his boot. It exploded on contact. "We need rain."

Grandpa's voice was oddly silent. Garahan men knew when to talk and when to keep silent. Obviously, it was time to ride it out. His brothers would either keep ragging him, busting his chops about stripping for a bunch of women… redheads at that… or they'd leave him alone.

Right now, Tyler couldn't say which he preferred, but he had hoped to talk to his brothers. A group of teenagers were running wild on the western border of town, roughing up other kids, shooting up the fence posts and signs hanging at the entrance to half a dozen ranches between Pleasure and Mesquite. Ranchers don't take kindly to having their property shot up. He and his brothers would probably do serious damage to anyone who took out the huge wrought-iron brand hanging on the gate to the Circle G. Timmy better not be running with that crowd or he'd skin him alive.

Finishing off the rest of his beer, he followed his brothers inside. He had just enough time to eat and get cleaned up before heading into town, to the job he hated and the woman he loved.

It had been a good day… with a great beginning. Her gaze flicked from the crowd up to the man on the stage, reliving the morning and the sweet love they'd made.

His gaze met hers, and it heated and lit a fire inside of her. Doing a hip swivel thing that would have rivaled Elvis had her thinking of how good it would feel if they were locked together instead of yards apart, with women hooting and hollering in between.

Tyler licked his lips and her belly clutched. From

the look in his eyes, he knew he had her full attention. His eyes darkened and the hint of desperate, dark desire pulled her in until she thought she'd drown in the twin pools of deep dark brown.

Later, he mouthed.

Her eyes widened and a shiver raced up her spine. He saw it all and flashed his killer grin right before he tipped his hat at her.

Scanning the crowd, relief washed over her when she didn't find the blonde they'd forcibly removed from the club the night before. No scenes, no distractions. Good; she planned to spend the night doing some distracting of her own. But right now, it was time to focus on working, or else she'd spontaneously combust. That thought had her grinning and turning back to let her eyes feast on the man who'd turned her heart inside out and her world upside down.

He reached for the rope coiled on the chair in the middle of the stage. Emily walked closer, admiring the smooth, easy motion of his hands as he lifted the knotted rope above his head in circular motions right before he let it go into the crowd.

Maybe she could convince him to teach her how to throw a lasso. It might add just the extra bit of spice to what she had in mind for her cowboy tonight. She had two more fantasies that they hadn't tried… hot coffee and ice cubes, and the silk scarves and the bedpost. As he reeled in the woman he'd been told ahead of time to lasso, Emily shook her head. It was time to stop thinking about what she wanted to do to Tyler and start thinking about collecting the receipts and getting the night deposit ready to drop off at the bank. With ten minutes to closing time, whatever receipts for drinks Gwen would be serving before last call could wait to be deposited with tomorrow night's receipts.

A few minutes later, she walked to the front door. "I'll be right back, Jo," she called out.

"Wait for me," her cousin called out hurrying to catch up.

They linked arms and walked toward the bank, chatting about their meeting earlier in the week and the results they'd had so far. There was no question that Mavis Beeton was definitely on their side, ready, willing, and able to lend the businesswomen in town a hand and lead the way toward keeping Pleasure and its heritage intact, while Tyler had agreed to round up the ranchers.

"So Mavis is ready to ride to the rescue?"

"Absolutely," Em said. "She's ticked at Frank Emerson, calling him high-handed and arrogant." Emily paused. "And a couple of things that'd make you blush."

"I'm glad she's on our side."

Once their money was safe in the night depository, they headed back toward the bar. They'd walked two and a half blocks when they noticed two tall men walking toward them. The light from the street lamp made it impossible to make out their faces, but the loose-limbed stride of the one and the purposeful stride of the other had them relaxing. "Looks like we were gone too long," Jolene whispered. "Here comes the search party."

"Ladies," Tyler tipped his Stetson and set it back on his head. Emily was close enough to see his expression change right before he asked, "What took so long?" Tyler's gaze met Jake's over the heads of the women. "Redheads are barrelful of trouble."

"But worth every minute of it," Jake added.

"Absolutely," Tyler agreed. He reached for Emily, and in that moment, holding Emily against his heart, he realized that nothing mattered… not the ranch, not his brothers… nothing. Because he realized that's what he'd be without Emily… nothing.

Emily sighed and snuggled closer, her delectable body rubbing against Tyler's worn jeans, stirring things best left alone until later to full attention. Tyler bent down and whispered, "You can't move now, or else everyone's gonna know how bad I want to get you naked."

Her low and sensual chuckle amplified the want that filled him to bursting every time he was near her. "Come on, sweet thing," he rasped, pressing his lips to her temple. She shivered, and he knew it had just as much to do with burning up the sheets as it did branding themselves on each other's hearts. It was in that instant that Tyler realized the real reason he'd never let Emily go. He loved every bit of her… temper, redhead, and all. She was everything to him. All he had to do was convince her that she loved him enough to take him, lock, stock, broken down ranch, and all.

They walked back to the bar, and once everyone was inside, Tyler locked the door behind them and walked down the darkened hallway to where Emily stood waiting for him. He was amazed that he no longer thought the mirrors or red velvet benches odd. The place had grown on him. He hadn't been working at The Lucky Star all that long, but long enough to put a dent in the mortgage and he was finally starting to chip away at the feed bill too.

"Hey, sweet thing." He walked over to where she

stood and pulled her into his arms. Once he had her there, he knew it wouldn't be enough. *Not tonight.*

"Mmmm..." he pressed his lips to the top of her curls and breathed in the scent that was uniquely Emily. "You ready to go upstairs?"

Emily leaned against him. "Not yet, but I think Jolene's done in."

He lifted his head and asked Jake, "You taking her upstairs?"

Jake nodded. "I'm taking Jolene to bed."

Emily's head shot up. "Did you mean that the way it sounded?"

Jake grinned at her. "Yes, ma'am," he said before his smile faded. "You have a problem with that?"

Emily snuggled closer to Tyler and answered, "I think you're just what my hardheaded cousin needs. You planning on doing something to change my mind about that?"

Jake scooped the tired woman into his arms. "No, ma'am."

Tyler laughed. "Go on, get a head start, we'll be busy down here for a while."

Emily shivered in his arms.

He rasped, "*Real* busy."

Alone, he eased his hold on her so he could watch her eyes. Grandpa always said the mouth might lie, but the eyes never would.

He placed a hand to the curve of her backside and pulled her hard up against his erection. His mouth covered hers, and he let himself feast. When he finally came up for air, he said, "You're like a drug. Each time I touch you or taste you, I want you more. I'm acting like a teenager… a walking, talking, raging hard-on. I can't get enough of you, and I can't wait to be inside of you."

"You sound worried. Wanting me shouldn't be a reason to worry, Tyler."

He clamped down on his libido and found the control he thought was just out of reach. Shaking his head to clear the lust from it, he realized he needed to explain. He wanted her to understand. "I've messed up before, Emily. By being too focused on the ranch and making ends meet. It's a demanding lifestyle even when times are going good. I'm not exactly relationship material… I know… I've been told that before."

Emily stared up at him and eased back until she was an arm's distance away from him. "I understand hard work and the endless hours. Since moving out to Texas, we haven't had time for much other than keeping the business afloat, and dodging the Preservation Society and those other groups hounding us for money."

"Em, I've failed in the past and it scares me that I might this time too." He held his breath waiting for her reply. Would she throw his ex in his face? Would she decide he wasn't worth the time or effort? She said she loved him… shouldn't that mean she would stick by him?

Grasping his hand in hers, she smiled and said, "I know you said you wouldn't ask me about my past lovers, and I appreciate that you haven't, but I have to confess that I haven't been able to make a relationship work yet. I'm scared that you'll walk."

"Away from you?" He shook his head, awed by the fact that the perfect woman for him didn't realize just how *perfect* she was. "I'd have to be deaf, dumb, and blind to walk away from the best damn thing that ever happened to me."

She squeezed his hands and brought them to her lips. "We're a pair, aren't we?"

His heart felt lighter, having shared his greatest fear with her. He tugged on her arm until she tumbled against him. "I'm sticking, Em."

"Thank God."

"Does that mean you are too?" He needed to hear her say it. It wasn't enough that she loved him. She had to like him and accept him for who and what he was; the Circle G was part and parcel of that.

"It's a no-brainer, Tyler," she said, pressing her lips to where his heart beat a steady rhythm. She looked up at him and must have seen the worry on his face because she asked, "Don't you believe me?"

His heart lurched and he hugged her tightly to him. "Yeah. I do, but I was thinking that I don't have a lot to offer you what with the way we're struggling to keep our heads above water out at the ranch."

She shook her head. "Is that what's worrying you?" Emily laughed. "I'm not exactly a high maintenance kind of woman, you know."

He nodded. "If you say so."

She laughed harder. "Was it all of those diamonds and jewels that I keep asking you for or the demands that you constantly take me out somewhere and spend oodles of money on me?"

He felt his lips lifting. The chuckle caught him by surprise. "Well, there is that."

She smacked him on the shoulder. "You're not thinking with the brains the good Lord gave you, if you think

I'm attracted to you because of what you have or don't have… it's who you are in here"—Emily tapped her pointer finger against his heart—"and up there," she said, pointing to his head, "that count."

His sigh of relief was loud enough for her to hear, but he didn't care. She loved him—him—and she'd take him just the way he was, ornery brothers and demanding ranch included. "I guess it's because the ranch means so much to me and is such a huge part of me that I was worried you wouldn't accept either of us if we were too much trouble."

"I already told you that I thought there was something really magical about your ranch. I meant it, Tyler, but even if you didn't have a penny in your pocket and only the shirt on your back, I'd still be in love with you."

He nodded, and she placed her hand over his heart again. "I mean that, Tyler Garahan."

"Same goes, Emily Langley." He dipped his head down so he could capture her lips and seal his words with a kiss. Confident and feeling better than he had for a while, he asked, "Would you dance on the bar for me?"

Her laugh eased the rest of his worry. "There was a whole lot of José involved," she said, "and I don't know that I want to drink that much again anytime soon."

He rubbed his hands up and down her arms. "So you only dance on the bar if you're drunk?"

She narrowed her eyes at him. "You really want me to get up there and dance?"

His heart stuttered. "I can't get the image of you up there in all your lace-covered glory, arms spread, singing your heart out from my mind."

"I don't remember singing."

"Jake said he would never forget the way you and Jolene looked up there with your—"

"Our what?"

"Hell, I really should have punched him."

"Whatever for?"

"He saw what I didn't, and I don't like sharing."

She frowned, and he wished he knew what she was thinking but didn't want to ask. Hell, for a man who didn't like to talk much, he used up his share of words for the week. "I'm talked out, Em," he confessed.

"Why don't you shut up and kiss me?"

Chapter 21

Emily's heart stumbled in her breast as Tyler's lips pressed against hers. *Lord, the man could kiss.* Her knees wobbled and her legs went limp as he plundered.

Nibbling and licking a path from just beneath her ear along the tendon in her throat to the edge of her scoop-necked top, his tongue skimmed there for a moment before slipping under to sample her. She pushed her worry aside. There wasn't any reason to worry that Tyler was jealous of the fact that Jake had apparently seen her and Jolene in their underwear dancing on the bar. Tyler stripped in front of dozens of women every night.

He lifted his head and the heat in his eyes seared her. "You don't have to dance on the bar if you don't want to." He reached out and grabbed a hold of her shoulders. "We could always use the bar for leverage while I take my time tasting you."

He swirled his tongue across her shoulder, flicking it along the length of her collarbone. When he reached the hollow of her throat, he pressed his lips to the wildly beating pulse point and then let the tip of his tongue slip up to her chin. Nipping it, he pressed his lips to the sensitized skin before sliding his tongue back down to the base of her throat.

"Tyler," she sighed, then she heard someone moan. It could have been her… maybe it was him. She didn't know or care. "I need you to touch me," she rasped.

"Tell me where, Em," he groaned as he slipped her shirt off and the straps of her bra down over her shoulders. Dipping his head down, he let his tongue glide along the edge of her bra, flicking it under the lacy edge, tormenting her. "You taste like heaven," he murmured, continuing his torturous path along the edge of her bra, teasing her nipples one at a time. "Will you let me look at you, Em?"

"Aren't you already looking at me?"

He laid his forehead against the top of her head and strained against the need to ravage. Once he had himself under control, he said, "I've never just looked at you. Will you let me?"

Her eyes widened as he reached for her. Her bra straps made it a challenge, but she slipped first one arm and then the other free, until her bounteous breasts were bared for him.

"My God, Emily," he whispered. "You're so beautiful." He hesitated before reaching out his hand to brush the back of it against her nipples. They hardened to peaks of perfection. The seducer became the seduced. "I've got to taste you."

She didn't say a word but didn't try to stop him. He flicked his tongue out to taste and was rewarded. Sweet and creamy with berry-tart perfection. "You're killing me."

"But I'm not doing anything."

"You beauty slays me, and the way you taste keeps me up nights when I should be sleeping."

"You're not alone, Tyler. When you're not with me, all I can think of is the next time we can be together. I really miss you when you're not in my bed."

He grinned, lifted her up onto the sleek ebony bar,

climbed up on the bar, and knelt in front of her, getting lost in the glorious depths of her whiskey-colored eyes. His heart stumbled, and his gut felt like he'd been head-butted by an angry bull. He swooped down and captured her lips in a tongue-tangling kiss. "I fall asleep thinking of you, and you're the first thing on my mind when I wake up."

Before she could respond, he kissed her again. Remembering the sensitive spot on her neck, just below her ear, he nipped the skin there, then pressed his lips to the spot to soothe it.

"Mmmm."

"Feel good?" He knew it did but wanted her to be open with him and tell him what was in her heart and on her mind.

"Yes," she hissed. He nipped her collarbone and dipped his head lower to tease first one nipple, then the other. When she was writhing beneath him, he drew her left breast into his mouth and suckled her.

She was bucking beneath him before he switched to her right breast and lavished it with the same tender attention. Emily gripped his head, holding him to her breast, but he wanted to taste more.

"I want to see if you're as sweet as I remember... right here." He slid a finger between her breasts down to her belly button.

He watched her eyes and knew she wanted him to. "Say it, Em."

"Please?"

"Close enough," he rasped, baring the rest of her to his eyes and then his lips, letting his tongue follow the path his fingertip had traced. Dipping his tongue into her belly button, he breathed in her scent. Womanly, a hint of lavender mixed with sandalwood, his aftershave. Hell, he wasn't done branding her with his scent yet.

"Let me taste you again, Em. I can't get enough of you." He slipped his hands beneath her curvy backside and lifted it up, waiting for her permission.

Amber fire scorched him, but he didn't let go. Now that he'd sipped, he needed to taste the very essence of Emily Langley again. He leaned down and blew a breath across the triangle of red curls guarding what he wanted her to yield to him. "Emily," he drawled out her name and dipped a finger inside of her.

She moaned out his name, long and low. He slipped another in and began to play her body, until she gasped out, "Yes, Tyler, now. Please?"

"Yes, ma'am," he grinned and lifted her to his mouth, plunging his tongue into her warm wet depths. It was his turn to moan. She tasted just like he remembered: heaven. He licked and sucked, nipping and tasting, until he was full to bursting, and she was writhing mindlessly beneath him, lifting her hips up off the bar letting him taste her more deeply.

"I'll be back for more later," he promised. "Maybe not just yet, but definitely soon." He leaned back on his knees, his boots scraping along the top of the bar as he reached into his pocket for a condom.

He ripped the top of the foil packet and pulled the latex out, but she stopped him. "Let me."

With a gentleness that had his heart tripping in his chest, she covered him from tip to base. Reaching up, she pulled him home and drove them both over the edge to insanity.

"Mmmm," she murmured a little while later. "What time is it?"

Emily's soft voice brought him back to earth. His back ached like a son-of-a-bitch and his knees felt raw, but when he opened his eyes, her face was the first thing he saw. Hell, he couldn't complain.

"Hey, sweet thing," he whispered, kissing her luscious lips. "Why can't I get enough of you, Miss Langley?"

"I don't know, Mr. Garahan," she said, "but I'm having the same problem.

"How did we end up on the bar?" he dragged his gaze away from her and looked around them.

Her eyes were alight with mischief. "It seemed like a good idea at the time. I'm just grateful the bar's a lot stronger than I thought it'd be."

He wished he didn't feel like he'd just been trampled by Widowmaker. He had the will, just not the stamina to go another round without eating. "You wore me out, woman. The body's willing but weak... maybe if you feed me first."

She drew circles on his pecs with her fingertips. The movement was making him crazy. "I mean it," he tried to sound stern, but she didn't stop. He grabbed hold of her hand, and she sighed. "All right, Tyler," she said. "What'll it be?"

"Got a side of beef you could fry up?"

She threw her arms around his neck and pulled him close. "I think I have a quarter of a buffalo in the freezer," she teased. Pressing her lips to his, she slipped her tongue inside to tangle with his. His mind fogged up and his dick sprang to attention. "If you feed me first with a side of aspirin, you can be on top."

Emily's wary look told him she either hadn't had a very patient lover before, or she wasn't used to talking about what she wanted her lover to do. Either way, he was going to get her to ride him later.

"You'll like it," he promised.

He eased out of her, rocked by how hollow he felt without that physical connection to her. "We'd better get you dressed." But he got hot all over again, fingering what was left of her lace thong underwear.

He slipped down off the bar, shifted himself back inside his jeans and started retrieving her clothes. Her shirt was hooked over the back of a barstool. He didn't have a clue where her bra had ended up. He'd find it later.

"Let me help you with your skirt," he said, pumped that she looked so totally disheveled and that it had been at his hands.

"How come I'm practically naked and all you have to put on is a shirt?"

He leaned close to her and pressed his lips to her shoulder. "You couldn't wait."

The dreamy look in her eyes only added to the euphoric feeling swirling around inside of him. It had been a long dry spell between women, but that wasn't at the heart of what he was feeling. *She was.*

Emily lifted her hopelessly stretched out shirt, and he wondered if it would shrink back when she washed it. "Do you want mine?" he scooped his shirt off the floor and handed it to her.

She reached out to take it from him, brushing her knuckles against the back of his hand. He felt the jolt shoot straight up his arm.

Emily must have felt it too, her eyes widened as she

slipped her arms into the sleeves. "You're positively lethal," she rasped, buttoning the shirt before scooting to the edge of the bar.

"Wait," he cautioned, "you don't want to scrape that lovely bottom on the edge of the bar."

She grinned and held her arms out to him. "Lovely?"

"Yeah," he scooped her up and held tight before letting her slide down the long hard length of him, setting her on her feet. His stomach rumbled breaking the spell she'd cast over him.

She laughed. "Come on, I'll rustle up some breakfast."

Half an hour later, he'd decimated the better part of a pound of bacon and a half a dozen scrambled eggs. Emily lost count of the slices of jelly toast he consumed along with about a gallon of coffee. Finally, the dark-haired hunk pushed back from the table and sighed. "I was hungry."

She couldn't keep from giggling. "I never would have guessed from the way you plowed through that meal." Tilting her head to one side, she asked, "Do you always eat like that?"

"Naw." He grinned and lifted his coffee mug to his lips. "I usually have steak with my eggs."

"If I hadn't been out to the ranch, I'd think you were kidding."

He swallowed the mouthful of coffee and set the mug down. "When you get up before dawn to tend to the cattle and horses, you have to eat enough to keep your body going until about noon."

She was beyond tired and achy in places that were just getting the hang of being used and abused… in a good way… again. "I'm going to bed."

Tyler stood when she did.

"Em," he said, "there's a couple of things I need to tell you."

"I'm too tired to talk now, Tyler." She really was. Besides if she rested up, she could take him up on his offer to let her be on top. "Talk and walk, babe." She spun on her heel and walked toward her bedroom, glancing at Jolene's closed door and the muffled sounds coming from behind it. *Sounded like Jolene and Jake were getting along just fine.*

"Emily, can you just give me a couple of minutes to get my head together?"

"I fed you."

He sighed. "Appreciate it, ma'am," he said, "but I need to you tell you something important."

It was her turn to sigh. "All right, but I wasn't kidding, you talk while you walk. I'm going to bed and it's in there."

He chuckled. "Yes, ma'am."

"And quit calling me ma'am all the damn time," she grumbled. "Makes me feel old."

"All right, darlin'."

How could she resist this man? "I'm halfway to that bed, and once I get there, I'm closing my eyes, so you'd best be getting whatever needs saying, said."

He spun her around and into his arms. "I love the hell out of you, Emily Langley." He locked lips with her and proceeded to kiss every last thought out of her head.

~

When he came up for air, she locked her fingers behind his head and pulled him to within a breath from her mouth. "I don't mind hearing you say it again, but you don't need to for my sake. I love you too."

"Why are we standing?" he asked, tugging her into her bedroom, tumbling her onto the bed. "When we could talk just as easily lying down?" He nipped her bottom lip and used her surprise to his advantage, delving deep, tangling his tongue with hers.

Instead of dragging her closer, he pulled back and cupped her face in his hands. "Do you know what scared me the most, Em?"

She shook her head, not wanting to break the spell of the moment.

"The thought of telling you how I felt and having you tell me you just love me for the sex and wouldn't want me if you knew I came with a broken down ranch and two ornery brothers."

She grinned, placed her hands on top of his, and confessed. "Well, I really love your talented lips and hips," she teased. When his brows furrowed over his dark expressive eyes, she laughed out loud. "I'd be crazy not to," she said. Before he could interrupt, she added, "It works both ways, Tyler. I'm a partner in a business that deals with pleasure—not just any man would be secure enough to get involved with me." When he stared at her, she smiled. "I'm crazy in love with you, and you can lasso me any time you like, cowboy."

His grin was lethal. Shifting his hands, pinning her arms at her sides, he smiled down at her, melting her heart. "Prepare to be hog-tied, ma'am."

Chapter 22

THE SOUND OF A DOOR BEING SHUT AND MUFFLED laughter woke her. She looked up. Tyler was awake and smiling down at her. Reaching out, she wrapped her arms around her man and slid them down to his amazingly taut backside, pulling him up to where she ached for him.

"Miss me?" Tyler bent to press his lips to hers.

She shifted until she was beneath him. "Mmmm." She wrapped her legs around his waist and poured everything she was feeling into her kiss.

"You're insatiable," he murmured, kissing a path of fire from her lips along the line of her jaw to a spot just beneath her ear. He nipped the skin then soothed it with a kiss.

"Are you complaining already?" Lord, she hoped he wasn't. She hadn't been this turned on since… she paused to think, but he was kissing her bare shoulder, and her mind went blank.

"Condom?" His rasped question broke through the haze of ecstasy enveloping her.

"Don't you have any more?"

"No," he groaned, taking her breast in his mouth. He suckled, pulling a moan from down deep inside of her. He shifted and poised above the other one long enough to say, "I didn't think we'd have enough time for more."

He latched on to her other breast and what she

was about to say ended up an incoherent gurgle low in her throat.

He drew her in and drove her up over the edge with his talented tongue and marvelous mouth. Drawing back, his eyes burned her with the dark, dangerous emotions swirling in their depths. "I was wrong."

When she could draw in enough air to speak, she mumbled, "There's a box in the bathroom."

Tyler was up and off the bed before she could finish.

"Where?" he demanded looking over his shoulder, pulling on his jeans.

"The closet."

He bumped into something solid. *Jake*. Hell. He saw that his friend had the box in his hand and felt the growl forming in his own throat. He swallowed it and asked, "Is the box full?"

Jake stared at Tyler, then down at the box. When he looked back up he drawled, "Yeah."

They grinned at one another, knowing the Langley women hadn't had the need or opportunity to open the box of condoms they kept in their bathroom, right next to the tampons, Midol, and Band-Aids.

"Pleasure pack?" Tyler's gut clenched. Man, it was a twelve pack of lubricated condoms, some ribbed, some twisted. "You gonna share?" Tyler knew he'd fight Jake for half if he had to.

Jake's eyes glazed over.

He probably just noticed he was holding a box of the variety selection.

"I probably don't have the stamina to use all of these before I go to work this morning," Jake admitted before tearing the box open like a kid on Christmas morning.

Tyler cupped his hands beneath the box to catch the ones that fell out. "Thanks," he said, turning around to sprint down the hallway.

"Hold on, lover boy." Jake had him by the shoulder. "We each get two three-packs."

Tyler looked down at the foil packets in his hands, then back up at Jake. "Sorry." He counted then tossed a pack at Jake before heading back into Emily's bedroom.

~

"What kept you?"

Tyler lifted his hand high, like a warrior returning from battle with the defeated enemy's sword.

Emily's heart skipped a beat when he lowered his hand, ripped off one foil packet, tossed the rest aside, and proceeded to open the packet with his teeth.

His gaze locked with hers. He shucked his jeans and sheathed himself before she'd managed to unbutton his shirt.

Stepping out of his jeans, he asked, "Have I told you how good you look in my shirt?"

He knelt on the bed, straddling her. Awed by the beauty of his musculature, she ran her hands along the breadth of his shoulders. Testing the elasticity and tensile strength of his muscles, she trailed her fingers slowly down to his glutes.

She smiled up at him. "And you have a seriously stellar set of abs and butt muscles."

He grinned, settling himself between her thighs. "I usually just use them for sitting."

"Not last night," she whispered, urging him forward,

pulling her knees up so he could go deep, right where she wanted him.

Words failed her as he pulled out, then plunged all the way to her core. He pulled out again slowly, dragging out her pleasure, until she thought she'd explode. She'd never been insatiable before, hadn't known she could feel this way.

"Tyler, please," she begged.

"Tell me what you want, Emily."

"You," she rasped. "I want you."

Like the flick of a light switch, Tyler stepped up the pace, plunging into her over and over until she went blind right before she splintered apart in his arms.

When she resurfaced, she heard him grumbling, "I think you just killed me."

"A big strong cowboy like you?" Her words belied the way she felt. Emily didn't think she could keep this pace up. Sore in places well used, somewhere just this side of exhausted, she moaned, "Even my fingernails are tired."

Tyler's answering chuckle cleared her head the rest of the way. Realizing that what she'd just said sounded ridiculous, she added, "Well, if they had muscles they'd be tired."

He laughed harder.

She smacked him in the shoulder.

"You are some piece of work, Emily Langley." He bent his head to press his mouth to hers. When he came up for air, he angled her chin so he could watch her eyes. "You think we can use up all of these condoms before I have to head back to the ranch?"

Tugging on his neck, she brought his mouth back down to where she could nip his bottom lip. She soothed it with the tip of her tongue then traced the rim of his mouth before molding her mouth to his.

She nipped his chin and grinned. "I'm game, but I probably won't be able to walk straight for a week."

His brown eyes smoldered with passion. He bent his head and traced his tongue along the tendon behind her ear before pressing his lips to one of her guaranteed trigger spots. Going with the flow, she tilted her head to give him better access.

"I'll make it worth your while."

Tyler's cell phone woke them. "Damn." He flipped it open. "This better be good."

He wiped the sleep from his eyes and shifted Emily so she was leaning against him. Tired didn't begin to describe what he was feeling right now, but it was a really good tired... a loose and sated kind of tired. Leaning down, he kissed her bare shoulder. "Are you sure?" Tyler shifted upright, jarring Emily. He soothed her with his free hand then slid his hand down to grab a hold of hers. Fingers entwined, he listened to the rest of what his brother had to say.

Flipping his phone closed he told her, "We have a buyer for Widowmaker." Pulling Emily back into his arms, he rested his chin on the top of her head. "You're a smart woman, Emily, and just because I haven't come right out to explain our financial situation over at the Circle G, I'm sure you know it's pretty bleak."

She nodded, waiting for him to continue.

"With O'Malley wanting to buy that bull, we could put a little more down on the feed bill; add that to what I'm bringing home from here, and we'll have the mortgage payment and start chipping away at the mountain of debt we still owe." His sigh was heartfelt. "Once we get a big enough chunk of the mortgage paid, I can quit this job and never have to go out onto that stage again."

He felt Emily stiffen next to him. "I'm not giving up what we have, darlin', so don't worry your pretty little head about that." Leaning closer, intending to capture her lips, he was surprised when she reared back and put a hand to the middle of his chest.

"What's wrong with working for Jolene and me?"

"Aside from the obvious?" He raked his fingers through his hair. Hell, his brain wasn't fully functioning yet; he could feel the gray cells misfiring from a seriously amazing bout of lovemaking with the gorgeous redhead glaring up at him.

Her eyes narrowed to slits of amber fire, but it wasn't passion fired in his direction; it was temper, pure and simple. "Maybe you'd better just say it plain out, Tyler, because I'm not sure I want to speculate and get angry with you for the wrong reasons."

"What the hell?"

"OK, so you don't like working for Jolene and me," she said, holding up one slim finger. "What else?"

"It's not that, Em, and you know it." A wave of uneasiness crept slowly up from his toes. "I don't like standing out on stage in front of those women."

"I thought you liked all of the attention."

He snorted. "You thought wrong."

"But you don't look angry like you did that first night you stripped on stage."

"There you go," he said, crossing his arms over his chest. "That one word in a nutshell."

Her eyes shot from angry to molten. "But you never said anything about it to me."

His temper simmered, and he put a lid on it. He didn't want to be angry with Emily. Hell, he wanted to kiss her sweet lips, even if they were spitting venom at him right now. "Jolene knows how I feel." He paused thinking back to that first day. "She interviewed me."

Emily shook her head. "Why didn't you tell me how you feel?"

"I thought it was obvious."

"Not to me."

Tyler drew her close again and pressed his lips to her hair, breathing in the faint scent of some kind of citrus. No matter how many times he'd been close to Emily, she always smelled good enough to eat. His gut clenched remembering how luscious she'd tasted last night. "I don't want to fight with you."

"You brought it up"—she squirmed out of his hold—"and we need to finish this."

Drawing in a deep breath, Tyler concentrated on distancing himself from his libido. "I think you and Jolene are the strongest, most resilient women I've ever had the pleasure of meeting."

Tears welled up in Emily's eyes. She blinked them away before he could comment on them. "Nice to know, but not the point."

He struggled with the simmering temper he thought he'd capped off. Finally, he decided there was no nice way to say it. *Best get it said.* "I hate stripping in front of that crowd of women." His gut clenched. "God, Em.

They make me feel like a piece of meat hanging in the butcher's window." He raked his fingers through his hair. "The Lucky Star is the kind of place I'd never go or want my woman to go."

"Do you have another woman?" she rasped, and he turned toward her again.

"Are you serious or just trying to piss me off?"

"If I'm your woman, then you'd better take a good look at who I am and where I work, because I like running The Lucky Star with Jolene and the girls, and I have no intention of quitting."

He opened his mouth to speak, but the glare she leveled at him had him chewing on his words and swallowing them.

"Not for you, the town council, or any of the precious societies that have been banging down our door demanding that we close them and reopen as an old-time saloon."

She folded her arms beneath her breasts, but he didn't think she plumped them up to purposefully distract him. "You finished?"

"No," she ground out. "If you feel that strongly about this job, then how can you love me, knowing where I work and that I don't intend to stop?"

"It's not the same," he matched her anger and raised her one. "You're not up on that damned circle of wood, strutting your stuff and stripping yourself bare."

"You wear briefs," she bit out, "you don't strip down to your birthday suit." She scooted to the edge of the bed and stood with her hands on her hips. "Are you telling me that you wouldn't be here with me right now if the tables were turned and you and your brothers owned a strip joint, and I was your headliner, shucking my clothes for all the men in town?"

Sharp pointed knives sliced his gut to shreds, and he lost the tenuous hold on his temper. "Damn it, woman, it's not the same and you know it!"

Tears welled up and spilled over. "It is," she whispered. "Why can't you see that?"

Undone, he reached for her, she stepped back, reaching for the shirt he'd left on the floor. Buttoning it up to the throat, she hugged herself as if she were cold.

"I don't want to fight with you."

"So you'd be with me if the tables were turned, and I was the one stripping for money?"

He couldn't speak. What could he say that wouldn't make her madder? Hell… could he tell her the truth right now? He didn't know how he felt; he needed time to think about it.

"I think you'd better go." She held the door open and waited.

"Don't you want to hear what I have to say?" he ground out, reaching for his jeans, picking them up off the floor.

"Your look says it all, Tyler." She sounded tired, defeated. "Please leave. I don't want you here right now."

He grabbed his socks and boots and stalked over to where she stood, trembling, and it was that one action that tipped the scales. His mad evaporated. His little redheaded filly standing her ground, eyes blazing but watery, chin held high. He loved her. He had to make her see his side without losing her.

"We'll talk about this later."

"Maybe."

"Hell, woman."

"Don't call me woman."

His lips twitched and he fought the urge to smile. "You won't let me call you ma'am, and I'd bet the ranch you don't want me calling you darlin' right now."

"Shut up and leave, cowboy."

The urge to smile shriveled up and died as hurt lanced through him. Jolene's nickname for him grated across his wounded pride. *Maybe it was time to step back and see what happens when the dust settles*. He loved Emily Langley, but he hated the job that brought them together. But if hating the job was going to drive a wedge between them, he had some thinking to do.

Her tears dried up, and he knew he wouldn't be able to talk to her right now when her temper was boiling over.

He had bigger problems right now. If he didn't get his ass over to the ranch and handle that sonofabitch bull, then they wouldn't be able to sell the animal to O'Malley. Too bad he was the only one who could handle the beast.

Their eyes met, and he prayed the trace of regret he saw there would be enough to keep her from making a hasty decision, one that included him being shut out of her life.

He nodded and strode through the door. He was leaving, but he'd be back.

Emily watched the stubborn man she loved to distraction walk out of her life unsure if he'd walk back into it. When she heard his footfalls on the stairs, she fell back against her door remembering a sad song her mother used to love about footsteps down the hall walking away. Tyler hadn't answered her. "What if he can't handle the idea I planted in his stubborn head? What if he couldn't handle if it were me up there on stage?"

She slid to the floor and the tears she'd been holding back pricked at the backs of her eyes. No need to be strong since she was all alone and nobody could see her break down.

Giving in to the ache in her heart, she hung her head and cried.

Chapter 23

"I'm gonna shoot the sonofabitch!" Dylan's voice broke through the haze of pain clamping around Tyler's middle, squeezing the breath out of him.

He got up on his hands and knees and tried to take a deep breath, but pain lanced through him, debilitating him. He collapsed and rolled over onto his back, breathing in and out in short, sharp, panting breaths. He heard his name being called, but just couldn't drag in enough air to speak. Dizzy from lack of oxygen, he fought to hang on and stay conscious.

"Forget Widowmaker," Jesse yelled. "Get the first aid kit."

Dylan ran to the truck, grabbed the toolbox they used to store the bandages, gauze pads, peroxide, and antiseptic ointment they used regularly, and skidded to a halt next to where his brother lay breathing like a freight train.

"Damned bull head-butted him and knocked him right into the fuckin' barbed wire."

Dylan frowned. "Shut up and let me think."

"What the hell do you need to think for?" Jesse demanded. "Our big brother just got the shit kicked out of him because he was too tired to pay attention and turned his back on that mean sonofabitch bull."

"We've got to get a good look at that gash to see if it needs stitches," Dylan sounded as if he were in pain.

Must be pretty bad if the middle Garahan brother was rattled.

Dylan's next words confirmed Tyler's fear of just how bad the cut really was. "Good thing O'Malley left the deposit and said he'd be back," Dylan ground out, "or else I'd shoot Widowmaker right between the eyes."

"Not worth it," Tyler rasped, finally able to drag in enough air to speak. He took a mental tally of his injuries. His ribs felt bruised, maybe cracked. He tried to take a deeper breath and groaned. Maybe broken.

"Lie still," Dylan bit out, "you're bleeding." His brother placed a wad of gauze against the worst of it all the while telling Jesse to pour peroxide onto a fresh piece of gauze.

Tyler finally had most of his wind back. He rasped, "Must be bad if you're willing to lose the money O'Malley's paying for that animal."

"Hell, bro," Jesse ground out, "no money's worth putting you in the hospital."

Before he could wrap his mind around that possibility, Dylan added, "You used to be pretty. Right now it's kind of hard to tell if you've spilled any of your guts in the dirt."

Tyler blanched, knowing his brother was doing his best to distract him while performing first aid and keeping Tyler from sitting up to inspect the damage himself. He fought against the need to do just that. He looked down at his gloved hand and saw blood… lots of it. He closed his eyes.

"I've cleaned out as much of the rust and corral as I can," Dylan rasped. "We've got to concentrate on getting the bleeding to stop."

Jesse knelt next to Tyler. "Brace yourself, bro," Jesse warned. "You're gonna need stitches."

"Shit." Tyler saw the blood covering both of his brothers. "Mine?"

"Yeah." Dylan narrowed his gaze at his older brother and demanded, "Stay with us, Tyler. We can't carry you and keep the pressure on the gash."

Tyler closed his eyes and nodded. "Use the ace bandage. Wrap it around the gauze. It'll hold me till we get to the hospital. When's O'Malley coming back?"

"After dinner," Jesse answered. "Hold this." He handed the edge of the bandage to Tyler. "And quit worrying about the money! You're getting us back on track with the money from your night job." Careful not to press too hard, Jesse wound the bandage around the wad of gauze and Tyler's ribs.

"O'Malley can find another bull," Dylan said, "I'm going to the truck for my rifle."

"No." Tyler didn't know whether to be worried about the possibility of bleeding out before they got him to the hospital and stitched up, or that his brother would follow through with his threat to shoot the bull.

"O'Malley wants Widowmaker," Tyler said. "He knows about the bull's bad attitude. That old man's smart. He knows that Widowmaker sires more steer than any other bull in the county."

He drew in a breath and clenched his jaw. Focusing to remain conscious took all of Tyler's strength. He could let the pain have him later. Right now, he had to help his brothers get him to the hospital and stitched up.

"I'm drivin'," Jesse muttered, helping Tyler to his feet. "Wait here." Jesse sprinted for the truck.

"He'll just grind the gears," Tyler rasped.

Jesse stopped the truck and hopped out to help Dylan get Tyler inside. "Let's go."

Braced between his brothers, Tyler ground his teeth all the way into Pleasure.

"Hang on, Ty, we're here," Jesse said, throwing the gearshift into first, pulling on the handbrake, and cutting the engine. "I beat my old record."

"Shut up and help me get him inside."

Tyler let his brothers talk while he focused on putting one foot in front of the other. He didn't want them to realize how weak he was. But one look from the woman manning the desk in the emergency room and he knew it was worse than his brothers let on. "Hell."

"Oh I think you've got a little more time here on earth," Dylan rasped, nodding that he'd go with Tyler and the triage nurse. "Jess you handle the paperwork."

"Divide and conquer," Tyler mumbled.

"Is he delirious?" the nurse asked.

Dylan shook his head. "He's fighting the pain. I'm pretty sure he's got a couple of cracked or broken ribs underneath that gash."

Two hours later, Tyler had been poked, prodded, stitched, and injected. "I still say I didn't need the tetanus shot."

"Wimp," Jesse mumbled halfheartedly. "You always did hate needles."

"I'd gladly have traded places with you and been the one filling out the paperwork."

Once again braced on either side by his brothers, the brothers led Tyler outside. "Easy," Dylan warned, "you don't want to rip out the doc's handiwork."

Tyler had felt the first couple of stitches while waiting for the local to take effect. It had hurt like hell, so he wasn't going to take a chance of ripping them out. "Remind me to punch you later."

"Done," Dylan agreed. "But I'll give you a couple of weeks to heal first."

"Appreciate it." Damn he hurt all over.

"Hand over the keys, Jess," Dylan said. "You barely kept the truck on the road."

"You just don't appreciate my style of driving," Jesse muttered.

If Tyler didn't hurt so damned much, he would have said something to back up Dylan. Their little brother still talked about making it big driving Craftsman Trucks for NASCAR out at Texas Motor Speedway.

Dylan held out his hand. "Gimme the keys so we can get this prescription filled. Then big brother here can call his boss and tell her he won't be at work tonight."

Later after they'd returned to the ranch he realized the pain from the stitches and his ribs didn't hurt as much as the pain in his heart. Emily didn't trust him because he hadn't answered her question quick enough.

Did he really want Emily to spend the night without him and give her time to come up with another convoluted reason not to trust him? It'd probably kill him if she rolled over into his side, but he was determined not to give her any more time alone to think. He'd spent too much time thinking already and all it got him was skewered into the barbed wire fence in the south pasture.

He needed Emily. He had to be with her tonight. "I've gotta go in." Tyler braced himself against the counter, praying he would make it upstairs. His nose hadn't been injured, and one whiff told him he needed to get cleaned up, because there was more than just Texas dirt ground into his shirt and jeans.

"Are you sure you didn't hit your head?" Dylan demanded getting right in Tyler's face.

"Pretty sure," Tyler nodded.

Jesse ranged himself next to Dylan and nodded. "Good because you're not going in to work tonight."

"But—"

"If we have to tie you to the damned bed to keep you here," Dylan ground out, "we will."

"You lost a lot of blood, Ty," Jesse said. "Give yourself at least a day or so to get your strength back before you go lifting cases of beer."

"Hell."

"Dylan or I could take over your job and give you a break," Jesse offered.

Dylan nodded. "One Garahan back is as good as another."

Tyler shook his head. "Amen to that," he said, easing down onto a chair, "but I already told you I don't exactly lift kegs or cases of beer."

His brothers looked at each other and then at him.

Damn. Why the hell couldn't they have believed him the other day when he'd told them the God's honest truth?

They waited expectantly. Shame filled his gut and iced it over, but then he thought of Emily's question. If the tables were turned what would he do? He remembered the way she'd stood by him when Linda Lee had tried to cause trouble and break them up. He'd be a fool not to trust that Emily would be as honest and trustworthy no matter if she stripped for money or he did. It was a job. Period.

"Gimme the painkillers," Dylan urged.

Jesse dug into his pocket for the bottle of pills while Dylan reached for a glass and filled it with water.

Grateful that he'd finally sorted it out in a way that made sense to him, he was ready to tackle the uphill battle of trying to convince one fiery-haired filly. Tyler took the pill and downed the glass of water.

"Whatever it is that you do nights, bought us time," Dylan said.

"Yeah," Jesse added. "We're gonna make the bank's deadline."

"O'Malley buying Widowmaker will push us closer to the black," Tyler agreed. "But I need to keep working for a couple more months to make sure we have a buffer. The roof on the barn's shot, the plumbing's shaky, and the damned furnace is older than O'Malley."

Dylan crossed his arms across his chest. "You're not going in tonight," he said. "I'll take your shift."

Tyler's gut clenched. No way could he imagine Dylan getting up on stage and shucking his jeans for a couple of greenbacks. Hell, the way the women crowd up to the stage, vying for position so they could stick dollar bills in his black spandex briefs would have his brother running for cover.

Dylan had gone longer without a woman than either of his brothers. It had taken a good eight months before Dylan had come around after his girlfriend had walked out on him. No way was Tyler going to do anything to force his brother back into his shell.

"You can't fill in for me."

Jesse and Dylan looked at one another, and then his younger brother crossed his arms across his chest and said, "Then I'll go." *Damned Garahan stubborn streak.*

"You're not irreplaceable, Tyler," Dylan said. "No one is."

Jesse was staring at him. Tyler shifted underneath his youngest brother's close scrutiny. "I didn't say I was irreplaceable."

"Are you serious about stripping?"

You could have heard a pin drop while his brothers worked it out in their heads. Finally Dylan swore, "Sonofabitch. Linda Lee wasn't lying… it's a ladies' club, isn't it?"

Tyler lifted his head and met his younger brother's steady gaze. He swallowed past the lump of shame in his throat and said, "Yeah I wasn't kidding the other night when I told you I stripped for money."

"The hell you say!" Jesse shook his head at him.

When Tyler nodded, his brothers looked at each other again. Jesse shook his head and laughed. "Man you really had me going there," he said. "Imagine my big brother getting paid to strut his stuff."

Tyler cleared his throat. When put that way, it didn't sound all that bad.

Dylan shoved Jesse. "He's not kidding."

Jesse shoved back. "How do you know?" He looked at Tyler, "You don't have to really… uh… strip. Do you? You just walk around without a shirt and let the ladies—"

When Tyler stared at him, Jesse visibly cringed. "Aw shit, Tyler," Jesse said. "We didn't need the money that bad."

Dylan walked over to Tyler and squatted down in

front of him. "Yeah," he said, meeting Tyler's shame-filled expression. "We did."

His brother put his hand on Tyler's shoulder, patted it awkwardly, and then stood up. "I don't know if I can fill your boots or step out of my clothes in front of a room-full of strangers, but I'll try."

"Are they all drop-dead gorgeous?"

Tyler shook his head at his brothers. "Hell." They hadn't reacted the way he thought they would. "Some," he answered, all the while wondering when Dylan would just say whatever was on his mind instead of flat out staring at him.

"Blondes, brunettes, or redheads?" Jesse wanted to know.

Tyler sighed. "All of the above."

"It's the redheaded boss's fault," Dylan said softly. "She wouldn't take no for an answer." He locked gazes with Tyler. "Am I right?"

Tyler wanted to say yes, but he'd lied to his brothers for the last time. Nothing, and certainly not his pride, was worth the guilt he'd had to live with for the past few weeks trying to hide the down and dirty side of his night job from his brothers.

He shook his head. "I could have walked away. But we would have had to give up Grandpa's dream… our dream… the Circle G." The ache in his heart doubled just thinking how close it'd been. "I'd do anything to keep the ranch…" he let his voice trail off. What more was there to say?

"Hell," Dylan mumbled, "couldn't you have just robbed a damn bank?"

Jesse started chuckling then Dylan joined in. Their

laughter soothed the worst of Tyler's guilt and loosened the knot in his stomach. He found his voice and a small piece of his pride. "Hell, and take a chance that one of mom's brothers would find out?" he cringed at the thought of it. "Besides, I couldn't be responsible for ruining the one-hundred-and-fifty-year-old sterling reputation of the Justiss men who've served as U.S. Marshals, could I?"

His brothers stopped laughing. "Uncle Matt would have skinned you alive," Dylan said.

"Yeah, and Uncle Ben would have nailed your hide to the side of the barn."

Relieved to have unburdened himself, Tyler leaned against the back of the chair and groaned. "Damn." His side hurt like a bitch. The local must be wearing off.

"It's got to do with Emily, doesn't it?" Dylan asked.

Tyler nodded. "I've got to get to town and explain. She put me on the spot and asked how I'd feel if our places were switched and she was the one up on that damn stage."

Dylan and Jesse looked at one another. "Hell, Ty. We like Emily."

Tyler sighed. "She told me she liked you guys too."

"Tough call though, Ty." Dylan shook his head. "How would you feel about it?"

"I trust her, damn it."

"Well then, that's all you need to worry about and all you have to tell her."

Dylan's gaze met Tyler's first and Jesse's second. "The Garahans are going to ride into town, to save Tyler's job, the lovely redheads who own The Lucky Star, and Tyler's ass where Emily's concerned."

Tyler's throat tightened. "Thanks, Dylan."

Jesse stared at him. "Two redheads?" Before Tyler could answer, Jesse said, "Man, redheads are the devil in bed and hell on a strong back."

Tyler played back last night's lovemaking marathon in his mind and grinned back at his brother. "Oh yeah."

"Hell," Dylan bit out. "We're gonna need a roll of duct tape."

Jesse backed away. "Hey, I'm not gonna let you to do that to me again… I was ten years old, damn it."

Tyler snorted. "Man, after Grandpa found you like that in the barn, Dylan and I couldn't sit down for a week."

Dylan smiled. "Use your head, Jess. We need duct tape so we can cover Tyler's bandages with plastic food bags."

"There's still that half a roll of plastic out in the barn from that greenhouse project we never had time to finish." Tyler hoped getting it wrapped around his midsection, so he could take a hot shower without getting his stitches wet, wouldn't hurt quite as much as piecing together a patchwork of the much smaller bags would be. Either way, he wasn't looking forward to either of his brothers pulling the duct tape off.

"You get the plastic, Jess," Dylan said. "I'll help Tyler upstairs."

"Don't start the show without me." Jesse headed for the back door.

Tyler was tired and sore. "What the hell are you talking about?"

Jesse was halfway out the door, but he stopped to answer, "I've got a couple of dollars upstairs," he said. "Don't strip 'til I get there!"

"I'm gonna kill him—"

Dylan grabbed a hold of Tyler's arm and chuckled. "You can kill him later."

"Man, you said that the last time."

"Yeah," Dylan said.

From the look on his brother's face, Tyler knew he was remembering the other time Grandpa took a switch to them. "If Jesse's leg hadn't broken, we might have convinced him to jump off the barn roof a second time." He grinned. "That was one hell of a homemade parachute."

"Jesse was having a good time, 'til the sheet tore right above where you'd knotted it."

"Yeah," Tyler said, "the sheet was old, but the knot held."

Helping Tyler toward the stairs, Dylan asked, "So just how far down do you strip?"

Feeling good enough now to razz his brother, Tyler drawled, "All the way."

Chapter 24

"Oh. My. God."

Emily turned to see what had her cousin resorting to one-word sentences and felt the blood rush from her head to her feet. Three gorgeous dark-haired hunks were walking down the hallway toward the bar.

Her heart skipped a beat. They were tall, they were good-looking, and the middle one was all hers… well, until he'd told her flat out that he was ending it. She'd thought long and hard about their argument that morning and it all came down to trust. She hoped she could get him to listen long enough to point that out to him.

As Tyler and his brothers got closer, she noticed that the men on either side of Tyler were actually holding him steady. Her heart plummeted to her stomach as she rushed toward him. "What happened?"

Standing close, she noticed his skin was pale and pasty, and there was a thin sheen of sweat covering his face. "Are you sick? Where are you hurt?" She reached for his hands and he all but fell into her arms. Tears pricked the back of her eyes, but she held steady. Something was wrong with Tyler, and until she found out what, she needed to stay strong and focused.

"Ladies," the two other men tipped their black Stetsons. "We're—"

"Dylan and Jesse," Emily interrupted. "Tyler's brothers. Tell me what happened."

"It seems Widowmaker had to get one last parting shot in," Dylan answered. "Tyler just happened to be standing closest when he let loose."

"Your ribs again?" Emily actually hurt thinking about it.

Jesse nodded. "This time he broke a couple... that and all of those stitches."

"From getting kicked?" Jolene sounded as if she didn't believe him.

But before Jolene could say anything, Dylan shook his head and added, "Damned bull head-butted him right into the barbed wire fence."

"How many stitches?" Jolene whispered.

"Enough," Tyler rasped. "I didn't want you to think I'd just desert you, boss, after all you've done for me." He looked down at Emily. "Em, I need to talk to you."

Emily nodded as Jolene asked, "Where are they?"

Tyler started to lift his arm, then stopped, wincing in pain. "From my side around to my back." Then he captured her gaze and whispered, "It ain't pretty."

Emily could not stop the tears from filling her eyes. She blinked, but her eyes welled up with more. "Are you really worried about that?" When he shrugged, she sensed that he was worried about her reaction. "Scars don't bother me." She laid her hand on his arm. "You should have stayed home tonight, Tyler."

"I tried to tell him that, ma'am," Dylan said, "but it seems our brother was worried about his job." He looked Jolene in the eye before looking over at Emily. "And setting you straight about how he feels about stripping."

Tyler stiffened. "I can handle this myself."

Dylan shrugged. "Why not go for sympathy when

you can?" he asked. "It'll soften her up enough that she'll listen when you finally stop thinking about how to tell her and just plain tell her."

"Sit down, Tyler." Emily eased him onto a chair.

Jolene followed and waved her hand toward one of the tables. "Please," she said to the men, "have a seat."

"Obliged." Jesse took the chair on one side of Jolene, while Dylan sat on the other side of her.

Jolene looked from one brother to the next. "Isn't this cozy?"

Emily ignored everyone but Tyler. Pulling her chair as close as possible, she laced her fingers with his. "Can I get you anything?"

Tyler's lips lifted on one side. "I really need to talk to you alone, Em."

Emily could see the lines of pain bracketing his mouth. "You could have called," she said. "It's a long ride into town."

Dylan turned toward her and said, "I told him that, but he's convinced he's irreplaceable and that you were dumping him."

Emily looked from one brother to the other. "He told you about that?" She wasn't sure how she felt about Tyler talking to his brothers about their argument. When Jolene reached over to touch the back of Emily's hand, she relaxed. She'd already told her cousin; why shouldn't Tyler do the same with his brothers?

"It was the only reason we duct taped him up and tossed his ass… er… butt in the shower," Jesse said.

Jolene raised one eyebrow. "Duct taped?" Her low laughter surrounded them. "You're full of surprises, aren't you, cowboy?"

"Damn, Jolene," Tyler bit out, "you know I hate it when you call me that."

She tapped her fingernail to the middle of her bottom lip. "You're hurting. Did you take any painkillers?"

He nodded.

"Well then," she smiled and turned back to his brothers, "how much do I have to pay you to shoot that damned bull?"

Dylan's chuckle was echoed by Jesse and then finally Tyler.

Emily sighed. Lord, the three of them were a sight, so darkly handsome and full of life. She'd seen how hard they worked their land and knew how tight they were as brothers. She didn't want to miss out on the chance to get to know them better, but more, she didn't want to miss out on the chance to have Tyler in her life. "You three must have broken quite a few hearts over the years."

"From the way Tyler dug deep for the strength to come here tonight," Dylan said, "I'm guessing his heart-breaking days are at an end."

Tyler squeezed Emily's hand then lifted it to his mouth, brushing his lips across the back of her knuckles. "You'd be right about that, Dylan." His gaze met Emily's, and she saw everything she felt for Tyler mirrored back at her.

"I'd never want to break your heart," she whispered, leaning close enough to brush her lips to his whiskered cheek. He looked like he needed to lie down. "Do you want to go upstairs?"

"Man," Dylan rasped, "give him a break; he's got three broken ribs and more stitches than I could count."

"Your brother needs to lie down." Emily's sharply indrawn breath had Tyler chuckling.

"You could take him out to the hallway," Jolene said. "It's closer. While you do, I'd like to have a word with his brothers in private."

Jolene had that look in her eyes… like she had the day she'd hired Tyler. He wanted to warn his brothers but thought it just might be interesting to see how they reacted to her little test. *Too bad he wasn't going to be around to watch them.*

"Go easy on them, Jo," Emily warned, taking Tyler by the hand and helping him to his feet.

"They can handle it," Tyler assured her. "We Garahans come from strong, stubborn stock."

"Come on then," she urged. "Let's get you settled on one of the velvet benches. You'll feel better if you can stretch out. You're way too pale."

"I hate missing all the fun, but…" he lowered himself onto the bench with her help.

Emily smiled. "I'm sure your brothers can handle themselves."

Tyler shook his head. "Dylan is easily distracted when it comes to redheads."

She grinned. "That's right," she said. "I forgot about that."

They rested for a few minutes, each lost in their own thoughts, until the sound of raised voices and furniture being bashed around had Tyler pushing to his feet. He swayed but Emily was there to brace him up. "I'll go see what's going on," she offered.

"Not without me."

"Fine," she bit out, "but if just one stitch rips out, I'm driving you back to the emergency room myself."

He looked at her, saw the worry in her eyes, and felt the overwhelming urge to soothe her fears mingled with the hope that they'd be able to work through the harsh words they'd exchanged that morning. "If agreeing will make you feel better, you've got a deal," he said. "Let's go."

They arrived in time to see a shirtless Dylan throw a punch and Jake dodge it.

"Hell," Tyler grumbled, "I didn't know he was here."

"He probably came in the side door."

"Jolene must have decided Dylan would do as my replacement tonight." Emily shook her head and Tyler grinned. "He must have walked in right after Jolene asked Dylan to take his shirt off." He nodded to his brother who managed to get a solid right in under Jake's guard.

"That's gonna hurt." He almost felt sorry for Jake. "If he's going to stick around, he'll have to get used to guys stripping in front of Jolene."

Emily shrugged. "From my point of view," she said, "it's hard to stay focused when the one you love bares it all for money."

Tyler stiffened, waiting to hear what else she had to say as their earlier words washed over him. "Some people don't have a choice, if they need to make ends meet, or dig themselves out of a financial hole—"

"I know that's why you're working for my cousin," she said. "So why wouldn't you be able to understand if I had to do the same thing?"

"Look, Emily," he rasped, "that's what I wanted to tell you. I trust you… no matter what you do for a living."

The sound of fists hitting flesh immediately followed by wood splintering distracted him. But when he turned around, he had to blink, twice. Jolene stood with her hands on her hips, tapping the toe of her boot against the floor. His brothers and Jake were lying on their backs in the middle of what used to be a table.

"You're all a bunch of morons!" Jolene shouted. "I don't need any of you to come to my damned rescue," she bit out.

"The hell you don't," Jake said, pushing to his feet.

"That's right," she said, "I don't because Emily's got my back."

Emily brushed her fingertips across Tyler's jaw. He snagged her hand and kissed it before she walked over to stand beside her cousin. "It's been the two of us for so long, it's hard sometimes to ask for help." She rubbed her hand on Jolene's back. "But deep down," she said, looking right at Jolene, "we're both scared."

"Jake's only trying to protect you, boss," he said, nodding at Jake who still had his hands fisted at his sides. "I'm guessing it must have looked pretty bad when he walked in just now, seeing you alone with two guys he doesn't know, with their shirts undone and their horns showing."

"He could have asked." Jolene brushed her hair out of her eyes. "But no." She glared at the man whose heart was in his eyes. "The big bad fire marshal made up his mind and just started swinging."

Dylan reached out a hand to help Jesse to his feet.

"Hey, we weren't poaching." He nodded in Jolene's direction. "We're only here to help our brother."

Jake looked from Tyler to his brothers and then back. "Shit," he ground out. "Why didn't you say so?"

Dylan grinned, wiping the blood from his split lip. "Hard to talk with your fist in my mouth."

Tyler shook his head. "My boss is one pretty lady," he smiled at her, "but she's taken."

"Could have used that bit of information before, big brother," Jesse said.

"Hell," Jake raked his fingers through his hair, "I'm sorry, Jolene."

Her sigh was long and low. "Next time ask."

"Damn," Jake said. "There's going to be a next time?"

Jolene crossed her arms beneath her breasts and stared up at Jake. "Probably. We don't plan on selling The Lucky Star anytime soon."

Needing to smooth things over between his brothers, his boss, and his friend, Tyler walked over to stand beside Jolene. "Jake Turner, Pleasure's Fire Marshal," he said with a nod before turning back toward his brothers, "Dylan and Jesse Garahan, my brothers."

"After what you've done to save the ranch," Dylan began, "we thought we could help out until your ribs mend and your stitches heal."

Jolene turned toward Tyler. "Ranch?"

"The Circle G," Jesse said. "It's been in the family for over one hundred and fifty years."

Jolene looked at Tyler. "You don't have a boss," she said, "do you?"

"Hell, no," Dylan answered for his brother. "The three of us are partners. Lucky for us Tyler figured out a way to dig us out of debt and save Grandpa's legacy."

There was no mistaking the pride in his brother's

words. "No wonder you got so hot under the collar when I first started calling you cowboy," Jolene chuckled. "You're the real deal."

"Why the secrecy?" Emily's voice had gone soft. He wished she'd look at him, but she'd backed away from him and now refused to meet his gaze.

He hadn't gotten around to discussing that part with her but he'd figured she already knew. "I wanted to talk to you in private, Emily."

Dylan crossed his arms over his chest and nudged his brother. "I think you should tell her now, while Jesse and I can back you up."

With a glance at his brothers, he dug deep for courage and pushed past his shame. "I was afraid to tell my brothers that the only job I could get was taking off my clothes."

His face flamed. The heat reminded him of the passionate fire burning inside of Emily. For her, he'd humiliate himself in front of his brothers and his friend. "I'd been to a strip club a time or two and never thought anything of it." He shrugged. "Hell, I'd even dragged Dylan with me once."

Dylan nodded but kept quiet.

"I never thought much about the women who got paid to strip. I figured they liked what they did, otherwise," he said, turning to look at Emily, then Jolene, "why would they do it?

"I was mad at first, when you asked me to take off my shirt"—he looked down at his hands—"I figured you were playing some kind of joke on me 'cause I was dressed like a ranch hand."

Jolene shook her head at him. "I'd never do anything like that."

"I know that now, but didn't at the time. All I knew was I needed the job." He looked over at his brothers. "The balloon payment on the mortgage and the feed bill were due." He looked back at Jolene. "I needed it bad enough to take off my shirt, and later on, my dignity along with my blue jeans."

Needing Emily to understand, he dug deeper. "I'm sorry I never looked hard enough to see past the glittering façade and curvaceous bodies of those women working in the clubs we'd been to. If I had, it wouldn't have been such a shock when the tables were turned, and I was the one who had to toss aside my manly pride to do whatever I had to in order to save our ranch."

He finally had the nerve to look at Emily. She was biting her lower lip while tears dripped down onto her dark blue T-shirt.

"Then why can't you understand that if I was in your place, I might have to do the same?" Emily asked. "What would be different aside from who's stripping on stage?"

Tyler started to reach for her but knew he'd end up kissing her instead of answering her. He looked over at his brothers. They both nodded, and he knew they had his back. "No difference, Emily," he rasped holding out his hand to her. "I trust you and that should be enough."

You could have heard a pin drop. He lifted his hands, but unless she acknowledged his words he wouldn't touch her again. He turned on his heel and walked away. Walking down the long mirrored hall, he was amazed that he'd lasted this long in a job he hated. *All for the sake of the Garahan legacy, the Circle G, and the woman he loved.*

"I never should have let her get under my skin."

"Then why did you?"

He turned and nearly fell over. "Emily." The way she was looking up at him had him swallowing against the lump of gratitude in his throat. She wasn't going to let him walk away from her. "I already told you why the other day."

She stepped closer. "Refresh my memory."

The hell with his cracked ribs; he was desperate to hold her. He wrapped his arms around her and laid his cheek on the top of her head, breathing in her unique scent: the citrus of her shampoo and the softer, sweeter essence that was pure Emily.

"I already told you… I fell so hard the first time I saw you standing there with chocolate smeared across your breasts."

"Did you?" she pressed her lips to his throat.

"You know I did."

"And if I had to strip for money?" she urged.

He lifted his head and looked down at her. "I'd trust you the same way you trusted me when my ex showed up and you cleaned her clock."

"I did," Emily agreed. "And I still do. Punching her in the nose was definitely a bonus."

"I'm sorry I let my being jealous get in the way of answering you quick enough."

Emily nodded. "I'm sorry I let my temper get in the way of giving you the time you needed to sort it out in your head."

"I'm done thinking, Em." Tyler shifted and groaned, but moved so their lips were lined up. "I love you and need you in my life."

"And?" Emily grinned touching her lips to his.

"If our roles were reversed, I'd still be jealous as hell of all of those guys getting a good look at what I'd want reserved just for me, but I know that's all they'd be doing is looking."

"I love you, Tyler Garahan."

"Praise the Lord, Emily Langley."

Lips locked, hearts linked, Tyler kissed her until her toes curled.

Emily laughed softly. "Do you think your ribs'll stand up to that kind of physical activity?"

He traced her lips with the tip of his tongue then parted her lips to taste her sweet mouth again. "They might, but the stitches probably won't."

"Then we'll just have to settle for a little mouth to mouth." Her smile was slow and hot. "Think you can handle that, Tyler?"

"You're killing me, Emily."

"Give me a little time, and I promise to make your eyes cross and your head spin." She kissed him back, tangling her tongue with his until he was so hot he thought he'd explode.

"Later," he promised, "Right now I need—"

"To kiss me, cowboy."

"Yes, ma'am."

Chapter 25

"OK, BOYS," JOLENE SAID, LOOKING OVER HER SHOULDER at Jake, then back at the dark-haired brothers. "Which one of you wants to be the first to take the test?"

Eyes narrowed, Dylan asked, "What kind of test?"

"The last one didn't turn out too well for us," Jesse admitted.

"Fire Marshal Turner promises not to interfere this time," she flicked a glance in his direction. "Unless you'd like to be included."

The men looked at one another, and she sensed they'd all take the bait. Their pride wouldn't allow anything less.

"We're in," Dylan answered for himself and his brother.

Jake met the challenge in her gaze. "Why not?"

Excitement tingled all the way to the tips of her fingers. "Just let me make a phone call." She pulled out her cell phone and flipped it open.

"Hey, Gwen." Jolene smiled. "Tyler's been injured... no, he'll be all right. But he can't go on stage for the next little while. Yeah," she said, looking in the direction he'd disappeared, "I'll tell him. I have a couple of good-looking men who are interested in taking the test," she said. "Can you, Natalie, and Jennifer come in early? Great. Now's fine."

She flipped the phone closed. "While you boys are waiting," Jolene said with a smile, "why don't all y'all help me clean up this mess?"

By the time she'd swept up and the men had hauled the broken table outside, Gwen was walking in with Tyler and Emily, with Natalie and Jennifer just a few steps behind them.

Relieved to see them together, Jolene called out, "You two sort out what you needed to?"

Tyler nodded. "But I was wondering if you'd mind telling me why you chose to open a strip club for women instead of a bar."

Jolene looked at Emily.

Emily walked over to stand beside her cousin. "You don't have to if you don't want to, Jo. Tyler would understand."

Tyler knew the women drew strength from each other. Hell, he understood and always felt invincible when his brothers had his back.

This time his boss surprised him and didn't hesitate. "I've always wanted my own place"—she looked over at Jake—"when I bought The Lucky Star, there were some code violations that I didn't know about." He nodded, and she continued. "Apparently the wiring was bad and the place was a firetrap. I had to come up with the money fast, or I'd lose everything we'd all invested."

"It's not just you and Emily?"

Jolene shook her head. "Gwen, Natalie, Jennifer, and I pooled our savings… all of it." She smiled at Emily. "When Em heard that we bought the place, she packed up and flew on out here to add hers to the pot. Can we move on? I've got to settle who's going to go out on stage tonight."

That got everyone's attention. Well, all least his brothers and Jake were hanging on her every word.

"That still doesn't answer my question."

"I didn't realize you were such an impatient man, cowboy."

"Jolene," he warned.

She grinned at Tyler. "Natalie and Jennifer actually gave me the idea. They'd both worked in clubs before and wanted to be on the other side for a change."

"Besides," Jolene continued, "being the only ladies' strip club in the county brings customers flocking to our place."

"So it's all about the money?" He didn't want it to be, but hell, who was he to judge? Without it, he and his brothers would probably be living in a cardboard box in an alley next to a dumpster.

Jolene folded her hands beneath her breasts. "Partly. Without it, you don't have a whole lot of control over your life." She looked at Emily and her friends, then back at him. "We all needed to take the control back."

"Tell him the other part," Emily urged.

Jolene nodded. "We wanted to offer a place where women could come and enjoy themselves in a safe environment. The women are in control here, but no one ever has the right to abuse my employees or my dancers." She looked at Tyler. "I'm still sorry that happened to you."

"Not that I'm sold on taking my clothes off for a living," he began, "but it helped keep our ranch afloat. I'm just sorry that I was caught off guard today when Widowmaker got the better of me." He wasn't going to be anything pretty to look at for a couple of weeks… if ever. "It might be awhile before anyone will want to look at me."

"I'm just glad you still walking and talking," Jolene

said. "If a bull knocked me into a fence, it'd probably kill me."

Tyler looked at her, sizing her up. "He would have done some serious damage. You don't have enough muscle and meat on your bones to handle getting abused like that."

Jolene nodded then turned toward the ladies. "Gwen's going to give the guys here a little test while Natalie, Jennifer, and I judge."

Tyler grinned. He knew exactly what kind of test that would be. "I hope you boys are up to it."

His brothers looked like they wanted to change their mind, but Jolene was already ushering them over to the other side of the bar. "I'd like to give each one of you the chance. Who wants to go first?"

Jesse answered. "I will."

Jolene grinned at him. "All right. Gwen, take him over to the stage. I want to have a word with Dylan and Jake in my office."

"Shouldn't we stay here with Jesse?" Dylan seemed unnerved.

"But that would be cheating," Gwen quipped, "and you don't look like the type who ever cheated on a test."

Dylan clamped his mouth shut.

Tyler was tired, but he wasn't going to miss this. "Emily and I will stay here with Jess," he said. "You go on with Jolene."

Dylan shrugged, let his gaze linger on first Natalie and then Jennifer, before following behind Jake.

When they were gone, Gwen grinned. "Stand on the stage.

Natalie and Jennifer watched Jesse like a hawk,

making him uneasy as he walked over to the stage and turned to face them. "OK."

Tyler couldn't help asking, "How's your back, Jess?"

Before his brother had a chance to answer, Gwen called out, "Catch me!" and launched herself at Jesse.

His mouth hung open in shock, but he braced himself and caught her against him.

"Ooooh baby," Jennifer crowed, elbowing her sister.

Natalie nodded and chirped, "Jesse gets my vote."

Tyler chuckled and Emily poked him. "You didn't think it was funny when it was you doing the catching."

"Yeah, but did you see his face?"

Gwen patted his brother on the shoulder. "You can put me down now," she said. "You passed."

Jesse set her down, shook his head, and walked over to Tyler. "Hell."

"Yeah," Tyler agreed. "It would have been easier to haul kegs."

"Be right back." Gwen disappeared only to return with his other brother.

From the look on Dylan's face, his test could go either way. His brother could be a pain in the ass if he wanted to. Tyler just hoped he wouldn't do anything stupid like refuse to catch the woman. She was sizeable enough to hurt herself if she hit the stage because his brother wouldn't do his part.

Gwen told Dylan where to stand and his brother was already mumbling. Not a good sign.

"How's your back?" Gwen asked, turning to face Dylan.

"Fine, why?"

Mindful of his ribs, Tyler leaned close to Emily and whispered, "I should have asked Gwen for a beer first."

Emily giggled. "Are you sure you're not the one with the mean streak?

Tyler shook his head. "This is my kind of entertainment. Brace yourself, bro," he called out.

Gwen launched herself. Dylan absorbed the impact and swore. "Sonofabitch. You could have warned, me," he bit out, awkwardly hanging on to Gwen.

Tyler shook his head. "Jolene wouldn't have liked it if I did."

Gwen leaned back and grinned. "Nice catch, cowboy."

"Dylan gets my vote," Jennifer crowed, doing a little boot-scootin' boogie in front of the stage.

"Hell," Dylan grumbled. "I need a beer."

"I'm buying," Gwen said, "just as soon as the big bad fire marshal takes the test."

"If he's so stuck on Jolene," Dylan asked, "why would he?"

Emily and Gwen turned to stare at his brother, and Tyler wondered why the women didn't answer. It was a logical question. Wasn't it?

"It's because he's so stuck on Jolene that he'd take the test." Emily paused, then asked, "Don't tell me that doesn't make perfect sense to you?"

Dylan shook his head at her. "Man, Tyler," he said. "Redheads are nothing but trouble."

"Just wait," Gwen said with a grin. "I think I'll go grab a couple of bottles of beer." Before Tyler could say anything, she called out over her shoulder, "Soda for you, cowboy."

She walked back over, expertly popping the tops off two brown bottles at once and one screw top as she carried them over… just in time… Jake and Jolene were heading toward them.

Jolene had a smug expression on her face that turned to one of intense interest as Gwen handed two of the Garahan brothers a beer and Tyler a soda.

His frown turned to a smile when she asked Jake, "How do you feel about being the entertainment?"

To give the man credit, he didn't miss a beat. "Just part of the package."

"What package?" Jolene grumbled.

Jake's gaze met hers. "Of tangling with one stubborn, gorgeous redhead."

Tyler and his brothers raised their bottles. "The winner gets the spoils."

Jake stalked over to the stage. "I'm ready."

"Are you ready, Gwen?" Jolene called out.

"Ready."

Taking pity on his friend, Tyler felt he ought to warn him. "Bend your knees and brace yourself."

Jake looked at him and opened his mouth to speak as the tall blonde bartender called out. "I hope your back is as strong as it looks."

His head whipped back around, and Tyler would later swear, the man looked like a Texas Ranger braced to meet an outlaw at high noon.

Jake caught Gwen easily; shifting to cup his hands under her backside, he bent his knees and dipped her down until her long blonde hair brushed the stage. Grinning first at her and then up at Jolene, he asked. "So did I pass?"

"Damn," Dylan murmured, pointing at Jake with his bottle. "You see that?"

"Yeah. The guy's got style," Jesse drained the rest of his beer.

Jolene seemed to be at a loss for words. From the confused look on her face, Tyler figured she'd been expecting Jake to be as awkward as he and his brothers. But the man surprised them all.

"You can put Gwen down now," she rasped.

Jake pulled her back up and set her on her feet. Instead of patting him on the back like she had the other men, Gwen grabbed a hold of his shoulders, yanked him close, and kissed him.

"Jeez, Gwen." Emily sounded exasperated. "That's poaching."

Gwen let go and grinned. "Mr. Turner," she said. "You seriously are the Big Bad Fire Marshal, and you get my vote."

Jolene sounded as if she were choking. Tyler walked over to where she stood and spoke quietly. "Only a man who's serious about a woman would go the extra mile to impress her with a move like that."

She squeezed Tyler's hand and let go, reaching for Jake. "I don't think I want you working for us."

Jake tilted his head to one side and grinned at her. "Why not? I passed the test."

She shrugged. "I don't know if I want to see you strutting your stuff in front of a group of women waving dollar bills."

His grin broadened. "Is that a fact?"

"I don't share," she told him right before she grabbed him and kissed him.

"Your cousin has style," Tyler said as Emily slipped her arm carefully around his back.

"They're good for one another." Emily smiled.

Tyler needed to know how she felt about him baring it all while she watched. "Do you share?"

Her look was a direct challenge. "What did you have in mind?"

He picked up her gauntlet. "Me."

Emily placed her hands on either side of his face, got up on her toes, and lined up their lips. "Not in this lifetime."

Tyler's head felt light. "Good to know. I don't either."

Mindful of his injury, she wrapped herself around him, like ivy on a tree.

"The only one you'll be dancing with on the bar is me."

"Looks like you'll be needing a permanent replacement for your headliner, Jo," Gwen called out.

Tyler lifted his head and looked down at Emily. "Did it bother you that I stripped for your cousin?"

Emily smiled up at him, "Yeah," she admitted, "but I only wanted to string up the big-busted bimbo who claimed to be your fiancée."

"We like you much better than Linda Lee." Dylan nodded at Emily.

"How do you feel about ranch life?" Jesse asked.

"Would you two shut up and let me be the one to ask?" Tyler ground out.

Emily's smile deepened. "I had a great time working with y'all." Her amber eyes darkened. "You thinking about inviting me out for a longer stay?"

"Yeah." Tyler placed his knuckle beneath her chin and tilted her face up so he could look into her eyes. "Come home with me."

"Are you asking or telling me?"

"Asking." He needed this woman in his arms and in his life.

"Well, then," Emily smiled. "I think I'd like to spend more time at the Circle G."

Jesse asked, "How long can you stay?"

"'Til I wear out my welcome," she answered.

"That's fine," Dylan chimed in. "You OK with that big brother?"

"Emily living out at the Circle G?" Tyler asked, looking down into the smiling face of the woman he loved. "I'm good with it." He pressed his lips to hers.

"So what about my new headliner?" Jolene demanded interrupting them.

Jake grinned at her and opened his mouth to speak, but she elbowed at him. "Don't even think about it."

He was still grinning when he told her, "Gwen liked me best."

Emily rubbed her hand up and down Tyler's spine and smiled at his brothers. "I think Dylan ought to fill in for Tyler."

Dylan blanched. "Why me?"

Emily shrugged. "You're the middle brother. Makes sense to me that it's your turn."

Jolene walked over to stand in front of him, eyeing him up and down.

Emily saw a tiny bead of sweat break out at the man's temple before trickling down the side of his face.

"What?" he finally asked.

Jolene grinned. "You're hired."

Emily chuckled. "Go easy on him, Jolene. Dylan's a man of few words, but I have a feeling he'll give you one hundred percent, just like Tyler."

Tyler laid his cheek on the top of her head. "Grandpa was right about redheads."

Dylan crossed his arms over his chest. "I haven't said yes yet."

Emily nudged Tyler, who straightened and let her go. She walked over to the middle Garahan brother and held out her hand.

Dylan scowled at her before turning to glare at Tyler. When Tyler nodded, Dylan grumbled and took her hand. "Aw hell."

Emily squeezed his hand once and let go. "If Tyler can pull double duty working here nights after putting in a full day at the ranch, you can fill in for him for a couple of days while Jolene and I look for a replacement." She paused and looked over at Jolene. "I don't think our cowboy's going to be easily replaced."

"Give it up, bro," Tyler called out. "No man can hold out against a Langley woman on a roll."

"But I can't strip in front of women I don't know," Dylan protested.

Jesse snorted. "Sure you can. Just pretend it's that little cheerleader. Man, what was her name, Ty?"

Dylan clenched his fists and stalked over toward the youngest Garahan.

Jesse danced backward but didn't turn his back on his brother. He grinned and called out, "You remember the one who used to practically drool watching Dylan strip out of his football gear after practice."

Tyler smiled and called out, "Sarah."

Jesse grinned. "Oh man, yeah. Sarah. She sure was cute the way her eyes would glass over and her mouth would drop open."

Dylan lunged at Jesse and took him out with an impressive flying tackle.

"Am I interrupting, ladies?" Mavis Beeton arrived on the scene.

Dylan's fist stopped an inch from Jesse's nose. They both looked up and swore.

"Really, boys," Mavis shook her head. "I know your mother taught you better than to fight indoors."

Dylan got off of Jesse's chest and helped his brother to his feet. "Sorry, Mrs. Beeton."

"Welcome to the madness." Jolene sighed. "We were having a discussion about who's going to be filling in for Tyler until we can hire a replacement for him."

Mrs. Beeton walked over to Tyler. "You poor dear, what happened to you?"

"I was trying to reason with a bull."

"Shouldn't you be sitting down?"

Tyler agreed. "Yes, ma'am, but we really needed to figure out what to do about tonight."

Mavis nodded. "That's part of why I'm here." Mrs. Beeton sighed. "Dylan quit elbowing your brother."

Emily smiled at the grumpy expression on the brothers' faces before asking Mavis. "What did you find out?"

Before she could answer a deep voice called out, "Ladies. You open for business early tonight?"

Emily and Jolene looked at each other and Jolene answered. "No. What can we do for you, Sheriff?"

"Mrs. Beeton called and asked me to meet her here."

She nodded. "Right on time too, Sheriff."

He smiled at the older woman. "I do try, ma'am."

"Well, after Emily called me the other day, I got on the phone with Lettie, Pam, and Minnie."

"And?" Emily prompted.

"Apparently, they'd already heard the rumor about Frank Emerson wanting to change the name of the town."

"Like I told you earlier, Mavis, that's hardly an issue for the law, ma'am."

Mavis frowned up at him. "I'm well aware of that, young man. But are you also aware that he hired those poor Baxter boys to use their new shotgun on the storefronts of three particular businesses in town?"

"Do you have any proof?" the lawman demanded.

Mavis smiled. "I'm sure Jim Dooley will be happy to back me up, after all, they are his nephews."

McClure nodded. "Appreciate the tip, but couldn't you have just told me over the phone?"

Mavis tapped her foot, impatience oozing from her pores. "I thought it would be best not to. Besides, there's more."

Emily motioned for everyone to follow her. "Why don't we all sit down?"

The Garahan brothers ranged themselves behind her. The need to protect must have been instilled at birth. Although she already knew the answer, she asked anyway, "Are you sure y'all don't want to sit?" Tyler shook his head and laid a hand on her shoulder and squeezed it. "We'll stand."

Mrs. Beeton cleared her throat to speak. "Aside from lobbying to change the name of our town, Mr. Emerson is embezzling funds from the Preservation Society."

Sheriff McClure slipped a hand into his breast pocket and took out a small black notebook. Flipping it open, he looked at Mrs. Beeton and nodded for her to continue. "I assume you have proof to back up your claim?"

She glared at the lawman. "I've been treasurer for the Preservation Society for the last ten years. Of course I have proof. I noticed a discrepancy in the bank statements recently and took a closer look. Between those statements and our books, I think I've pinpointed the time it all started… right about the time Mr. Emerson began to campaign to bring tourism back to Pleasure."

McClure frowned but kept writing. "Can I see the statements?"

"They're in my car." She paused. "But there's more. I don't have any proof, but I think he might be behind the anonymous phone calls trying to extort money."

Tyler and Jake glanced over at Emily and Jolene, waiting while McClure asked, "What calls?"

Jolene frowned at Mavis. "I didn't tell you I'd received any calls."

Mrs. Beeton frowned at her. "Did I mention your name, Jolene?"

The sheriff shut his notebook and nodded. "I'll be in touch."

"Let me get those statements for you." Mrs. Beeton rose to follow the sheriff.

Watching them leave, the middle Garahan brother groaned. "Tyler—"

"Suck it up, bro." Jesse shot a grin at Jolene. "I can't wait for my turn."

Tyler shook his head at his brothers, pushed to his feet, and pulled Emily with him. "How about it?" he asked. "Will you come with me to the Circle G?"

"Jolene," Emily said, taking a hold of Tyler's hand, "I'm going to need a couple of days off."

"I guess we can get along without you for a day or so."

Emily looked up at Tyler. "I'll see you next week."

"But Em—" Jolene began.

"Just kidding, Jolene," Emily said. "I'll be back to check up on Dylan."

"Want to drive?" Tyler asked, pressing his lips to Emily's temple.

"Sure—"

"Hey, Emily," Jesse called out. "Catch!"

She looked up and held out her hand, snagging the keys Tyler's brother tossed at her.

"She sticks a little when you shift into third."

"How are we going to get home?" Dylan grumbled.

"I can give y'all a lift," Gwen said, walking back into the bar. "After your shift's over."

Natalie tucked her hand through Dylan's arm. "Ever dirty dance before, cowboy?"

Jennifer slipped her hand in the crook of Dylan's arm on the other side of him. "What size briefs do you wear, honey?"

Dylan's mumbled reply wasn't fit for polite company.

Emily tugged gently on Tyler's hand. "I think we should let your brothers and the ladies get better acquainted." When he resisted, she lifted his hand and turned it over, pressing her lips to the palm of his hand. "I'll make you steak and eggs for breakfast."

Tyler grumbled, "Nothing special, it's what we usually eat."

Emily's grin was positively lethal. "With a hot cup of coffee and ice cube chaser?"

Tyler's dark eyes gleamed, and Emily knew he'd be able to stand up to the gentle loving she had in mind for him tonight.

He pulled Emily toward the hallway and grinned. "Grandpa's right... redheads are twice the trouble." When Emily opened her mouth to protest, he claimed her lips, "And worth every damn minute of it."

Acknowledgments

As always, I need to thank my family for their unending support. I can be difficult to live with when I'm working through difficult phases of the creative process. My family, Lord love them, have developed certain routines that make living with me, while I'm on deadline, possible. They by turns, look at me oddly and avoid me like the plague, or light the candles in our living room so our house is filled with the soothing scent of vanilla and hazelnut.

Either way, their love comes through, reminding me of how lucky I am to have married the man I fell in love with at first sight. After all these years, he still makes my heart stop with one look… I'd be lost without him. It's hard to believe, but our three children are adults now and equally talented in their own right. I'm so proud of you guys! Thank you for allowing me to pursue my dream.

Thanks to my wonderful editor, Deb Werksman, and her vision. I'm grateful for the chance meeting at a writer's conference where Deb and I were both desperate for caffeine and exchanged business cards waiting for it to arrive.

A special thank you to two well-meaning friends, Tara and Pat, who dragged me to a strip club in Houston. I really did think I was old enough to attend; apparently I was wrong, but the material I gathered from that experience far outweighed my embarrassment at the time. To Anne Elizabeth who inspired my curvy red-heads… you're fabulous, my dear.

To the real Natalie and Jennifer… reviewer friends who have been behind me since they reviewed the first book in my Medieval trilogy. Nat and Jen are consummate professionals when writing reviews; they never trash a book or its author. Natalie reviews for Romance Junkies at www.romancejunkies.com and Jennifer for her own website Wild on Books at www.wildonbooks.com. Their dedication to the genre is absolute, and for that I'm forever grateful. You two ladies are THE BEST!!!

About the Author

C.H. Admirand is an award-winning, multi-published author and has published ten novels in mass-market paperback, hardcover, trade paperback, magazine, e-book, and audio book format.

Fate, destiny, and love at first sight will always play a large part in C.H.'s stories because they played a major role in her life. When she saw her husband for the first time, she knew he was the man she was going to spend the rest of her life with. Each and every hero C.H. writes about has a few of Dave's best qualities: his honesty, his integrity, his compassion for those in need, and his killer broad shoulders. She lives with her husband and their three adult children in the wilds of northern New Jersey.

She loves to hear from readers! Stop by her website at www.chadmirand.com to catch up on the latest news, excerpts, reviews, blog posts, and links to Facebook, MySpace, and Twitter.

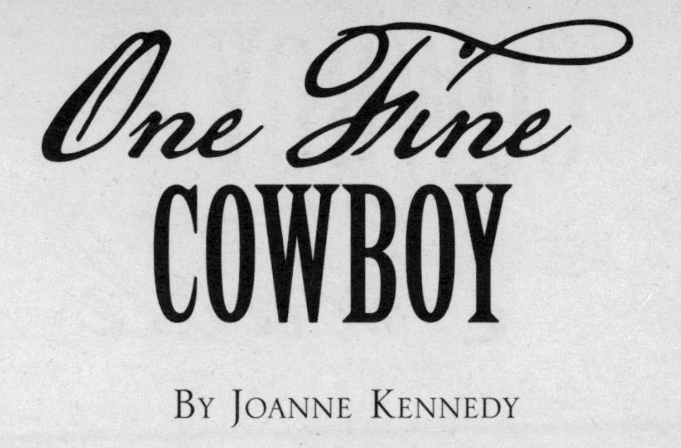

By Joanne Kennedy

The last thing she expects is a lesson in romance...

Graduate student Charlie Banks came to a Wyoming ranch for a seminar on horse communication, but when she meets ruggedly handsome "Horse Whisperer" Nate Shawcross, she starts to fantasize about another connection entirely...

Nate needs to stay focused if he's going to save his ranch from foreclosure, but he can't help being distracted by sexy and brainy Charlie. Could it be that after all this time Nate has finally found the one woman who can tame his wild heart?

Praise for *Cowboy Trouble:*

"A fresh take on the traditional contemporary Western... There's plenty of wacky humor and audacious wit in this mystery-laced escapade." —*Library Journal*

"Contemporary Western fans will enjoy this one!" —*Romantic Times*

"A fun and delicious romantic romp... If you love cowboys, you won't want to miss this one! Romance, mystery, and spurs! Yum!" —*Wendy's Minding Spot*

978-1-4022-3670-9 • $6.99 U.S./$8.99 CAN/£4.99 UK

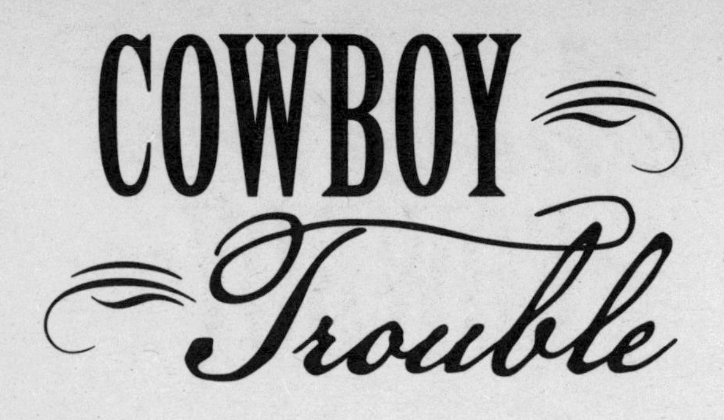

By Joanne Kennedy

All she wanted was a simple country life, and then he walked in…

Fleeing her latest love life disaster, big city journalist Libby Brown's transition to rural living isn't going exactly as planned. Her childhood dream has always been to own a farm—but without the constant help of her charming, sexy neighbor, she'd never make it through her first Wyoming season. But handsome rancher Luke Rawlins yearns to do more than help Libby around her ranch. He's ready for love, and he wants to go the distance…

Then the two get embroiled in their tiny town's one and only crime story, and Libby discovers that their sizzling hot attraction is going to complicate her life in every way possible…

"I'm expecting great things from Joanne Kennedy! Bring on the hunky cowboys." —Linda Lael Miller, *New York Times* bestselling author of *The Bridegroom*

"Everything about Kennedy's charming debut novel hits the right marks…you'll be hooked." —*BookLoons*

978-1-4022-3668-6 • $7.99 US / $9.99 CAN / £4.99 UK

Beau hasn't got a lick of sense when it comes to women

Everything hunky rancher "Lucky" Beau Luckadeau touches turns to gold—except relationships. Spitfire Milli Torres can mend a fence, pull a calf, or shoot a rattlesnake between the eyes. When Milli shows up to help out at the Lazy Z ranch, she's horrified to find that Beau's her nearest neighbor—the very man she'd hoped never to lay eyes on again. If Beau ever figures out what really happened on that steamy Louisiana night when they first met, there'll be the devil to pay…

Praise for Carolyn Brown:

"Engaging characters, humorous situations, and a bumpy romance... Carolyn Brown will keep you reading until the very last page." —Romantic Times

"Carolyn Brown's rollicking sense of humor asserts itself on every page." —Scribes World

978-1-4022-2435-5 • $7.99 U.S. / $9.99 CAN

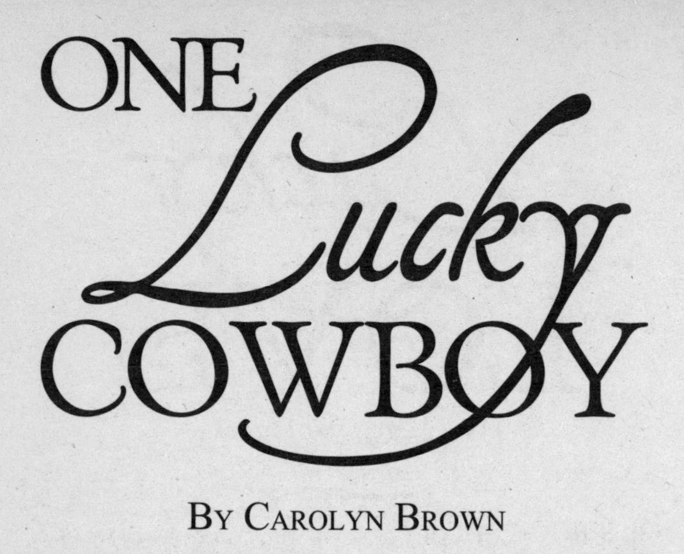

BY CAROLYN BROWN

No big blond cowboy is going to intimidate this spitfire!

If Slade Luckadeau thinks he can run Jane Day off his ranch, he's got cow chips for brains. She's winning every argument, and he's running out of fights to pick. But when trouble with a capital "T" threatens Jane *and* the Double L Ranch, suddenly it's Slade's heart that's in the most danger of all.

Praise for *Lucky in Love*:

"I enjoyed this book so much that I plan to rope myself some more of Carolyn Brown and her books. Lucky in Love *is a must read!"* —Cheryl's Book Nook

"This is one of those rare books where every person in it comes alive... as they share wit, wisdom, and love." —The Romance Studio

978-1-4022-2437-9 • $7.99 U.S. / $9.99 CAN

BY CAROLYN BROWN

Griffin Luckadeau is one stubborn cowboy…

And Julie Donovan is one hotheaded schoolteacher who doesn't let anybody push her around. When Griffin thinks his new neighbor is scheming to steal his ranch out from under him, he's more than willing to cross horns. Their look-alike daughters may be best friends, but until these two Texas hotheads admit it's fate that brought them together, running from the inevitable is only going to bring them a double dose of miserable…

Praise for Carolyn Brown:

"A delight to read." —Booklist

"Engaging characters, humorous situations, and a bumpy romance… Carolyn Brown will keep you reading until the very last page." —Romantic Times

"Carolyn Brown's rollicking sense of humor asserts itself on every page." —Scribes World

978-1-4022-2436-2 • $7.99 U.S. / $9.99 CAN / 4.99 UK

BY CAROLYN BROWN

Saddle up, cowboy...

She doesn't need anything but her bar...

Daisy O'Dell has her hands full with hotheads and thirsty ranchers until the day one damn fine cowboy walks in and throws her whole life into turmoil. Jarod McElroy is looking for a cold drink and a moment's peace, but instead he finds one red hot woman. She's just what he needs, if only he can convince her to come out from behind that bar, and come home with him...

Praise for *One Lucky Cowboy:*

"Jam-packed with cat fights, reluctant heroes, spirited old ladies and, of course, a chilling villain, Brown's plot-driven cowboy romance...will earn a spot on your keeper shelf."

—*Romantic Times*, 4 stars

"Sheer fun...filled with down-home humor, realistic characters, and pure romance."

—*Romance Reader at Heart*

978-1-4022-3926-7 • $7.99 US / $8.99 CAN / £4.99 UK

BY CAROLYN BROWN

She's finally found a place that feels like home...

When Cathy O'Dell buys the Honky Tonk, the nights of cowboys and country tunes come together to create the home she's always wanted. Then in walks a ruggedly handsome oil man who tempts her to trade in the happiness she's found at the Honky Tonk for a life on the road with him.

Gorgeous and rich, Travis Henry travels the country unearthing oil wells and then moving on. Then the beautiful blue-eyed new owner of the Honky Tonk beer joint becomes his best friend and so much more. When his job is done in Texas, how is he ever going to hit the road without her?

Praise for Carolyn Brown:

"Carolyn Brown takes her audience by storm... I was mesmerized." —The Romance Studio

"Carolyn Brown creates a bevy of delightful and believable characters." —The Long and Short of It Reviews

978-1-4022-3927-4 • $7.99 US / $9.99 CAN / £4.99 UK

BY CAROLYN BROWN

He's just doing his job...

If Hank Wells thinks he can dig up dirt on the new owner of the Honky Tonk beer joint for his employer, he's got no idea what kind of trouble he's courting...

She's not going down without a fight...

If any dime store cowboy thinks he's going to get the best of Larissa Morley—or her Honky Tonk—then he's got another think coming...

As secrets emerge, and passion vies with ulterior motives, it's winner takes all at the Honky Tonk...

Praise for ***Lucky in Love:***

"A spit-and-vinegar heroine...and a hero who dances faster than she can shoot make a funny, fiery pair in this appealing novel."

—Booklist

"Carolyn Brown pens an exciting romance... This is one of those rare books where every person in it comes alive."

—The Romance Studio, *5/5*

978-1-4022-3928-1 • $7.99 U.S/$9.99 CAN/£4.99 UK